Return to Ithaca

BOOKS BY RANDY LEE EICKHOFF

*denotes a Forge Book

Return to Ithaca

A Confessional Novel

RANDY LEE
EICKHOFF

A TOM DOHERTY ASSOCIATES BOOK

NEW YORK

RETURN TO ITHACA: A CONFESSIONAL NOVEL

Copyright © 2001 by Randy Lee Eickhoff

Design by Heidi Eriksen

A Forge Book
Published by Tom Doherty Associates, LLC
175 Fifth Avenue
New York, NY 10010

www.tor.com

Forge® is a registered trademark of Tom Doherty Associates, LLC.

ISBN 0-312-87446-4

First Edition: June 2001

Printed in the United States of America

0 9 8 7 6 5 4 3 2 1

for Dianne

IN MEMORIAM
RAYMOND
JUNIOR EICKHOFF

Of Special Note

I owe a special debt of gratitude to Father Ray Smith, who told me about *Man's Search for Meaning* in Huron, South Dakota, in the spring of 1964, and later sent Viktor Frankl's book to me in June.

Ithaca is an imaginary place that is based upon the stories told to a young boy by his grandparents, Bruno and Elsie Jeitz. The countryside is real, though, and one may travel it if one follows the Bad River Road west from Fort Pierre. Van Meter is now only a cow pasture and Capa is a ghost town. Midland is still there, as are the hardy ranchers who make up several of the characters in this book.

My parents, Raymond and Eldina Eickhoff, deserve a special thanks for the many patient trips back to that country to show me my youth time and time again.

A special thanks to Robert Gleason and Jacques de Spoelberch, who alternately talked me through the various drafts, offering their wisdom and guidance cheerfully and frequently.

Thank you, each.

R.L.E.

ómoi, péplegmai kairian plegén éso

—AESCHYLUS
from *Agamemnon* (line 1343)

We are not now that strength which in old days
Moved earth and heaven, that which we are, we are.
One equal temper of heroic hearts.
Made weak by time and fate, but strong in will
To strive, to seek, to find, and not to yield.

—ALFRED, LORD TENNYSON
from *Ulysses*

L'homme n'est ni ange ni bête: et le malheur veut que
qui veut faire l'ange fait la bête.

—BLAISE PASCAL

Drink a health to the wonders of the western world,
the pirates, preachers, poteen-makers, with the jobbing
jockies; parching peelers, and the juries fill their stom-
achs selling judgments of the English law.

—JOHN MILLINGTON SYNGE
from *The Playboy of the Western World*

The Past as Preface

There comes a time in an author's life when he must reexamine the life he has left behind. If he has left a war behind as well, the examination is, at times, painful, but there nevertheless, cropping up unbidden in serene times like an old debt that one cannot repay. And then the memories come crashing in one by one upon each other and all one's yesterdays become todays that he tries to put to rest by writing about them. Some stories, however, simply cannot be told, for there are times when the truth is so exceptional that it lends itself more to fiction than nonfiction. And sometimes the memories of others are equally long and it is better if some things are left unsaid.

The Montagnards in Vietnam comprise many tribes. In the days of the last emperor, Bao, in the late fifties and early sixties, the Montagnards were the quarry for hunting parties much in the same way the fox is the quarry of hunt clubs in England, Ireland, and Virginia.

Compared to the aristocratic culture of the Vietnamese, the Montagnards were a primitive people. Their laws were simple and direct—the guilty were punished quickly and severely by their standards. Their way of life was casual and scandalous to some. Sexuality was simply a matter of life and was not ceremonial. Their gods were functional, not aesthetic, and the individual was only a part of the village or tribe, not an island apart from the main. The entire village raised the child and for a child to go against the village was an affair that would bring dishonor not only upon the father, but upon the entire village as well. Guilt was collective in that respect.

In some ways, the Montagnard life was similar to that of the

Lakota. There was a certain nomadicism to the Montagnard, but it was the generosity of the spirit, the willingness to care for others and to accept responsibility for others, that was remarkable to each tribe separated by hundreds of miles.

Yet, when war came to Vietnam, it was to the Montagnards that the South Vietnam and American governments turned to for help with guerilla attacks upon the North Vietnamese armies moving down along the infamous Ho Chi Minh Trail. American teams, very similar to the Deer Teams of World War II, were sent into the mountains to recruit the Montagnards with supplies and promises that they would have a place in the new government that would be formed once the war was over. Some of us didn't realize the lies until they became fact. The Montagnards displaced by the war were placed in *agrovilles* where their culture and way of life was taken from them, where they withered and died.

Some of the Montagnard tribes realized this and headed north, deeper into the mountains, searching for a place to belong. Some of them came into contact with the Shans of Burma and minor skirmishes were fought there. Others simply melded back into the forest and the mountains and disappeared, taking refuge in the darkness of the jungle and the craggy mountains where, French engineers and cartographers had claimed thirty years before, no one could live.

Much has been written about various syndromes the Vietnam veteran brought back with him from the war, about his inability to cope with the world after being at war. In many cases, this has become a fashionable excuse for not getting on with one's life; in some cases, however, it is a reality. The world I left in 1965 to go into the mountains of Vietnam was as different as night and day from the world to which I returned in 1966. In 1965, the war was a romantic vision and we were warriors going into that vision to save the world from Communism, an evil that was threatening the American ideal—baseball, hot dogs, and Mom's apple pie. There was glory to be found in war, then. Sherman's comment that "war is hell" was a reality that we cheerfully embraced, for we had seen enough of war on the silver screen to realize that heroes were those who were meant to succeed in our society, in our culture. Most of us had been raised with the war stories of our fathers and grandfathers (I remember one young man whose father had been Rommel's aide when the Desert Fox was in Africa) and that provided us with a universal identity.

The trouble was that the Vietnam War was in its infancy and when we returned, it had matured into a perceived evil that revolutionized American society. We went over to Vietnam heroes; we came back as perceived "baby killers" by bored students looking for a cause against which they could rebel. Within two hours of stepping onto the streets of San Francisco after returning from Vietnam, I was first praised by an adult who thanked me for doing my duty and then spat upon by a protesting student from Berkeley.

The entire world had changed and I found it extremely difficult to cope with it. The music was different, styles were different (miniskirts, of which I approved, and long hair on men, of which I didn't), and what had happened to the straight-laced moral dictums about sex I met with mixed feelings. The United States was now the foreign country to me, and I was going to have to relearn my culture, much in the same way that Odysseus had to relearn what had happened to his home on Ithaca after his return. My homecoming was not "honey-sweet" either, as Teiresias cautioned Odysseus when the Wanderer journeyed to the Land of Hades. Our Poseidon—the American populace—was not finished with us either, and the people's revenge upon us for doing our duty caused us much suffering. We had inherited the wind and that wind blew us in many different directions as we sought a place to which we could belong. Our journey after our return was similar to that of Odysseus, yet we could not find a land where our oars would be recognized as winnowing shovels. Our journeys were sometimes physical; always they were mental.

At last, my journey ended with my wife and my family, who had stayed with me through the five years that I wandered in the blackness of despair. Then I tired of using the war and my country as an excuse for not getting on with my life. In December, I said to hell with both and planted my winnowing shovel by rebuilding my life at the University of Nebraska.

But I couldn't forget what had happened to me. I felt the agony of defeat long before our government made my sacrifice meaningless. I came out of the despair into which my government threw me.

Many veterans did not. Some have yet to return to Ithaca.

RANDY LEE EICKHOFF
January 1, 2001

Invocation

I am called Dog, but that is not my name. The priests at the St. Francis Indian Mission named me John Crow Dog after the man who found me in a wicker basket woven from red sumac branches on top of a hill on John Morgan's ranch. Ancient warriors had built a ceremonial ring out of red stone on top of the hill, but no one knows why. When I grew older, I would often go to that ring during the Moon When the Cherries Turn Black and listen to the warriors' voices as they spoke to me on the wind.

They would tell me what to do.

This made me different from the others at the mission who did what the priests told them to do and watched, laughing, when the priests would beat me for doing what the ancient warriors told me to do.

Crow Dog was a *wichasha wakon* for the Lakota Sioux. Touch the Clouds, his father, was also a *wichasha wakon*. He rode with Crazy Horse and it was he who was trusted to take the heart of Crazy Horse into the Badlands to bury secretly, away from the eyes of the *Wasichu*. I say his father but one who is a *wichasha wakon* never marries. His sons are always orphans selected to learn the secrets of the *wichasha wakon*. The Oglala Sioux believed that such children were sent to the people by Sacred Woman, who came out of a white cloud to give the medicine pipe to the Oglala. The pipe had twelve eagle feathers, one for each of the moons, tied to it by woven sweet grass. Then, she changed into a white buffalo and galloped away over the plains. Each time a hoof touched the ground, a brown buffalo sprang from the earth, shaggy and snorting, and on the wind came her voice singing sweetly and telling the Oglala that this was her gift to them.

All this Crow Dog taught to me as Stepping Wolf had taught it to him. We were the Keepers of the Pipe. It took many moons to learn everything from the Thunder Beings to Mother Earth and this was something that could not be taught outside of the Oglala tongue. So, I did not speak English until I went to the mission. The priests did not think that I knew English, since I never spoke it, but I did, for Crow Dog had made sure of that as did John Morgan and his son Tom Morgan. But it is not for a *wichasha wakon* to speak outside of the Oglala tongue so I received many beatings from the priests until John Morgan took me from them and brought me back to his ranch where I lived with Crow Dog and worked the cattle with him.

But this is not my story. I cannot tell it, for a *wichasha wakon* should not make much of his winters, even when they bow him like heavy snow lying on willow branches. One man's life is the life of all men and animals and birds of the air. Each is a child of Sacred Woman.

Yet, this is a tale of a great hunter, a great warrior, a great traveler. It is the story of the vision of a man who was too weak to use it, yet the vision did not wither and die as many visions do. Instead, it became a holy tree that flourished in the hearts of people it touched, nourished them, and in its withering years, saved them. It did not die, for it was of the spirit and will forever be in the darkness of their eyes.

This is the story of Henry Morgan.

Henry was born in the Moon of the Changing Seasons. On the day of his birth, I went to the ring of stones on top of the hill to seek a vision for him. I stripped myself naked and purified myself by washing in soapweed and sage before entering the ring. There I found a medicine hoop, quarter-woven in red and black. A hunter's moon rose above the horizon and I held the medicine hoop so the moon could be seen through it. The moon turned dark as if blood were being poured over it. Then, a roan horse rode down from the sky. Its rider carried a bleached steer skull and when the rider laughed, I felt the breath of doom wash over me, pebbling my flesh. The roan and rider reached the earth and galloped away to the west toward the Badlands, disappearing into the night. I sang to the moon and prayed to Sacred Woman that I might see other riders, but none came and a great sadness entered me.

When Henry's mother died, I took Henry into the Badlands to the sacred place where the heart of Crazy Horse lies. There, I washed him with smoke from burning goldenpea and sage and gave him the medicine hoop that I had found in the ring of stones on the night of his birth. I told him about the vision I saw for him. I roasted the fruit of the prickly pear in the fire and we ate it. Then we ate pemmican I had made from beef after I had mashed golden currant berries and pin cherries and buffalo berries into it and dried it over a hickory fire. When we were finished, I brought out the pipe and we smoked kinnikinnick from it, blowing the smoke to the four directions. And I named him for the warrior whose heart lay buried in the hills around us and once again that warrior lived, for the dead live on in their names. I knew that once I had given Henry his sacred name that I could talk with him in ways that I could not talk with others. And if I talked long enough with him, then the ancient ones whose names he bore would reappear, claiming their names through him. He had become a child of the past as well as now.

And so, I had my son.

Ithaca

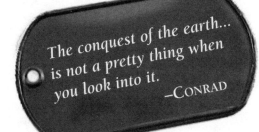

The conquest of the earth...
is not a pretty thing when
you look into it.

—CONRAD

Chapter One

She raised her summer-sky blue eyes to look out the window above the zinc sink over the sun-burnt grama grass waving in tufts of honey, gold and white, over the prairie before the shale hills marking the beginning of the Dakota Badlands. Here and there, clumps of dark-green soapweed dotted the pale blonde prairie. She lifted the cup of coffee, sipping, looking down the long, gentle slope to where tall cottonwoods stood on the banks of the creek and shook their golden leaves with the slightest breeze. Giant bur-reed and narrow-leaved cattails, the downy spikes once used by Indian women to line diapers for their babies, clumped at one point where the creek washed back from the bank.

A small Indian village once stood there, but the United States cavalry had ridden through the village a hundred years ago, killing everyone—man, woman, and child. After a rain, she would walk the banks, looking for whatever might have been uncovered: arrowheads, pot shards, a rusted cartridge, a stone axehead. Once, she found a fetish carved from sandstone, but she did not know what it signified. Sometimes when the rain came hard and washed rivulets down the banks, bleached white bones would appear, the bones of those Indians. She would carefully gather them and carry them to the lightning-struck cottonwood that grew on the hill above the stock tank where she buried them deep with a spade in a line down away from the tree. Sometimes, she would go up to that tree and sit beneath it on the grass and close her eyes and imagine ancient voices whispering to her on the wind coming through the branches. But no rains had come for a long time, now, and she knew if she walked the banks, she would find only dry shale that would crumble in her fingers if she picked it up.

She sighed and smoothed her black hair with its iron-gray streaks back from her high forehead covered with a faint network of wrinkles. Her head began to throb and she gently rubbed her temples, hoping she could ease the throbbing away before it worked its way into a blinding headache. Overhead, she heard her father-in-law's boots kicking along the hard wooden floor before he walked into the kitchen and sighed again, turning away from the window.

"Mornin', Kate," Tom Morgan said, yawning as he entered, tucking the tail of his blue denim workshirt into faded jeans fitted low and loose over his narrow hips. A worn brass buckle held an ancient brown belt around his waist. He lifted a chipped cup, its faded DAYS OF '76 legend barely readable, from a hook beneath the cupboards and filled it with coffee from the pot on the stove. He cautiously sipped, then grimaced as the coffee scalded his tongue.

"Hot," he complained.

"Twenty years," she said.

"Huh?" he asked, trying another cautious sip.

She sighed. "For nearly twenty years, now, you been doing that."

"Doing what?" he asked, frowning.

"Burning yourself with the coffee. A dog only sticks his nose into a fire once, but you been doing it every day for nearly twenty years."

"Maybe," he grunted, miffed. He blew on his coffee before taking another cautious sip. He looked fondly at the fine lines etched in his daughter-in-law's face, noting the square shoulders and deep breasts. She wore a plain blue denim workshirt, the tails tucked into faded jeans pulled down over scuffed brown boots. Her hands were large and square, the nails cut short. Her nose was bold and her gray-streaked black hair had been pulled back and rolled into a tight bun at the base of her neck.

A handsome woman, he thought. Not beautiful, maybe, like those in town, but store-bought beauty ain't worth a damn anyway. Not one of those hanging around Myrtle's Beauty Shop could even saddle a horse let alone ride it out to check the stock. Or throw a calf and hold it for branding, for that matter. Yes, Henry could have done worse.

She stirred and pulled herself away from the window, and turned to face him. He smiled into her startling blue eyes. Her full lips tilted in a brief smile, then she moved to the cupboard and set out a box of cornflakes and two bowls. He moved to the refrigerator and took a pitcher of orange juice and milk from it, hipping the door shut, and brought them to the table.

They heard the clang of the triangle down at the cookhouse as Cookie called their foreman, Seth Williams, and two hands, Sam and Joe, to breakfast. Kate poured the cornflakes into the bowl and reached for the bowl of sugar from the ledge above the table. Old Tom glanced at the white plastic clock on the wall above the refrigerator and clicked on the radio on the ledge. Paul Harvey was just finishing the "Rest of the Story" and the farm and ranch news would be next. He hooked a chair with the toe of his boot and pulled it out from the table as Kate brought the pot of coffee from the stove and placed it on a trivet on the table and sat opposite him.

"Think I'll ride over to the west pasture and check on the cattle there," he said. He picked up his mug of coffee and blew across it before cautiously sipping. "I ain't too sold on mixing the breeds. I spent a lot of time building up a pure-bred reputation. Don't know why that ain't good enough for you."

She shrugged. "Wasn't my idea. You forgot that Bill had decided to break the herd apart when you turned the ranch over to him. His idea, his herd."

"Yeah, but that don't make it right," Tom grumbled.

"You going to take Dog?"

He grunted. "No. He left last night for White River. Be gone two, maybe three days. A Sun Dance is scheduled down there."

She smiled fondly at him, noticing for the hundredth-some time the gnarled fingers and rope-scarred hands, the heavy lines grooved into his tanned face as if by a bailing hook. His bushy eyebrows stood out like barbed wire over his hooded, sun-bleached gray eyes the color of a blue norther. His white hair was neatly combed straight back and she could smell the faint rose scent of the lotion he used to keep it plastered in place. His shirt had been buttoned full against the sagging flesh of his throat. The tin of Union Leader tobacco bulged one of the button-down pockets of his denim workshirt.

She sighed silently and allowed her mind to drift back to when his son, Bill, had brought her home from Pierre after a long train ride from the state university in Vermillion. She had been excited, then, and apprehensive at meeting Bill's father who had been too busy with spring roundup and branding at the time to come to their wedding in Yankton. Not, she reflected, that there had been much of a wedding. A justice of the peace had presided with just one other couple present as witnesses. But she could sense that Bill had been disappointed when his father had not made the effort to come to the wedding.

I suppose it was your fault. Or, at least partly your fault getting pregnant. Starting from scratch like that is hard on a young couple. Damn hard. But you have to give him credit; he's never mentioned his disappointment to you. And when Timmy was born, well, that seemed to make things all right. I wonder if it would have been different if you hadn't miscarried the first child.

And then, unbidden, her mind slipped to Bill's brother, Henry, and she felt her face grow warm, remembering his square jaw, his blue eyes and how they seemed to bore to the back of her brain and read her thoughts there and how excited she had felt and she saw that excitement mirrored in his eyes—

Stop it! This is not the way to begin the day! Those times are past and should remain in the past. You have Timmy. I won-der if Bill would have stayed home if Timmy had been a girl? No, he wanted to go where his brother had gone. Two brothers have never been that close. And then, there was the romanticism of the war. But what about Henry? Why didn't he come home?

He spoke, but it took a second for the words to break through her thoughts. She blinked and looked at him. "What?"

"You gonna dream like that you might stay in bed a little longer," he said grumpily.

"Then who would make the coffee for you to burn your lips on?" she asked.

"I can make coffee. I had been doing it for years ever since—" He let his voice trail off and Kate nodded, patiently waiting for him to continue. Nearly thirty years had passed since his wife had died from cancer, and he still could not mention her name without a catch in his throat.

"Anyway, as I was saying," he grumbled, "I gotta check the west stock. And there's a section of fence and a couple of posts could stand replacement up there."

"Better take along Timmy to help you. Wire's a two-man job," she said. Then, remembering her daydream, she added acidly. "Of course, if you hadn't glorified the war, we would have both Henry and Bill here and things would be a lot smoother."

His faced reddened as he puffed out his cheeks and exhaled loudly. "I didn't—"

"Of course, you did," she interrupted angrily. It was an old argument between them, yet she still couldn't put it to rest. "I remember how many times you told them the Morgans had always done their duty for their country. Your father went to World War One while your grandfather stayed at home and took care of the place. Of course," she added, feeling the spite building up within her, "his father didn't have a place to tend while he went off with Sherman on the great Georgia raid, right? And you, well, somehow you always managed to make Anzio sound like a great glory while your father stayed at home. And of course, you were willing to do the same when Vietnam came around for Henry and Bill." She blinked back angry tears that sparkled in her eyes. He looked away. "The ranch wasn't good enough for them by the time you had finished with it. There was a magic monotony, then, between the prairie and the sky and they couldn't bear the criticism that they heard in your voice behind your stories of war. The daily task of chores could not compete with the romanticism of war that you spun with your stories."

"I didn't tell them to go," he said defensively.

"Of course you did, you old fool," she said, suddenly weary with the argument. "Your stories did that." She glanced toward the window over the sink. "The earth here hasn't the bewitching breath of the Far East. Going to bed at night, knowing you have to get up in the morning and take care of stock, string wire, or work on old windmills isn't the same as the dark mysteries of the imagination." She paused, thinking. "I guess it's because they didn't know fear."

She finished her cereal and rose, waiting patiently while he scraped the sugar from the bottom of the bowl and licked it from his spoon before handing the bowl to her. A tiny grin twitched her full lips. He might be one of the roughest ranchers around, but he still had a sweet tooth.

She carried the bowls to the sink and rinsed them, stacking them neatly on the drainer. She glanced out the window again. The leaves of the cottonwoods down by the stock tank were changing to gold. Across the yard, the bunkhouse door stood open, and she could see the men readying themselves for work. She frowned.

"Think we'll have enough time to finish haying before first snow?" she asked.

The old man shrugged. "You do what you can. That's the way it is, nothing more. You try to fight for more than what the prairie's willing to give you and you'll get nothing. But as for haying"—he rubbed his hand across his lips—"I don't know. Ain't much more out there to warrant cutting and wasting fuel sweeping and stacking. Certainly not enough to run the bailer. This damn drought's pretty much stumped the growing season."

She shook her head. "Gotta put up as much as we can. It'll be expensive trying to buy feed for the stock through the winter."

"Can't put up what you ain't got," he said. He drained his coffee cup and leaned back, the chair creaking under his weight. "The prairie's like a cantankerous woman; you gotta treat her right and respect the way she is or she'll make sure you regret it later."

He rose and stamped his feet to settle them in his boots

before crossing to her by the sink. He paused and kissed her forehead, startling her.

"What's that for?" she asked, drawing back, her hand instinctively touching her forehead.

"Been a while since we've been in town," he said. "Let's go to Ithaca and take in the Saturday night dance."

"What dance?" she asked.

"The square dance," he said patiently. "Saw in the *Captial City Journal* that the American Legion's having one to raise money for the new school. Blue and Dolly will be there. Should be fun."

She laughed. "You old coot. You know that if we go in you'll settle yourself down in front of the courthouse with the other old coots, and I'll sit in the hall with Mary Seiberts and Widow Terry and pretend that my husband's outside between sets nipping at the jug. No thanks."

"Well, you think about it," he said. "Do you good to get away for a bit. I'll even buy you an ice cream cone at Bob Steiner's Emporium, if you like."

He stepped out into the porch and took his weather-stained Stetson from its hook by the door, and slipped it on. The right brim curled higher and bore a grease stain from being handled so much. He lifted down the old .308 Winchester from the rack beside the door, and slipped the clip from it, checking the loads. He slipped it back in, seating it with a hard slap.

"What about Timmy?" Kate asked as he opened the door. "You going to take him? Or you want him to go over to the south pasture with Seth and the boys?"

"I suppose I'd better take him or else I'll have to listen to your complaining all evening when I get back. Better get him up," he grumbled. "I want to drop down to Bad River and check on the windmill there. One of the boys said he thought the pump leathers were shot. I'll come back through before heading over to the west pasture and pick him up."

"No, you wait for him," she said as he stepped through the door. "We don't need you climbing a windmill today, either. Besides, he has to learn what it is to stay at home. I don't want him to become like his father and uncle. Or you." He muttered a reply she couldn't hear as he slammed the door behind him.

She turned, walking resolutely to the hallway. Slowly she climbed the stairs, the boards creaking under her feet as they slid across the worn boards, her hand resting lightly upon the well-rubbed banister. She breathed deeply, smelling the light lemon still clinging to the polished oak.

She walked down the short hall to the room at the end and knocked lightly, waited for a moment, then turned the knob and walked in. Her nose wrinkled at the stale, night smell. She crossed the room and opened the curtains, sliding the window up. A fresh breeze blew in, carrying a scent of sunburned grass with it. She breathed deeply, then looked over her shoulder at the bed. A bare arm stretched out from a pile of blankets and hung over the side of the bed.

"Timmy," she called. A grumble rolled up from beneath the blankets. "Timmy, get up."

"Go 'way," he mumbled. The arm disappeared back under the blankets.

She reached out and swiftly yanked the blankets back. White, naked skin shone briefly as he sat up and yanked the blankets back, exclaiming, "Ma! I'm naked!"

"I've seen you that way before," she said dryly.

"Yeah, but things are different now," he said surly, holding the blankets tightly to his chin. She reached for them again. "Mom!"

"Are you getting up?"

"Yes!"

"You have five minutes," she said sternly, heading for the door. "Your grandfather said he was going down to Bad River to check the windmill, but I don't want him climbing that tower alone, so get a move on."

"He's climbed that tower a hundred times," Timmy answered sullenly.

"Well, he isn't climbing it today; you are. He'll think he's taking you along to keep you out of mischief." She shut the door behind her, cutting off his retort. She waited until she heard his bare feet strike the floor, then smiled and returned to the kitchen.

It took him fifteen minutes. She looked up from the sink as he entered the kitchen, his hair still gleaming damply from its quick combing. A touch of shaving soap still showed behind one ear. He wore faded blue jeans sensibly cinched at his slim waist by a common brown belt, the cuffs pulled down over scuffed and scarred brown boots. A blue denim workshirt, a carbon copy of his grandfather's, fitted loosely across his slim chest. He crossed to the toast she'd made and picked up two slices as he continued toward the door.

"Don't forget your wire gloves! Tom's going out west to check those heifers and fix some fence after he looks at the windmill!" she called.

"Okay, okay!" he said. He paused at the door to pull his hat from its peg and to take a pair of scarred, yellow leather gloves from a shelf. He waved as he edged around the door.

She watched as he ran toward the old washed-out blue Ford pickup parked next to the machine shop, then sighed and turned back to the sink. Absently, she reached up and fumbled at the dial on the radio on a shelf beside the window, her fingers automatically switching the dial to FM and Public Radio. The strains of a Bach concerto echoed through the house.

Chapter Two

Tom sat in the pickup, waiting impatiently for the young boy to come. He turned the key to the ignition and when the engine roared, he turned on the radio. He recognized the tunes of "Jambalaya," an old Hank Williams song, and leaned back in the seat, tapping his fingers in time upon the Bakelite steering wheel.

When the short days of fall come there will be frost. Yes, there will be frost and that will put some moisture back in the ground. But it won't be enough. No, not nearly enough.

And although the space of the sky above began to turn ever-changing violet and the cold air snapped against his cheeks, he knew that the lanes down from the house would still be dry and dusty in the morning and the cattle would begin to die again slowly from thirst. But they did have water from a natural spring that Heinie Koch had dammed for them with his caterpiller back in the fifties before he was killed in an airplane crash while dropping supplies to folks cut off from town by the '55 blizzard.

Timmy smiled as he stepped from the house and saw Old Tom waiting patiently in the pickup. He hurried across the sun-baked yard to the pickup. He could hear the radio playing as he approached. The old man always listened when an old Hank Williams song came over the radio.

Senior, not Junior. Grandpa couldn't stand the son.

"Just like the young squirts to think they can improve on the old ways," he'd say. He'd frown and turn his head and spit, sometimes forgetting that he was sitting in the kitchen and drawing Ma's scathing comment about barns and hog pens although it'd been a long time since they'd kept a hog on the place. Grandpa thought they were just too damn much trouble.

"Hogs are too damn smart," he'd say. "Sumbitch's always trying to outfigure you instead of living and letting live."

They bought what pork they wanted from Whitey's Locker, paying the few cents extra a pound in town for a whole lot of peace of mind at home.

"Took you long enough," Tom grumbled as Timmy opened the door and slid in on the frayed seat beside him. He crammed the last of the toast in his mouth and turned to glance at the bale of wire and fence posts the old man had thrown into the bed of the pickup. A posthole digger lay beside them. "That all you having for breakfast?"

"Ma said you were in a hurry. She don't want you climbing that windmill tower," Timmy replied around the mouthful of toast. The old man ground the starter and shifted into first.

"I told her that I could do it myself. Just taking you along to keep you out of mischief," he said.

"Yeah, she said that too," Timmy answered.

"I know she did. You think you're telling me something I don't already know?" He dropped the clutch and the pickup jerked forward, nearly stalling. He shoved the accelerator to the floor, and they roared across the yard in a cloud of dust. For some reason, he had a terrible time getting started in first gear but only ground second or third once or twice before catching onto the rhythm of shifting gears.

They rode silently along the country road, listening to the radio, comfortable in each other's silence. Timmy leaned back against the seat, grateful for the respite from going out into the hay fields with the hired men. They were halfway through the second month of haying and he was bored with running the thirty-foot dump rake back and forth across the fields, forming thick windrows for the sweep or bailer coming behind him. Today promised to be a hot one too. A trickle of sweat already ran down his sides and no cloud hovered in the sky. By noon, the wind would be a breath of furnace heat blowing across the fields and pastures.

"Think it'll rain today?" he asked. He looked over at his grandfather's seamed face and the gnarled fingers firmly gripping the steering wheel. The old man glanced at the sky and shook his head.

"Nope. Not today, not tomorrow either. Ain't no water in the air, boy. Can't you feel it sucking the water out of you? That's how you know it ain't gonna rain. Damn. When you gonna learn?"

Timmy ignored the old man's patronizing tone. He'd be twenty in a few days and had already decided that he wasn't going to change his grandfather's ways. "Been a long time since a rain. Tanks are drying up fast in the hills. Bad River and Deer Hollow Creek are almost all that's left in all of Haaken County."

"It's been a bad one," Grandpa conceded. "Snow will be welcome when it comes. At least it'll put something down into the water table. That is, if it comes," he added.

"What'll happen if it doesn't?"

"What the hell do you think will happen?" the old man snorted. "The damn cattle will die. 'Cept ours. It'll take something for Hollow Creek to go down. Best thing we ever did was to let Heinie Koch build that stock tank for us. At least we've got water now." He stayed silent for a long moment, then added: "If old Heinie hadn't got himself killed in that fool airplane of his I'd probably have him out now, trying to bulldoze up another tank just to spite that sumbitch Reynolds."

They passed Old Man Stone's place. Timmy could see grouse strutting around the hedge row of Osage orange and Russian olive and remembered that hunting season was only a week off. He made a mental note to come back on opening day and twisted his head to make sure the NO HUNTING signs were still attached to the gate leading in to the abandoned home site.

"Reynold's gonna have a hell of a time real soon," the old man commented with satisfaction as they passed another gate leading up to a grove of trees tucked in a cut between two hills. His hands wrung the steering wheel, and he turned to grin at the young man beside him. "All his damn money ain't gonna put water in the bellies of those cattle. Fool should've known better than to put so damn many head on those pastures. Too many for the land to support, and he can't truck enough water in to keep them now. Maybe if he had brought in fewer he'd still have enough water to keep half, but what the hell? His problem, not ours."

Timmy looked thoughtfully back at the burnt grass and the white-faced herefords standing, watching the truck go by. Several head already lay on the cracked clay where water should have stood but now wisps of wiregrass had begun to grow, spreading down from the overgrazed rangeland. A small puddle lay in the middle of the near-empty tank, but there wasn't enough water in the puddle for all the cattle crowded into the pasture, filling rapidly with sourdock growth. Nor, he discovered as he looked into the next field, enough hay to make more than one or two bales an acre.

He glanced again at his grandfather and noticed the satisfied smile clinging to the old man's lips. Don Reynolds had been trying to buy the old man's land for over ten years, ever since the banker had moved into Ithaca and bought out the Stockman's Bank, renaming it Haaken County Bank and raising interest rates on loans and dropping saving interests by a full percent. The old man had promptly pulled all Morgan money out of the bank and transferred it to the First National Bank in Pierre. Reynolds had bought up or leased most of the land around the Lazy M, until the Morgans were almost an island in the middle of Reynolds's holdings. The only land that Reynolds didn't control besides Morgan land was Old Man Stone's and that was on a fifty-year lease to the Lazy M, giving the Morgans control of the best bottom land and water rights in the county. Over the past few months, Reynolds had stepped up his campaign to buy out the Morgans, but the old man stubbornly refused to sell.

And a good thing, too. Otherwise, what would there be for Uncle Henry to come home to?

Not, he thought bitterly, that there was any hope that Uncle Henry would come home at all. He had never seen either his father or Uncle Henry, having been born two months after his father had left for Vietnam, following Uncle Henry who had been at the start of President Lyndon Johnson's full commitment of troops. He had a vague sense of his father from the few photographs in a frame on top of the piano in the living room of the house and the large framed picture on top of his mother's bureau in her bedroom. Short, blond hair, piercing blue-gray eyes, and a square chin with high cheekbones. Not all that different from his own features which resembled more his uncle, but what was in the man behind the pictures? That, he had no way of knowing despite the stories his mother and grandfather told him.

The worst is growing up without a father.

He had fought many fights over that on the playground and after school in the willow stand down by Froggy Bottom Creek that ran behind the schoolhouse before his classmates finally decided to leave him alone.

"Well? You gonna sit there or you gonna open the gate?" Grandpa growled.

Timmy blinked and looked foolishly from the old man to the gate in front of the pickup. He opened the door and scrambled out and hurried to the barbed wire gate. He put his shoulder to the end post and pushed to ease the tension, then slipped the bale over the post and hastily pulled the gate open. His grandfather gunned the truck through the gate and stopped and waited as Timmy hooked the gate back to the bale.

"Daydreaming again," the old man said disgustedly as he climbed back into the front of the pickup. "Get that from your Ma, no mistake about it. Always dreaming about one thing or the other."

"You never dream?" Timmy asked defensively.

The old man shook his head. "Ain't got time for it. Dreaming's for fools what's got too much time on their hands and no intentions of spending it wisely."

They bumped along a few minutes before the old man turned off the path leading down the hill to the windmill standing in the middle of a grove of cottonwood trees beside Hollow Creek, cutting instead across the field toward a fence line that rose up a hill and disappeared over the crest.

"Think it better to check the fence first," he said matter-of-factly. "If we gotta dig new post holes, it's better doing so before it gets any hotter."

"You mean if I gotta dig," Timmy said.

"Someone's gotta be the boss," the old man said. "That goes with age."

They grinned for the first time at each other as the pickup labored up the hill. Suddenly the old man slammed on the brakes, nearly throwing Timmy through the windshield. He looked increduously in front of the pickup.

"What the hell," he said. "Son-of-a-bitch!"

Timmy looked out at a massive herd of herefords moving across the fenceline where two sections had been pulled down. Three cowboys on horses looked back up the hill at them, then reined in their horses and sat, silently watching.

"Goddamn that Reynolds!" Tom exploded. "He cut our wire!"

"Maybe the fence just came down," Timmy said soothingly. "Those posts are pretty old."

The old man gave him a furious look. "Then, why the hell are they driving the cattle over into our land instead of back to their own?" he demanded. He slammed the pickup into first and spun the wheels as he sped down the hill toward the men on horseback.

Recklessly he pulled around in front of the cattle, trying to head them off, but the cattle had smelled the water and simply swung around the pickup, heading for the stock tank. The riders pulled up their horses and sat loosely in their saddles, grinning at the old man. Tom swore and stepped stiffly from the pickup, glaring at them.

"What you sumbitches think you're doing, Grayson?" he demanded from the leader.

Grayson pushed his hat back, exposing the white of his forehead where the sun did not touch. He grinned and wiped sweat from beneath his nose with a thick forefinger.

"Taking our cattle to water," he said laconically.

"That's our water! Not yourn!" Tom said furiously.

The riders laughed. Timmy watched as a dull red began to move up the old man's stringy neck. Carefully, he lifted the Winchester from the gun rack behind the seat and quietly opened the door, easing out, masking his movements with the door.

"Yeah, I know," Grayson answered. "But it's the only water around and our cattle need it. You got too much of your own."

"Our cattle need it too," Tom said. He hawked and spat. "And as to how much I got, well, that ain't any of your business any more than how many cattle you got is mine. Now move your damn herd off our land!"

"I don't think so," Grayson said easily.

"What?" Tom cocked his head. "What did you say?"

"What are you going to do?" Grayson said mockingly. "By the time you get the sheriff out here, the cattle will have drunk their fill."

"Then we'll shoot them," Timmy said, stepping from the cab. He levered a shell into the chamber of the Winchester. "That'll stop them, won't it?"

"And what do you think the courts will do about that?" Grayson sneered.

"We still have laws about trespassing here," Timmy said. He draped the Winchester through the crook of his arm, keeping his hand loosely cupped around the action. "And that goes for men as well as cattle," he added pointedly.

"Talk's cheap," Grayson said.

"Uh-huh," Timmy said. He triggered the rifle, sending a bullet into the shale in front of Grayson's horse. Startled, it reared and Grayson swore, grabbing for the saddle horn. Old Tom grinned.

"Now move your cattle!" Timmy said tightly. He levered another cartridge into the chamber and raised the barrel to center on Grayson's chest. "This land's posted!"

"All right!" Grayson said, yanking hard on the bridle. The horse stood still, legs quivering, eyes walling nervously. He gestured at his riders. "Get the cattle."

The others glanced at Grayson then moved around in front of the cattle, bunching them and turning them back toward the hole in the fence. They swore and yelled. Dust swirled around them. Slowly, reluctantly, the cattle turned and began moving back despondently to Reynold's land, their hooves powdering the grama grass and saltgrass.

"This isn't over," Grayson yelled. He spurred his horse, moving hard on a couple of laggards, turning them away from the hole in the fence.

"He's right," Timmy said as the last of the herd swung through the fence. "This isn't over, you know." He handed the rifle to Tom and pulled on his wire gloves.

"I know," Old Tom said. He sighed and took his hat off, mopping his forehead with a calico bandana he pulled from his back pocket. He resettled his hat and stared as Grayson and his riders disappeared over a small rise.

"Reckon we'd better tell Sheriff Wilson," he said. He set the safety, then placed the rifle back in the gun rack. He reached beneath the seat of the pickup and took out a pair of wire gloves and pulled them on.

"Don't think that will do any good." Timmy grunted. He turned to the bed of the pickup and lifted a bale of barbed wire out, dropping it on the ground. "Reynolds's got Wilson in his back pocket, you know that. Wilson owes him money. Lots of it. Wonder why Wilson went so deep into hog futures?" He reached behind the seat of the pickup and took out a pair of wire pliers and went to the fence, pulling the cut strands together to splice them.

"Trying to get rich quick," Tom answered. He pulled a fence stretcher from the back of the bed and moved to a fence post, laying the stretcher out on the ground beside it. "Men like Wilson are always into shortcuts. They don't have any staying power for the long run."

He grunted as he wrapped the station rope around the fence post and clamped onto a wire. Quickly, he took up the slack in the rope and tightened the wire while Timmy pegged it onto a fence post. The old man released the latch and paused to stare off across Reynolds's land.

"Seems like I've either been fighting this land or someone every day," he mused. "Always something. Never any peace."

"It isn't the land," Timmy said, gathering the tools. "It's the people."

The old man nodded. "Yep. Something to what you say. But

the land brings out the best and the worst in each person. More often than not, the worst. Leastways that's the way it seems lately. I remember when a man's handshake was all the contract a man needed. Now"—he shook his head—"I take a close look at a man's hand before I take it."

"We gonna stand here jawing all day or you figure on getting that windmill checked sometime soon?" Timmy asked. His lips spread a grin across his lanky jaw.

The old man sighed and shook his head. "Another thing I don't need is a young calf just off the teat telling me what I should or shouldn't be doing."

He scowled and stumped back to the pickup, leaving the stretcher for Timmy to bring. The young man grinned at his grandfather's back and gathered the stretcher and roll of wire and threw them into the bed of the pickup before climbing in. The old man ground the gears and the pickup lurched, then gathered speed as he shifted into second.

Timmy looked out across the prairie to the gray shale hills and burnt grama grass that belonged to Reynolds. Midmorning was an hour or two away, but a southeast wind blew hot against his face and heatwaves rose simmering in the sun. No rain today, he told himself, gnawing at his inner lip. Then he swiveled his head to look at the lush, green meadow, filled with cordgrass and side-oats grama, below the stock tank where whiteface cows stood. "Turkey-foot" seed heads from big bluestems shot skyward from the meadow. A dark premonition touched him briefly. He shook his head, trying to tell himself he was whistling at shadows.

Dog

The day I was to leave for the Sun Dance at White River, I walked in on her crying. I went up to the big house to tell her that I was going and she was sitting in the armchair in the living room and crying. A record was playing but I did not know what music it was. I knew it was not Hank Williams or anything like that music, but I did not know the name of this music. When I asked her why she cried she said it was because she knew there wasn't anything as beautiful as Ferras playing Beethoven's "Concerto for Violin and Orchestra in D Major."

I did not think the music was beautiful but I could understand the music helping her to see something beautiful and this was a good thing to see. It had been a long time since her husband, Bill Morgan, and his brother Henry, my godson, had left. A very long time. And she had not known many moments of happiness since his leaving.

Perhaps if there had not been Vietnam there would have been happiness for them, but this I do not know. Bill went to Vietnam only because his brother had gone. He should not have gone. He was not a warrior. Henry is a warrior and such people are not placed on this earth by Sacred Woman for their pleasure. We all have duties, reasons for being here, but for the warriors, the duty is much harder for they cannot have what others have. It was not in Bill to be what his brother was although he wanted to be like his brother. There was a tenderness in him that was not in Henry. He liked people. He liked the land. He liked the ranch and the cattle and working the cattle.

So she cried when she heard music that told her there was something beautiful on this earth. And I was happy for her, but I knew that happiness would not last. Perhaps if the rains came the happiness would last, but I knew that the rains would not come, for the leaves of the cottonwood trees had begun to change a full moon before the Moon When the Cherries Turn Black. This meant that the roots of the trees had already drunk the water from the soil and since there was no more water, the trees had decided to die their little deaths early.

I worried too about Henry Morgan for it had been a long time since I had seen him. Except in the smoke of my fire. Sometimes I can see things in the smoke of my fire. It is a gift that I have had from Sacred Woman since I was taken to Harney Peak in the Black Hills—the sacred *Paha Sapa* of my people—and there stood on the place where Black Elk stood many years before and had his vision. It was there that I had my vision too and knew that I was truly blessed by Sacred Woman, for although many have stood in my steps in Black Elk's steps, not many are given a vision by Sacred Woman.

I, John Crow Dog, was the first to have a vision at this place in many years and for that, I was both blessed and cursed. Blessed for I would be able to help my people in a way that they had not been helped for many years. Cursed for I would never be like other men.

When I left, I heard the record change and strange dance music trickle out the open windows of the living room. I knew that music because I had heard it once many years ago and had asked her the same question. She told me that it was Liszt's "Mephisto Waltz"—the dance of the dead. She did not play it very often because it was not music to be listened to for pleasure but music that would allow one to see inside oneself. It was music for one alone. That was the music for Henry.

Stepping Bull was waiting for me when I drove into White River and made my way to the camp down by the water. I could smell whiskey on his breath and knew that I would have to dance the Sun Dance alone the next morning as he would be too sick to dance. Stepping Bull knew that I was not pleased by this and followed me down to the water where I stripped and walked out into the rushing water and let it numb me.

"You are late," he said, and I knew that he was trying to blame me for his own drunkenness. But I did not listen to him as he tried to work his way into an argument. He sat on the bank and watched as I washed.

"Billy Spotted Horse and Tom Standing Bear are in jail down in Gordon," he said.

I paused, staring up at him. "Why?"

He shrugged. "They got drunk and decided to square things for George Little Pony." He laughed. "They found Eterskel and beat him pretty bad. They should have come back to the reservation, but they didn't. The sheriff caught them when he found them passed out in Tom's car at the state line." He chuckled. "About fifteen more feet and they would have been safe."

I nodded, remembering when Phil Eterskel and some of his friends had beaten George Little Pony after he refused to let them hunt pheasant on his land. They were drunk and beat him for that and because they needed someone to beat at the moment. Then they had shot his cattle and drove their pickup through his cornfield. His cousins, Billy and Tom, were big and powerful and did not like many white men.

"Is anyone going down to get them out?" I asked.

He shrugged. "Not now. The whole town is very angry with them for beating Eterskel. It isn't safe."

At last, he left me alone and weaved himself through the darkness back to his tent where I knew he had hidden a bottle of whiskey.

I did not remain alone in the darkness for long as Little Bird, his woman, came down to the river and stripped and walked out into the water with me. I saw the light play upon her heavy breasts and the thick bramble bush between her legs. She smiled and handed me a cup. I sniffed cautiously for I do not drink whiskey and am afraid that someone will someday steal my medicine by playing a bad joke upon me. But I smelled only coffee and thanked her. I drank while she moved around me, washing me carefully with soap made from the root of the soapweed.

She took my hand and led me to the bank. Moonlight glimmered from her skin and drops of water shined like tiny quartz from the hair of her dark triangle. She put her arms around me and rubbed her heavy breasts against my chest. She smelled fresh and clean and I followed her as she pulled me down onto her upon the ferns. Her tongue touched mine and then she guided me between her legs and I entered the soft center of her.

Later, I entered the sweat lodge that had been prepared for me to cleanse myself of her. I washed myself with sage and smoke before entering, then sat and listened to the heat rising from the stones in the fire in the center of the lodge. I stared into the coals of the fire and found myself within the thoughts of Sacred Woman and listened to the sadness of her thoughts which are the thoughts of the earth which are the thoughts of the men back in Ithaca. I listened to their thoughts and suddenly a man stood in front of me and I knew him to be Touch the Clouds.

Listen to your grandfathers, he said to me. A great sadness

rested upon his face and I asked him why he was sad. This you must know, he said. He stretched his arms wide and a great cavern appeared in his chest. I watched and a bay horse with night-black mane galloped from the darkness of the cavern, moving slowly as in a dream. He stopped in front of me and spoke.

Look!

And he turned slowly to where he came from and I looked back into the darkness and watched a red sun creep slowly out of the darkness, driving before it twelve black horses. Sparks flew from their hooves and lightning crackled and streaked toward me from their noses. I cried out in fear and they disappeared and the bay horse with night-black mane appeared again.

Why are you afraid when I am here? it asked me.

Because I am man, I answered.

It turned toward the north and six white horses galloped toward me, hard snow flying from their noses. The bay turned again to the west and three sorrel horses galloped toward me. Where their hooves touched the ground the grass withered and died. The bay turned again to the south and a roan horse galloped toward me and thunder and lightning followed it. The earth trembled and the sky split open and fire rained down from the sky. Then darkness fell and Touch the Clouds stood again before me.

You have seen, he said, and disappeared.

I rose and walked from the sweat lodge and ran to the river. I plunged into the waters and felt the coldness drive hard against my flesh. I stood in the waters, facing east, waiting for the sun.

Chapter Three

Kate Morgan sat on the wooden bench swing hanging from a gnarled branch of the large cottonwood that sprawled up and over the old ranch house. She sipped coffee from a chipped mug with the faded legend CASEY TIBBS, WORLD CHAMPION COWBOY as she idly pushed against the ground with one booted foot. A long strand of hair lay plastered across her wide forehead. A breeze blew across her flushed face, cooling it. She pulled her shoulders back, trying to work a kink out of her back. She looked down at the dishpan filled with string beans she had picked and a few carrots, the last of the year. She glanced over at the garden behind her. Time to lay the mulch and till it back into the ground.

As always, she felt a twinge of sadness at the end of the growing season, leaving her feeling empty and hollow inside as if a part of her had been taken away. A gold leaf fell onto her lap. She picked it up between dirt-stained fingers and brushed it against her cheek.

Twenty years.

Had it really been that long since Bill left for Vietnam, following Henry? 'Sixty-five. At least twenty.

I think Bill loved the idea of marriage and the idea of family. Perhaps it was because he lost his mother when he was very young to a sickness that he could not understand and could not protect her from. By taking a wife he replaced her with the only magic he could conjure from his world. He was made for marriage. But Henry was not made for marriage and although Bill tried to be like Henry, there was too much against him from the beginning. The five years after his mother's death he spent alone in the big house with only his father and Henry. They took most of their meals in the cook house with the three hired hands and cook. It was a male world and as a male world there was no softness in it, no compassion which must be taught.

And then, she told herself, there was the war and in 1965 the war was not an evil thing for the people in South Dakota still remembered World War II and all the romantic foolishness that went along with it, from the music to the loyalty everyone felt for their country and their country's soldiers. The Korean War dampened that spirit a bit but by the time the Vietnam War came, the memory of World War II was still current enough that Henry and others like him went willingly to Southeast Asia because their country had said it was necessary for them to go. And because Henry went, Bill went. To be with his brother. To be like his brother. To see people's admiration in their eyes like they looked when they thought about Henry and others like him before times changed.

But Bill never came back again to see the change. And Henry never came back after Bill was killed. And now, he will never come back again. I was here then. But I was not their mother; I was only the idea of what she stood for—the family. And with the distance that was between us came the awareness of the idea. And the awareness touched some dark secret place within him and then came despair and guilt and he buried that guilt in the war.

At first letters came frequently and I sent letter after letter to the anonymous APO address, not certain where he was except somewhere in Southeast Asia. Then the letters came less and less and I wasn't even certain that he was still in Southeast Asia. Then for a long time the letters stopped altogether.

She shook her head irritably and took a large swallow of coffee. The war. Almost fifteen years had passed since the last American troops had been pulled out of the country. Fifteen years, and still the war claimed its victims.

She raised her eyes to look at the iron chanticleer atop the weathervane on a cupola of the house. A west wind, she reflected automatically.

Her eyes burned with sudden tears. Damn. I thought I had

finished crying. But I guess one never is—there is always something to cry for.

She heeled the tears away with the palm of her hand and finished her coffee, dropping the mug on top of the beans and carrots. She rose and picked up the dishpan, balancing it easily on one hip as she walked back to the ranch house. A meadowlark sang from its nest in a bunch of buffalo grass on the prairie and she stopped to listen, turning automatically to the stock tank down the hill from where the home place stood. The cottonwoods glowed golden in the afternoon sun. A mourning dove called, whooo-oo-oo-oo. A lonely sound.

She sighed heavily. Lonely doesn't get the beans snapped, she told herself. She stepped inside the house, letting the screen door bang shut behind her and moved to the sink. She placed the dishpan in the sink, ran cold water over the beans and carrots, then quickly snapped the ends of the beans, working automatically, letting her fingers take the memory away from her.

She heard the sound of the pickup roaring up the small hill toward the ranch yard as she finished the last of the beans. She smiled slightly and wiped her hands, glancing at the clock. Five P.M. The day had gotten away from her. She shook her head, irritated at herself, and crossed to the refrigerator, opening it. She clucked her tongue in disgust: she had forgotten to set the roast out to thaw before going out to her garden and now it was too late. She bit her lip, considering.

The door slammed open and shut behind her. She cocked her head and looked over her shoulder as Tom slumped in, limping on his scarred old leg torn when a steer had horned him during branding season years before. His face was grim, a smudge of grease streaking one leathery cheek. He slapped his hat on its peg and crossed to the sink.

"Don't you use my good towels, now, you hear?" she said sharply as he turned the water on and picked up the gray bar of pumice soap. He grunted and began scrubbing his hands under the water. She looked at Timmy and arched an eyebrow. He shook his head.

"We had a little run-in with Grayson," Timmy said. He hung

up his hat and moved over to stand beside his grandfather. He took the beans from the sink and turned the faucet over to his side, wetting his hands before picking up the soap. He ignored the old man's growl and vigorously soaped his hands before dropping the bar back in its dish beside the sink.

"What happened?" Kate asked.

"They cut the wire to drive their cattle over to our water," Timmy said. He smiled at her. "They left when we reasoned a little with them."

"I'll bet," she said dryly. "Who did the reasoning? You or your grandpa?"

The old man snorted and plucked a towel from the rack beside the sink. "I don't need anyone to talk for me. Been doing all my own talking for nearly sixty-five years, now. Words are words. I still know enough of them to talk to people."

"Uh-huh," Timmy said laconically. "You surely do."

"Smart ass," the old man snarled and crossed to the refrigerator, peering inside. "What's for supper?"

"How about omelets?" she asked, reaching for the cheese and eggs.

"Forgot to lay the meat out, huh?" the old man said with relish. He took the eggs and cheese from her and placed them back in the refrigerator. "Now that's as good an excuse for going into town as I can find."

"What's that?" Timmy asked.

"I been trying to talk your ma into letting me take her in to the dance tonight in Ithaca at the American Legion."

"I don't—" she began protesting, but Timmy broke in.

"I think that's a fine idea," he said enthusiastically. "We could all use a little time in town. Shake the shackles off and kick up our heels."

"This wouldn't have something to do with Mort Swanson's daughter Penny, would it?" she asked. He blushed and she grinned at him. "You men go on ahead. I've got a few things to do around the house."

"Ain't nothing that can't wait," Tom said stubbornly. He grabbed her shoulders and gave her a shove toward the stairs.

"Now the three of us are going into town and have a nice steak and do a little heel-kicking. That's all there's to it. You've got one hour."

She laughed and reluctantly climbed the stairs to her room, her mood suddenly lightening. Perhaps the old coot was right. A little fun never hurt anybody.

She heard the radio click on downstairs and a twangy voice sing:

> Now, I keep drinkin' malt liquor
> Trying to drive the blues away—

She smiled to herself and opened her closet, critically eyeing the dresses hanging neatly at the back of the walk-in closet.

Tom stared out the window over the sink. The late afternoon of the day held deep to its dappled east-borne clouds. Over at Old Man Stone's place the abandoned orchard would be deep in russets and greens but the apples would be small because there was not enough water to make them full-bodied and round. The crabapples would be more sour than ever and the entire poise and balance of the period itself would be out of whack and the rhythmic rise and fall of the days would be jarred and jangled. A faint noise came to him and he leaned forward over the sink and looked up into the deep blue that hurt his eyes. He saw the V-flight of geese heading south for the winter, ever south in search of water. A faint click in his heart, a faint throb along the pulse of his throat, told him that this was the last fabric of his days and he heard a confused music within himself that suggested names, but he could not remember the names and stood in the growing darkening silence listening to the nebulous music that trailed itself south, ever south, with the flight of the geese.

He sighed and left the kitchen and walked into the living room. The room through the lace end of the curtain seemed suffused with dusky golden light amid which the lamp by which she read appeared a pale flame. The windowpanes of the house looking to the west reflected the tawny gold of the great bank of clouds heaving up from the horizon. But there was no rain in those clouds despite their bulk and the dry air that blew through an open window into his face burned his cheeks and watered his eyes. He shook his head. Nothing good gonna come of this, he told himself.

Overhead he heard water beginning to run in the bathtub and grinned. At least they could have a bit of fun tonight. He walked to the stairway and climbed up to his bedroom, unbuttoning his shirt as he went.

Chapter Four

Ithaca was what some people called a "spit-'n-holler" town—just long enough to give a spit and a holler and one would be through the town. Trains slowed only long enough for the engineer to make sure the red-eye wasn't out before roaring through. Every year at the annual town meeting, Winifred Grubber, the town librarian and a fervent postmillennialist, raised a protest about the Chicago & Northwestern's lack of respect for the townspeople by not going slow enough for people to get out of the way if they were making the crossing from the river to town across the tracks. Old Man Buelow, who had been section foreman for so many years that people called the section house the Buelow Place, always protested that no one had been killed at that crossing since the thirties when ol' Tom Yellow Eyes had gotten drunk and lay down on the track to rest a minute.

"Found pieces of him from here to Phillip!" Buelow would cackle, then snicker maliciously as Winifred Grubber shuddered. " 'Course, that don't count the time that Howard Levins was crossing the track with his wagon of melons, but no one got killed then. Sure had melon all over, though. Why, those things went flying from here to Timbuktu! Sure enough! Levins never was the same after that. Town wasn't neither! Those melons splattered around enough that we never found half those damn seeds. We had volunteer vines coming up all over! Damn near took over the town. 'Course it was wetter then. That was the year that Jimmy Watkins ate deathcamass thinking it was wild onion, remember? Died 'fore they could get him to the hospital in Pierre. Tch. Tch."

A man of wit, some people claimed, while others thought

the old section foreman should have been pensioned off years before and sent to live in Pierre in the old folks' home at St. Mary's Hospital where he could wander around in the Municipal Park next door to his heart's content. But most people were afraid to make their feelings known outside of the meeting hall for fear that the Chicago & Northwestern would remove Old Man Buelow and close down the section, bringing about the final end of the town. For all his faults, Old Man Buelow could still be counted on to turn on the red-eye and pull the train off to a siding for someone to get aboard or get off if that person had remembered to call him from Pierre or Rapid City before boarding the train.

And there was also the matter of loading stock from the stock pens to the west of the town. If the train went, cattle costs would nearly double by the time the ranchers shipped their cattle to the Fort Pierre stockyards on truck instead of train. And then the town would die for sure because there would be no use for the town without the periodic cattle shipment from the ranchers.

The only brick building in town was the small post office where Clara Hubbard worked, sorting mail and bagging it and making her rounds through the countryside before returning to Midland where she lived. Once, the postal service thought to discontinue the Ithaca line and run everything out of Midland, but Clara crammed her six-foot frame and two hundred pounds behind the wheel of her postal jeep and drove in to Pierre where she had a private chat with the postal inspector, a small, balding weasel of a man who sweated through his shirt every day of the year despite the temperature by noon. When Clara left, no more talk was heard about closing the Ithaca line, which would stay open, it was understood, until Clara decided to close it by retiring.

The only highway through town, a narrow two-lane, black-topped road that had not been repaired in thirty years, ran east and west, paralleling Bad River, before making an abrupt ninety-degree turn to dive down a short hill and rattle across a single-lane girded bridge heading south.

Dougie Miller's gas station, half stone and half wood, stood at the far end of the street with a faded Skelly sign stuck up on a creosoted wooden pole marking the gravity-fed gas pumps. Miller stubbornly refused to replace the pumps with electric ones, positive that to do so would cut into his profits. Dirt had crusted over the floor of his garage so thickly that the hydraulic lift stopped two inches shy of the floor when it was lowered, and no one could remember the last time Dougie had cleaned the washrooms although all agreed it had to be sometime before Roosevelt sent the boys overseas to fight. But he let anyone pick the chokecherry bushes that grew behind his station down to the river so all kept pretty quiet about Dougie's lack of hygiene.

Although the town had municipal mains for water and a sewer system that dumped the sewage into a slough north of town well beyond the water table, most of the houses had their own wells, sandpoints drilled down to the water table thirty feet beneath the clay soil.

Steiner's Emporium, a large wooden building that was a combination dry-goods store and food market with a small drug counter and fountain in the back, gave the folks what they needed in the way of emergency items, running credit lines on three-by-five cards Eddie Steiner kept in a recipe box under the counter below the nickel-plated cash register.

Next to Steiner's store was a small grain elevator with twin steel tubes that stood taller than anything else in town except the water tower where Lon Moore had forced Dwight Bode to climb to the top, carrying a gallon of white exterior paint, and paint over Linda Moore's name and the legend he had attributed to her lapsarian habits.

The town had mainly one culture—German—although most of the people who lived there had other blood running through their veins as well. Yet most of the older ones remembered how the World War II years had been miserable years indeed with rowdies from the nearby towns rolling through in bobtail trucks in the wee, small hours of the morning, firing rifles and yelling curses at the "krauts" who lived in their midst and surely had business with the goose-stepping son-of-a-bitch overseas. The toughest times came when one of the nearby hometown boys got killed and the children would return home from school in Midland, bloody and beaten by the sons and cousins of whoever managed to get himself killed.

The American Legion hall was built right after the Korean War and named after Klaus Koch who had been given the Silver Star posthumously after being killed at the Chosin Reservoir. The rowdies no longer drove through the town after that save once, making the mistake of trying to hoo-rah the town when Tom Morgan had stopped at Miller's to gas-up his pickup before heading back to the ranch. What followed was still spoken about in hushed tones whenever it was talked about at all. Tom had taken his .308 Winchester from the rack behind the seat of his pickup and shot out the tires of the pickup. The rowdies' truck started to swerve and started to roll over, throwing those in the bed out onto the roadway. When the driver crawled out of his truck and started cursing Tom, the rancher slammed him in the mouth with the stock of his Winchester, shattering his teeth. The others, shaken and bruised after being thrown from the truck, paid Dougie ten dollars to pull the truck back over onto its wheels with his wrecker and drove silently from the town, the owner lying in back on the bed, moaning through a bloodied mouth.

Music swelled and broke from the American Legion hall as the Morgans left Elsie's Café. Old Tom worked hard with a toothpick at a piece of meat lodged between two back molars. Timmy handed a hard peppermint to Kate as they stood for a moment, savoring the cool fall night. People called to them as they crossed the town square and they waved back, pausing to exchange pleasantries with a couple before moving on.

"That old Homer doing the call?" Tom asked one of his cronies—Arch Rankwell—as he tossed the toothpick into a brown spirea bush. A slight breeze rustled the dry limbs together.

Arch nodded. "Yep. Came down from Midland on account his grandson's band is gonna play the last set for the younger crowd. Sort of moral support, you know?"

Tom shook his head. "More of that damn rock-and-roll racket, I reckon?"

"I don't know," Arch confessed. "Ain't country, that's for sure."

"We'll be gone by then," Tom said firmly. He started to move past, but Arch reached out and grabbed his arm.

"I heard you had a bit of trouble with Reynolds's man, Grayson," he said in a low voice.

Tom's eyes narrowed, and he motioned for Kate and Timmy to go on ahead of him. "What'd you hear?" he growled.

"Enough to tell you not to go in there," Arch said. "The Rafter R is in there. Almost the whole lot of them. Dodd Black hit the hooch a bit over at Fatty's place up by Four Corners before they came on in. Got to blowing what they would do to you and the boy if you should show up. Mentioned something about Kate as well, but I ain't gonna repeat that."

"What'd he say?" Tom asked, a hardness coming into his voice. Arch shook his head.

"Nope. They's killing words, and he wouldn't of said them if he wasn't whiskeyed up with that Who-Flung-John. But I'd gather your folk and head for home, Tom. You won't find many friends in there, tonight. A lot of them want to see you get hurt 'cause you got the only water around. You and the Bledsoes, only they ain't comin' in. Will won't let his people into town until the drought breaks, you know. Comes in himself with his oldest boy, Ken, to get supplies, then heads back out promptly."

"Be a cold day in hell when I run from the Rafter R," Tom said tightly.

"It's more than them. A lot of people are in danger of going under and they look at you and Bledsoe and the water you got and it makes them feel helpless. Man can only feel like that so long before he gets to hating the person that makes him feel that way." Arch shook his head, the lines in his wrinkled, weather-beaten face deepening as he pulled a cigarette from a pack in his shirt pocket. "People normally your friends won't do much to help you, now."

"I'll think about it," Tom said, pulling away.

"Yeah, you'll think about it, but you'll go in there anyways, won't you? Stubborn jackass."

Arch turned away and walked over to a bench under a cottonwood and sat next to two old men. He took out his knife and a piece of wood, spat, and leaned back, carefully shaving tiny curls from the soft pine. For a second, Tom was tempted to join him on the bench, telling the old stories about the thirties and the forties, but he turned and hurried to catch up with Timmy and Kate. They eyed him curiously as he clomped up.

"What'd old Arch want?" Timmy asked, frowning. In the distance, they heard the 9:00 P.M. train whistle its way through town, the sound rising and falling to warn Ithaca traffic that it wasn't stopping at the small depot as it rocketed toward Rapid City. The noise cut through the shadows of the streets like the train itself.

"Not much," Tom said. "Just to warn us that the Rafter R's in town."

"Maybe we should just go back home," Kate said, stopping. She fingered the pink sweater around her shoulders nervously. "We don't need any more trouble."

"That's what Arch said. But I'm in the mood for dancing a set or two and that's what I intend on doing," he finished stubbornly. He linked his arm through hers and pulled her into the hall. They paused, blinking in the dimness made from the low wattage bulbs overhead. A cowboy band stood at the far end of the hall with Homer Atchison clutching the microphone in his bony fingers. His cowboy hat had been pushed to the back of his forehead and light glistened from the sweat shining from the white scalp beneath his thinning hair. He wore a blue shirt with imitation pearl snaps instead of buttons. Two roses had been embroidered on the front of the yoke and a bolo tie with a steer head clasp that reminded Tom of Hopalong Cassidy's tie hung around his neck.

Tom's eyes flickered around the room, catching the wallflowers sitting patiently in folding chairs along one wall, waiting for when the men got drunk enough to see the beauty beneath their homeliness. To their right, a long wooden bar curved down to the door. Men leaned elbows on the bar and lifted glasses of beer as they talked about the drought and cattle prices. Heads turned and looked curiously at them and he felt Kate's hand tighten nervously on his forearm. He ignored them, absently patting her arm to reassure her.

"I'll see you later," Timmy said beside him. He walked across the hall, swaying easily around dancers. Tom grinned as he saw Penny Swanson, wearing a yellow dress with a neckline swooping low enough to expose the tops of her young breasts, smiling at Tim's approach. Good to see life in the young ones, he thought with satisfaction. The smile disappeared as his eyes shifted to the group standing beside her, recognizing Grayson and other Rafter R riders. The skin tightened across his cheekbones, the corners of his lips drawing down into deep parentheses.

"Oh God," Kate murmured.

"Come on," he said roughly, dragging her out onto the floor as the band swung into "Leaving Cheyenne" and Homer began singing in his cracked voice.

> "Goodby, Old Paint,
> I'm a-leavin' Cheyenne"

Kate tried to push away, but he pulled her close, and swung her out into the circle going clockwise around the room. His boots clumped noisily on the floor as he moved into his own version of the waltz-two-step and circled the room, slightly out of time to the music.

"You stubborn old coot," Kate said, taking two steps to his one as she tried to keep her toes from being trod upon. "You're just aching for trouble, aren't you?"

"If it's gonna come, it's gonna come," he returned. "Maybe it's better here where there's witnesses."

"To what?" she asked. Her eyes flashed angrily. "The Morgans aren't the most popular around Ithaca, right now."

"We got friends here," he said.

"No, we got *acquaintances*," she emphasized. "There's a difference. If everyone had water, then we might have friends. But they don't and we do. That makes for bad feelings."

"It'll be all right," he said soothingly. "Now just concentrate on your dancing. We're here for a good time, remember?"

She sighed and followed him through the dance. When the band finished, she quickly excused herself, glanced over at Wallflower Row, saw Annie Boskins grinning at her, and resolutely headed her way. A square dance started and Homer's voice slipped into the call:

> "Here we go with the old chuckwagon.
> Hind-wheel broke and the axle draggin'
> Meet your honey and pat her on the head."

He laughed and leaped up in the air, cracking his heels together. A cowboy let out a *whoop*! from across the room. She hurried off the floor, then pulled up short as Grayson stepped in front of her.

"Like to dance?" he grinned. His eyes glinted moistly and she could smell the whiskey on his breath and the rose oil he had used on his hair to plaster it in place. A light flush glowed from his high cheekbones. He held out a calloused hand. She stepped aside.

"No thanks," she said. "I need to say hello to Annie." She nodded in the woman's direction, noticing how the smile had slipped into a frown on Annie's face.

"You can always talk to her," Grayson said. "The night's still young." He took a slight step to block her again. She stepped back to stare at him.

"I don't want any trouble," she said.

"Who's causing trouble? All I want is a little dance." He grinned recklessly at her, his eyes staring hypnotically into hers. For a moment she wavered, then shook her head.

"I don't think that's a good idea," she said. She tried to step around him again, but he blocked her and she took a quick step back. The color mounted to her face as a hot retort leaped to her lips. Then Annie Boskins slipped between them, linking her arm into Kate's and bumping Grayson out of the way with a fleshy hip.

"Come on, Kate," she said roughly. Her eyes sparkled behind her steel spectacles as she fixed Grayson with a hard stare. "I want to hear what's been happening out at the ranch. Been a long time since you came into town."

"Catch you later." Grayson called mockingly as Annie dragged Kate away toward an empty table. He sauntered over to Wallflower Row and led Sarah Hopkins, a plain-looking girl from a small ranch down on the Bloody Run onto the floor.

"What's with Grayson?" Annie asked, her blue eyes squinting through the stale, smoky air. "He's coming on awfully strong."

Kate hesitated, then sighed. Her shoulders slumped. "He had a run-in with Tom and Timmy this morning when the Rafter R tried to move in on our water," she explained. She glanced over to where the Rafter R cowboys sat around a long folding table. Bottles of Jim Beam and Sunnybrooke bourbon shone in the dim light. "I think there's going to be trouble."

Annie shook her head. "There's always trouble when the Rafter R is in town. That's nothing new. Those boys think they have a hard lien on life once they start working for that outfit. There's something else. What is it?" She leaned her head back and stared suspiciouly at Kate. "He coming around again?"

Kate blushed and looked away. Grayson had been one of the cowboys who had made overtures to her after Bill had been dead five years. At first she had been flattered by the attention they had given her: bouquets of wildflowers left in the mailbox or on the porch, boxes of Russell Stover candies, bottles of perfume from Steiner's Emporium, all left with awkwardly written notes. Then the invitations began to arrive to go to dances, all tactfully refused. Most of them had taken their disappointment with grace, but not Grayson. She glanced involuntarily at him as he wheeled his partner around the floor, his handsome face flushed from the whiskey and dance and remembered how he had caught her coming out of the chicken coop with a basket of eggs and tried to kiss her. Tom had been working in the machine shed and saw her struggling with him and came up behind Grayson with a hotshot, stabbing the cattle prod into his backside and hitting him with the electric charge. Grayson had howled and leaped away, his hands clapped to his buttocks and old Tom had stepped in close and hit him again with another electric shock in the belly that had doubled him over. Then Timmy galloped up on his horse and roped Grayson and dragged him down the lane and out onto the road, leaving him there. She had had a hard time to keep Tom from going after Grayson with his rifle.

"No," she said. "No, he hasn't been around again. Not since Tom—" She hesitated. Annie quickly patted her hand.

"The bastard got off lucky. He deserved horse-whipping," she said. "Now if that had been my Nancy, Grayson would've found himself in the hospital with a broken leg."

Kate gave her a twisted smile. Annie didn't know about the October day three years earlier when Grayson had caught her in the barn and pulled her into an empty stall. She remembered his hot breath, his black eyes glinting, as he tried to kiss her. Then she heard a solid *thunk!* as a two-by-four connected with his head and his weight sagged heavily upon her, smothering her for an instant before Tom pulled him off her.

"It wouldn't have made any difference," Kate said.

"No, that one is pure mean," Annie answered. She raised her head, looking around, then clucked her tongue disgustedly. "And ain't none of these yahoos gonna help if trouble breaks out." She took a handkerchief from the sleeve of her dress and blotted the perspiration from her beefy face. "Damn drought." She cocked an eye at Kate. "These really are good people, Kate. You know that. You've lived around here twenty years. It's just that, well, you got water. Some of the ranchers around here have been in business all their lives and now they're about to lose everything their grandparents built up from nothing and all because of no rain. It don't make them feel any happier when they look at your place and see that water." She held up her hand as Kate started to speak. "I know. I know. They could've settled that land the Morgans did. But they didn't. And that don't help neither. They took the land closest to the town and the railroad. Back then, it made sense. Now"—she shook her head—"a little water's all they need."

"Yes," Kate said. "No rain doesn't help, that's for sure."

"You heard anything from Henry?"

The question came suddenly, casually. She glanced at Annie and saw the change working in her face and wondered again what had been between them before she had come to the ranch as Bill's bride. She shook her head. "No. Nothing. Vietnam's been over nearly twenty years." Her voice thickened and she looked quickly away before her eyes teared.

"I don't understand that man," Annie said brusquely. "It just plain don't make any sense. Why not come home after all this time? Just don't make sense to me."

Kate shrugged and looked at the dancers. Timmy gave a quick wave as he pranced by, swinging Penny on his arm. She waved back.

The tears had dried in her eyes and she felt herself calm again.

"It doesn't matter," she said. "I gave up on him coming home a long time ago. The war did strange things to a lot of people. I suppose."

"Nonsense," Annie said stoutly. "That's just an excuse. Why, look at how many men around here fought in World War Two and Korea. They all came home and came home thankfully once the war was over. Wasn't any floating around the country searching for something for them. No sir. They came home, packed their uniforms into the trunk in the attic and got down to running their lives again."

"Their war was a popular one," Kate said. She looked at Annie. "When Henry came home the first time, he landed at Oakland. A bunch of college kids linked arms and sat down in the road and wouldn't let the taxis bring Henry and the others off base. Did you know that? When Henry finally got into San Francisco, he went shopping for some civilian clothes. When he walked down Market Street, people spit on him."

Annie looked away from her, drumming her fingers on the table top. "California ain't here," she said. "People around here are different. Nobody around here would have spat on Henry. They're real people."

"Are they?" Kate smiled wryly. "They sure didn't make him feel welcome when he came home on leave the first time, did they?" Annie looked away. "What was it Betty said to him? 'I don't understand how you can do that?' Remember what happened when Henry told her to go to hell?"

"People change," she said defensively. "And you know why Betty Rogers came on to him that way. He and she were an item together when they went to high school here. Her old man was the barber, then, and I tell you she was one wild little thing. Still is," she added, nodding across the room. Kate followed her motion and caught Betty looking at them. She tossed her head and leaned over the table, pretending interest in the cowboy sitting across from her. His head tilted down automatically as he took in her large white breasts bubbling over the top of her low-cut cotton dress, the pale blue discolored by patches of perspiration that hinted at the naked woman beneath.

"She thought that she and Henry would be getting married. No"—she shook her head—"most of the folks around here are good folks."

"Then why are we having so much trouble with them? I don't think we can blame it all on the drought, can we?"

"Well I never been to college like you, but I know these people. I ain't never been nowhere else all my life, but here. And I tell you that these are good people. Good country people."

"Yes," Kate echoed. "Good country people who blame us for their difficulties."

Annie's lips thinned and she started to answer, but a commotion on the dance floor drew her attention. Kate shifted and looked over her shoulder as the music trickled off. A small crowd had gathered around Timmy and Dodd Black. The Rafter R rider swayed on his high bootheels, grinning crazily at Timmy. Penny stood behind them, her face white and drawn, her eyes darting nervously around the room, seeking help.

"Be careful, Black," Timmy said in a neutral voice. "You're drunk. Don't say anything you'll regret."

"Regret? Why should I regret anything?" He reached out suddenly and grabbed Timmy's shirt in one meaty fist, balling it up and pulling him close. "You Morgans think you can run rough over everyone, don't you?"

"I'm not looking for any trouble. Take your hands away," Timmy said quietly. He kept his hands down by his side, his eyes steady on the cowboy's.

"You man enough to do that? Without your grandpa around?" He laughed and shook his hand back and forth. "Come on, boy. Let's see you do it!"

"I don't want any trouble," Timmy said quietly.

Kate rose and started for the floor. A hand reached out and grabbed her, pulling her back. She tried to turn, but a strong arm looped around her shoulders and held her tightly. A heavy scent of English Leather aftershave wafted over her. She looked up into Grayson's face. He grinned down at her. She struggled.

"Let go of me!" she said furiously. She tried to stamp on his foot, but he shifted her away, holding her easily, but firmly.

"Let it be," Grayson said lowly. Suddenly he bent his head and kissed her hard on the lips. She went rigid, paralyzed by shock, then tried to push away from him.

Timmy's eyes caught her struggle. His face tightened, then his knee came up hard into Black's groin. The cowboy's face turned ashen. He groaned and spun away, falling on his knees to the floor. He bent over until his forehead touched the floor, moaning. Timmy pushed through the crowd and grabbed Grayson, spinning him away. His fist lashed out and cracked against Grayson's jaw, knocking him backwards into a line of folding chairs.

"Get him!" someone yelled, and the crowd converged on Timmy. Three reeled away. Someone knocked hard into her back, and Kate felt herself falling. Someone grabbed her and steadied her. She saw Grayson push himself up out of the pile of chairs and step forward, grabbing Timmy's shoulder. The young man spun around. His fist lashed out again. Grayson staggered away, his hands cupping his nose. Blood dribbled down upon his shirt. Tom gave a roar and came bulling his way through the crowd. He followed Grayson, swinging wildly. A fist bounced off Grayson's temple, then a cowboy spun Tom around and punched him low in the stomach. Tom sagged, then gamely struck out. Two others grabbed him and held him tightly while a third grinned and began raining blows upon him. Kate's fingers closed around the folding chair. She raised it high, then felt it being pulled from her grasp. She whirled around and slammed into the bulk of the sheriff. She looked up into Kelsey Wilson's face. His jowls shook beneath his chin.

"Do something!" she demanded.

"What do you want me to do?" he asked in a high, thin voice.

"Your job!" she snapped.

"Looks to me like they asked for it," he said.

"Kelsey Wilson, you don't do something right now, we'll see what you do next November's election!" Annie snapped.

"Now, Annie," he whined.

"Don't you 'now Annie' me! Get in there and stop that before someone gets hurt, you worthless piece of trash!" She grabbed a whiskey bottle from a table and waved it threateningly at him. "Why, if Henry Morgan was here, he'd kick your fat butt around the dance hall for you, just like he did thirty years ago when you tried to take a few liberties down at Miller's Pond! Remember?"

"Annie—"

"I remember that! What do you think he'll do to you this time? Take that tin star and put it where the moon don't shine?" She stepped forward and waved the whiskey bottle under his nose. "I'm gonna count to one!"

He flushed and stepped resolutely forward, pushing people apart. "All right! Break it up, now! Come on! Enough's enough! They've learned their lesson!"

A loud cry of pain came from the group, and Kate spun back around. The men holding Tom let him go, stepping back. He fell next to Timmy, cradling his ribs, his face gray with pain. She ran to him and knelt.

"I'm all right," he gasped. He winced in pain, but nodded at Timmy. "See to Timmy." She rose and bent over Timmy. Lumps formed over his face and a tiny trickle of blood came from his nose and lips. She gently touched his face and he moaned, moving away from the pressure of her fingertips. She looked wildly around at the ring surrounding them. Unfriendly faces stared back.

"I'll take care of him," Annie said to Kate. "Someone bring me some water." No one moved and her eyes narrowed. "I ain't asking again." Her eyes fell on Homer. He flushed and picked up a glass and handed it to her. She poured it on her handkerchief and began to wipe Timmy's face. His eyes fluttered open, looked around dazedly, then sharpened. He pushed her hands away and sat up.

"He'll be all right," she said soothingly. She nodded to Tom. "You see to that old man. Way he's holding onto his ribs they might be broken."

"Good country people," Kate said bitterly, and rose, stepping to Tom and helping him to his feet. Her eyes fell on Grayson. Her lips tightened and spread into a thin line. He smiled back, mockingly. She paused to grab a glass half-full of whiskey from a table and threw it into his face. He yelped as the whiskey struck his eyes and began to rub them furiously.

The crowd parted as she silently led her father-in-law from the hall. Timmy pulled himself to his feet, glanced around at the circle, then his eyes settled on Grayson.

"Don't come around the Lazy M again, Grayson," he said, his words ringing out over the crowd. "You stay away from us, Grayson. I ain't telling you again."

A laugh rose from the group. Someone made a raspberry, and Timmy turned, walking painfully after his mother and grandfather. Behind him, men slapped each other on the back and the group broke apart, the Rafter R riders heading back to their table and bottles of bourbon. Homer climbed back onto the small stage. The musicians quickly spun into another song. Men grabbed their partners and began to dance, their steps more feverish with excitement and triumph than before.

Annie Boskins shook her head and stomped back to her chair. She settled herself and used her damp handkerchief on her face. She glanced at the woman beside her.

"Ain't nothing good going to come from this," she said.

"Them uppity Morgans had it coming," Helen Jackson said. "Time they were taken down a peg or two. Too bad Henry the War Hero wasn't here to get a bit of it too."

"I don't think that would be a good idea, Helen," Annie said. "I'm not certain Ithaca would outlast him. He came back once and there's a few out there that still bear a couple of scars he left." She nodded at the dance floor. "He was bad news then, and I don't think he's the type to go soft with time."

"I don't know why you're holding out for them, Annie Boskins! Drought's hit you as hard as it has the rest of us."

"The Morgans don't have nothing to do with the drought," she said stoutly.

"They got water," Helen sniffed, looking away. "Least they could do is to share their good fortune with those who don't."

"And sacrifice their own cattle?"

"Gotta rain sometime," Helen said defensively. "Meanwhile, they could be helping out."

"And suppose it don't rain, what then?" Annie said. "They'd go under just like the rest of us are." She shook her head. "I don't like it neither, Helen. But that's just the way things are. If the calf was in the other pasture, I wouldn't do any different than the Morgans. And neither would you. You wouldn't!" she snapped when the other woman tried to protest. "Times like this, a person's gotta look out for himself."

She stared at the dancers, her mood darkening. Boots thudded against the hardwood floor as women danced lightly around their partners. A certain gaiety seemed to have penetrated the hall following the Morgans' exit, but a dark forboding settled over her, and she watched moodily, deep lines forming in her fleshy cheeks as her lips drew down into a frown and the dancing became more frenzied.

Chapter Five

"Jesus Christ!" Old Tom groaned. "Do you have to hit every god-damned bump in the road?"

Kate took a deep breath and let it out slowly as she eased back on the accelerator. The Buick slowed as she tried to avoid the potholes in the graveled road leading from the highway to the ranch. The drive back from Ithaca had been silent until they turned off the main road. Doc Adams had wanted to keep Old Tom for observation over night, but the old man stubbornly refused.

"Sorry," she muttered.

"Isn't your fault," Old Tom grumbled. He tried to draw a breath and winced as his sides pressed against the heavy tape wrapped around his trunk. "Damn painkillers ain't worth a shit. You'd think Doc Adams would've given me something a little stronger."

"I guess he didn't think you needed anything stronger," she said automatically. She glanced into the rearview mirror. Timmy sat quietly in the backseat. The gauze and tape over the stitches in his face, shone brightly in the darkness. "You okay?"

Timmy's eyes caught hers in the mirror. He nodded and looked out into the darkness. The prairie appeared blue under the silver moonlight, the gullies, dark scars slashing across the land.

"You're awfully quiet," she said.

"Nothing to say," Timmy said. His eyes flickered back to hers and away. She glanced back at the road, and touched the brakes briefly as the gray shadow of a coyote drifted across the road in front of them.

"My fault," Tom said. "We should have come home when Arch told us about Black."

"We should have stayed home in the first place," she said angrily. "But you got on your high horse, wanting to show everyone that you weren't afraid. Now look at you! Cracked ribs and Timmy with six stitches in his face! I guess you really showed them."

"We got in a few licks," he protested feebly. "They didn't get away free from it. That one lost a couple of teeth and I think Grayson got his nose broke for his trouble and—"

"And you're lucky that it ended when it did or you could've got seriously hurt!" she snapped. "I don't know what got into you."

"About three or four boots," Tom said, trying to laugh. He gasped painfully.

"See?"

"What's that?" Timmy said suddenly from the back of the car.

"What?"

"Over there. The ranch. Looks like a fire."

They looked off into the darkness at a glow showing over the crest of a hill. Kate slammed her foot down upon the accelerator. The Buick leaped forward. Tom hissed loudly through clenched teeth as the car roared over the hill and bounced hard into a pothole. Flames leaped high from the bunkhouse as they pulled in through the gate. Cookie and the two hired hands, Sam and Joe, raced back and forth from the tank by the windmill to the bunkhouse, throwing buckets of water on the fire. Seth Williams, their foreman, held a garden hose, directing a thin stream of water ineffectively onto the roaring flames.

Timmy leaped from the car as it skidded to a stop. Seth glanced over at them then turned his attention back to the flames.

"What happened?" Timmy yelled.

"Dunno for sure! Thought I smelled gasoline!" Seth hollered back.

"Everybody get out?" Timmy asked.

"Yeah! They're trying to keep it from spreading." He glanced at Timmy, his eyes taking in the bandages, then flickered over to Tom limping up. "What the hell happened to you?"

"Rafter R," Timmy said.

"And others," Tom said. "I think everybody was waiting to get in a few licks."

"Yeah, you look like it!" Seth said. He turned his attention back to the fire, shaking his head. The roof suddenly fell in with a loud crash. Flames and a column of sparks leaped high. "Shit! Forget the bunkhouse," he yelled at the men. "It's lost! Stop those sparks before they get on the grass and the hay!"

Obediently the men ran after the sparks, stamping them out and pouring water on them as they landed. Cookie filled a bucket from the windmill and ran after a series of sparks flying toward the haystack next to the barn. Sam and Joe followed, pausing to stamp out sparks as they lit in the brown grass. Seth kept the hose trained on the bunkhouse, waving it in an arch back and forth, directing the stream high so that it fell back onto the flames. They watched as the flames danced away from the water, climbing up the skeleton framework of the bunks. A box of cartridges exploded suddenly, causing all to crouch. Bottles of aftershave blew up, the alcohol burning blue briefly. The men renewed their efforts, throwing buckets of water onto the flames, working from the outside in to the middle. Slowly, the blaze burned its way down to embers.

Gray light showed in the east when Seth at last tossed the hose aside and stared glumly at the skeleton timbers in front of him. Silently, the men, faces black with soot, gathered around him. Someone hawked and spat. Seth sighed and ran his hand across his lined face, smearing the soot.

"Well that's that," he said. "Reckon we've lost it."

"Yeah," Tom said. He took a deep breath. "Any ideas?"

Seth shook his head. "I thought I smelled gasoline just before it went up, but I can't be certain."

"The Rafter R," Tom said bitterly. "Took advantage of us being gone."

"You don't know that," Kate said.

"The hell I don't!" he flared.

"You don't," she said harshly. "All you've got is Seth saying he thought he smelled something. Wilson won't even give that a thought. Anything could've caused that. Faulty wiring, someone smoking in bed, any number of things could have started it."

"Yeah," he said, "but any number of things didn't start it! You know it was the Rafter R."

"Knowing isn't proving," she said. "Now, get up to the house and get into bed, you old fool! Standing around like this isn't helping matters one bit!" Tom opened his mouth to argue.

"Come on, Grandpa," Timmy said quietly, taking his arm. He tugged, and Tom winced, then his shoulders slumped. He turned toward the house and painfully hobbled toward it with Timmy helping him. She watched their progress for a moment, the old man leaning heavily on Timmy's arm, limping suddenly as he remembered his tired legs. She turned back to Seth.

"The boys get anything out?" she asked.

He shook his head. "Some. Not much. We pretty much lost everything in there."

She looked at Sam and Joe waiting quietly beside Cookie. "Well, looks like we gotta take the day off. Send Cookie and Sam in to Pierre to pick up new gear today. You and Joe can go in tomorrow. Meanwhile, we need someone to watch the west place until Dog comes back from White River. Then we'll send him over there. I have a hunch that Rafter R will try to move cattle across to the tanks after this. Dog will stop them," she added grimly.

"What about haying? We've still got half of the south pasture to bring in," Seth said.

She shook her head, brushing a strand of hair from her face. "We'll have to leave it for now," she said tiredly. "Tom's going to be laid up for a while. Broken ribs," she added to his raised eyebrow.

"Rafter R?" She nodded. He hawked and spat. "I guess they're startin' to get serious."

"Looks like it," she said, turning away. "I'll have the checks ready for Cookie and Sam when they're ready."

"Mrs. Morgan?"

She paused and turned back to the men. They shuffled their feet and looked away from her. Then Seth cleared his throat and said apologetically. "Ma'am, I think we all would just as soon have our time."

"If it's because you've lost your belongings, I'll make good on them," she said.

"No, ma'am, it ain't that alone," Seth said, flushing through the soot covering his face. "It's how everything is shaping up. We could take all the cracks people make when we go into town and, well, hell, the fights are nothing more than we'da got in Fort Pierre at the Hop Scotch on Saturday night. But it's been gettin' worse the past couple of months and all. And this—" he turned, gesturing at the glowing embers—"well, who knows what's next? Someone took a pot shot at Sam on the tractor today. Didn't hit him," he added hastily as she looked sharply at Sam, "but it did hit the tractor. We figure that was warning enough. We was thinking about pulling out but this, well, I guess it just decided things for me. Sorry, ma'am."

She stared at them, but they looked away from her. She sighed heavily. "All right. I'll have your checks drawn up when you're ready. I just wish one of you at least would wait until Dog gets back from White River before pulling out."

"Yes, ma'am," Seth said. "I reckon I can wait that long." He glanced at the others, but they looked away. He shifted his feet and ran his hands through his hair. "Well, one'll be enough for now, I 'spose. I sure hope Dog don't take it to mind to go visiting long."

She turned and walked up the slight hill to the ranch house and climbed up onto the porch. She opened the door and walked into the house and into the kitchen. She drew a glass of water from the sink and drank it, then drew another, staring out over the plains as the sun rose. Down in the draw, a small fog rose from the creek, hovering around the willows. She raised her eyes and looked across the prairie. The grass seemed burnt and withered except for the green patches of wooly verbena around the tank and the creek.

"Mom?"

She turned and looked at Timmy standing in the doorway. She drank the water and put the glass in the sink. She heeled her shoes off and stood on the cool linoleum floor. She leaned back against the sink and crossed her arms under her breasts. "You put your grandpa to bed?" He nodded. His red-rimmed eyes stared back at her. "That's good. The boys will be pulling out soon. They've asked for their time." She shook her head wearily. "Seth said he'd hang around until Dog got back from White River before going. He'll watch the fenceline. I suppose Cookie or the others would stay too until then. But—"

"Mom," he said again. She raised her head and looked at him, waiting. "Maybe it's time we asked Uncle Henry to come home."

Her lips thinned into a tight line. "We can make do. We have these past years and we can again."

"But—"

"I said no and that's it," she said fiercely. She turned away from him and poured another glass of water. She sipped it, staring off into the dark.

"I know it's been hard with him gone," Timmy said quietly. "But we need help. With the help quitting and everything, Grandpa and me will need every hand we can get to handle the cattle over the next few months."

"I'll ride with you," she said quietly.

"And who will watch the place when all of us are gone?" he demanded. "They burned down the bunkhouse. Someone's not here, what's to stop them from burning down the barn and the house? Then what next? The grass? The hay?" She looked at him sharply. He nodded. "Yeah. That's what I would do: burn the grass, if I wanted to force someone out. Don't make any difference at all how much water we got if we ain't got the grass for the cattle. Or the hay. Mom, we need another person around here and I don't exactly think anyone's gonna want to come to work for us and go up against Reynolds after the others leave. We need Uncle Henry."

"He won't come," she said. Her shoulders sagged and she hunched over the sink. She shook her head. "If he was going to come, he would have come a long time ago. But he didn't. We weren't what he wanted when he came back from Vietnam. Not what he needed. Or something like that. I never really understood why he didn't stay here. Something happened to him over there. I guess it happened to a lot of soldiers, though. I've been reading about all the troubles they've been going through since they came back. But your uncle had a family, and he had a ranch. He had obligations that he avoided. And so he took up some fancy footloose ways. But it was his choice. Neither your grandpa nor I stood in his way. That wouldn't have been right. A person has to want to belong before he can belong. And your uncle didn't."

"Times have changed, Mom," Timmy said quietly. "A lot has happened since then."

"Not enough," she said, turning around to face him. She heeled tears from her eyes and shook her head. "I don't want him here. We'll be all right. We'll make do."

She walked past him, heading for the stairs. Timmy listened to her climbing the stairs then sighed and went to the sink and drew a glass of water and drank it down. He stared out through the window into the blackness and thought about what she had said. Tiny muscles worked along the point of his jaws, then he turned and walked upstairs. He knocked quietly on his grand-father's room and opened it. The old man was in bed and rolled over, reaching overhead to turn on the bed lamp clamped to the iron railing of the headboard. He looked at Timmy in surprise.

"Well, now, I know it ain't time to get up. I ain't heard the rooster yet."

"A coyote could've gotten him," Timmy said.

The old man shook his head. "That old bird's too ornery to let that happen. No self-respecting coyote would sink a tooth in that bird. What is it?"

"The boys are leaving after Dog gets back."

The old man's lips thinned into a hard line. "Goddamn," he said wearily. "What next?

"Where's Uncle Henry?" Timmy asked.

The old man sighed and pushed himself up, pulling the

pillow behind him. He looked at Timmy and scratched his jaw. "Now why would you want to know that?"

"I think it's time that we ask him to come home," Timmy said. "We need him."

"What's your mother say about that?" Tom asked.

"No."

"Then, I guess that's it." He sighed.

"Grandpa, we need him. We need help. And you know that no one will go up against Reynolds. Not after tonight. We have to ask Uncle Henry. He ain't coming home on his own or he'd be here by now. So where is he?"

"What are you going to do? Call him up?"

Timmy shook his head. "It's easy to say no over the telephone. I want him looking in my face when he says no this time. I want to see—"

"What? What do you want to see?"

"I want him to tell me why," Timmy said. "I want to see him and watch him tell me no. Then I'll believe that he really doesn't want to have anything to do with us. Maybe he just needs to be asked."

Tom stared silently off into the distance for a long minute. "Son," he said at last, "there are just some people who aren't meant to be in one place. Your uncle's one of them. He just wasn't meant for family life. He's been asked plenty to come home by both me and your momma. If he was gonna come home, he'd be here by now."

"Yeah, I can see that," Timmy said drily. "But if he won't do it for Mom or me, maybe he'll do it for the land."

"I don't know," Tom said, scrubbing his hand wearily over his face. "Sometimes, I wonder if all of this is really worth the trouble."

"You don't mean that."

"No, I guess I don't."

"But you know where he is?"

He nodded. "He's at Gethsemane. A monastery in Kentucky."

"A monastery? He's at a monastery? Been there all this time?"

"For about five years, yes," he said.

"All right," Timmy said. "I'll leave at first light." A grin spread across his lips. "Don't tell Mom until after I've gone. I wouldn't put it past her to come after me and try to drag me back home."

Tom nodded. "You need any money?"

"Can always use some money," he said.

Tom nodded and rose, his joints popping, his knobby toes cracking on the floor as he crossed to the big mahogany bureau. He opened the top drawer and took out a box. He opened it and removed a sheaf of bills, handing them to Timmy. "There's about a thousand dollars. Better if you fly down to Kentucky."

"I'll be back as soon as possible," Timmy promised, taking the money. "Anything you want me to tell him?"

"No," the old man said. "I said it all once. That's enough. If he's coming, he's coming. Ain't nothing more to be said about it. I guess you need to hear it, though, and that's good enough for me. I'll make sure the boys hang around until Dog gets back, and I'll keep Seth here until then. He owes me that. Go and see your uncle. Get it out of your system."

He crossed to the bed and climbed in, pulling the covers to his chin. He reached up and turned off the light and rolled away, facing the wall. Timmy walked quietly from the room and closed the door softly behind him. His heart beat rapidly.

Dog

It was the Moon When the Cherries Turn Black when Timmy left for him. He was gone when I returned from White River where I danced the Sun Dance. But I already knew that Henry was coming home. I heard it in the song of a meadowlark while I was dancing and trying to pull free from the wing bone of an owl that had been shoved through the flesh of my chest and tied with long leather straps to the sun pole. The meadowlark's song came through the song of the Indians who beat the drums for me, but I heard it just the same.

Return home, it said. Return home for you are needed.

And I stopped the dance and cut the leather straps, freeing me from the sun pole. I left the others there and rode away from the silent drums.

When I returned, she came and told me that Timmy had gone to Kentucky for Henry but she did not think he would come home. I did not tell her about the meadowlark's song. She did not need to hear that. I listened to her as she told me about the dance and the fire. We sat in front of my cabin and smeared a paste I made from meadow anemone upon the wounds on my chest to help them heal. Dragonflies danced around me, hovering in the air, and I knew the sadness was coming home with him.

The next day I rode my pinto horse out to the ring of stones, purified myself with smoke and sage, and sat in the center of the ring of stones, listening to the sounds the earth makes. And the sounds were warm. Yet there were other sounds, sounds of the night that came and went and these sounds I knew to be whispers from the past.

The next morning, a roan horse stood at the bottom of the hill. I did not know where he came from, for we did not have a roan horse on the ranch, but he was there. I walked naked down the hill to him. He waited for me, watching me with liquid eyes. I stroked his long nose and blew my breath gently into his nostrils. He pushed me away with his nose and I knew then that he had come for Henry.

Chapter Six

Timmy stepped from the taxi and stood for a long moment staring at the forbidding stone wall and solid iron gate topped with spearheads. The hinges showed streaks of pale green and the black paint on the individual spears had blistered in places with red rust running out from under the blisters like old blood. The monastery, set deep in the valley along a narrow road that twisted among loblolly pines, looked cold and forbidding, grimacing at any would-be visitors. Behind him, the driver hawked and spat through the window.

"Not many people allowed in there," he said laconically. He wiped a thick forefinger over his bushy mustache streaked with gray. His porcine eyes looked sunken into his suety cheeks. Thick black caterpillars crawled above his eyes. He shifted his weight, his leather jacket cracking, the taxi groaning on its springs.

"Not since Thomas Merton died. Lot of people came at first, but now there's only a few. Reckon a couple more years and won't be any. More's the shame."

Timmy ignored him and walked to an intercom placed conspicuously on one of the stone pillars. He pressed a button, waited, then pressed again. He traced the galvanized piping that ran from the intercom box up the pillar and around the corner before disappearing. The voice came on a wave of low static.

"I am sorry, but visitors are not allowed at this time. Have you made an appointment? If you have, press again. If not, we apologize for any inconvenience we have made for you, but this is a holy retreat and we are in silence at the moment."

"My name is Tim Morgan," Timmy said. "I called from the airport this morning."

A long moment passed. Timmy resisted the temptation to press the button again. He looked up at the top of the iron gate and wondered if he could climb over it without impaling himself on one of the medieval spears. At last, static erupted from the box and the disembodied voice said: "Please follow the drive to the front door. There is a small, graveled, parking area available. Do not drive off the road. If you have taken a taxi, please inform your driver to remain in his taxi. You will be met by Brother Paul." The gates clicked and a loud hum sounded as they slowly swung open.

Timmy returned to the taxi and stepped in back. He closed the door. "He said—"

"I heard," the driver grunted. He slipped the gears and drove carefully through the gate. Timmy stared silently out at the trees at the edge of a long, green swath that stretched down from the road. Late Indian rod volunteered their red blooms here and there along with contrasting bluebells. The driver caught Timmy's stare in his rearview mirror.

"Been pretty warm. Unseasonally," he offered. "Had a cold snap the other night so reckon those flowers will be the last 'til spring. More's the pity, but fall's sorta pretty around here. More so up in the hills where the hardwoods are. But it's pretty enough around here. 'Spose that's why they built this place here. Real peaceful. And pretty. Look over there." He pointed off to the right. Timmy obeyed the thick, jutting finger. He could just see the peak of a roof covered with old gray shingles. "That's where Merton lived. He was different, you know. Wanted to be more alone than any of the others, I'm told."

"You seem to know a lot about this place. I thought the monks discouraged visitors," Timmy said.

"They do," the driver answered. "My sister's boy thought he wanted to be one of them. Came out after six months. Said he missed the noise. He's at the university, now. You got any family here?" He looked in the mirror at Timmy.

"My uncle," Timmy said.

"Your uncle?" the driver asked. He waited for an explanation, but Timmy stared out the side of the taxi. Finally, the driver shrugged and pulled onto the graveled patch cut into a carefully manicured lawn. He turned the engine off and pushed his seat back, taking a newspaper from the seat beside him.

"I'll be here when you get back," he said. He turned off the meter. "Take your time. You must have a lot to talk about. I ain't got nothing else to do for a while." He grinned and opened his newspaper.

"Maybe you'd better go," Timmy said, handing a twenty dollar bill over the seat. "I have your number. I'll have someone give you a call."

"It could take a while for me to get back out here," the driver warned.

"It could take me a while in there too," Timmy said. "I've got twenty years of catching up to do."

"Think you'll get it done?" the driver asked. He took the twenty and reached for his change bag. "People in there don't have much to say."

"We'll see," Timmy said. "Keep the change."

The driver shrugged and stuffed the bill into his change bag and dropped his newspaper back onto the seat as Timmy stepped from the taxi and walked to the front door, huge and timbered, studded with large-headed iron spikes. A knocker in the shape of a cruciform hung in the center of the door. He lifted the knocker and let it drop. The door opened immediately and an elderly man, thin to the point of emaciation, the crown of his head fringed with gray hair cut short, stared owlishly at him through thick-glassed, horn-rimmed spectacles. He wore a cowled cassock, the hem barely touching the ground. Bare feet with thick, yellow toenails, long and curling, peeped out from sandals beneath the cassock.

"Tim Morgan," Timmy said. "You're expecting me?"

The man blinked and shuffled aside, motioning for Timmy to enter, Timmy turned and waved to the driver. The man saluted with a cocked forefinger and pulled out of the parking area, the back wheels spinning slightly, throwing gravel. Timmy turned and stepped through the door.

The vaulted entry was dark and gloomy and at least ten

degrees cooler than outside. He shivered. Dim light shone from electric sconces anchored in the walls. Old paintings, dusty with fine lines radiating through the paint, of cowled men hung on the walls. An ancient coat tree stood to his left, the wood worn white. To his right stood an old umbrella stand with three elderly umbrellas standing upright in it next to a small table with a dusty register opened to a blank page. An old-fashioned Waterman pen stood in a penholder beside it. Timmy picked it up and dutifully filled out the entry below an indecipherable scrawl dated four months earlier.

"Not many visitors, I see," he said.

The man shook his head, gave a thin-lipped smile, then motioned for Timmy to follow him as he shuffled down the cavernous hall, the leather of his sandals slapping gently on the old stone floor. Timmy moved easily, unconsciously timing his steps to the man's.

At the end of the corridor, the man stopped beside a heavy door made of black walnut and opened it with difficulty. He motioned for Timmy to enter.

"My uncle?" Timmy asked. The old man nodded and motioned again and Timmy stepped through the doorway into a small room. Bookshelves neatly filled with books circled the room and beneath the leaded window in the wall opposite. A lone table, massive and solid, stood in the center of the room. Six chairs surrounded it, high-backed and austere. He looked around the room: he was alone. Slowly, he crossed to the table and placed his hat upon it. He glanced at the titles of the books, then crossed to the window and nudged it open. He looked down upon a garden. A lone worker wearing a brown cassock slowly worked with a large pair of pruning shears, carefully cutting grape vines back to the main stalk. The silence was heavy and Timmy began to hum softly under his breath.

Behind him the door opened and he turned to stare at the brown-cassocked figure that took two steps into the room and stopped. Thin, but broad-shouldered, a long jaw that ended in almost right angles. The nose had been broken at least once in the past and gray eyes stared impassively out at him from beneath wiry brows. His blond hair had been closely cropped. Timmy took a deep breath, suddenly feeling like he was staring into the future at a reflection of himself.

"Hello, Uncle Henry," he said. The figure nodded and Timmy took an automatic step forward, then stopped. They stared silently at each other for a long moment, then Timmy laughed, the sound harsh and cracked in the oppressive silence of the room.

"Well isn't this something?" he said. "My uncle. At last. How long has it been?"

"You were five when I last saw you," the figure said softly. "We were at the state fair in Huron."

"Strange that I don't remember that," Timmy said quietly. "I remember other things. I remember you reading to me and telling me stories. You know what I liked the best? The one about Odysseus coming home. But I don't remember the state fair."

The figure's eyes shifted away to the window. He glided silently across the room and shut the window, firmly latching it. He turned and faced Timmy again.

"I'm sorry," he said. His voice whispered. A thin rasp came beneath the words. "What happened to your face?"

Timmy gently touched the stitches and said. "That's part of the reason that I came."

The figure nodded, waiting for him to continue. Timmy took a deep breath, feeling the awkwardness between them. "So how've you been?"

The figure shrugged. A tiny, sad smile touched the corners of his lips. "All right. It's . . . peaceful, here."

"I'm glad for you. It isn't peaceful at home," Timmy said. "What's wrong?"

"Lots," Timmy said. "There's a drought, and we have the only water. A lot of people resent that."

"I can imagine," the figure said mildly.

"Can you? Well imagine our bunkhouse being burned down. Imagine Grandpa and me getting beaten. Imagine Mother trying to keep the whole ranch together by herself."

The figure's eyes slipped away from him. "How is your mother?"

"As well as can be expected. The men are leaving. Seth said he would stay until Dog got back. Grandpa said he'd make certain that he stayed until I got back too."

"How's Dog?"

"At a Sun Dance when I left," Timmy answered. "He comes and goes as he pleases. Still lives alone in that tiny shack down by the creek where the chokecherry bushes are. You remember them?"

"You don't lose your memory," he said. "You always remember the things you want to forget, yet those are the things that you always remember." He turned to look at Timmy. "And you always remember the things that you should remember."

"Which are we?" Timmy asked. "Have you tried to forget us?"

"Yes," he answered softly. "I've tried. Not because I wanted to, but because I had to."

"You had to," Timmy said. He shook his head. "Why did you have to?"

"You'll have to ask Dog that," he said.

"Dog," Timmy said. He shook his head. "He doesn't say much anymore. Just goes to that hill of his and sits and stares."

"In the ring of stones?" he asked.

"Yeah." Timmy's eyes wandered to a painting of a man hanging over the door. His eyes were sharp and black. His hand was suspended in mid-air as if ready to offer a blessing. Timmy nodded. "Looks like something from the French Renaissance."

"You know art?" Henry asked. An eyebrow quirked in question. Timmy shook his head.

"No, but Mom keeps trying."

"You haven't gone on to college, then?"

Timmy laughed. "Home educated. Mom's a bit reluctant to let me go. She's afraid I might turn out like Dad. Or you."

The figure smiled gently. "You might. But that's a chance we all have to take. It's part of life. But there isn't any hurry. You have plenty of time."

"Yes."

They stared at each other for a long moment. Then Timmy spoke.

"Why? Will you just tell me that? Why did you run away from us?"

"I don't think you would understand," the figure said softly, regretfully.

"Try me," Timmy said. "I really want to know."

"I didn't fit in anymore."

"You're right: I don't understand."

The figure shook his head. "There's a whole world between us," he said.

"I suppose you're going to blame it on Vietnam, right?" Timmy said, sarcasm dripping from his voice. "That seems to be the general excuse with you people, isn't it? 'Nobody can understand me because I fought in a war.' "

"Partly," the figure said. "But it isn't that alone. It's everything that happened not only in the war, but here, in the United States as well."

"And what was that?"

"The whole culture changed. Everything." A hint of bitterness could be heard in his voice. "When I returned, I no longer recognized what I had left behind. Can you understand that? War changes people, yes, but the biggest change was within people themselves."

"Pardon me if I don't sound sympathetic, but everybody changes. That's the nature of the world."

"Yes." The figure turned away from him and looked at the window, touching the glass with his fingers. "But the big change was in the society. There was no longer a place for me."

"In Ithaca? In South Dakota? Not much change there in the past hundred years."

"That was part of the problem because, you see, I had changed." He turned and looked at Timmy, pain evident in his eyes. "I told you that you wouldn't understand. You have to see what happened from both sides. Can you do that?"

"No," Timmy answered bluntly. "I can't. I don't care about the other side. We needed you and you didn't come home. That's the plain and simple of it. I don't understand all of your reasons and the ones that I'm hearing don't make one bit of sense to me."

"Then why are you here?"

"Now there's irony for you," Timmy said. "You think it's a war that kept you from coming home? Well we have a little war of our own and we need your help. It's time for you to come home, now. You can't declare your separate peace any more."

A sadness filled his eyes. He turned to leave, but Timmy stepped around in front of him.

"No, no. You don't get off that easy. I want to know why you didn't come home, and I want to know why you won't come home now that we need you. We ain't asked anything of you until now. So tell me. And don't give me your homespun I'm-a-victim philosophy."

The figure backed away from the pressure of Timmy's hands. His face suddenly looked old, drawn and worn. "I don't think so."

"Then, there's not much for me here, is there?" Timmy said.

"I'm not Odysseus, Timmy."

"This was a big mistake," Timmy said bitterly. "A big mistake. Mom tried to tell me that, but I came anyway. Do you know I had to sneak away to get here? Oh Grandpa knew I was leaving, but Mom didn't. Now I'm damned if I know why I bothered." Angry tears sparkled in his eyes. "Ah, the hell with it!"

He turned and stormed from the room, slamming the door behind him. The figure stood quietly for a moment, then his shoulders sagged and he moved to the rectilinear window and watched as Timmy emerged and stood indecisively in the yard. A pang went through him, but he could not recognize what he was feeling. Once he could have understood the pang, but not any longer. He had lost that long ago.

A weary smile touched the corners of his lips then flitted away on moth wings. He closed his eyes and leaned his forehead against the cold window.

Once you would have known. Once when you thought that life was a pirate's booty, treasure for the taking. But that wasn't only your fault. The whole country encouraged that type of excess. There were treasures, but at what a price: misplaced allegiance and patriotism, a misplaced sense of identity in the cumbersome machine clumsily working its way through the war. That was when you discovered that myth carried more weight than reality, but you did not recognize that in time to do anything about it. The old and venerated truths steadily disappeared to be replaced by lies and inventions that took the place of real events.

He sighed and opened his eyes, looking again for Timmy, but he had disappeared. He turned away from the window.

Gone. It's better this way. Yes, much better. How easy it would be to forget the war, to forget our part in the war. But some things must be remembered. Some things need to be remembered. Not all of us can afford the luxury of living in vacuums.

He turned from the window and looked around the room, at the high, exposed beams, nearly black with age, the flagstone floor, the heavy, academic bookshelves. The room smelled of knowledge, dusty and stale, and dimly he thought he heard the dry clicking of ancient rosary beads. A bell sounded faintly somewhere, calling for an hourly prayer for those who still prayed for world peace. He did not attend those prayers: to do so felt too much like hypocrisy. Instead, he walked to the bookshelves and absently ran his fingers over the titles stamped in gold, registering them dimly.

How many of us were arrogant with our own immortality before we heard a shot fired and were aware that we were all too mortal? How many of us saw our deaths in the eyes of those we killed? And, because of our fear, we cannot go home. What irony!

He closed his eyes, remembering, hearing the screams, smelling the air filled with acrid cordite and rank blood, swallowing against the coppery taste of fear like new pennies. Raw images crept behind his eyelids, dark shadows moving in their own dance—

"Try me."

He opened his eyes and slowly turned to face the door. Timmy stood in front of him, his eyes burning angrily.

"Try me," Timmy repeated. "I really want to know."

Morgan pursed his lips, then shook his head. A deep sigh crept raggedly from him. "I didn't fit in any more," he said wearily. "The war used me up. There was nothing left there for anybody. Not your mother, not your grandfather—not even you."

"That wasn't your decision to make," Timmy said. The figure shrugged. "So you just stopped loving us. Is this what you're saying?"

"No. Maybe. I don't know. I lost feeling." He spread his hands wide, a tentative smile touching the corners of his lips. He shook his head. "I wish I could. But there's a whole world between us," he said sadly. "A form of ethical mandarinism." He turned to leave, but Timmy stepped around in front of him. He stared at him for a long moment, then shook his head. "You don't know what you are asking."

"Were you afraid? I could understand that if you were afraid."

He laughed mirthlessly and his eyes became dark. "Perhaps. There are many different types of fear in the danger one anticipates. It is the imperfect vagueness of human thought. Imagination is the father of all fear. It lives in the shadows and comes out only in nightmares and daydreams when your thoughts are filled with valorous deeds. When I was your age, I loved those dreams. They were the best part of my life—a secret truth, reality hidden beneath the humdrum of chores, stringing wire, working the cattle. They were intoxicating and I became drunk with confidence in my own mortality. So did your father."

"All dreams end," Timmy said.

"Do they?" he replied.

His eyes turned blank for a moment, remembering.

Dog

I dreamed the warrior's dream that night and knew that Timmy had found him. In my dream a thunderstorm appeared, but it did not rain. Instead, men fell like spears from the sky slanting down into the earth where they struck, quivering, before falling limply to the earth. And then the grass burned away from the earth and the water evaporated into a mist and I knew then that the earth had forsaken us and we were alone.

The Journey

We live, as well
dream—alone.
   —Conrad

Chapter Seven

A lone kite circled high overhead in the unclouded sky, enveloped in a fulguration of sunshine, dropping lower and lower in graceful swoops, drawn to the still figure below.

He lay flat on the jungle floor, pressing his chin hard against the rich, black dirt and the thick muggy air lay heavily on his back. Beads of perspiration popped out on his forehead, trickling across deep furrows down frown lines to drip off the end of his nose. A bee, drawn by the sour-sweet smell of the perspiration, buzzed curiously around his head and disappeared, but there was no other sound. He wished the birds would sing and make things seem normal. It was very important to him that everything seem normal, but the birds did not sing and had not sung for a very long time, and now an eerie silence hung around his ears like a shroud. He forced himself to be patient and lie still and concentrate on the elephant grass and liana vines crawling thickly over the ground in front of him. Twenty feet beyond the grass and vines a sharp break sliced deeply through the vegetation. During the rainy season, waters rushed noisily through the cut toward the Don Nai River and down to the Mekong Delta. The thought of water made him thirsty, and he wished he could unscrew the cap of his canteen and drink deeply of the tepid water. But he could not drink the water yet, and this made him thirstier. He thought of cold waterfalls high in the north mountain country and the ice-cold bottles of beer with the sides of the bottles dripping with condensation served on the terrace of the Continental Hotel in Saigon. But now dust lay like sifted flour on the leaves and vines, and the bed of the break was heavy with dust and rotting leaves. A dead tree gleamed whitely in the sun and rested across the break like a huge, prehistoric bone. The man felt a pressure on his foot and cautiously turned his head to the left to look at the brown, wrinkled face of Nguyen Duc.

"They come," he said softly, and Henry Morgan turned his attention back to the break. Slowly they came into view: black pajama-clad figures with wide, woven bamboo hats like saucers on their heads, their shoulders hunched under heavy loads. They moved with great difficulty through the dust and dead leaves of the break. The first passed, and Morgan read the black letters on the side of the cardboard box on his shoulders: U.S. ARMY/CON-DENSED MILK. The others shuffled by, the carriers concentrating on the ground in front of them, each step stirring the fine dust into small clouds that rose above their ankles and turned their brown feet gray. He could hear the tiny plops of their sandals. Above, the kite whistled once and startled itself into silence, and Morgan silently blessed him as a good omen.

The figures moved slowly up the break as Morgan quietly counted to himself, five-six-seven-eight. He felt the old man's black eyes staring steadily at the back of his head and grimly smiled. Timing was very important. He waited and wondered at the foolishness of the men in front who moved tiredly through the break without posting a point guard. The heat did this; the heat and the jungle lulled men into carelessness and made wise men fools and fools dead.

The twelfth man passed the tree. Morgan hesitated, then quickly wrenched the handle on the detonator. The claymore mine exploded. A deadly tidal wave of hot metal rushed at the startled figures, cruelly slicing into brown flesh. Morgan instinctively ducked his head at the explosion, then quickly raised it as Nguyen Duc's rifle began to bark. He thumbed the safety off his Thompson, rose to his knees, and sprayed a short burst into the quivering figures. Movement flickered at the corner of his eye. He whirled to see one of the figures sprinting toward a thick clump of elephant grass. He swung the Thompson toward the figure but something sped past his eyes and the figure screamed and fell forward on its face, reached back and frantically clawed at the quarrel sticking between his shoulderblades, convulsed, and died.

Morgan turned back to the break. Brown, twisted figures lay in the break like gnarled tree roots. Cautiously, the Montagnards moved from concealment and warily approached the still figures. Morgan became conscious of a humming in his ears and yawned deeply to ease the pressure. Beside him, Nguyen Duc noticed the yawn and grinned.

"It is good," he said, his voice carrying the musical lilt of the North people. "We have killed many today."

"And captured much food," another added eagerly. Nguyen Duc looked sternly at the speaker. The young man realized his mistake and immediately dropped his eyes, flushing with embarrassment for having spoken without permission. Morgan felt a brief flash of pity for the young man, but the code of the hills was rigid. The young man would have to suffer his embarrassment for having spoken without the old man's permission.

"Take it," Morgan said, sweeping his arm generously at the break. "Take the guns and the ammunition and food and strip the bodies and leave them naked."

"And the heads?" the old man asked.

"Do what you must," Morgan answered. "But remember that you are a soldier."

The old man nodded and spoke over his shoulder at the men watchfully waiting by the bodies. They began to rapidly stack the weapons and contraband on the bank. Morgan moved to the shade of a large baobab tree and sat, easing his back against its trunk. He pulled the black British Commando beret from his head and rubbed his hands vigorously over his shaved scalp. Nguyen Duc slung his rifle across his back and moved to Morgan's side and squatted.

"Dai-uy," he said, and Morgan rolled his head against the trunk of the tree to look at the thin, emaciated figure that could trot all day through the jungle heat and still fight a day's battle at the end. He reached into the button-down pocket of his jungle fatigues and pulled out a crumpled pack of Salems and proffered them. Nguyen Duc made the okay sign with his thumb and fore-finger, bent to light the cigarette from the flame of Morgan's Zippo lighter and pulled the smoke from the cup formed by his fist. His lips never touched the cigarette for the old man was superstitious and currently very religious. Periodically the old man would embrace one religion or another, usually when his arthritis reminded him he was old, and make dutiful offerings to whatever gods he happened to think about at the moment.

"*Ong o' Viet Nam bao lau roi?*" the old man asked.

"*Lan lam,*" Morgan replied. "A long time."

"*May mom?*" Nguyen Duc asked. "How long?"

"Four years," Morgan answered automatically, and pulled a green paisley scarf from around his neck to wipe his face. The old man had asked this after the first ambush when they had been very lucky and found the bags of script meant as payment to the Viet Cong in the Mekong Delta to the south. Now they repeated it after every ambush to keep the luck with them.

"That is a very long time," the old man said respectfully. "Your woman does not complain?"

"I have no woman," Morgan said shortly. He shrugged. "But if I did, would it not be the nature of women to complain?"

The old man laughed appreciatively at this and coughed as the smoke choked him. Morgan pounded him on the back until the spasm passed, then pulled a battered silver flask engraved with his initials from his thigh pocket. The old man's eyes lit with pleasure, and Morgan smiled.

"Will you join me?" he asked politely. The old man made polite sounds of refusal, then reached for the flask and drank the Johnnie Walker Scotch with relish. Morgan smiled and saw the others looking longingly at them out of the corners of their eyes as they gathered the supplies and weapons.

"*Cai nay tot,*" he called. "Join us."

They flashed quick grins and quickly crowded around the cigarettes and Scotch.

"This is not good, Dai-uy," the old man protested. "They forget their places."

Morgan felt a moment's annoyance at the old man's reproach,

then remembered the old man was the chief of his village and the young men with whom they had made the ambush had yet to earn their right to a place on the council.

"I am sorry," he said. "You are right, of course, but with your permission, I think the day has been long and hot, and the ambush was successful. They all fought with much valor. Do you not think a reward is needed?"

The old man pretended to think, then nodded his head in agreement. "You are wise, Dai-uy," he said magnaminously. "Such valor should be rewarded."

"And an eighth share of the spoils for each?" Morgan suggested wickedly. His eyes danced with laughter, but he kept the smile from his lips.

"Too much," the old man objected quickly. "A twelfth. And that is too much as they will trade their shares for much beer and will be useless to us for a week. Better a twentieth."

"But, some have families," Morgan protested gently. "I agree. A tenth is enough. Just right."

"*Aiee*, Dai-uy!" the old man groaned. He rocked back and forth on his heels and rubbed his hands in distress through his gray hair. "You will make a poor man of me. But, again, you are right. A fifteenth it shall be." He turned to give the orders.

Morgan leaned back against the tree and stared at the blue sky. Not a cloud in sight and the sun held still at high noon, a hot orange that pulled the juice from the bone and burnt the unwary to a black crisp. He listened to the old man order his villagers and squinted through the film of perspiration over his eyes as the old man suspiciously inspected each bundle to make sure the division was correct. Dimly he remembered it was Christmas Eve, his fourth Christmas Eve in Vietnam. What day was it back in Ithaca? Was it snowing? Were excited high schoolers skating on the mill pond and was a bonfire burning on the shore for the skaters to seek warmth? What was Kate doing? And Timmy? He shook his head and stared up at the sky. What difference did it make now?

He felt the warmth of the earth against his back and the warmth of the sun against his face and thought about the snow back home and the decorations on the Christmas tree in the old ranch house, and the smells of the turkey and stuffing, the brandy and cinammon breads, and the hot rum punch his father would mix after he came in from checking the stock. He could see his father's eyes shining as he walked through the door, hear Kate complaining about the turkey, and a twinge of guilt ran through him as he thought about Kate and the rainy day in April when his father and Billy were in Fort Pierre with a load of cattle. He had been in Philip, picking up wire and parts for the windmill on the south place.

Where's Dad and Billy? he asked, coming through the door.

She was standing on a chair, cleaning the top shelf of a cupboard. Startled, she dropped a cup and saucer, scrambled, trying to catch it, then lost her balance and fell backwards. Morgan rushed forward and caught her, his hands sliding up to cup her breasts.

"Thanks," she said shakily. She turned her head and her lips were close to his. And then he was kissing her and she was kissing him back—

He shook his head, driving away memory. You have been away too long. Too long. And how old is Timmy now? Five? Yes, five. I wonder if he remembers me? You need to go back. You sorry son-of-a-bitch, you can't go back. It's Billy who should go back. You should never have written that letter.

He closed his eyes, remembering the letter he had written after the old man led the raid on the camp where the Viet Cong had been holding him. He shook his head. That had been a close call and he had been very lucky. He had been waiting for his turn at questioning, remembering the lieutenant from Wisconsin who had been stretched between two trees and flayed. But the lieutenant had known nothing and his screams had not convinced the Viet Cong that he knew nothing because he had only been in the country three weeks. The old man and his men had come too late for the lieutenant whose luck hadn't been with him.

He sighed, remembering again the letter he had written to reassure Billy and Kate and his father that he was all right after the close call. He had meant the letter to be nothing more than that, but it had been the final letter that brought Billy to Vietnam. He remembered the strained letter Kate had written to tell him that Billy was in Bien Hoa, assigned to Headquarters, 173rd Airborne Brigade (Separate), ending with the final note that Timmy was beginning to look more and more like him every day.

Well, he told himself, at least Billy's safe in his office job, even if it chafes him knowing that big brother is out here. But it is better that you stay back there, little brother. You have a wife to go home to. Timmy needs a father. And it can't be me. Besides, there's too much remaining to be done here. A bitter wave swept over him. And I've done enough back home already.

He reached over and picked up a chunk of earth and crushed it between his palms, quickly inhaling the rich smell. There is magic in the land, much magic. This is where you belong, now.

But he knew that wasn't the answer just as he knew he didn't know the answer. Perhaps it lay halfway between wanting to go back and knowing what remained to be done in Vietnam and what waited for him back at the ranch. By coming here, he had made an obligation to the villagers and himself. And that, he could not violate.

He took another drink of Scotch and breathed deeply, then grimaced. Already the bodies were beginning to spoil. Nothing lasted long in the jungle heat. He looked up at the tree tops and marked the kite swinging slowly overhead and the vultures waiting patiently in the trees. It was no good. They had been here too long and too many vultures had gathered. For those who knew the jungle, that many vultures meant only one thing: a large kill, much larger than any kill by any animal. He clapped the beret back on his head and picked up the Thompson, wincing as his fingers touched the hot metal.

"*Mau len*! Hurry!" he called to the old man and pointed at the trees. "We have been here too long."

The old man glanced at the birds, frowned, and nodded at him, then turned to swear at the men to finish their work. Smiles disappeared, and the men worked faster. Within minutes the loads had been evenly distributed and the men waited to march out. Morgan drew a deep breath and shrugged into his harness,

Chapter Eight

The village had no name. According to the topographic maps drawn by French engineers twenty years ago and still in use by the U.S. Army, no village existed here or anywhere near here for the topographic lines of the map bunched so tightly together they looked like one.

The fault lay with the wary cartographers who had little desire to plunge into unfriendly jungles during the rebellion of the fifties and had relied, instead, upon interviews with friendly Vietnamese more than eager to impart information on their country to the map-makers. But the cartographers were not that judicious with their selection of information and much of the information given them was false. This village was just such an example. According to the map, this was a mountainous region bordering the jungle with the heavy forest parted only by the Xang Xi River.

The village perched on a large shelf jutting from the side of a mountain and could be reached only by a narrow footbridge spanning a deep gorge cut by the river in its rush to the South China Sea. Two hundred feet below, the waters crashed over jagged rocks in frothy madness, and those crossing the footbridge carefully timed their steps to coincide with the pendulum swing of the bridge as it swung back and forth.

Although Morgan was not very excited about crossing the bridge, he appreciated the defensive position of the village. A frontal attack by the enemy would be suicidal and only a fool would want to risk climbing the west face of the mountain to get to the village from behind. Mortars could reach the village, but Morgan guarded against that by selecting guards to be permanently located on the only route an enemy could take. The guards, he was positive, were reliable for he had chosen the old man's son and one of his nephews to command the guards. Blood was still the oldest obligation in Vietnam, and the only guard against the fashionable treachery practiced among the hill people who admitted allegiance to no one. But it was also necessary to go back to the village for the trip up the long trail out of the thick jungle with its heavy canopy of leaves that turned everything into night by midday, dark and steamy, filled with a rotting stench that cloyed to the nostrils and clothes, until they at last emerged on the rocks high above the canopy of trees where the air was cool and clean, purifying the soul, was just as important to him as the descent into the jungle. There, high on the mountain, he could look back down upon the jungle and know that in a brief hour he could travel back down into the dark heart of the world. Then he could feel the madness of the land enter his soul, his mind remaining clear and detached as he analyzed his feelings, feeling the corruption make its way deep into him, nudging insistently at his last sense of rational thought.

At such times, scraps of old poetry filtered into his mind:

> We are the hollow men—
> —headpieces filled with straw—

He shook his head, driving old thoughts away, focusing upon the problem of now.

Why aren't there any birds?

Maybe a predator? Perhaps. But unlikely. The predators that would drive the birds quiet seldom came up this high for the only game for them were small mice. No, probably not a predator.

He frowned, shaking his head. He was making too much of it, surely. The problem now was to get across the bridge after the ambush. Although there had been twelve in the party and twelve bodies counted, Morgan felt uneasy and deliberately swung back and forth across the column's trail time and again as they neared the bridge. He looked carefully for something, but found nothing and this bothered him. There should have been a branch broken from some animal's passing, a vine untimely torn from its grip, a pile of leaves disarrayed. But there was nothing. Not even a sound. Normally birds would scold them as they left the jungle to climb to the forest of the hills, but none were visible. Nothing.

He frowned and slowed his approach to the path twisting its way up the side of the mountain to the footbridge and looked harder. All he could find was a fresh pile of jackal dung, and he worried what had caused that nocturnal animal to move during the day. Perspiration flowed faster down his face and stung his eyes, but he ignored it and examined the ground as carefully as possible. But there was only that pile of jackal dung and nothing more. Finally he shrugged his shoulders and moved up to join the old man impatiently waiting by the bridge.

"What is wrong?" the old man asked. Morgan shrugged his shoulders and looked back at the jungle.

"I do not know," he said. "It is not right."

"What? What did you find?" the old man asked. He straightened himself, bones quietly popping, and stared down the trail. Morgan debated whether to tell the old man about the jackal dung but decided against it. The old man would see that as an omen and refuse to lead his people out on any raids for at least a week. Then, too, what was significant about a pile of jackal dung?

"Nothing," Morgan said. "That is wrong." The old man shook his head and reslung his rifle.

"Sometimes there is nothing to see," he said, and spread his fingers in the French manner of dismissal. "Perhaps it is the heat."

"Perhaps," Morgan said, but he couldn't relax the tension between his shoulderblades. The old man looked shrewdly at him, then stepped deliberately onto the footbridge.

"Come," he said. "Tonight we shall eat good and drink *ruro'u uyt-ky* for the Christ child. Much *ruro'u uyt-ky*."

He grinned a gap-toothed smile and walked carelessly across the footbridge, his knees dipping automatically to compensate for the violent swing of the bridge. Morgan waited until the old man was across and the bridge had slowed its swing before he stepped out on it. Perhaps the old man was right; he probably had been in the bush too long. He smiled wryly at the old man's sly suggestion and mentally counted how many bottles of whisky he still had in his hut. He would probably need a case for this feast, but what the hell, it was Christmas, wasn't it? He stepped lightly on the planks of the bridge. It would be good to get drunk and forget where he was and why he was there. But not too drunk. It would not do to forget too much of one thing and remember too much of another.

He frowned as he stepped off the bridge and a figure in a new uniform stepped out of his hut and came toward him. Then a smile broke over his lips as he recognized the soldier.

"Billy!" he exclaimed as his brother came up to him. He grabbed his brother's hand, squeezing it. "What are you doing here?"

Billy grinned, his eyes crinkling merrily at the corners. "I had some time coming so I decided to slip up here and see you. I came up on the supply chopper."

"How are things back in Bien Hoa?" Henry said. "You rear echelon folks don't get out much, do you? That what you're doing up here? Trying to put enough time in the bush to get the Combat Infantryman's Badge?" he added teasingly.

Billy laughed and shook his head. "No. One hero's enough for any family." He smiled. "Damn, it's good to see your ugly face." He reached out and took the Thompson from Henry's shoulder. He lifted the Thompson, smelling the barrel. "Any luck?"

Henry nodded. "We caught a few bringing supplies down the line." He nodded at the men clustered around in front of the old man's hut. Then he remembered the old man and turned quickly to him. "Forgive my manners, Old Man," he said. "This is my brother. We have not seen each other for two years."

"He is your brother," the old man said, eying Billy critically. "One can see the same father and the same mother in both of you."

Henry laughed. He looked at his brother. "He says that he can see we have the same father and mother."

Billy nodded and held out his hand. "Tell him that I'm pleased to meet him."

Henry nodded as the old man took Billy's hand. "He says it is an honor to meet an old man like you, but wonders why you let the young men do all the work."

"He did not say that," the old man said. He pumped Billy's hand once, then released it. "But it is good that he is here for you at this time. It is good to have one's family with him at such a time."

"Yes," Henry said, grinning at his brother. "It is good to have family for Christmas."

The old man nodded then gestured at the men waiting in front of his hut. "I must go and divide up the goods before they become too impatient and decide to do it themselves." He nodded at Billy and hurried off. Henry grinned.

"What did he say?" Billy asked as Henry turned toward his own hut. He fell in beside him.

"That it was good to have family here for tonight," he said. He laughed. "So, what do you hear from home?"

"Not much," Billy grinned back. He wiped his hand over his face and dried the perspiration on his trousers. "Kate sent a picture of all of them. I left your copy beside the radio for you. The old man looks like he's sucking on a lemon. I don't know how she got him to put on a tie."

"He's wearing a tie?" Henry said. He shook his head. "It really must be Christmas."

They laughed and went into the hut. Henry dropped his pack in a corner and went to the radio, picking up the small leather wallet lying there. He opened it, staring at the photo, Kate held Timmy on her lap and smiled into the camera lens. Behind her, Tom stared grimly at the camera, his head held rigidly above a snow-white collar, a tie carefully knotted below his chin.

"You're right," Henry said, shaking his head mockingly. "Dad looks like someone's strangling him."

"Yeah," Billy said, coming up behind him, looking over his shoulder. "I think that's the first time he's worn a tie since Mom died."

"At least," Henry said. He closed the wallet and placed it back beside the radio. "So, what do you hear?" He crossed to a small table and poured water into a basin there. He splashed water onto his face and across his chest. He took up a small bar of soap and worked up a lather.

Billy shrugged and sat on a chair beside the radio. "The usual. Cattle prices are holding steady, but Dad's thinking that Johnson needs to bring the prices up through government supports."

"Ninety percent parity," Henry said. He scrubbed the lather over his face and across his chest. "I can hear him now."

Billy laughed. "Yeah, he said that, too. Kate says that Timmy's growing like a weed. Looks like it, anyway. I can't believe how much a kid can grow in six months."

"That how long you been here?" Henry said. "I forgot."

"Time passes when you're having fun," Billy said. He sighed, looking around the hut. Two small, rough-hewn tables, one holding the radio, another serving as a washstand. A larger table used as a field desk that held maps, pads and pencils, a small, portable typewriter, and a line of paperback books neatly stacked at the back. A cot with a folded nylon poncho liner, and two tin chests used as foot lockers lined one wall. A larger wooden chest painted olive drab held medical supplies. Stacks of cardboard boxes holding c-rations and Scotch whisky and ammo boxes completed the hut. "You sure can't be accused of living like a warlord."

Henry glanced at him and laughed. "Is that what people are saying about me?"

"Among other things," Billy grinned. Then, the smile slipped from his face. "So, when are you going home? Kate keeps asking that in her letters."

Henry turned away from him and took a towel, drying himself. "When my job's finished," he said casually.

"You like living this way?" Billy asked suddenly, gesturing at the hut. "I don't get it. You could have gone home a long time ago. Why didn't you?"

He shook his head. "Just seems like one thing after another comes up. Besides," he added, glancing at Billy frowning in his camp chair. "I don't work for the same boss as you. Mine's a little more demanding. Not all of us can be Remington Rangers," he teased.

Billy flushed and looked away. "That wasn't my idea," he protested. He hawked and spat disgustedly through the doorway. "I didn't ask to be made a clerk."

"At least you have showers and movies and clubs and—"

"Yeah, yeah."

Henry's face sobered. "You have the family, Billy. One of us in the field is enough. It's better this way."

"I know," Billy said. "But sometimes I just wish—"

"This isn't what you think it is, Billy," Morgan said, interrupting him. "You do not want to be here with these people. It's not what you think it is. We've been lucky. Very lucky."

"Yes, and your luck can't last forever," Billy said soberly. "At least if I was here I could watch your back."

"But who would watch yours?" Morgan flared. "One bad ambush and we'd both be killed. And then who would take care of Kate? There is nothing here for you."

"And there is for you?" Billy challenged.

Morgan stared away for a moment, then turned back to him, his lips set into a grim line. "This country can get into your veins, Billy. And that is something terrible. It's as if—as if the powers of darkness own you. There is the danger, because once that happens to you, you feel as if you have become—I don't know what—a supernatural being. You *feel* invulnerable, but you *know* that you are not! And you know that it is dangerous to feel that way, but you can't help it. Have you seen the old man's house?"

Billy frowned. "Is that the one with the skulls on sticks?"

"That's the one," Morgan said. "Yes, that's the one. Do you know why they are there?"

Billy shrugged. "Trophies?"

"Yes, trophies," Morgan said shortly. "But more importantly, the old man believes that the skulls can speak to him in his dreams. Advise him. It's diabolic! But there's a grandeur, too. Do you understand?"

Billy grinned. "Sounds exciting."

Morgan shook his head, his lips drawing down. "No," he said harshly. "No, I can see that you do not understand. This is not a place for everyone. You are still South Dakota and you have right already figured out. There is no right out here. None."

"You stay here," Billy said.

"Because I have to."

"Surely you've been out here long enough that you could get reassigned if you wanted to."

Morgan shook his head. "You don't understand, I don't think I can make you understand. But it's not for you. That you must know; it's not for you."

Billy lifted his head stubbornly. "I think I can decide what I should be doing."

"So, how long are you staying?" Henry said quickly to avoid the argument he could see coming.

Billy shrugged. "Just a couple of days, I'm going back on the next chopper. I'm only on a three-day pass. But," he added, hinting significantly, "I've put in for a transfer."

"They won't let you come out here," Morgan said. "They frown on brothers being in the same place."

"It's happened before."

"A clerical accident. My people don't make that kind of mistake. But enough of that. Let's don't spend the time fighting. You're just in time for the party."

"Party?" Billy said, puzzled. "What party?"

Chapter Nine

"*Xin can ly,*" the old man said, and lifted his tin cup high. Henry sighed and untangled his legs. He glanced at Billy sitting beside him. His brother's face seemed glazed. Henry pushed himself up. The temperature had fallen rapidly as the sun disappeared behind the mountains. At first the cool air felt good, but now there was just enough chill in the air that a fire was needed. The flames danced in the shadows where the women waited. Some of the men had already lurched to their feet and staggered into the darkness where giggles greeted them followed by low murmurs of welcome.

"Jesus," Billy muttered. "Don't that old man ever slow down?"

"Tradition," Henry said. He turned his head and looked at the clear sky and full moon. A vague uneasiness stirred in his stomach, and he pretended to drain his cup with the old man in response to his toast. The old man was too drunk to notice and sighed happily as he watched Billy gamely drain his cup.

"Ah, it is good to be among friends and family," the old man said. He gestured with his cup, and Henry lifted a bottle to fill it. The old man peered closely at the contents and, satisfied that the cup was filled, carefully lowered himself to the ground by the fire. Henry looked at the bottle in his hand, gauging. It was three-quarters empty. Another hour and he and his brother could safely slip off to his hut.

"We are pleased that the Dai-uy and his brother are here with us." He raised his cup and sipped. Henry and Billy lifted theirs in answer. The old man smacked his lips and looked fondly at Henry. "I dreamed you here, and you are here. That is a blessing for us." Murmurs of agreement followed his words. "I did not dream your brother here." He frowned, searching for words, then smiled. "But you are welcome as well and if you are as good as your brother, perhaps I should have dreamed you here after all."

He sighed and stretched and took another sip. "Many years ago, our people were very numerous, very numerous," the old man began. Henry sighed and eased his legs.

"What's he saying now?" Billy said, his words slurring.

"A story," Henry said.

"Jesus," Billy said. He held out his cup and Henry poured a small jot and politely turned his attention to the old man's familiar story.

"They were very brave and fought many glorious battles with the *ngur bi Trung-Haa* in the south." The old man spat contemptuously into the fire and waited as the others imitated him. "The *ngur bi Trung-Haa* wanted our land, not so much for its value, but—"

Flares suddenly lit the sky overhead, and everyone froze in the eerie white light. A hut exploded just beyond the circle of fire. Henry burst into action.

"Mortars!" he screamed, and rolled swiftly away from the fire. The villagers began to mill in confusion.

"What the fuck?" Billy said, blinking stupidly at the flares.

Henry swore long and fluently as he peeled a screaming girl away from him.

"Come on!" he yelled. He hauled Billy to his feet and gave him a shove. He crouched, and ran to his hut. He dove through the doorway and scrambled wildly in the dark for the rocket launcher and Thompson and hung a sack filled with .45 caliber clips around his neck. He grabbed Billy's AR-15 and harness and thrust it into his brother's hands as he stumbled into the hut.

"We've gotta get to the bridge!" he yelled. He shook his brother. "Are you all right?"

Billy pushed him away and shrugged into the harness. "I'll make it! You go on! I'll join you!"

Henry nodded and dashed back outside. Some of the villagers had started to fire random shots into the darkness across the gorge. It seemed lighter and he looked up at enough flares to light a gigantic Christmas tree.

"Shoot the flares down!" he yelled. The old man looked at him blankly. "The flares! Shoot them down!" He sensed Billy beside him. His brother raised his AR-15 and started shooting. The old man clapped two of the villagers on their shoulders and raised his own rifle. The four of them began shooting at the parachutes holding the burning sticks aloft. Another round exploded near him, and Henry ducked as wood and hot metal showered down upon him.

Jesus Christ! The bridge!

"Get those goddamn flares down!" he yelled at his brother. Billy nodded and rammed another clip into his AR-15. Henry leaped to his feet and ran to the bridge. He sensed the old man beside him. They dropped down beside the bridge. The Viet Cong were halfway over, and Henry blessed the stubborn faith the villagers had in the old structure that had kept them from making it sturdier. The Viet Cong, unused to the sway of the bridge, moved awkwardly toward the village. Henry took a half-turn around the sling of the Thompson, knelt, and carefully squeezed the trigger. Surprised screams came from the darkness. The structure began to sway violently as those on the bridge turned and tried to run back. They bunched in confusion, and Henry braced the Thompson against a bridge upright and emptied the clip into them. Bullets richocheted around him, and he hastily rolled out of the way and scurried to a pile of boulders that served as an anchor for one of the bridge supports.

A flash across the gorge caught his eye, and he heard the explosion behind him. He swung the rocket launcher around in front of him, ripped off the safety wires and held the tiny crosshair sight where the flash had been. He waited for the next flash, made a minor correction and fired. A loud whoosh! momentarily deafened him, and he saw the rocket explode. He swung his Thompson, recklessly spraying the area across from him.

The firing stopped, and he waited cautiously, aware that the fires behind would silhouette him if he stood. Minor explosions came from the village as dry timbers cracked and fell, and the odd cartridge exploded in the heat. Shrill wailing rose and dipped as mothers and wives found their dead children and husbands and coarse cries of warning as the men, finally organized, spread out through the darkness to find the enemy. Then all was quiet except for the crackling flames and wailing.

Henry carefully stood, body tense and ready to drop at the first flash, but none came. He sensed, rather than heard, Nguyen Duc as the old man moved to his side.

"It is over," the old man said quietly. He was no longer drunk. Henry nodded and spat, the taste of Scotch sour in his mouth. He slipped the sling of the Thompson over his shoulder. The grip dangled near his hand; he caressed it absently with his thumb.

"For now," he said. "But they will come back. Some got away."

The old man scrubbed his hands across his face and stared into the darkness.

"The bridge?" he asked.

"I think it is secure," Henry said.

"Good," the old man said. He hesitated, then moved out onto it. Henry let him go alone. It would be better that way.

He looked down the gorge into the darkness. Moonlight glinted off the water of the river. He thought that he had never seen such a shabby sadness. He turned back to the village. Broken bodies lay like twisted dolls in the shadows.

"Billy?" he shouted.

"Dai-uy! Dai-uy!" weak voices called.

"Billy?" A sudden coldness came over him. He ran back into the village. He found his brother, lying face down. The two men who had been helping him lay in crumbled heaps next to him. He fell to his knees and gently rolled his brother over. Sightless eyes stared back at him. He felt a warmness on his hand and looked down at where the shrapnel had ripped his brother's chest away.

"Billy!" he screamed. Tears came to his eyes.

"Dai-uy!"

He swallowed and draped the Thompson over his shoulder by its sling. He gathered his brother's body and rose, staggering under the sudden weight. He stumbled back to his hut and lay his brother down gently upon his cot. He sighed. His eyes blurred.

"Dai-uy!"

He took a deep shuddering breath and pulled the poncho liner up, covering his brother. He bent and dragged the tin locker filled with medicines and bandages from beneath his cot. He swept his table clear, lit his lanterns, then turned to treat the first of a steady stream of wounded.

The sun was high in the sky and the inside of Morgan's hut a sauna when he finished wrapping gauze around the leg of a small girl, neatly tore and knotted the ends and dismissed her with a tired smile. The young girl shyly smiled back and limped out of the hut. Morgan yawned and stretched. His shoulders cracked, and he dug his knuckles hard into the small of his back to remove the stiffness. His eyes were scratchy, stinging from lack of sleep. The long night was over, and he had lost track of the number of wounded he had helped and tried to help. The hut stank of blood, and he could taste the brassy flavor of death in his mouth.

He glanced at the shape of his brother lying on his cot under his poncho liner. His eyes burned. He walked out of the hut and squinted and shaded his eyes against the brightness of the morning sun as he crossed to the Lister bag hanging in the shade of a baobab tree. He lifted the cover and splashed water on his face, then drank deeply and sighed as the coolness spread through him. He saw the old man wearily approaching and drew a cup of water, slowly sipping as he waited.

"*Chao ong,*" he said formally.

"*Chao co,*" the old man answered. He accepted the cup of water Morgan offered gratefully and drank it solemnly. His red-rimmed eyes filled suddenly, and he turned quickly away. Morgan pretended to be interested in something high up the mountain. The old man sniffed, blew his nose between two fingers, and turned back to Morgan.

"Your brother?" he asked. Morgan shook his head. "I am sorry. That is one of the noble truths about pain. Death."

"Will you have a cigarette?" Morgan asked, and held out a crumbled pack of Salems. The old man formed the cup with his thumb and forefinger and smoked quietly.

"My shame is deep," he said sadly. Morgan grunted sympathetically and waited. The old man looked up at the sky. "It must have been the birds."

"Yes," Morgan said. "The birds."

"Yes," the old man echoed. "We should not have waited for the birds to gather. That was very foolish."

He fell silent, and Morgan waited for him to continue. A small bird chirped cheerfully in the distance, and Morgan tried to identify it. Overhead a kite spiraled lazily. The old man nervously chewed his lower lip and tried to maintain his dignity.

"My son," he said quietly, and the anguish in his voice struck Morgan hard. He shivered at the pain etched in deep lines around the old man's eyes, his cheeks.

"We shall have to move," he said.

The old man looked around him at the broken village. He threw back his head and stared at the huge creepers clinging to the side of the mountain and the brush that waited patiently on the outskirts of the village. The village was older than the old man and had been the home of his people for many generations. They had resisted all attempts to take the village and land from them. Not even Diem's decree in 1956 that no individual could own more than a hundred hectares of land had kept them from grimly holding onto their ancestral homes. But now, now there was nothing left for them but to leave, and the old man knew that only faint traces of the village would be seen in a few weeks and by the end of the year, after the side of the mountain was washed clean by the monsoon rains, nothing would be left but old bones rising from eroded graves and maybe a copper bracelet or the shards of a broken pot. For these more time would be needed, but the jungle was patient, patient and always there and always the victor. Now the old man felt the added pain of the leader for his people to the shame he carried.

"Yes," he said. "Yes, we shall have to move. Perhaps north—" His voice trailed off, and Morgan watched him carefully.

"He went north," the old man said harshly. "There is no other place for him. He would have to go north. Far north. The others in these mountains will hear about what he has done and there will be no place for him but the far north." He turned to stare at Morgan with cold and terrible eyes. "My son—" His voice cracked. He coughed and looked away. "I knew the Viet Cong had offered him money. I should have known it was only the first of many offers."

Morgan nodded, remembering the time he had caught the son cutting the arms and legs off a screaming monkey, laughing as the monkey writhed in pain. He had knocked the son to the ground and shot the monkey. Now, he remembered the son's eyes burning hatred at him.

"We are not given to know everything," Morgan said.

"Yes," the old man said. "But there are things that we should know. I should have known his weakness. That money would give him things that he could not have here. I should have known that. Sons do not live their father's dreams."

"Yes," Morgan said. He gave the old man the rest of his cigarettes and rose. He waited uncertainly beside the old man for a moment, then pressed his shoulder and walked back to his hut. A lump formed in his throat, and his eyes watered. He felt like a stranger and tried to shrug off the feeling. He had to radio Colonel Black and report and knew he would be taken away from the village and the people as a precaution. Perhaps the four years were over. He looked at the village, at the broken people who would now have to leave their homes as the Viet Cong had learned where they lived. Then, he turned and looked back at his brother. A hardness formed in his throat.

No! Not this way! he thought savagely. He stared around at the wreckage.

"Boy!" he called. A slim brown youth, naked save for a

loincloth, appeared in the doorway. "Crank the generator." He waited, impatiently fiddling with the microphone cord of the radio as the youth laboriously began turning the handles of the generator. Morgan wiped the sweat from his face and sniffed his armpits. He grimaced at the sour smell and pulled a bottle of Johnnie Walker Scotch from a bag hanging from a rafter, uncorked it and drank deeply. He splashed some of the Scotch under each armpit, preferring the sting of alcohol to the threat of fungus. The radio crackled. He made a tiny adjustment and spoke into the microphone.

Chapter Ten

Morgan squatted on his heels in the shadow of the quonset hut and traced curious designs in the dust with his forefinger while he waited patiently for his ride. A great weariness draped itself over him. Colonel Black had not been in when he reported to his office after the helicopter dropped him off. He had filled out the paperwork, identifying his brother and a report on what had happened at the village. He had started to use a telephone to call home, then hung up and left. A letter would be better, he told himself. Later. Then, he had walked over to Colonel Black's office, but the colonel was in a meeting. He had told Black's aide to tell Black that he would return at 0800 hours the next day and asked that a jeep be called to take him into Saigon.

On the way out he had suddenly become aware of the pretty blonde who stared in fascination at his shaven head from her desk by the door. Her eyes, he noticed, were gray with tiny flashes of brown, her bosom deep, and she colored prettily when she realized he had caught her staring.

He could hear the clamor in the office behind him as the first lieutenant shouted for Lieutenant Holmes. He made a mental note of her name. He allowed his mind to sort out the details he had noticed about the woman. She wore no rings, she smoked too much, and her fingernails were chewed to the quick. One button on her blouse had been cracked from an ironing, and she had plucked one black eyebrow a shade higher than the other which suggested she was probably impatient and a bit careless with her private life. Probably had nylons hanging from the shower and bobby pins in the sink if she shared an apartment with an officer or her blanket carelessly tucked around the issue mattress if she lived in one of the new two-story concrete barracks. He favored barracks rather than the apartment supported by some officer: her desk top showed too many bad habits resumed for her to live in orderly barracks.

A jeep screeched to a halt in a cloud of dust and a young sergeant untangled long legs and stepped from behind the wheel. He looked left, then right, noticed Morgan, and shrugged.

"You looking for a ride, sir?" Morgan nodded, and straightened from his squat. "Stephens. With a 'ph.' This it?" He hefted Morgan's backpack, started to swing it into the back of the jeep, and caught himself when he heard glass tinkle. Gently, he lowered it onto the cushion and climbed behind the wheel. He looked curiously at Morgan as he slid into the passenger seat beside him. He drove off, shifting smoothly through the gears as he accelerated.

"What's your preference, sir? Most people in from the bush stay at the Continental or Caravelle. Some stay at the American, but that isn't its real name, the American, that is. We just call it that because there's an MP station there. You check your weapons into the armory when you sign in. Going to be in town long?"

"Not long," Morgan said, and settled himself against the hot canvas of the seat. "A week or two. The Continental sounds fine. Did you know Graham Greene wrote most of *The Quiet American* while he stayed there?"

"Really? That's nice to know, sir," Stephens said, his voice neutral. Morgan concealed a grin with a last draw on his cigarette before flipping the butt onto the pavement. He would be willing to bet that the young soldier had probably never even heard of Graham Greene and could care less if he had been a writer. Those stationed in Saigon read even less than those in the bush. The exotic city held too many fascinations for one to spend idle hours curled up with a book instead of a young Vietnamese woman eager to indoctrinate them into the mysteries of the Orient. He frowned. The irony of Greene's work was not lost upon him: Americans were seldom quiet. Even their silences spoke volumes.

Stephens drove past the sentry box, carelessly flicked his forefinger at the guard, and slipped easily into the heavy traffic moving toward Saigon. Morgan settled back and took a good look at Saigon. Much had changed since his last visit to the city nearly a year ago.

Saigon was an exploding metropolis of nearly two million people and growing rapidly as displaced refugees swarmed down from the north in search of the legendary city of flowers and peace. They found, instead, slums built from packing crates or *agrovilles* filled with lice and rats and cornucopias of rotted food to eat. Unless they had money, that is. Then, it would be Dai Nay Boulevard where they would live in luxurious villas behind concrete walls with broken glass imbedded profusely on top and the Cercle Sportif, the old French club still clinging desperately to colonial splendor. It didn't matter. Everyone appeared to live in a crazy conglomerate of plans, hopes, dangerous enterprises, far ahead or behind in the shadows of civilization, shuddering at the thought of hard work, leading precarious lives of leisure in a place of decay.

Stephens expertly wove his way past rusting buses, small white Lambrettas, and woven bamboo rickshaws jamming the brick-paved streets, and turned into a little-traveled side street. Tall palms drooped delicately, elegantly, and trailing vines of scented flowers crawled gently along the walls. Morgan heard birds singing and the bustle and snarl of the main boulevards seemed far away. The iron gates anchored in the cement-covered brick walls here were more delicately wrought with fine patterns like filigreed lace. The richest were monogramed with signature initials and the rich of the rich had two letters separated by a hyphen. The houses were hard to see and Morgan had to content himself with quick glimpses of red-tiled roofs and, once, a vine-covered veranda, and he half-expected a white-suited Frenchman and his wife, dressed in yellow chiffon, to step from the house into a chauffered automobile and be driven away. Then, he saw two officers, a Vietnamese and an American, step into a staff car and he leaned back against the thin cushion of his seat and stared at the clean gutters of the street. He smelled himself and became aware of his tattered appearance and the difference between being the poster soldier he had just seen and the soldier he was. For a brief moment, he felt ashamed, then grew angry at himself for his feelings.

"Let's try somewhere else," Morgan suggested. "Some place without an MP station."

"Beg pardon?"

"Anywhere but the Continental. I'm afraid it's lost its charm," he said. "How about the old Villa Jacques? Out on Plantation Road?"

"Anything you say, sir," Stephens said.

Without braking, he wrenched the jeep into another side street and the cool palms were exchanged for blinding sun that reflected off tall, concrete buildings.

Morgan squinted against the sudden harsh sunlight, and a slow, dull ache began to mount behind his left eye. He focused his attention on the palm trees and slumped in his seat. He pressed his knees against the dashboard. Suddenly, he remembered his brother and felt very, very tired.

"Are you married, sir?" Stephen asked.

"No."

"Someone waiting for you back home?"

Morgan didn't answer, his thoughts turning toward Kate. It was going to be hard to write the letter, but it had to be done. An ache rose in his throat. He squeezed his eyes shut, pinching the bridge of his nose. For a brief second, he thought he smelled lavender. If I returned to the ranch, would the same feelings I left come back? No, because you are not the same person who left the ranch. And that is the tragedy of war: becoming different. And not now. Not with Billy dead.

Stephens glanced sideways at the man sitting beside him, but Morgan stared through slitted eyes at a world of his own. Stephens drove the rest of the way in silence. When he turned into the pink graveled drive that led to the Villa Jacques, Morgan jerked as if he had been sleeping and turned to him.

"Do you know a woman named Holmes?" he asked.

"Lieutenant Holmes? Sure." Stephens said. He wrinkled his brow. "Why do you ask, sir?"

"Would you see if she's busy tonight? And if not, ask her to join me for dinner?" Morgan swung his legs out of the jeep and reached for his backpack and Thompson before Stephens could gather them. "And I have a foot locker stored at the Bachelor Officer Quarters back at Ton Son Nhut. Sorry. I should have thought about it sooner, but I didn't. Would you mind gathering it for me?"

"Not at all, sir." Morgan turned to go. "Excuse me, sir?" He turned back and looked at Stephens. "Well, uh, sir, what if Lieutenant Holmes says no? Would you like me to—well, I know a couple of nurses—" He met Morgan's stare and silently swore at himself. Christ! What had he been thinking? This was an officer, not a sergeant!

"She'll come," Morgan said at last. "She's curious."

He turned to the portico of the Villa Jacques, ignoring the white-coated doorman who raised his nose at Morgan's appearance and made half-hearted gestures at relieving him of his burden. Morgan stepped past the tall, white columns glistening with fresh paint and entered the heavily-carpeted foyer. He paused in the cool interior to let his eyes adjust from the blinding sunlight. Potted palms flanked him. To his left, a short stairway led to the dining room and bar. Overstuffed chairs and a sofa clustered around a fireplace to his right. He glanced overhead at the heavy mahogany fans turning slowly, smiled, and walked to the desk. His steps were silent on the deep, mauve carpets. The deskman raised a solemn eyebrow, but Morgan ignored him, spun the register around and signed his name.

"A suite," he said bluntly. The man raised both eyebrows this time and looked at Morgan carefully. The cool interior began to make Morgan's eyes feel heavy.

"*Toi muon thue phong,*" Morgan said impatiently.

"I speak English. And French," the man said pointedly. His voice carried only the slightest accent. Morgan nodded.

"Good. A suite, please," he repeated. "With a bath. And please telephone MAC-V, Colonel Black's office, and inform them where I'm staying."

The mention of central headquarters broke the man's solemn composure. He smiled thinly and turned to the keyboard behind him, smoothing his carefully oiled hair with one hand as he studied it for a moment.

"Very well, sir. And as for a suite—I have a small bungalow near the pool. Would that be satisfactory? It is a little more, uh, quiet."

Morgan nodded at the man, knowing he was more concerned with the rest of the guests in the hotel than he was with Morgan's comfort. All of Saigon is military now, he thought. He half-expected the deskman to bow stiffly and click his heels.

"Satisfactory," he said aloud, and the deskman slapped the bell in front of him and stood at attention in front of him as the bell boy leaped smartly to his bidding. Morgan turned and saw Stephens standing in the doorway.

"Tell her it's the Christmas season," he said.

Wordlessly, Stephens touched his brow with his forefinger and left. Morgan smiled faintly and followed the spotless white back of the bell boy. First, a bath and then a couple of drinks. And then the letter. He suddenly felt old, very old.

"That's what he said, ma'am," Stephens said. He spoke in a low voice. Others in the office cast sidelong glances at them and worked as quietly as possible in an attempt to hear what was being said. The First Lieutenant watched them suspiciously as Second Lieutenant Rachel Holmes pretended to check the trip ticket Stephens had handed her. She pointed with a pencil to an item and Stephens leaned closer. He smelled her perfume, stale cigarettes and peppermint lifesavers.

"What does he—who—did he say anything else?" she asked. She kept tapping the spot with her pencil. Stephens shook his head.

"No. Just dinner, sir. Oh he did say to tell you that it's the Christmas season."

She frowned.

"What should I tell him, sir?" he whispered.

"Oh, damn it, tell him yes," she said. She looked down at

her desk to cover her confusion. She shivered and she squeezed her legs together to keep them from trembling.

"Yes, ma'am," he said. "I'll phone you and let you know time and everything, okay?"

She nodded and Stephens picked up the two trip tickets she had placed on her desk and left. The door snapped shut behind him. She opened her mouth to call him back and cancel, then shook her head.

"Damn him!" she said. A chubby girl with deep acne scars turned from the next desk.

"What'd he do?" she asked.

"Nothing. Just nothing," Rachel said furiously, and pushed a pile of papers aside and slammed a ledger sharply on her desk top. She opened it and began to furiously copy figures from one sheet onto another.

"Something, I think," the girl said.

Rachel drew a deep breath and leaned back in her chair. She pushed her hair back and held it briefly off her neck to let air blow across the damp ringlets. "I just did something damn foolish," she said. "I told him I would have dinner with him."

"The driver?" the girl asked.

"No, no," Rachel said impatiently. "The one who was just here. You know, the jungle bunny. Oh, forget it."

She bent back over her desk and picked up her pencil. The point snapped and she tossed it aside, opened the tray of her desk, selected another, and began transferring numbers. The chubby girl pursed her lips and arched an eyebrow. She collected a sheaf of papers from her desk and briskly crossed the aisle to another girl. She bent close and began to whisper in her ear. The second girl looked at Rachel in surprise, then hurriedly rose and crossed to another girl.

Rachel pretended not to notice, but she could feel the curious looks and knew what they were thinking.

Chapter Eleven

High in the mountains to the north, the old man sipped sour coconut beer and listened to the jungle. His wife slowly stirred a pot of vegetables over a tiny fire. Scattered throughout the bamboo grove, other old women moved stiffly as they prepared food for their men, but there were no young men. The old man frowned: the Dai-uy was not going to like this. But how could he have stopped them? They melted into the jungle like shadows. One minute there, the next, gone. No shots, no screams, nothing. Just clamoring monkeys. The spirits, he decided, were to blame: the old ones were very patient but would not be patient forever. Perhaps it was not too late. They had salt and the new scarf the Dai-uy had given him was almost like silk. The hammered brass bracelet around his wrist would help too.

A small breeze rushed through the clearing and stirred the leaves of the bamboo. He raised his head and sniffed. The rains were not far behind. The horizon was strung with rain clouds. The sun that morning had risen over the hills like a mist-shrouded egg yolk. The Dai-uy had better hurry or the trail would disappear. He turned and faced the north and breathed deeply.

Up there. Yes, up there. In the mountains. That is where *he* waited. The old man did not permit himself the mention of his son's name, Bao. Instead he drank the coconut beer from his bamboo cup and threw it violently from him.

Haw! Even the thought of *his* name soured the beer. He rose, knees popping with the effort, and moved to the monkey-hide Ca and poured more of the coconut beer into the metal canteen cup the Dai-uy had given him. He made a face and swallowed.

He would be glad when the Dai-uy returned and brought more of the *ruro'u uyt-ky*. This stuff tasted like monkey piss. He walked to the old woman's pack and removed a small sack of salt and carried the salt and the beer into the jungle with him. When he was hidden from the others, he untied the scarf from around his neck and carefully folded it and laid it under a flat rock. He broke four twigs from a branch of a tree, bent them in half, and placed them north, south, east and west of the rock. He stepped back and looked carefully at his offering.

The gods may be pleased with this. It is a poor offering, but it is the offering of a poor man. Were we back in the village I would leave the fat from the back of my fattest goat, but we are not in the village, and I do not have any goats. But here is beer for you to drink, and although it is the beer of a *Hon Bo* gambler, it is all that I have.

He poured the beer on the four sticks and waited for a sign. He heard a voice within him and concentrated.

You search for your son. Why?

There is honor—

Is your honor a god?

No. I am not a god.

A heavenly spirit, then?

No.

A demigod?

No.

Then, your honor is a human being?

No. All is gone.

Not all. Not yet.

A kite whistled, and the old man frowned and uneasily scratched his neck. It was not a good sign, for the kite was a messenger of the *Diem Vuong*, the Lord of Hell.

He bowed thrice toward his offering and backed from the clearing. Carefully he made his way back toward the camp. Half-way there, he stopped. Before him lay a fresh pile of jackal dung. It was the worst possible sign. He turned to his left and began to work his way around the droppings. It was the only thing he could do.

The unforgotten son with the unspeakable name smelled the same wind and frowned. He too knew the rains were not far behind. This morning, the sky had looked as brightly grained as polished bone, as if all color had been drained out of the sun. In fact they were too close for him to continue north. He *had* to cross the Red River, and that was impossible now, for the river north of where he now stood would be swollen with the waters from the north, and he dared not use any of the bridges. He swore, long and violently. Very clever of the northerners to make this arrangement and very stupid of him not to see through their plans. But he would show them. He would make it. First, though, a slight detour south until the rains stopped, then back north.

He turned and shouted orders, and the young men from his village turned and began plodding back to the south. They were weary and moved like cattle to the market. Still they were his, and their numbers made him very powerful. Bong Dien began to angrily push his way through the column of villagers, stripping off sweat-stained bandoliers and equipment as he approached.

Bao pulled a U.S. Army canteen from his pack and drank deeply from it. He dropped to his haunches and poured some of the water on top of his head. He sighed. Another confrontation. How did those in Hanoi ever manage to make a decision? He remembered the early teachings of his father before he became friends with the Dai-uy and the teachings dwindled to nothing. Patience was the necessary virtue, even before honesty and desire. With patience and time, anything could be obtained.

He forced the irritation from his mind and reached for his pack and removed the last of the Salem cigarettes he had taken from the Dai-uy's bag. He scraped a small hole in the earth with his fingers, crumbled the cigarette pack into a ball and dropped it into the hole and covered it with dirt. This was as far north as any *linh my* would ever get. He felt a small sense of satisfaction at that.

Chapter Twelve

Morgan awoke, dry-mouthed and sweating. A heavy, mahogany fan clicked slowly over him, sluggishly pushing the heavy air through the room. His head pounded from the intensity of his dream and he smelled stale fear in his sweat. He swung his feet off the bed, bracing them on the sisal rug covering the floor like a mat. He reached for the bottle of Scotch on the nightstand beside his bed. He ignored the glass and drank deeply from the bottle. He gagged, breathed deeply and swallowed convulsively until the beating of his heart slowed. He pushed himself shakily to his feet and looked at his naked self in the mirror above the bureau. He smiled ruefully at the incongrous figure he presented: the pale, catfish-belly white of his hips and thighs contrasted with the deep bronze of his chest and shoulders, marred only by the dark-green fungus that crept around his armpits. He looked down at his pale feet and frowned at the spongy, wrinkled skin and knew he'd have to peel them soon. He sniffed the air in the suddenly stuffy room and grimaced. He smelled like a day-old corpse left out in the sun.

Or a cow, he thought, and his mind turned unwillingly to the ranch near Ithaca in South Dakota. He closed his eyes.

The image flickered and grew in his memory: a sunny day in autumn, for those were the best, and he was riding with his father slowly along the east fence that bordered the Rosebud Indian Reservation, not because there was a need to do so, but simply because it was an excuse to be riding on a warm, sunny day in the fall.

Looks like we got a death, the old man said. Henry looked at his father, eyebrows lifted in question. The old man pointed at the sky and he looked up to see the turkey buzzards circling lazily high overhead. Something large to draw that many buzzards, that's for sure, the old man added.

Together they heeled their horses and trotted up and over the ridgeline. There, at the bottom in a backwashed gully lay a dead heifer. Five or six buzzards were already at her, one with his head up her anus. Henry reached automatically for the Winchester in the saddle boot, but the old man placed his hand on his arm, staying him.

You don't want to shoot a buzzard, the old man said quietly. Bad luck. 'Sides, it's against the law. They're only doing what they're supposed to be doing. Nature's disposalers, you see. They clean up after the mess we make of our prairies.

I just wanted to scare them away, he said defensively. I wasn't going to shoot them.

Accomplish the same thing by riding down there. Might as well save your bullets, the old man answered. He gigged his horse and the old buckskin moved obediently down the shale toward the heifer. Henry followed, neck-reining the sorrel when it shied away from the smell of death.

Easy, easy, he murmured, and the sorrel stood still, nostrils flaring red, eyes walling toward the heifer. Its skin shivered, and Henry soothed it, speaking calmly until it relaxed and bent its neck, taking a clump of grama grass in its mouth. He dismounted and tied the reins to a large lump of shale. The shale would not hold the sorrel if it wanted to leave, but it would remind it that it was hitched.

He pulled up his jeans and walked across to the old man who already squatted on his boot heels. His nose quivered from the smell of rotting flesh. The old man seemed oblivious to it as he studied the head. The buzzards had already taken the delicacies: the eyes and the tongue. He looked up as Henry stopped next to him.

Looks like a poacher, he said quietly. He pointed to a spot behind an ear where a bullet had entered the brain. The earth was dark with dried blood beneath the head.

A single shot. Close, too. You can see the powder burn. He

bent the ear back and showed Henry where the hide was darker than the rest.

You want me to ride back and phone the sheriff? Henry asked.

The old man pulled a stem of grama grass out and put it between his lips, mincing it with his teeth, thinking. At last he shook his head and rose stiffly.

Nope, he said. Don't think so.

But why? Henry asked. Ain't it just like stealing?

Oh yes, it's that all right, the old man said. He removed his hat and wiped the inside of it and his forehead with a bright-red bandana before resettling. His pale eyes looked over the fence across into the reservation. And I expect that we could probably follow that trail and find out it was Amos Yellow Feather who took it, he said.

If you know who, then let's get him, Henry said eagerly. He turned to leave, but the old man's voice pulled him up short.

Nope, don't think so, he said softly. Henry turned around and watched as the old man took a tin of Union Leader from his shirt pocket and slowly built a cigarette. You see, Amos has had a run of bad luck, lately. Wife's been sick and so has three of his five kids. He doesn't have much to begin with—just a spit-and-piss one-loop operation—barely enough to feed his mouths during good times. Reckon he needed meat mighty badly to do this, he mused.

If'n he's so bad off, why don't he kill one of his own beeves? Henry asked. Why come all the way over here and kill one of ours? That's what ain't right. If'n he didn't have any of his own, then I could understand. But this, he shook his head. I don't follow your line of thinking. Just plain stealing, it looks like to me.

Yeah, probably you're right, the old man said. He popped a kitchen match with his thumbnail and bent his head into his cupped hands, away from the small breeze gently curling the grass. He inhaled deeply and let out a thin stream of smoke. He broke the match, then wet the tip of his thumb and middle finger and pinched the burnt head of the match before dropping it to the ground where he dug it into the shale with the toe of his boot.

But, I expect he needs his own cattle to sell for the bills, he said. His pale eyes caught Henry's and held them. Amos ain't been a bad neighbor. None of the Indians been bad to us, son. This ain't the first time one of them has been hard up enough to sneak a beef. Probably won't be the last. But they'll make good on it, somehow. You wait and see.

If you say so, Henry said doubtfully. The old man heard the doubt in his voice and smiled. Sunlight glinted from the silver stubble around his chin.

You got a bit to learn about human nature, Henry, he said gently. And what's right. Take a good look at the cow.

Henry turned back and stared, not sure what he was looking for.

Notice that he took everything he could carry on his horse—front and back quarters are gone. That tells you he needed the meat. Was he just after a steak or two, he'da carved them out and left all the rest for the buzzards. But he didn't. Notice the wire, too. Henry's eyes lifted to the fence. He didn't cut the wire to come across like he would've if'n he'd just been after enough meat for a Sunday barbecue. No he pulled the staples out of the fence posts, lowered the wire to get his horse across and back, then hammered the staples back in. Real thoughtful, that.

Why didn't he come and ask for help instead of just taking it? Henry asked. That's what I would've done.

It is, is it? The old man smiled. Well, that's the difference between you and the Indians. They got a whole lot of pride. It's hard to admit that they need help. Most of them, that is, he added. 'Course, you always got a few like ol' Slope-Nose and Owl Face who drink everything from Thunderbird wine to hair oil and shaving lotion, including squeezings from canned heat. They don't amount to much and never will. Lot of white folks like that too but we don't make such a hey-do about them around here. We just pretend they don't exist like ol' Ted Miller and Howie Shaw. Don't think either one of them's drawn a sober breath in twenty years. Most likely got livers like pumpkins about now. But we pretend there ain't nothing wrong with them. Indian behave like that, on the other hand, and we hold 'im up to ridicule.

He sighed, finished his cigarette, and carefully pulled it apart, pinching out the coal. He shook his head and stared back across at the reservation. Wasn't too many years ago that they owned all this land, Henry. Their ancestors are buried in it. You gotta respect that too. Don't just look at the man, Henry. Always look at the reason for the man. That's what's important. Remember that now.

No, he added, turning toward his old buckskin. We'll leave Amos alone and pretend that we never found this. It don't hurt us none. And I expect we won't have to ride this fence for quite a while.

Why's that?

The old man paused and looked at him, his eyes smiling. Well I think Amos will probably watch our east line here pretty closely and keep it up. Just his way of paying us, you could say. He'll find a few other ways too. In the long run, we'll probably come out ahead.

And they had, he reflected, smiling at his image. When it came time for fall branding, Amos had ridden over with his two oldest boys and pitched in to help. His father offered him wages, but Amos simply shook his head. His father didn't push it, but politely thanked Amos for being neighborly. That Christmas a package mysteriously appeared by their door. When they opened it, they found a deerskin shirt for his father and a pair of deerskin gloves for him.

A pounding on the door shattered the memory and he blinked, slowly bringing himself back from his thoughts.

"Captain Morgan?" The pounding began again.

"Yes?" he called. He rubbed his knuckles hard against his eyes.

"Message, sir."

"Shove it under the door."

A scratching like mice came from the bottom of the door and a small sheet of yellow paper slid into the room. He rose on unsteady legs and stumbled to the door. He bent, picked it up, and leaned against the door while he read, "My office. Eleven hundred hours. Black."

He crumbled the paper into a tiny ball and tossed it toward the small, wicker basket by the bed. He missed. He picked it up and dropped it into the basket, then placed the basket closer to the bed. He took a towel and sat naked in the middle of the bed and began to peel the dead skin from his feet in thick, curling layers, wetting the towel with Scotch and pressing the dampness against his feet.

Chapter Thirteen

Morgan rose as Rachel walked across the dining room to his table at the Circle Sportif. He smoothed his white dinner jacket and touched the knotted tie, making sure that it was straight. Eyes turned to watch her covertly as she made her way across the room. The Circle Sportif was the oldest club in Saigon, built by the French colonials before the war and still snobbish enough to have only a token number of Vietnamese, professors and those who could trace their lineage to the Nguyens, the last dynasty, numbered among its members. The few Americans who held membership in the elite club did so from the influence their departments wielded: the embassy members and the intelligence community comprising the majority of those.

She looks like a Modigliani. No, more like one of the pre-Raphaelites. Rossetti would have loved to paint her, but I am thankful that he did not paint her for he would have corrupted her.

She halted before him and held out her hand. He clasped it gently. His palm rasped like a file against hers and her flesh tingled. She tried to smile and the corners of her eyes fluttered like butterfly wings. She forced the smile wider until her face felt like cracked porcelain.

"Good evening," he said politely, and moved around the table to hold her chair for her. She sat and smoothed her dress over her thighs. Her stomach muscles quivered. A delicate, purple-tinged orchid lay by her table service. He returned to his seat as a waiter materialized by the table, a cloth-covered bottle in his hand. He poured wine in their glasses, placed the bottle in an ice bucket, its silver sides covered with a light, cold mist, and disappeared.

"I'm sorry about the orchid," he said. "I didn't know what color you'd be wearing." She realized the purple clashed with her orange dress and she felt a small delight in this weakness of his.

"That's fine," she said graciously, and a small, warm glow formed in her stomach as she awkwardly pinned the orchid to her dress. "I don't receive many." He grinned and rubbed his nose with the palm of his hand.

"I don't give many," he said sheepishly, and picked up his glass. His eyes sparkled, and she realized that he had drunk a lot already. "Actually, I think this is only the second one I've given."

"Let me guess," she said, and leaned forward. Her dress gaped and his eyes flickered automatically to her breasts. She hastily sat back and picked up her water glass, sipping. "The other one was to your prom sweetheart."

"Right. I suppose you received your first one then?"

"No. Actually, this is my first. I didn't go to my prom." She drained her glass and absently twirled it by the stem. He took the bottle from the ice bucket and refilled their glasses.

"I see," he said. Silence gripped the table, and he shifted uncomfortably. They sipped their wine and smiled self-consciously at each other. Rachel became conscious of the wooden fans clicking overhead, the ferns and bougainvilla in one corner of the room, the black and white tiles on the floor. She shifted her weight and the bamboo of her chair creaked, and she suddenly realized that it would leave a pattern on her velvet-covered behind when she stood.

"More wine?"

His voice startled her and she realized that her glass was empty. She nodded, and he motioned to a waiter and spoke rapidly to the black-tied Vietnamese who came to their table.

"You speak the language very well," she said after he left.

"Thank you," he said. "I've been here long enough that I should." He smiled and took a package of Salems from his pocket and offered her one. She took it and leaned across for a light.

Too late, she remembered her dress and blushed furiously as his eyes dropped.

"Oh?" She sat back and puffed furiously on her cigarette to cover her embarrassment. She waited for him to continue, but his eyes became distant, and he toyed absently with his butter-knife, tracing the design on the heavy silver handle with his fingernail. Silence gathered around the table. She tried desperately to think of something to say. It occurred to her that of all the arts, the art of communication was the most important and seldom taught. But what could you say to lift him from his melancholy? You have a nice tan? I know what you're thinking because I have spent a thousand hours thinking the same?

The waiter arrived with another bottle of wine and refilled their glasses. She seized hers and raised it in salute.

"May you be in heaven two days before the devil knows you're dead," she said, and quickly set her glass down and covered her mouth in horror at what she had said. "I'm sorry, I didn't think."

"Irish?" he asked, and raised his glass and drank. His eyes smiled at her discomfort.

"On my mother's side," she said. She fidgeted and sipped from her glass, swearing silently at herself. Act natural. Act natural, she told herself fiercely.

"How long have you been over here?" he asked.

"Too long." The answer was automatic. "Seven months. And you?"

"Longer. Much longer." He laughed and his teeth flashed white against the deep tan of his face. "Where are you from? Where's home?"

"Nowhere." She felt her face tighten.

"Career woman?"

"For now." She puffed nervously at her cigarette. She blinked, realizing Morgan was staring curiously at her.

"I'm sorry, you were saying?"

"I asked if you would care to dance?" He raised his left eyebrow and smiled.

She looked, confused, at the small dance band, then back, recognizing the tango. She shook her head.

"I can't dance to that," she said. She smiled tentatively at him. "Sorry. Wish I could."

"Then, I'll teach you," he said firmly. He rose and took her hand, pulling her protesting to the floor. "Now, follow me."

He gently, but firmly took her hand and slowly led her through the introductory steps. She stumbled, at first, then caught the rhythm and the step, and soon they were gliding across the floor. She felt the music work within her, the subtle backbeat, the intensity, the suggestion of the dance. Perspiration dotted her upper lip, and she lost herself in the sensuality of the dance, his gentle smile, the time and the place. For a brief few minutes, the war ceased to exist and she imagined herself in the arms of an attractive man with nothing to do for the rest of her life but dance.

All too soon the dance was over, and she tucked her hand inside his elbow as he led her back to the table and pulled her chair out for her.

"Thank you," she murmured and sat. She reached out for a cigarette, lit it and dropped the match in the ashtray between them. He caught her hand before she could bring it back across the table. She pulled, but he held firmly.

"Please," she said, and bit her lower lip. He smiled and turned her hand over, intently studying her palm. She felt naked and her cheeks and ears reddened and she squirmed uncomfortably in her chair.

"Thank you for the orchid," she said weakly.

"I should have brought you white lilacs," he said, continuing to study her palm. His thumb brushed over the Venus mound and her stomach fluttered.

"They're out of season, aren't they?" she said. He raised his head and she swallowed heavily and forced herself to meet his eyes. In this light, they seemed gray, but on the dance floor, she would have sworn they were blue. His grip loosened, and she snatched her hand back, disguising her urgency by lifting her wineglass.

"Hungry?" he asked.

"Aren't you?"

He laughed. "Yes, I am. And I'm afraid I've left my manners behind."

The tension disappeared between them and the comfortable awareness of man and woman grew in its place. They relaxed back in their chairs. Morgan picked up the bottle of wine and refilled their glasses.

"Do you always ask strange women to dinner?" She blew a cloud of smoke across the table at him. The band began to play "The Last Time I Saw Paris."

"Constantly," he said poker-faced. "It's my greatest sin."

"Perhaps you should do penance," she suggested lightly. Her eyes crinkled with laughter.

"I already have," he said dryly. He motioned for the waiter. "I'm good for the next thousand years or so. Shall we order?"

Stephens drummed his fingertips in boredom on the Bakelite steering wheel of the jeep and slid down in his seat. He yawned and tried to focus on the front of the club where he had delivered Lieutenant Holmes two hours ago. Thunder rumbled distantly and lightning flickered over the tops of the trees. He sighed and slid down in his seat.

Jesus! How much longer would they be?

He yawned again and reached beneath his seat and brought out a pint bottle of whiskey. He unscrewed the cap and started to take a sip. The bottle stopped halfway to his lips as he became aware of two khaki dressed figures standing beside the jeep. Resignedly, he raised his eyes to the black military police brassards. He sighed, lowered the bottle, screwed on the cap and handed it to the nearest MP. Neither smiled as they inspected the bottle.

"Out," one said, motioning with his baton. Stephens took a careful look around: no other MPs where in sight. For the moment, they were alone. With exaggerated care, he swung his left leg out of the jeep.

"Do you know MAC-V orders regarding the consumption of

alcoholic beverages in a military vehicle?" the MP asked sternly.

"Oh yes," Stephens said, swinging his right leg out. "I do." He continued the movement, pivoting smoothly on the ball of his left foot, driving the toe of his right into the MP's groin. He grunted and doubled up in pain. The bottle smashed against the concrete of the street as his hands automatically dropped to cradle the pain. Stephens grabbed him by the collar and shoved him into the path of the other MP. He staggered backwards, the raised baton windmilling as he tried to maintain his balance. Reflexively, he grabbed his partner to keep him from falling. Stephens stepped neatly to his right and hooked his left fist against the exposed jaw of the MP. He crumbled over the back of his partner, driving him face first onto the concrete. A bone snapped and a sunrise of blood appeared. Stephens cast a quick look around and discovered Morgan and Rachel watching from the doorway of the club. Morgan's face was impassive, calculating. Stephens swallowed and forced a grin.

"Just give me a minute, sir," he said. Without waiting for a reply, he picked up the two MPs, unceremoniously bundled them into the jeep and sped off.

"What do we do now?" Rachel asked. A smile tugged at the corners of Morgan's lips.

"Let's wait a couple of minutes and see if he returns," he suggested.

"Do you think he will?"

"I think so," Morgan answered.

"Why?"

"Because there's nothing left for him to do," he answered.

Minutes later, Stephens slid up beside him in the jeep, stepped out, and pulled the seat back. He reached for Rachel's arm to help her into the backseat.

"Well?" Morgan asked.

"Yes sir?" Stephens said. Rachel stepped into the back of the jeep and sat, carefully arranging her dress around her legs.

"What did you do with them?" Morgan asked as Stephens pulled the seat back, locking it in place.

"There's a house of, well," he paused, glancing at Rachel. He quirked his head. "You know, sir. *That* kind of house?" Morgan nodded, holding his face impassive. "Well, I left them there. They'll be all right," he added.

"I take it you are well acquainted with the personnel of this 'house'?" Morgan asked.

Stephens flushed. "Well, sir, I, uh, that is, yes. Sir."

"What did they want?"

"Oh, just hassling, sir," Stephens said, inventing quickly. "One of them lost quite a bit of money in a poker game to me and this was his way of trying to make up the loss. You know how it goes, sir."

"Uh-huh," Morgan said dryly and stepped into the passenger side of the jeep. Stephens hurried around and settled himself behind the wheel. "I think you're lying," Morgan added.

"Yes sir," Stephens said. He started the jeep and put it into gear. "Now where would the captain like to go next?"

Morgan eyed him for a minute, then sighed and leaned back against the seat. "Down to the Eve Club on Tu-Do Street. Do you know where that is?"

"Yes sir," Stephens said and gunned the jeep away. Rachel grabbed the back of Morgan's seat to keep from flying backwards. She glared at the back of Stephens's head.

"Take it easy!" she snapped.

"So," Morgan said. "What's going to happen now when those two wake up?"

"Nothing, sir," Stephens said, shifting smoothly and weaving in and out of the traffic. "They won't want to admit that one person took them both. A matter of pride, if you know what I mean, sir. Oh, I'll have to do something for them one way or the other, but there won't be any repercussions. I hope. Sir," he added, giving Morgan a quick look out of the corners of his eyes, but the officer sat quietly, not rising to the unspoken question. Stephens swore silently to himself and drove the rest of the way in silence to Tu-Do Street.

"Wait for us," Morgan ordered as he helped Rachel from the backseat of the jeep. "We shouldn't be long. I want to see if an old friend is here."

"Yes sir," Stephens said. He kept his face expressionless, looking over Morgan's left shoulder. Morgan nodded and turned to help Rachel into the club.

"What are you going to do about that?" Rachel asked as the door closed behind them.

"I'm not sure," Morgan said. He looked around the interior of the club and shook his head. "Nuts. I thought Maurice would be here."

"Maurice?" Rachel asked, cocking her head quizzically.

"An old friend," Morgan said. He motioned toward a table. "Let's grab a drink and see if he shows up, all right?"

She shrugged and walked toward the table as Morgan motioned to a waiter to follow them.

Outside, Stephens frowned irritably at the front entrance to the club.

Damn fool. Now, you've really gone and done it. You'll be lucky to get away with an Article 15 court martial, now. Maybe not, though. There's something different about that guy. Other officers would have had you back on base and in the stockade for sure by now. I wonder what he has in mind?

He gnawed at a fingernail, frowning. How long would they be? At that moment, fat raindrops splattered against the jeep's windshield. He sighed and stepped out to raise the canvas top to cover the jeep as rain began to fall in torrents.

"So," Rachel asked. "Have you decided what you are going to do about Stephens?"

Morgan shook his head. "No. Probably nothing."

"You know he was lying," she said.

"Yes."

"And—" She motioned with her hands. Morgan grinned.

"I never was that fond of MPs anyway," he said. "But I think he needs to sweat a little before I let him go."

"Do you think he will?" she asked.

"No," Morgan said. "But I can hope."

The passenger seat flapped forward, startling him, and he straightened as Morgan handed Rachel into the back and stepped quickly into the front seat.

"Sorry, sir," he said, reaching for the ignition. "I guess I was thinking about something."

"That's all right," Morgan said. He glanced at Stephens. "Looks like you were caught with the top down," he said. "You're soaked."

"Yes sir," Stephens said. He shifted the gears and drove quickly away. "I had trouble getting the top up. Where to?"

Morgan turned in his seat and looked at Rachel. "Nightcap somewhere?"

She studied him for a moment, her eyes smoldering with a luminescence as if scorched by a pitiless flame from heaven. Then, she smiled apologetically and shook her head. "No, thanks. I'm a working girl and tomorrow comes early. I'd better get back."

"You heard the lady," he said, leaning back against the seat. "Take us home, please."

Stephens drove down Nguyen Hue past the flashing lights of the Shack and the Capitol bars and turned over to Vo Thanh Street and passed the 147 Club where the prostitutes gathered. He glanced across the river to where Cholon lay, dark and torpid in contrast to its sister city across the river where lights shined garishly and music pulsed and throbbed from seething gin mills where anything could be bought. B-girls, dressed in shimmering Suzie Wong dresses, carried sharp razors in their long hair and wandered the streets looking for marks; contraband whiskey was unloaded off stolen army and navy trucks; cartons of cigarettes were exchanged for marijuana, and gun runners exchanged their wares for heroin shipped down from Thailand and Cambodia. The very buildings seemed built with gray bricks of opium, he thought. He turned and rounded a corner and wove his way to Le Qui Don Street and headed for Ton Son Nhut.

The rain had stopped and fog began to roll up the river and stretch clammy tentacles out over the city when Stephens left Morgan at his bungalow. Morgan thanked him and told him to pick him up at 0700 hours. Stephens drove away and waited until he had turned onto the road leading back into the heart of Saigon before reaching beneath the seat and pulling out a pint of whiskey. He took a long drink and shuddered as the whiskey bit through the cold and hit his stomach, warming it.

Christ, it's cold! He shivered and took another drink, feeling the warmth of the whiskey curl through him. Damn glad that they decided to call it an evening. Don't know what the hell I would have done if I had to hang around in these wet clothes. He took another drink and turned onto the old Rue Richard, newly named Phan Dinh Phung, and headed south past the old colonial villas cloaked in darkness behind heavy walls and tamarind trees. He glanced at his watch, noted the hour, and swung down along the river. Curfew had long passed and, although he had a Class A ticket that allowed him out past hours, it was still best to avoid the military police. The river road was best for that. Late at night, it was always damp along the road, a clinging dampness that seeped in through heavy starch and wilted collars and destroyed creases from shirts and trousers. The MPs hated that, preferring the drier streets where the lights were brightest and the young girls flirted with them as they drove by.

Stephens dropped his headlights to blackout glints. No sense in taking any chances. A new MP who hadn't figured out the routine might be on duty, and he would be very conscientious and suspicious as to why Stephens was six miles out of his way. He sniffed deeply, appreciatively. The rain washed the smell of garbage and exhaust from the air, leaving behind the smell of many flowers. Not, he reflected, that there was much smell of garbage and exhaust in this section of the city. The people who lived here were too rich and politically correct for the smell to work its way up the river from the city.

He took another drink and accelerated as he headed into a ball of fog that lumbered slowly across the road. A dark shape suddenly loomed in front of him. He swung the wheel sharply to the left and there was a sharp *thunk!* and the wheel jolted and jumped in his hands. The jeep careened into a trishaw and came to rest. He switched off the ignition and listened to the engine ping in the cool air. He could hear the gentle lapping as waves licked gently against the stone quay. The fog was like cobwebs against his forehead, his mouth, and then he heard the moaning. He reached under the seat and pulled out a five-cell flashlight. Carefully, he stepped from the jeep and made his way toward the moans. His foot struck something soft and, shielding the light with his free hand, he knelt and quickly flashed the light on and off after he examined the man on the ground. A young Vietnamese clutched his groin and writhed in pain. His leg was broken and in the brief flash of light. Stephens had caught the white thigh bone poking through torn flesh. He turned the light on again, cupping his hand around the lens to shield the glow. Blood ran freely and flecks of foam spotted the man's lips. He lifted quivering fingers to Stephens. Pain shined from his black eyes.

"*Curu toi voi!*" he gasped. "Help!"

Stephens rose and groped his way back to the jeep. He made his way to the front and flashed the light quickly through the wreckage of the trishaw. One headlight had been broken and the hood dented. It wouldn't take much for the motor pool sergeant to piece together what had happened. It was not uncommon for the Vietnamese to throw themselves in front of cars and try to gauge the speed correctly so the car would run over their shadows and kill the *ma-qui* or evil spirit that had attached itself to them. A lot of them misjudged the speed of the car and the car usually looked like the front of his jeep did now. Stephens shook his head. He knew a court martial and reduction in grade waited for him. The U.S. Army had strong feelings about its drivers helping the Vietnamese to rid themselves of the *ma-qui* at the expense of striking them. And he knew the liquor on his breath wouldn't help him at all.

The moans grew louder and he returned to the man. He squatted beside him and flashed the light again. Bright black eyes, filled with pain, looked up at him. His hand tightened on the flashlight.

"*Curo toi voi!*" the man gasped again. "You help!" he added in English as he recognized the American.

Stephens sighed and reached into his back pocket. He removed a knife and pressed a button, flicking it open. The sharp blade cut quickly, cleanly, through the Vietnamese's neck, and Stephens leaped back as the man thrashed and blood spurted from the severed jugular. A horrible gurgling bubbled from the man's lips, then all was quiet. Slowly the body ceased twitching. The legs twisted once again, the broken one flapping on the ground, then the Vietnamese lay still. Stephens listened carefully to the night, then grabbed a foot, the sole hard and horny against his hand, and dragged the body to the edge of the quay and rolled it over and into the water. He listened again, and moved back to the jeep, backed away from the wreckage of the trishaw, then drove quickly away.

Two miles down the road, an emaciated dog showed in the light from the single headlamp. Quickly, he twisted the wheel, swerving to hit it. The dog flew through the air and Stephens stopped, got out, and walked back to the quivering body. He plucked a few tufts of hair from it, walked back to the jeep, and carefully stuck them into the blood around the broken headlight.

That should buy you some time. Not much, but a little to let you try and figure something out. Damn! Damn! Damn!

He slid again behind the wheel, took a quick drink from the pint of whiskey, then drove carefully back to base, desperately trying to think of his next move.

Chapter Fourteen

Colonel Black flipped the file he had been studying onto his desk and leaned back in his chair with a growl. His throbbing temples threatened to burst. He slid open the middle drawer of his desk, removed a bottle of aspirin, shook six out, and popped them into his mouth, chewing them. He grimaced at the alkaline taste and washed it away with a glass of Perrier, belched, sighed, then again picked up the file and tried to focus upon it. But his mind kept wandering back to the meeting the day before with the Central Intelligence boys at their "Lincoln Library" headquarters in the U.S. Information (USIS) agency building on Le Qui Don Street. They were sympathetic to his plight but could offer no help on maintaining surveilance over the Ho Chi Minh trail. Tiny muscles worked hard at the corners of his jaw as he remembered how the "boys" had brushed off his argument for their support.

"Come now, Black," Gordon Jorgenson, the station chief, had said. "You really think we have the manpower for that? We're stretched as thin as we can get, right now."

"Besides," Tom Donohue, in charge of the newly formed Political Action Teams (PAT), said, "we're rebuilding, changing our approach. We've decided to go through a pacification program instead of inserting teams. That may have worked with the OSS and its Deer Teams during World War Two, but not now. We're trying for a more passive intelligence approach."

"Passive intelligence?" Black felt the back of his neck grow warm. "What the hell is passive about military intelligence?" His heavy brow thickened as he glowered at the man across from him. Jorgenson smiled.

"We tried it the old way, Black," he said softly. His fingers reached up automatically to pat the flesh beneath his right ear-lobe. The war and heat appeared an aesthetic, metaphysical exercise form in the cold, air-conditioned room. Black shivered as the sweat dried on his back. "But that doesn't work. You have to move on, find other ways. Besides, you still have a couple of those teams left, don't you? Why don't you use them? This sounds more like one of your piratical raids: slash, bam, run."

"More than what?" Black asked heatedly. "Pampering your powdered political friends?" He shook his head. "Jesus! At least my men aren't hanging around with Big Minh and his toadies!"

A hard mask slipped down over Donohue's face. The professional smile disappeared. "I think you've said enough, Black," he said quietly.

"Have I?" Black leaned forward over the desk, his eyes flat and opaque. "You think I don't know about the Nugan Hand Bank accounts in Australia? You don't think I don't know about the payments to those bandits in the Golden Triangle who call themselves war lords? You boys got a lot to learn, I think. Sometimes slash and run tactics are better than selling our honor and integrity."

And that had been the end of the meeting and any help he could expect from that part of the Langley boys. It would have been nice if they could have taken some of the heat off; as it was, he could spare only one man himself.

The intercom buzzed. He rubbed heavy knuckles across his eyes and licked alkaline residue from his lips. The intercom buzzed again, and the first lieutenant's nasal voice made him wince. His headache began to pound again. Tension, he thought. He slapped at the toggle switch and growled, "Send him in."

He sat up, straightened his sweat-stained khaki shirt, and poured another glass of Perrier. The door opened and Morgan walked in.

Black heaved a sigh and took a cigar from the humidor on his desk. He took his time lighting it.

"Close the door," Black said. Morgan heeled the door shut and crossed to the chair in front of the desk and sprawled in it without invitation. "Sit down," Black said dryly. Morgan nodded. Black sighed. "I'm sorry about your brother."

Morgan nodded. Tiny muscles worked along his jaw. "It was a mistake sending him out. Why did you?"

"It was Christmas," Black answered. "I thought it would be good for you to have someone around beside your Montagnards. Why the hell didn't you call for an evac when the village was first hit?" He leaned meaty arms upon the desk and glowered at Morgan.

"There wasn't time," Morgan said. "You know how such things are." He looked significantly at Black. "We could sure use a doctor. I've asked for one repeatedly."

Black shook his head. The complaint was an old one. Morgan had been asking for a doctor to be assigned to them, but MAC-V claimed every doctor had been assigned. Yet whenever he went to the Officer's Club or the Circle Sportif, he saw a large number of doctors flirting with the nurses or drinking gin and tonics around the tennis court.

"The Montagnards got along very well without a doctor for a couple thousand years with cowshit and leeches. Enough," he said, raising a hand as Morgan opened his mouth to argue. "What happened?"

"The village leader's son went over," Morgan said. He picked up Black's silver letter opener from the desk and began to toy with it.

"That tears it. Goddamn!" Black fell back in his chair, staring at the map. He belched and took a hard puff on his cigar. He shook his head wearily. "Well what are they going to do?"

"Relocate." Morgan tossed the letter opener back onto the desk and straightened in his chair. "Farther north. They want to avoid the *agrovilles*. The Strategic Hamlet Program would mean the death of the old ways."

Black shook his head. "You know the policy. They've gotta come in. We resettle them after they've been compromised."

"Crap," Morgan argued. "You know what that means. They'll be placed in a relocation camp for a year or so and starve while

Ky and his boys find ways of shagging the money we give them for relocating our friends into their private accounts outside the country. Most of my villagers will be dead by then and Ky's boys will jam them into another village where they'll be outcasts. No."

Black raised his eyebrow. The veins in his neck swelled like a lusting bull, his face reddened, and his huge hands slowly clenched. "You're getting a little overbearing, Morgan. I've taken a lot from you, but by God, you'd better remember who's running this show!"

Morgan's face tightened and Black sighed and scrubbed his hands across his face.

"I like you, Morgan," he said quietly. "You're the last of the group. Twenty-seven handpicked men as team leaders and you're the last one left. We ought to give you a promotion for longevity, Morgan."

Morgan remembered the training—secretive, no one knowing exactly what was happening to him until the last week at Ft. Holobird at the special intelligence school when they were told they were each going to command a five-man team somewhere in Vietnam for special guerilla activities. After five months, only four of the original twenty-seven were left.

"You seemed to adapt quite well, Morgan. Why is that?"

Morgan shrugged. "Just lucky, I guess."

"No, luck may give you six months. You've had four years. There's something more to it than just luck. You seem to be particularly well-suited for it."

"It's over, isn't it?" Morgan said suddenly. Black stared at him for a long time, his eyes expressionless. Then he sighed and placed his cigar in the cut-glass ashtray on his desk and leaned back in the chair. The leather creaked in protest as his weight pressed against the springs. "Yes it is. Why don't you send me home? It's over."

"It looks that way," Black said quietly. "Oh we'll play this war for a while because we've gone too far into it to bail out right now. But there it is: sooner or later, we'll pull out. It's coming. We can only play god so long. There's a conflict in every human heart between rational and irrational. Sometimes the dark side overcomes the better angels of our nature. Every man has his breaking point. That's what happened with Connors and Mc-Laughlin. They reached their breaking point and that is what ended them. You haven't. And that's why you haven't gone home. We can't let you go home yet. We still have need of you. Sorry. I know what with your brother—"

"I understand," he said quietly.

"Do you?" Black asked. "I wonder." He shrugged. "Maybe we can arrange an R and R in Bangkok or Hong Kong. We could bring over your father. Your sister-in-law? Maybe a brief vacation with your family?"

Morgan shook his head. "Forget it."

"It's really no trouble."

"Why don't you just send me home? I've been here longer than the others. I think I deserve an end to this damn thing." Suddenly he felt tired. He leaned back into the chair. Lines suddenly appeared around his eyes, the corners of his mouth. He seemed to age rapidly in seconds.

"We can't," Black said. He shook his head. "We need you. I can let you go for a while, a month, maybe, but you're too good. You know what's going on out there. A month in Hong Kong. How about it?" Morgan stared at him for a long moment, then heaved a great sigh and shook his head.

"Forget it. I'll go home when I can stay home," Morgan said. "I don't want to go home then have to come back here. There's too much danger in that. I'd lose my edge."

Black grinned, tiny muscles working at the corner of his jaw. "You see? You can't go home?"

"Perhaps," Morgan said. He lifted his eyes and stared unseeing at the map, picturing the mountains and the valleys, the clean sweep of fields. Black let a silence build between them, then picked up his cigar again, relighting it.

"Why north?" Black asked, smoking quietly on his cigar. "That's sort of jumping from the frying pan, isn't it?"

"The son went north." Morgan smiled thinly as Black's eyes began to glitter. He recognized the look and knew that Black had decided on how to use the Montagnards.

"Stop them," he said flatly.

"What's up?" Morgan said. "What is it you want, now?"

"Drugs." Black said flatly.

"Drugs?"

"Yes." Black rose and moved to the large map. His eyes darkened and deep lines curved down like horns from his nose to his chin. "We've got a big problem," Black said. He swept a huge hand over his close-shaven head. "We've had a few desert, go over to the Viet Cong, but lately a lot of soldiers have been going into drugs for their escape. Marijuana can be bought in almost every shop in the city, ten cents a cigarette, a 'joint.' Maybe as high as twenty-five percent. MAC-V has been trying to stop it by infiltrating the troops with CID boys. Jesus! Isn't that a hoot? As if we don't have enough of a problem with the Viet Cong and the hard-asses from up north, now we have to wage a war on our own boys."

"Marijuana's not all that bad," Morgan said. "It's better than opium and a lot of them use that. Maybe you should be grateful that they're not haunting the opium parlors off Tu-Do Street."

Black glared at him. "That's on the increase too but more than that we've got heroin suddenly putting in an appearance. It's coming down from here." He turned to the map and traced a route with a thick forefinger. "From the mountains up here across the borders of Laos, Burma and Thailand. The 'Golden Triangle.' The CIA boys have identified twenty-one opium refineries there that produce about seven hundred tons of opium annually. It's become big business, now, coming out with the Royal Thai Air Force and our soldiers returning from R and R in Bangkok. And it's cheap. Opium goes for about a buck a hit, morphine five bucks a vial, and a heroin habit can be supported for two bucks a day. We've got fourteen-year-old girls selling the shit at roadside stands like the kids do lemonade back home."

"Why?" Morgan asked.

Black shook his head. "Time." He smiled thinly at Morgan's frown. "Soldiers whose tour gets short, use the dope to make the days go faster. Marijuana slows down time, but horse makes it go fast. Psychologically, that is. A lot of them don't have any idea why they are here. They feel like they're in a dream. Life's unreal, values crazy." He shrugged. "They just want to get through it as painlessly as possible. But it's not helping matters any. Officers avoid disciplining them to keep from being fragged, having grenades tossed in their tent while they're sleeping. The army's set up a drug rehabilitation center in Can Tho, but that's not the answer. We've got to stop the run down from the Golden Triangle."

Morgan frowned. "Why not let the Langley boys do it? You said they've found where the shit's being processed. Why not send in a strike force and take them out?"

Black smiled grimly. "Who do you think set them up in the first place?"

"What do you mean?"

"How do you think the CIA boys get those bandits to patrol their borders? They pay them for their opium crops."

"Jesus," Morgan said. "What a shining little war this is. How did it get started?"

"The protest movement back home," Black said.

"Protest? What protest?" Morgan asked, perplexed.

"Against the war. Bunch of goddamned college students smoking marijuana and opium, shooting dope, that sort of thing. Goddamned draftees bring their habits with them. It's spread like a cancer through the troops. That's where you come in."

"Me?"

"And your Montagnards."

"They've been hard hit—"

"I *know*, Morgan," he said. "But they will follow you. You've already proven that. Now what we want is for you to stop the drug running from the north by cutting their lines here"—he jabbed the map—"and here."

"That's over thirty square miles!" Morgan said in protest. "I know that country. That map isn't a true reflection of what it's like. That land is a hodge-podge of broken terrain, rocks and chunks as big as houses, vines as thick as a man's body, trees so close together that the day is only a gray light and a constant drizzle from the heavy dew." He fell silent, remembering the quiet, then the slow, deep pulsing of the jungle as if the earth were breathing in fast, deep pants, as if it lived in a dark dimension of its own. It smelled like slow death.

"You can't do it?" Black said. His lips pressed tightly together in a thin line. Morgan stared back, unflinching.

"There's a price," he said quietly.

"I don't bargain, Captain Morgan," Black said angrily, his nostrils pinching whitely.

"Not for me," Morgan said. "For my Montagnards."

"What is it?"

"A new village," he said quietly. "We owe it to them. They've done everything we've asked for four years. Now they've lost their village to the Viet Cong."

"We don't owe them anything," Black said, turning away.

"Yes, we do. I have to have a lever," Morgan said, inventing quickly. "They have to know that they can depend on us for something."

"We're freeing their goddamned country," Black began, then stopped and turned red as Morgan laughed.

"You just told me the whole thing is lost," Morgan said. "But that doesn't matter. What does matter is that these people have lost their homes. Do you know what the word is for village? *Xa.* That means 'land, people, sacred.' These people have lost the home of their ancestors and the village *dinh*, or shrine, which is the god of the earth to the village. The land is sacred, Colonel. Sacred. Before the French even got here their religious life centered around the village and the god of the village. When the French tried to take that away from them, they had a revolt they had to put down."

"All right, all right," Black said.

"Besides, we're not freeing the Montagnards, we're freeing South Vietnam, if you want to be technical about it," Morgan continued. "These people down here have treated the Montagnards the same way we did the Indians. They hunted them for sport during the reign of Bao Dai, even though he was only a figurehead for the French. The French raided their villages for slaves on their rubber plantations."

"Come on, Morgan," Black said roughly.

"They used to put bounties on them. The Rands, the Moi, all had bounties on their heads. The same as they had on the jackals that raided their chicken coops."

"All right," Black said resignedly, holding up his hands. "We'll relocate them. After the operation."

"I'll take it to them," Morgan said.

"Now then," Black said briskly, turning again to the map. "There is absolutely no use in trying to break up the suppliers here in Saigon and Cholon. We don't have enough men for that. Instead, we have to try and close the main trails that the suppliers follow down from the north. About here"—he jabbed the map— "is where the trail divides and spreads throughout the country. The Mekong, Da Nang, Nha Trang, Bien Hoa, and Cholon. What are you smiling at?"

"You've forgotten something," Morgan said. "That country is home to a lot of different tribes. Some of them have been fighting longer than you can imagine. And that trail you're pointing at comes out somewhere near that point, not necessarily at that point. You are talking about a thirty mile square area in the roughest mountain country you could hope to see. Chances are slim that we will even be able to find the trail let alone be in the right place at the right time to catch some smugglers."

"Nonsense," Black said gruffly. "Every one of your villagers is a trained guerilla. They could find a monkey turd under a pile of leaves if you made them want to. I want those runs stopped." He poured another drink of Perrier and sat behind his desk. "Stop them."

Morgan rose and crossed to the map and studied it closely for a long moment. Then he spoke, his back still to Black. "There's more to it than that, isn't there, Colonel?"

Black nibbled at his lower lip for a second. Morgan turned and leaned up against the map, crossing his arms. He waited. Black nodded. "There is another reason. A rumor is going around that Nguyen Cao Ky and a few of his closest confidants were members of a secret society in the north before the war. So was Giap, the NVA leader."

Morgan whistled and shook his head. General Vo Nguyen Giap, the brilliant guerilla leader from North Vietnam, one of Ho Chi Minh's closest friends, and Ky, the vice president and prime minister of South Vietnam, fraternity brothers? Good God! If the press got hold of that, heads would roll back in Washington. The Directorate of Generals would be forced to take action and the country would surely fall in the wake of another coup.

"We suspect that secret society was the start of the Binh Xuyen which controls the black market and smuggling in Saigon and the B-girls, the opium traffic, and gambling in Saigon. I know, I know," he continued, holding up his hand as Morgan attempted to break in. "The Binh Xuyen was thrown out of Saigon years ago when Diem's forces drove them in the Rung Sat swamp east of here. But they never caught the leader. Le Van Vinh or Bay Vinh. Everything simply moved underground. We can see the old Binh Xuyen hand in quite a few incidents around the country.

"Last week, two politicians involved in the assembly were assassinated. They were trying to set up a task force to infiltrate the Binh Xuyen through the operations in Cholon. Their plans were known to only a select few. Ky was among them. If Ky is deposed, the government and armed forces will be thrown into chaos and the time will be right for a massive push from the Viet Cong on Saigon and Nha Trang. We think that may be coming due to the increased Viet Cong activity near Chon Thanh and Tala and Khel farther north. If they are building forces for such a push, they stand a good chance of being successful."

"There seems to be a lot of armor and men based here," Morgan ventured. "I saw the General and several newsmen touring when I came in on the chopper."

Black made a face and looked distastefully at the end of his cigar. "That's a sore point. The general has a penchant for flamboyant gestures. He likes to use the press, and consequently, keeps a lot of the Vietnamese troops and armor around that could be used in the field. *But*," he emphasized, stabbing his cigar in the air in Morgan's direction, "most of the *Americans* are scattered around this god-forsaken country while the ARVN sits on its ass here. The brass excuses that by claiming we can't be sure how many of the ARVN troops are really North Vietnamese Army infiltrates. Outside of Colonel Vann's Tiger Corps, I don't know of any that I would give two cents and a rat's asshole for."

"Then why are we bothering with the drugs?" Morgan asked. "It seems to me you'd want the Montagnards to begin harassing the Viet Cong around Chon Thanh, Talal, and Khel."

Black shook his head. "No, there's a massive operation under way for that. That's why I can't get regulars to do this job. The Tactical Air Control Center is holding all aircraft back for strike support except for the B-52s which will continue bombing Haiphong to keep suspicion down.

"It is imperative now to stop the smugglers from bringing the dope down from the north to help dispell the rumor about Ky. That is urgently needed. Stay close to the Ho Chi Minh Trail. Do not engage any of the regular troops. We can't afford casualties. Concentrate on the smugglers."

"We need supplies," Morgan ventured. Black stopped him.

"Make out a request and have it on my desk by noon tomorrow. I'll have it processed, and you can take them back with you."

Morgan nodded. "One more thing. The provinces are still headed by the leaders of the Regional Forces—Diem's old Civil Guard—who have authority over the Popular Forces. The leaders of the Regional Forces have established themselves as the old war lords of China did during World War Two. This complicates our problem because each regional leader demands we clear any of our patrols through him before we begin operations. The Viet Cong do not operate out of a single province and roam at will while we get bogged down in local politics."

Black chewed reflectively on the end of his cigar. "Any of the leaders demanding tribute from you?"

"Yes. Two weeks ago we ambushed a supply train in the Tuyen Doc Province and cut it in half. The survivors fled, and we chased them into the Quong Duc Province where we caught them. After the battle was over, the regional commander appeared, demanding we turn over all the contraband and pay him fifteen thousand piasters for not informing him of our operations within his province. I refused. He got a little ugly about it."

"You think he might have informed on you?"

"Maybe," Morgan said. "I do think he helped Bao set us up. It fits. Bao was there three days after the ambush to trade."

"I'll take care of it," Black said. He jotted a note on a pad. "Anything else?"

"Yes," Morgan answered. "These people are used to village government. The Vietnamese sees the province as a large village. The war doesn't affect him at all as long as it doesn't come to this province. These province chiefs are autonomous. I don't think you'll get far going through the local government."

"We might be able to change that soon," Black said. "But right now, our hands are tied. The rumor against Ky has harmed his credibility. If he tries to make any policy changes now, his detractors will have a field day. Thic Tri Quang would love that."

Morgan frowned. Thic Tri Quang and his militant Buddhists had been challenging the elections scheduled and calling for a boycott at the polls. Ky was in trouble, for about a third of the population was Buddhist and several of the bonzes, the Buddhist monks, had killed themselves in protest, soaking their robes in gasoline and setting themselves on fire. It was effective, Morgan had to admit, for the entire world pays attention to martyrs. And some of the Catholics, he remembered, still thought of Diem and Nhu as martyrs for being assassinated during the military coup. That too could harm Ky at the polls.

"How about appointing the Montagnards to govern themselves?" Morgan asked. "Not one Montagnard is invovled in the government now, and they are doing the dirtiest job in the war. They've been ruled by the Mandarins, the Chinese and the Japanese, but have never controlled themselves in a unified state. Of course, they have their own village, but they have never been united. You could start by building a solid army with the various villages and eventually give them self-control. That would be much better than putting them into one of those refugee camps like we had at Bien Hoa and Rach Bap back when Diem was around."

Black flinched, remembering the uproar that had followed Gertrude Samuels's visit to a camp in Rach Bap when she described the camp as being filled with thousands of tents that covered the ground while people huddled on rice mats on soggy earth under canvas, waiting dully for food and medicine and water, often going days without them. When the U.S. government stepped in and gave the peasants money to rebuild their homes, they had, digging nearly fourteen miles of canals, draining thirty thousand acres of land, and planting rice before building eight thousand houses on an expansive swamp. They had expected to be given the property after they had cleared it, but Diem's government thought otherwise and forced the refugees to sign tenancy contracts for the land in which they promised payment over time in return for the title. Many left and joined the Viet Cong.

"Impossible," Black said, waving his hand in dismissal. "That's precisely what I meant when I said we couldn't push for any governmental changes. That could split the country four ways between the Buddhists, the Catholics, the Montagnards, and the Cao Dai and Binh Xuyen who would come out of the shadows and join forces. They might even swing an election as dark horses. But maybe we can do something about getting a few of them appointed as regional commanders with American advisors. Military and civilian."

"That's a start," Morgan said. "But pick the advisors carefully. Especially the civilians. The Montagnards are hill people and very proud."

"I'll take it up with Washington," Black said. "I won't promise anything," he said cautiously, "but I'll see what can be done."

Morgan nodded, climbing to his feet. "I'll have the supply requisition on your desk first thing in the morning."

"Tomorrow's Saturday," Black said. "Make it Monday. You could use a little rest."

"Thanks. Maybe I'll visit some friends."

"You have any left?" Black asked, smiling.

"A few," Morgan laughed, and opened the door. He stepped through, closing it behind him. He leaned against the door and

Chapter Fifteen

Morgan paused to let a procession of saffron-robed monks pass in front of him. Their shaven heads gleamed, and they tapped the pavement in front of them with long, wooden staves as they walked, holding out wooden cups for *sous* to buy their evening meals. They had little trouble finding the money they needed for an old custom held that anyone who gave money to a monk would be blessed with good luck. In time of war, people needed luck more than ever. Morgan dropped a five piaster note in two of the bowls. The monks ignored him and slowly moved after the procession. It was not for them to be gracious; he had merely done his duty. Morgan was amused at their calm assuredness.

"Doesn't do to trust fate. Always best to aid the odds a bit. Never lose your faith in mysticism," he said aloud. A young man hurrying by paused to give him a questioning glance, but Morgan shook his head and the man hurried away. An air-conditioned limousine escorted by four jeeps of military police eased by. He glanced into the rear seat of the limousine and saw Westmoreland, haughty and arrogant, medals flashing from the rich, carefully tailored khaki shirt, and a group of senators wilting in the heat despite the air-conditioning. The group passed and across the road, Morgan saw an old man dressed in rags, staring at him. The old man's face looked like a skull. Even from this distance, Morgan could see the hatred burning in the old man's eyes. He turned away and hurried down the street, past the American Embassy. Large oil drums filled with sand and cement marched in military alignment across the street behind a long roll of concertina barbed wire arching thirty feet in front of a gray building. The stars and stripes hung limply from a flagpole attached to a ledge on the third floor. The white pole gleamed like a bone, and a gold eagle stood arrogantly on a round globe at the end of the pole. Two marines stopped their pacing inside the wire and fingered their AR-15s until he passed. Morgan ignored them and hurried down the street to the quay and walked by the river down to Le Loi Boulevard before crossing to Tu-Do Street and the Club Eve.

Two large palms stood guard before double doors mounted on heavy iron hinges. The doors were made from ironwood and practically impregnable. Two large glass windows bearing shutters locked nightly at curfew carried a second skin of steel mesh to keep hand grenades and molotov cocktails from being thrown inside. A small brass plate discreetly mounted to the right of the doors read EVE. Other clubs, he knew, were more popular with the young soldiers who flocked to the loud music grinding from jukeboxes and flashing neon lights in the bars like the Casino where they could fondle the bar girls, who wore short dresses and tight blouses and wobbled on stiletto heels into which they had crammed their naked feet, for the price of a shotglass of tea that the girls insisted on calling whiskey.

He pulled the door open and walked inside, pausing to let his eyes adjust to the dim lighting. Three tall, white columns stood evenly-spaced on the first level in front of a kidney-shaped bar. Overhead, large mahogany fans turned slowly, silently, on well-oiled bearings. Rattan tables and high-backed fan-shaped wicker chairs stood tastefully scattered across the black and white tiled lower floor. A long, low couch piled high with white cushions and pillows stood at the far end of the room. Blooming mimosa scented the air from a planter next to the couch. A lone woman sat at the couch, smoking a cigarette. A martini in a stemmed glass stood in front of her. A carefully groomed man dressed in a white suit sat with legs elegantly crossed at the ankles at the corner of the bar, quietly concentrating on a bottle of vermouth. A cocktail shaker, its sides frosted, stood next to it along with a bottle of gin. Morgan smiled and moved quietly behind him. He leaned over and spoke softly into his ear.

"The secret is in the vermouth, not the gin."

Maurice spun on his stool, his watery blue eyes breaking into a warm glow as he recognized Morgan.

"Henri!" He threw his arms around Morgan's shoulders. "It has been too long, my friend."

"Much too long, Maurice," Morgan answered. The old man beamed at Morgan, and the tension eased from Morgan's shoulders as he slid onto the stool next to Maurice.

"How is your wife?" he asked. Maurice shook his head and motioned for the bartender. He ordered shaved ice and Pernod, then turned back to Morgan.

"Ah, my friend." He clicked his tongue against his teeth, sighing again. "The arthritis has her hands so swollen she cannot lift a spoon. And the pain!" Tears glistened in his eyes, and he quickly patted them with a handkerchief drawn from inside his jacket. "She is so brave, that one. No crying, but I can tell when the pain is too strong. The eyes, I can see the pain in her eyes."

"I am sorry to hear that," Morgan said. The concern in his voice was real, and the old man patted Morgan's knee. The bartender silently slid the bottle of Pernod and two tall glasses filled with shaved ice in front of them.

"We are old," Maurice said, shrugging. "One must expect some things when one gets old. She wishes to go back to France, but—" He waved his hands and glanced around at the club. "What are we to do with this? No one can give the money to buy this. No one wants to give the money to buy this," he amended. He sighed. "Ah, the war. The war."

"This country has always been at war," Morgan said, smiling at Maurice's minor drama. The old man shook his head vigorously.

"But it is a different type of war, my friend," he protested. "And we have different people fighting it. They do not have the—" He paused, brow furrowing as he tried to find the word that had escaped him.

" 'Style,' " suggested Morgan. Maurice's eyes blinked, then he nodded.

"*Oui. Exactement.* Everything is—*détraqué.*"

"Out of order," Morgan said automatically. The bartender

silently slid a plate of shelled shrimp and lime wedges in front of him and set a glass of cold white wine beside it. He raised an eyebrow in question as Maurice carefully poured the Pernod over the shaved ice, filling the glasses half-full.

"You are too thin," Maurice said. "Eat. Drink the *sáncerré*. It will take a few minutes before the Pernod is ready."

Morgan smiled, selected a large shrimp, squeezed a wedge of lime over it, and popped it into his mouth. He sipped the wine and smiled as it cut through the sharp lime tang and flowed coldly down his throat. The heat melted from behind his eyes and the back of his mouth. Maurice smiled with pleasure as he quickly ate five more, washing each bite down with a swallow of wine. He sighed.

"The whole world is that way, *mon ami*," Maurice said. "Before, we had soldiers who liked fine wine, soft music, beautiful women, but now, it is beer, music of drums and no song—"

"But the women are still beautiful," Morgan said, nodding toward the lone woman sitting at the far end of the room, Maurice frowned.

"That one?" He shook his head and took a small strawberry pastille from a tin and placed it carefully between his lips. "A *poule*. No, the old days are gone. How is your war?"

"Not so fine, my friend," Morgan said. He reached for the glass of Pernod. Maurice nodded, and he sipped and smiled appreciatively. "Too many people are being killed for such a small return."

"Freedom is a dear price," Maurice said. He slid his stool closer and tapped Morgan gently on his wrist. His skin was the color of dried parchment, his fingernails beautifully shaped and lacquered. "You remember Josef? He owned the tailor shop on Rue Catinat?"

Morgan smiled. Like most of the French still in Vietnam, Maurice stubbornly refused to recognize the new names of the streets which had been changed following the expulsion of the French Colonial government after Dien Bien Phu. Rue Catinat had become Duong Tu Do or Freedom Street. Rue Richard, where the old colonial villas were, had become Phan Dinh Phung, the main north-south street through Saigon.

"The one with the globe in the window? How is he?"

"A fire bomb burned his shop and son," Maurice said solemnly. "He killed himself after the burial." He leaned closer to Morgan and whispered: "They say that his son was one with Le Butcher, the Frenchman who fights for the North Vietnamese." He shook his head. "Why a man would betray his own, I do not know."

"Does anyone know this man?"

"No one," Maurice said. His eyes flicked uneasily to the bartender and back. "It is not wise to speak thus of him, *mon ami*," he said cautiously.

"There is no need to speak of him at all," Morgan said. "I am sorry." Maurice shrugged a shoulder, and raised an eyebrow to show no offense had been taken. "What about the lame man? Daniel?"

"Yes, that is his name. He is dead also."

"And François? Richard?"

"Dead. All dead. It has been a very bad year for friends."

Morgan raised his glass in salute. "To old friends." They clicked glasses and drank and Morgan set his glass on the bar in front of him.

"Have you finished? Good. You have time to get ready. You must have dinner with us. Judith will be so pleased. It is Friday and tomorrow will be a long day for me to be away from her."

Morgan laughed. "I'll dash and get my tie." He slid off the stool, pressed Maurice's hand, and turned to the door.

"At the villa," Maurice called. "Five of the clock. Do not forget!"

Morgan waved and stepped out, squinting as the harsh sunlight stabbed hard behind his eyes. He hailed a small Lambretta and directed the driver to the Villa Jacques. He settled back against the badly sprung seat and stared morosely at the colorful shops modeling the latest fashions as they passed. It would be good to see Judith again.

The house was spacious and cool with high vaulted ceilings and a majestic teak stairway winding gently to the bedrooms on the second floor. The study was to the left of the door as he stepped into the foyer, and Morgan caught a glimpse of filled bookcases running along the walls to a large stone fireplace before he followed the silent butler to the anteroom. He could see a long table set with snowy linen and sparkling through a door at the far end of the room. Shutters had been thrown back from long, narrow windows, and the evening breeze flowed through the rooms, cooling and scenting the air with perfumes lifted from carefully tended beds filled with exotic flowers and groves of lime and pineapple, and jackdaw sent their scents as well. Fresh flowers blazed from vases set on every flat surface, making the house seem artificially alive.

In the middle of the anteroom, Judith half-reclined gracefully on a long, paisley sofa in a cloud of blue chiffon. Maurice hovered anxiously over her, sipping from a glass of cold sancerré. A plate of sugared strawberries rested within easy reach on an end table.

Morgan crossed to her and bowed over her outstretched fingers. He touched them briefly, feeling the dry and brittle flesh beneath his fingers. The veins were close beneath the surface and the age spots like overdone liver. His fingers felt dusty from the contact.

"*Enchanté*, Madame," he said. "Thank you for having me to your home."

"You are welcome," she said graciously, her voice thin and high with a slight tremor, but birdlike in its charm. She turned to Maurice. "Is he not handsome in his jacket? Not like the other one who smelled of stale socks." Maurice squirmed, smiled ruefully and looked at Morgan. He shrugged.

"Some of my friends have not the proper wardrobe," he said apologetically.

"Nonsense," she sniffed. "They simply have no manners. The

graces have been assigned to the balcony from the vulgarities approved today. It is a shame, don't you think?"

"People change with the time," Maurice murmured defensively. He winked at Morgan and offered him a glass of the sancerré. "Don't you think so, my friend?"

"Perhaps," Morgan answered. He raised his glass to Judith. "But gentlemen fight wars, too, and don't forget their shaving kit."

"Touché, Maurice," she laughed, and placed her hand on his sleeve. "Our friend has touched the pulse. There is no excuse for bad manners."

Morgan smiled as Maurice graciously bowed his head in surrender and touched her hand with his fingertips. His collar was stiffly starched and chafed his throat, his tie threatened to strangle him, but he refrained from tugging at it and remembered to sip and not gulp from his glass. The wine slid smoothly, fresh and tart, over his tongue, and he complimented Maurice on his selection.

"Aren't strawberries rather hard to get this time of year?" he asked. Maurice smiled and shook his head.

"I had them brought down from Dalat by a friend," he said. "The wine was brought up from Vung Tau."

"Isn't that a perfectly dreadful name?" Judith asked. Her mouth twisted with distaste as she pronounced the word. "Vung Tau. It makes one think of a horse barn. Cap St. Jacques was much more beautiful."

"It is still the same place," Maurice said gently.

"No." A cloud passed over her face as she stared into the distant past. "Without the name, a part of the beauty disappears. I can remember the white, clean beaches and bathing houses where we used to change into our costumes and the beach chairs and cold sangria the natives would bring us. The sea was so beautiful like—like—" She blinked her eyes and carefully dabbed them with a lace handkerchief. Morgan smelled a faint scent of lavender. "But that was all when it was Cap St. Jacques. What is Vung Tau like, Henri?"

"The last time I was there the sea snakes were migrating and everything was gray. The sea looked like lead." He sipped from his glass.

"And the waiters?" She pressed him gently.

"They were gray as well. The young are in the army."

"You see?" She turned in triumph to Maurice. "You see? Beauty lasts only as long as the name."

"You mustn't excite yourself, my dear," he said concernedly. She smiled and patted his hand to reassure him.

"My dear Maurice! I know I am no longer beautiful, but my name has not changed." She turned back to Morgan. "And now, I believe we have teased our guest long enough. He must be hungry."

"Famished," Morgan said, and swallowed the last of his wine. He placed the glass upon the small mahogany table next to the strawberries and moved to the center of the room.

Maurice helped Judith to her feet. She leaned heavily upon his arm as he escorted her into the dining room. Her lips tightened from the pain. She sensed Morgan looking at her and turned calm eyes upon him.

"Tell me, Henri, Have you seen the latest fashions? Maurice tries to describe them, but I'm afraid he is more interested in his scruffy friends," she said.

They moved into the quiet elegance of the dining room. Morgan looked around him. It was a world that belonged to the 1930s and the romantic mystery of French Indochina and plantations and veranda parties. He began to speak about what he had noticed the women wearing in the streets and at the Caravelle Hotel and since he had been in Saigon only two days, he made wild guesses on what should be. He spoke of bright colors, blues and reds and oranges, deliberately failing to mention black, the national color that seemed to be everywhere. He spoke of the light and the bright flowers in the park near the cathedral and carefully deleted any mention of the dark world, the invisible shadows lurking in the mouths of alleys. Dreams still lived in his story and time stood still among the clinking of crystal and fine dinnerware for a brief moment.

Chapter Sixteen

Rain poured through the leaves and needles of the trees and the creek bed, once filled with fine, powdery dust, now roared with angry currents flowing ever southeast to the South China Sea. Bao stopped beside the creek and stared sourly at the rushing waters. His hair, thoroughly soaked, lay like heavy oil over his forehead. His shirt hugged clammily about him and the inside of his thighs tingled from being rubbed raw by his wet pants. Mud squished between his toes, and the backs of his calves ached with the thought of forcing a way through the raging torrent. He could not remember when he had last tasted hot food, and he knew from the silence of the others that they, too, could not remember. Usually, they would carry abundant food and needed only a moment to have a fire going in the ovens made from biscuit tins they carried with them. But since the night of the ambush, the number that followed him had grown three times, the people filtering in by twos and threes, all young, all eager to be with him. He turned to look at the others. They stared impassively back at him, crouched on the backs of their heels, waiting. He bit the inside of his lip and fingered the small pouch filled with tightly rolled bills belted snugly around his middle inside his shirt. There was more money in the pouch than his father collected in any of the raids he had led with the Dai-uy. And much easier to get. He smiled as he remembered the regional commander handing him the money and promising them he would not pursue them with the Regional Forces. Bao, however, led his band away from the route the regional commander had traced for him with a well-manicured forefinger over the map.

Temptation, he knew, spoiled many plans. A wise man did not tempt others. But now, this whore of a creek—

Anger began to boil through him as he looked at the brown, boiling water. They could cross it, but the loss of men might be high. Too high. A good leader must be patient. Besides, the Cambodian border lay only twenty or thirty kilometers in front of them within the Halls of the Gods. Aieee! Climbing those would wear one down! He smiled to himself. Perhaps that would be a good idea. That would leave little doubt as to the identity of the next chief. But pushing the men that hard could also be dangerous. The elections had yet to be held. But to let them rest, yes, much better. Let them think he had stopped to make them stronger and more fit to fight the Roundeyes should they be surprised.

He chuckled. Yes, that was the way it should be done. And here comes that fool Bong Dien. Well, he could use him to let the others know. If he explained loud enough.

"*Do'i day!*" he said loudly. "We rest here. Bong Dien, it is good you are here. The men are tired and the Roundeyes may be close. Send four men around us to watch and let the others rest beneath the trees until this unspeakable rain slows and the current lowers."

Bong Dien's eyes narrowed and his lip curled. Bao bit his cheek to keep from laughing at the frustration in Bong Dien's face as he shrugged, and turned from Bao and shouted through the dripping curtain. Vague shapes collected weapons and disappeared into the forest. The rest crawled beneath the low branches of trees. He turned back to Bao and smiled, then stooped and wormed his way beneath a cluster of vines.

Bao laughed, and crawled under a pine tree. He pulled a U.S. Army poncho from his pack and quickly stretched it from branch to branch and squatted beneath it. He unclasped a canteen from his hip and drank deeply from it. The Dai-uy's whisky burned through him, and he smiled happily.

Poor Bong Dien. Did he really think he could win the election? Poor fool! The son of a goat herder would never win while he, Bao, the son of a chief and the grandson of a grandson of a warlord, stood against him. Ah, futility, futility!

The old man wiped the rain from his upturned face and turned to the shrunken man waiting patiently, respectfully, beside him.

"It will end soon," he said. "The young ones will not know this or do not care and will make camp for it is not pleasant to march in the rain. They do not have the years to know when one should rest and one should march. We must move fast or we shall lose them. Tell the women to move back and follow. We shall leave signs like this for them."

He picked up a dead twig from the ground and broke it into a rough square.

"This will be easy for them since they are women. But," he continued, "they must bring the branches with them so others will not follow us. That is very important. Be sure they know this."

The shrunken man nodded, and silently limped down the trail, speaking in a low voice to those on either side. The old man pulled his shirt over his head so the rain would not strike his face.

The young ones would not march in this rain. He could feel that in his bones. Familiar old pain began to throb in his joints, but he ignored it. They would march. The young ones would not be expecting them to march so they would march. The young ones forgot the story of the plodding ox who walked all day and the young deer who spent itself in quick spurts.

A clap of thunder rolled from far ahead. The old man laughed. *Aiee!* A good sign. The gods beckoned to him from halls. Now if only the rain would stop. But not too soon. No, that would be too bad.

He sneezed and eased his rifle from one shoulder to the other and started down the trail. The others stirred themselves and shouldered their packs to follow him. Rain began to fall faster, but the old man ignored it. He was walking in a hidden valley high in the mountains while goats and lambs played at his heels in the bright sunlight.

The tiger coughed in the night, and the old man strained to place the direction through the slanting rain. A very bad omen. The tiger must be very old and tired to come this close. Or else young and foolish. The old man hoped for young and foolish as that made him less dangerous. He pulled the army poncho tighter around him and tried to concentrate on being warm, dry and warm.

He is probably very young and foolish. An old tiger wouldn't be up this high in this rain. Even if his belly was empty the old tiger would rest in a dry cave and lick his aching joints. No, this is definitely a young tiger, proud of his youth and strength, and that will kill him some day. He will become too proud and too sure, and one day, he will do one foolish thing, and then it will be too late for he will be dead, and there will be one less tiger to grow old and tired and wise and dangerous.

He fingered his pipe. How nice it would be to smoke one of the little pellets of opium and wait for the rain to stop. His joints ached, and his muscles stiffened against the cold. The old man felt his age and knew what the young men would do. He sighed and regretfully placed his pipe back in its pouch. There would be time for that later. He struggled to his feet, slipped in the mud of the trail, and caught himself. A muscle in his back began to throb. He turned and called to the huddled forms squatting as he had on the trail.

"Up, you lazy sons-of-pigs! May your parents and grandparents return as worms for creating such lazy men. How do you expect to get from here to there? Maybe the gods will move the earth and bring you with it?"

The old men smiled gap-toothed smiles and straggled into a line. They moved down the trail, and the tiger coughed again at the movement.

Young and foolish. Very young and very foolish. What game will he hunt tonight in the rain?

Bao rolled from his pallet in the cold and damp early morning. He rose yawning to his feet and scratched his groin. He sniffed and smelled rotting wood and shivered. The day of his grandmother's funeral had smelled the same, and he shivered again, this time not from the cold, and looked around the camp.

Smoke from the cookfires hung low to the ground. The young women moved silently through the smoke and damp, their upper bodies only visible, like spirits. Bao picked up his rifle and moved to one of the cookfires and squatted tiredly on his heels, rifle carefully balanced across his knees, and waited for his morning bowl of rice. He remembered the long night and the tiger roaring and wondered if he had dreamed the tiger roaring or if one had actually roared. He decided a dream tiger had roared for although he didn't believe the old stories anymore, he still felt nervous and uneasy for the legends sprang too easily to his mind. A muscle jumped spasmodically in his arm, and he pulled the tail of his shirt from his trousers and carefully rubbed the morning mist from his rifle.

It was a fine rifle, and he was very proud of it for he had taken it from a dead Viet Cong. Unfortunately, he found it very hard to get ammunition, but that, he was certain, would soon change after they had crossed the mountains and worked their way back north to their new friends. Affectionately, he rubbed his fingers over the Russian markings, feeling the steel, cold like a whore's skin. The thought soothed him, and the muscle in his arm ceased jumping. He smelled roasting pig, and his mouth watered as he remembered one of the scouts shooting a wild boar and bringing it into camp the day before. Angry at the shot and wasted ammunition, he had lashed out at the scout, but now he had to admit this was much better than rice. A farmer could live on rice, but a soldier had to have meat in his belly to give him strength.

He heard the others as they began to move around the camp, easing the morning stiffness from cramped muscles. Bao smiled to himself as he heard someone mutter curses at a foot that refused to wake up. Da Soo moved through the smoke and handed him a bowl of rice with generous chunks of meat chopped into it. He thanked her, and she smiled at him, her moon face wrinkling pleasantly. He admired her roundness as she moved from him, then sighed and quickly ate. The food warmed his stomach, and he rose and contentedly stretched.

A group of men squatted on their heels by one of the fires. They seemed to be arguing, and Bao frowned. This was not good. The day was too young for arguing. He moved toward the group. One of the men noticed him and made a quick, chopping motion with his hand. Bao's eyes narrowed watchfully, and he casually moved his rifle, holding it by the pistol grip, barrel pointing down and a little forward.

"*Chao oom,*" he said. "Good morning."

A few grunted and pretended to be absorbed in their eating.

"Yes," Bao continued. "Yes, it is a fine morning. A man feels good on such a morning as this. But, as I approached, I thought I heard angry voices and I worry. These are strange forests and filled with strange spirits. A man must be careful or the spirits may seize his mind and soul."

One of the men made a rude noise, and Bao turned to him. The man who had brought the meat to camp stared sullenly at him. Bao kept his face impassive as he spoke.

"Sometimes one does not even know when the evil ones are present for they are very tricky."

"What do you want?" the rude one asked. "You do not speak of the spirits truthfully. What do you want with us?"

"I worry for your souls, my friend," Bao said. He casually turned his body so he could watch the entire group.

"We have done nothing," protested another. "You worry needlessly."

"Ah," Bao said. He shook his head in sorrow. "Yes. I suppose it was nothing. Probably just the wind. But I worry when I see someone shoo flies when there are no flies. I think that just perhaps a spirit has entered his body, and he is now feeble. Tell me, my friend, tell me. Are you feeble?"

"No." The rude one stood. He held a machete close to his

leg. "No. I shall answer. It is you. We question you."

"Me?" Bao opened his eyes wide, pretending dismay. "Why should you question me? Have I not taken care of you? Are any of you hungry?"

"The food is not of your bringing. You assume too much, Bao. You were not selected, but took. That is not our custom."

"Custom? What custom? We left custom dead at the village."

"Some things are ever with a man," the rude one said. "Those can never be changed any more than a man can change his skin like the snake. We demand our right."

"So-o-o-o." Bao took a deep breath and slowly let it out. "How say the rest? Do all wish this?" Out of the corner of his eye, Bao saw Bong Dien move casually up on his left. Where does he side? With me? Against me? Bao shifted his stance to keep him in view.

"Speak!" he snapped. "How do you wish to be done with this thing? The day grows no younger."

"We must meet in council," the rude one said. "That is the way."

"Fool!" Bao snapped. "There is no council. Where are the old men? The priests? Do you wish to be leader? Stop prattling like an old woman and take what you want."

The man hesitated and looked into Bao's eyes and knew he was going to die. He screamed and swung the machete in a savage arc as he leaped for Bao. The scream died in his throat as Bao's rifle cracked and three bullets tore through his chest, his throat. He crumbled in a heap at Bao's feet. Blood fountained from his torn throat and his heels drummed briefly against the ground, then stilled.

"Ah." Bao shrugged his shoulders and lowered his rifle. "It is too bad. The spirits were too—"

Bong Dien's rifle quickly raised, and Bao cursed himself for forgetting. He watched as the bore grew larger and larger until it seemed to consume his whole world, and he looked into the terrifying blackness of the abyss. His legs moved dreamily, and he felt himself falling slowly, too slowly. He tried to bring his rifle to bear, but his fingers were thick sausages and fumbled at the safety, the trigger, and he knew he would be too late. Bong Dien's rifle belched and Bao felt the searing heat as the bullet burned past his shoulder and simultaneously heard a meaty chunk! as when a butcher clubs an ox. He wondered why he felt no pain. Bong Dien fired again, and again Bao flinched and rolled and wondered why he was not dead.

A low moaning came from behind him. He turned slowly to it. Da Soo lay curled on the ground, her round face twisted in pain. She clenched her hands tightly against her abdomen, but Bao could see the gaping holes the bullets had made where they exited above her kidneys. A sharp cleaver lay on the ground beside her. She opened her eyes and stared at Bao. Her mouth twisted, and a clout of blood gushed forth. Her legs writhed in agony, and she died. Bao rose and faced Bong Dien.

"How—" He swallowed, and tried to clear his ears form ringing. "How did you know?"

Bong Dien smiled, but the smile never met his eyes.

"She carried his blankets," he said. Bao slowly nodded and silently cursed himself for not being aware.

"I should have noticed, Bong Dien," he said formally. "A good leader should know things like that."

"You have been very busy. There are many to care for," Bong Dien said graciously.

A red rage seethed through Bao at Bong Dien for his reply made Bao seem careless and careless men were not to be trusted with leadership. He looked at the others watching them carefully and swallowed his anger, forcing himself to smile. Bong Dien's simple face broke into an answering grin.

"This is true," Bao agreed. "There are so many that I must have a good man to be my *trung-úy*. That is why I have chosen you."

"I thank you, Dai-uy," Bong Dien said humbly. "It is a great honor. I shall try to be worthy."

The others looked at each other. Dai-uy. Bong Dien had called Bao Dai-uy. Eeeah. The elections are over. So be it.

Bao looked down at Da Soo. A piece of bright-red cloth fluttered in the breeze. He reached down and pulled it from the body. Carefully, he folded it into a scarf and wrapped it around his head.

"A man must remember his beginning. This is my beginning and your beginning and this marks the end of treachery. We are one."

Bao smiled and grasped Bong Dien by his right shoulder and placed his fist over his heart. Dai-uy. The word carried stature and class and made him an important man. It made him respected and honored.

The old man hesitated, and stared closely around him at the huge fir trees, gnarled and twisted, standing in clusters along the spine of the mountain. He did not like this place. Quiet pressed heavily upon his ears, broken only with a heavy drop of water sliding from a needle of a tree and plopping on the forest floor. Too quiet. Now that the rain had stopped, there should be movement—birds fluttering from branches, monkeys, the distant grunt of pigs or a tiger cough, even the silent pattering of hooves and sweep of branches or a squirrel chattering—anything—but there was nothing except the drip of water from the branches of the trees. Everything was dead. The old man sniffed and grimaced at the dank and sour air.

Twenty meters in front of him jutted a huge outcropping of gray boulders fallen from the cliff above. He studied them carefully. A malevolent force seemed to emit from them. He could feel hard eyes watching him and his skin quivered. Phantoms moved at the corners of his eyes, but when he turned to them, they disappeared.

Eeeah. This is a very bad place. Very bad. It is a place of dead thieves and murderers and any who come this way are very foolish or crazy. But I come this way for he-who-was-my-son, who is both foolish and crazy, and is not dead, has come this way, and now he is among the spirits of thieves and murderers and they will help him so I must be very clever or they will kill me. Look. Look carefully, old man, for things are not right here.

The old man ran his tongue along the gap between his teeth,

sucking it as he stared in concentration at the boulders and to the right and left, looking for anything out of place. The gray day offered just enough light to catch movement and small reflections and the old man had that instant warning, the small movement made by a soldier before he presses the trigger, and the sound of metal scraping over granite.

He dropped flat on the forest floor and scurried like a crab behind the thick bole of an old pine. Bullets thudded into the wood and the old man heard the asthmatic coughing of a Soviet Kalashnikov AK-47 and the startled cries of the old ones behind him as death rode down upon them.

"*Nam xuong*!" he shouted. "Down!" Cautiously, he poked the carbine around the trunk of the tree and fired rapidly at the rock outcropping and ducked back as wood chips flew from the base of the tree from return fire. Calmly, he drew a second clip from the ammunition pouch attached to his web belt, rammed it home, and readied the carbine. He peeked quickly around the tree and drew back as bullets hammered the bark like woodpeckers. He rolled onto his back and looked down the trail. Lau Duc sprawled on the ground, his white hair showing red from a gaping wound in the back of his head. Another man lay behind him in a pool of blood, his chest cut away by a hail of bullets. Then, the old man's heart saddened as he saw Ngoc Thieu crumbled by her burden, her old fingers locked deeply in the soft earth. A bandolier lay on the ground in front of her, halfway between them.

"Ahhh!" His breath whistled from him and a thickness rose in his throat. "You were a good wife. It was not your fault the seed went bad."

Then whose fault was it? Neeeah. That was hard to answer. There had been no bandits in either line and their lines were among the oldest in the village, in the province. His line could be traced to the fifth cousin of the Emperor Le Thai To who kept the skulls of his enemies in a room next to his bedroom and had them painted in bright reds and greens and yellows with their names lettered upon the dome of the skull in thick, black letters. That was truly old. Somehow, somewhere, the blood had gone wrong. There must have been an ill-chosen consort somewhere.

The AK-47 chugged again, and the old man frowned and forced his thoughts back to the present.

"*Lui lai!*" he yelled, and motioned for his men to move down the trail. "Back, you turd-eaters! Back!"

Slowly, the old ones crawled back down the trail. Nguyen Duc fired another burst around the tree to let them know he was still there. Then, he settled himself behind the tree and filled his cheek with betel nut. It was a foolish ambush. They should have all been killed. But there had been no flankers and for this the old man blessed his son's stupidity.

Bullets hammered the tree again, and the old man smiled.

Use your ammunition. Kill this tree many times. You will not be able to lead my people. Not as long as I am here and I am here because your will not let me go. Eeeah. Who will last longer? How is your patience, man-who-was-my-son?

"Old man!"

He hunched himself up the trunk of the tree and peered cautiously around it. The voice seemed to come from two rocks leaning together like tired soldiers. A stone ledge covered with moss and lichen hung over them like a roof.

"Old man! Can you hear me, old man?"

He recognized Bao's voice, distorted like an echo, arrogant with conceit, and he bristled at the taunt and lack of respect.

"Old man! Where are your men? Your legions? Again, tell us how the French were defeated at Dien Bien Phu!"

He was behind the rocks, under the ledge. The old man was sure of that. But was there stone at the back as well? He frowned.

"Speak, old man! Speak! How great are you now, old man?"

Nguyen Duc leaned out away from the tree, quickly aimed at the dark underside of the ledge, and fired rapidly. He leaped down the trail and jumped behind another tree, and listened with satisfaction as his bullets ricocheted from the hard granite and buzzed like angry hornets under the ledge. There was a surprised howl and yelp of pain and bullets slammed into the tree he had left.

The old man rolled to his back and laughed quietly at the

sky. Night was far off, but they wouldn't come for him until dark and then he would not be there.

Thee was very foolish, my former son. You should have used flankers. Now, I will have another chance to kill you. And I shall. I shall kill you, make no mistake about that. You are dead now as surely as you will be then.

He composed himself and made himself as comfortable as possible. He watched the trail carefully.

This is a good place. It is too steep on both sides for you to come around me and I do not think you will be so foolish as to come down the trail for me. But I will wait and see. There is no hurry. The forest spirits will give me time and they will take that time from you. Can you feel it yet? How older you become? How short your time is growing? Think about that, my former son. Think long and often about how your days draw shorter and the nights longer. Soon, the cold rains will start and that will be the time and you will look down my rifle and you will know that you will die. Then, I will cut off your hands and feet and you will crawl painfully through the Dark World forever in accordance with our laws for treachery and betrayal.

In the distance a kite called and the old man nestled his cheek against the stock of his carbine and sighted carefully up the trail. The smooth wood felt good against his skin, and he concentrated on it and the sharp tang of cleaning oil and forgot about the cold ground beneath him.

Chapter Seventeen

The first lieutenant waited nervously while a sleep-rumbled Colonel Black blearily read the dispatch the lieutenant had brought him. Silently, Black swore at the security that demanded he be found twenty-four hours a day and reflected briefly on the bed behind him in his villa. It didn't look like he would be returning to it this evening.

Goddamnit. You'd think once in a while somebody could not fuck something up in this man's army. This is the third night this week. Now, you're going to have to shower and shave and climb back into uniform and go back to the office just because some Major Asshole thinks a new shipment is about to slip over the border.

He sighed and rubbed his hand over his bald head and tugged furiously at his wiry eyebrows. He peered at the lieutenant and almost laughed out loud. The lieutenant was trying very hard not to stare at Black's very hairy legs sticking out like thick stumps from under his silk sleeping jacket.

"Do you know what this is about?" Black asked.

"Yes, sir," the lieutenant said. "Major Haversham explained it to me on the nightline."

"Okay," Black said. He sighed. "I guess Morgan's vacation is about to be cut short. Do you know where he's staying?"

"Captain Morgan? Yes, sir," the lieutenant said. "I can send Stephens for him after he drops us off back at the office."

"No," Black said. "Have Stephens take you back to the office, then go get Morgan. I need to freshen up a bit. Send another jeep for me when you get back to the office. Check also with Colonel Reid and see if he's got a Caribou that he'll be able to spare in twenty-four hours and alert Supply to stand by for Morgan to run through. Got it?"

"Yes, sir," the lieutenant said. He saluted, but Black ignored him, shutting the door in his face. The lieutenant shifted his weight from foot to foot for a second, then turned on his heel and ran angrily through the rain to the jeep.

"Where to, sir?" Stephens asked.

"Back to the office!" the lieutenant snapped. "Then go get Captain Morgan and bring him to the office. Tell him that Colonel Black needs to see him immediately."

"He's gonna ask why, sir." Stephens said.

"I think that Captain Morgan will be able to figure it out," the lieutenant said. "And if he can't"—he stared at the villa's closed door—"then, we'll just let Colonel Black tell him."

Stephens sighed and put the jeep into gear, pulling away from the small villa. He drove carefully back to Ton Son Nhut, his mind suddenly filling with an idea that would get him away from his Saigon troubles. He smiled to himself in the dark. Now all he had to do was to convince Morgan.

Morgan stood on the balcony of his room, sipping from a glass of Johnnie Walker Scotch. He watched the flash lightning and listened to the rain driving hard against the tiles above his head. A warm melancholy settled over him, and he thought about the old man and his people and wondered if they were at the meeting site yet or if they had to circle around enemy troops to make it to the abandoned temple.

He stepped back into the room from the balcony and crossed to a table and chair and sat. He glanced at a book lying on the table—*Kim Van Kieu*—*The Tale of Keiu*—and pulled it to him, opening it. His eyes fell on the words, reading:

> Inside the silent, gloomy room,
> all night I listen to the rain.
> Its dirge disturbs an exile's pillow.
> It drips and drops as wane late hours.

It drums on windows and bamboos.
With tolling bells, it enters dreams.
I've hummed a song and stayed awake.
Sleep comes by bits and shreds till dawn.

Except no sleep comes tonight. No, not tonight. Billy should be home by now. I wonder— He finished his Scotch and was about to pour another when he heard a knock at the door. He rose and crossed to it. He opened the door and stepped back as he recognized Stephens. "Yes?" he asked.

"Pardon me, sir, but I was instructed to pick you up and take you back to Colonel Black's office," Stephens said.

Morgan frowned. "What's up?"

"I really don't know, sir. The lieutenant got a message from a Major Haversham tonight and had me drive him over to the colonel's villa. Then, he had me take him back to the office and come get you."

"I see." Morgan drained his glass, then crossed and placed it on the table. He paused for a moment, then opened a drawer and removed a shoulder holster from the drawer and shrugged into it. He took a Colt .45 from the drawer, checked the clip, and slipped it into the holster, then slipped into a jacket, settling it over his shoulders.

"Well, let's go," he said. "We can't keep the good colonel waiting."

"No sir," Stephens said.

Within minutes, they were driving carefully through the slanting rain back toward Ton Son Nhut. Stephens cast a quick glance at Morgan, then mentally shrugged his shoulders.

"Ah, I was wondering if I could ask you something, sir," Stephens asked. He kept his eyes on the wet pavement in front of them.

"What about?" Morgan asked. He coughed and wiped his hands over his face, flicking the water onto the floor of the jeep.

"I heard—through the grapevine, you understand—that you might be going out again—in the bush, I mean—and I got to wondering if you could maybe, well"—his face turned a faint pink—"maybe you could use another set of hands?"

Morgan leaned back against the seat and considered him for a long moment. "Was that in Major Haverhsam's message?" he asked quietly.

"I don't know, sir," Stephens said, choosing his words carefully. "But I've got a pretty good idea what's happening."

The enlisted men's telegraph. Black will be glad to know that his plans are probably out and about already. Aloud he said, "And what might that be?"

"Well, it's no secret, sir, that we've got a big drug problem here. And it ain't likely to get any better. The Saigon police ain't doing much to stop it but then again, they probably are getting a lot of money from the dealers to look the other way, so why should they? So it stands to reason that we gotta stop it outside of town, right?"

"And how did you come to this?" Morgan said.

"I got my sources, sir," Stephens said. "Colonel Black's been getting a lot of traffic from Nha Trang and other points about the problem. He calls you in." He shrugged. "Doesn't take much to put it all together."

"I see. All right. What is it you want?" Morgan said.

"Well, sir," Stephens took a deep breath. "I'm thinking that you might have need of another man out in the bush. I'd like to go back out with you."

"Why would you want to go out in the bush? You've got it made here. Saigon duty's every man's dream."

"Well . . ." Stephens paused, touching the brakes as a dog ran in front of them. "I haven't made up my mind what I wanna do. That is, I don't know if I want to stay in the army or get out and go back to school. I wasn't so hot when I was in school and so—"

"How much school do you have?" Morgan asked.

"Mainly hard-knocks," Stephens said with a quick laugh. Then he sobered and glanced quickly at Morgan, then back to the road. "I went through the Vietnamese language school at the Presidio. I thought I would be used elsewhere, but"—he shrugged—"I guess they needed someone like me in Saigon. It isn't bad, I guess, but if I decide to stay in the service, a little time in the bush would be beneficial, I think."

"Yes, it would," Morgan said. He studied Stephens for a long moment, seeing in the young man's enthusiasm himself four years earlier. He thought about the village and the old man and how alone he had been even though he had been among the villagers for five years. "Look, I could use you, yes. But it's hard work. You won't like it, I guarantee. Unless you're a crazy, and you don't strike me as one of those. I can guarantee you one promotion only, and you might make that anyway staying in Saigon. Back in the States, the promotion boards won't know if you've been in the bush or not. They'll just see Vietnam stamped on your service record and presume you were in the field. So if that's your sole concern, I'd say stay here in Saigon."

"Thanks, sir, but I've already considered that. I don't want to go to a line outfit or anything like that, but out there"—he hesitated—"it can't be any worse than the reservation." He nodded at Morgan's quizzical look. "Yeah, I know. I don't look Indian. It's a weird gene pool. My grandmother was a Blackfoot. I grew up in Montana. The mountains there can't be easier than the ones here. When I was young, I spent a lot of time with my grandmother. Mom and Dad"—he shook his head—"they spent more time crawling inside cheap wine bottles. I haven't seen them in years. I don't think I would recognize them if I saw them. I'm not even certain they're alive. My grandmother died two years ago when I was at Montana State. Football scholarship. I could pass as a white. I was one of the lucky ones." He drew a deep breath. "Besides, I would like to work in the field doing what you do."

"Do you have the slightest idea what I do?" Morgan asked dryly.

"A pretty good idea, sir," Stephens said. "I've been driving for Colonel Black and his people for quite a while."

Morgan pursed his lips, studying him for a long moment, then shrugged. "All right, I've seen how you can handle yourself with the MPs." Stephens flushed. "And if you're crazy enough to volunteer to go back in the bush with me, I'll see what I can do. I still think you're making a mistake, though."

"Thank you, sir," Stephens said.

"You won't be thanking me in a week or so. *If* Colonel Black okays your reassignment to me. And," he said deliberately, "if you try to walk away from it out in the bush, I'll kill you." Stephens turned his head to stared at Morgan. "Be aware of that. Out there is a different world. There are no rules as you know rules."

"Yes, sir," Stephens said. "I understand that."

"Then, why do you want to go?"

"I told you—"

"You've told me only part of it," Morgan said bluntly. "You've told me the gloss. Now, tell me what you are glossing over. What are you running away from?"

Stephens flushed and bit his lip. "There was an accident," he said slowly, then stopped, glancing sideways at Morgan.

"A bad accident?" Stephens hesitated, then nodded. "Someone died." It wasn't a question, but Stephens nodded anyway. "I see." Morgan stared out at the street. "And you could be found at fault for this 'accident?' " Again, Stephens nodded, tiny muscles knotting and unknotting at the corners of his jaws. "All right. *Ông nói tiêng gì?*"

"*Tôi nói tiêng Viêt tiêng-Căm-Bôt,*" Stephens replied quickly. He shrugged. "*Tôi nói kém lam. Tôi tiêc.*"

"*Có phài không?*"

"*Tôi tuóng thê.*"

"*Tôi thâv rôi,*" Morgan replied. "You're not bad. But the Montagnard language is not the same."

"I'm a quick study, sir," Stephens said. He glanced at Morgan and turned a faint red. "Uh, sir?"

"It's all right, Stephens," Morgan said. "I'll talk with Black."

Stephens slowed as they approached the MP stand, then shifted and sped through as the MP glanced into the jeep and waved them on. A strange euphoria swept through him.

Chapter Eighteen

"Come in, Morgan," Colonel Black grunted as Morgan tapped on the door. He leaned back in his chair and looked with tired eyes at Morgan's damp shoulders. "Still raining, I see."

"It's out of season," Morgan said. He crossed to the desk and sat in the chair in front of it. "The Montagnards believe it to be the tears of the souls who are doomed to wander the earth for their sins of betrayal. It is a most unlucky rain."

"Uh-huh. I hope you don't believe in that mumbo-jumbo," Black said. Morgan shrugged.

"Doesn't matter one way or the other if I believe it," he said. "The thing is, they won't do anything while it is raining." And that much is true. Although when they no longer have a village, it doesn't matter to them.

"Damn," Black said. He drummed his fingers on his desk top, considering. He shrugged and said. "Well, can't be helped. Maybe it will have stopped by the time you get ready to go back out there."

"I thought I was to have a little R and R," Morgan said. "Your idea. I was just asking."

"My ideas have been changed by a listening post up around Dong Phieu," he said. "It seems that a small party of smugglers has come across the border from the Golden Triangle and is making its way down here."

"Raw opium? That's what usually comes out of the Golden Triangle. At least that isn't as bad as heroin."

Black grimaced. "Yeah, that's what it used to be. But I understand that one of those war lords has installed his own cooker.

What we are getting, according to Major Haversham, is first-run stuff. You can imagine the market on that."

Morgan nodded. One hundred percent heroin would street-cut to almost ten times its size with the price going up at each exchange. Somebody was about to become very, very rich.

"And you want me to go up there and stop it before it gets to South Vietnam," he said quietly.

"Jesus, yes," Black answered. "Once it comes across the line, there's no telling which province commander will take it in. Even if they stumble across it accidentally, it would be early retirement for the commander up there."

"Yes, I know," Morgan said. "If you remember, I warned you about Big Minh and some of his boys. Corrupt as the day is long. And they're still walking around as cocky as the day I came here."

"Big Minh can't be touched," Black said quietly. "He's too powerful. Ky would like to replace him, but a lot of Vietnamese are loyal to that fat queer. Especially here in Saigon."

Morgan nodded. The war had changed Saigon from the jewel often referred to as Paris of the East by the French before Dien Bien Phu to a great evil whore; painted, primitive, hypnotic, the Whore of Whores. Anything could be purchased in its streets. Everything from forbidden ivory, to drugs, to little girls or boys, to live "snuff" shows where a woman endured every sexual act imaginable and finally was killed.

"I know," he said quietly. "The war makes strange bedfellows. Pardon the cliché."

"Clichés become clichés because they are true," Black said. "When the truth becomes too predictable, you have a cliché. And we can't get rid of clichés because people insist on using them."

"Getting philosophical, now, are we?" Morgan grinned.

"It's goddamned late," Black growled. He rubbed his hand across his unshaven jaws. It sounded like sandpaper scraping across a table. "You need to go to supply and pick out what you need. Anything. Medical supplies, C rations, ammunition, what-ever. We'll drop you in when the rain lifts."

Morgan nodded, chewed on his lower lip for a moment, then

said, "And what about my Montagnards? What guarantees will you give them?"

"I ran the idea by Ambassador Lodge and he took it to Deputy Premier Nguyen Van Thieu who reluctantly agreed."

"You're kidding." Morgan shook his head. "I'm sorry, but I don't trust them. Thieu, I mean. And his people. They belong to the same family that used to hunt the Montagnards for sport. And now, they're willing to give them a voice in the government and control over the Highlands in exchange for their help in the war? Excuse me, boss, but it sounds wrong to me."

Black leaned back in his chair, a smug look on his face. He opened a drawer and slid a sheet of paper from it and flicked it across the desk to Morgan. "I anticipated you would say that and I had this drawn up and signed by Thieu."

Morgan picked up the paper, reading, and as he read, misgivings filled him. The paper gave the Montagnards almost exclusive control over the Highlands, stating that all the territory in which they operated was to be considered under their own martial law. They had the right to try criminals and to execute them. They could levy taxes within 10 percent of the yearly worth of which 18 percent of the accumulated monies would be remitted to the Saigon government. In exchange, they were to assume control over the area in question and all joint operations in that area between the United States, Australian, and South Vietnamese forces would be conducted through them. On the surface, it appeared that the Montagnards would finally have a land of their own, but Morgan noted that the paper, although bearing the signature of Thieu as deputy premier, did not carry any seals of office. The Vietnamese, with their tradition and love of pomp and circumstance, made everything an elaborate ceremony. Still, it was better than he hoped.

"You will notice," Black said dryly, "that it is all contingent upon their keeping the Highlands free from infiltrators."

"And you know that that is impossible," Morgan said. "There are a lot of Montagnard tribes up in those hills and each has a chieftain, a headman. Each will want to have a say in the government."

"That's your problem. And theirs," Black said. "I've simply given you the paper that you need to begin work on putting everything together."

"So it all falls back in my lap," Morgan said quietly.

"What the hell did you expect?" Black demanded, suddenly angry. He clenched his fists and furiously scrubbed his knuckles over his head. "You come in here giving me ultimatums, well, goddamnit, I did my best. If that isn't good enough for you, then maybe you'd better remember that you are a soldier. A soldier, damnit, and not a fucking politician. Follow your orders! And *that* is an order!"

"Yes sir," Morgan said. He handed the paper back to Black. His face showed hard planes in the yellow light of the room. Black took the paper and shoved it into the desk drawer, slamming it shut. "But I want you to know that if you decide to abandon these people because it becomes politically expedient, I'll go to the press with it. The French colonists did that when things became too hard for them. I won't have that. We started something here and although I don't understand everything about it, I do understand what has happened to those people. I won't walk away from it."

Black stared at him thoughtfully for a long moment. "You are close to stepping over that line, Captain Morgan."

"Frankly, Colonel, I don't care. Do you want to send me home?" he challenged. "I don't think the war is very popular over there right now, is it? What do you think would happen if I went public about the wet work we've been doing out there?"

"All right. You've made your point. Now," he said. "Let's get down to business. You have to make contact with your people and convince them that they must stop this latest infiltration. It shouldn't be a very big problem if the early reports are correct. A small party only. But it will serve as a demonstration to the Vietnamese government that the Montagnards are willing to patrol their own territory and work on behalf of the government. It is a start. I've alerted supply to give you carte blanche. Pick out whatever you need. The lieutenant will take you over there when we are finished here and sign for you. Anything else?"

"One more thing, sir," Morgan said. Black leaned back in his chair, his eyes narrowing in warning. "I want the man who's been driving me around."

"Who?"

"Stephens."

"He's just a kid," Black said.

"Old enough to have been drafted and to wear the uniform. I need him."

"Look: I can give you a lieutenant from one of the old teams. At least, he'll have been trained. That kid hasn't been trained in anything but a basic course in the Vietnamese language and driving a jeep, as far as I know. He's got only a temporary clearance for this office."

"You said 'anything,'" Morgan reminded.

"There's something else, isn't there?"

"Yes. He was involved in an accident."

Black waved his hand in dismissal. "You drive in Saigon traffic, you can expect to get in an accident a time or two. We have motor pools to take care of that."

"I don't think it's that kind of accident," Morgan said quietly. "And if it's as bad as I think, I don't think it would be good to let it get out. If we're in the bush, then he's out of the way of any investigation that could be coming."

"Jesus Christ," Black said wearily. "One damn thing after another. All right. Take him. I'll clear it through personnel."

Morgan shrugged. "I have a feeling that he'll be good for me."

"Can we get down to business, *now*?" Black growled. He rose and crossed to the map and, using a thick forefinger as a pointer, outlined where the group had crossed down from the Golden Triangle and the route that they would probably follow. Morgan followed attentively, refraining from reminding the Colonel that he was well out of the boundary of South Vietnam where, if discovered, an international incident would be created. That was not Black's concern. He was a soldier pursuing the enemy. Politicians created boundaries and soldiers fought wars. That was enough for him. A half-smile flitted across Morgan's face. He knew, however, that if he was caught outside South Vietnam territory that he would be hung out to dry by both the army and politicians. Judas goats are not claimed by anyone.

Chapter Nineteen

Nguyen Duc squatted on his haunches and sadly looked around the tiny clearing in the middle of thick pines. The others patiently waited for his orders, but he did not speak and brooded on the emptiness inside him from the mistake he had made. The ambush had been costly. They had been thirty-two; now only eighteen waited and the old man knew the pain they felt and tried to put his pain behind him.

It is not so much that we lost most of our supplies. And the radio. *Eeeah*. The gods must have been very angry indeed with us to send a bullet through the radio. The Dai-uy will be very mad at us for this foolishness. You should have waited for him. He is very young, but he has been long in the mountains with you, old man, and he has become very wise. Remember the punji pit? Ahh. That was an excellent ambush. He made us dig a big hole and stand sharp bamboo inside it and cover it with a mat woven from the bamboo leaves and covered with dirt strong enough for a man to walk upon. Then, while he ambushed the Viet Cong down the trail, we uncovered the pit and when the Viet Cong ran back, they fell in.

He shook his head and the others waited for him to speak. He cleared his voice and fingered his rifle. Perhaps someone else should lead them now. He would hate to give up his rifle, but he had been very foolish when he should have been very wise. He had let his anger rule him and a wise leader never did that. No, it would be better if someone else led them. But who?

He twisted his head and slowly looked around the clearing. They stared back at him, patient, passive. He could not read anything behind their eyes. Who could lead them? He cleared his voice again.

"I have been very foolish," he began. "I have let my anger rule my judgment and a wise leader does not do that. Perhaps someone else should lead you. Someone whose thoughts have not grown soft with age."

One of the old men, Loc Thien, sighed and eased his position. His knees popped in the silence and he grimaced from the sudden stab of pain.

"Perhaps someone should," he said scornfully. "When a man cries about his mistakes instead of correcting them, then it is time for him to wear the *ao dai* and clean pots with the women."

Anger flashed through Nguyen Duc and his fingers tightened convulsively on the stock of his rifle, then relaxed. Loc Thien caught the movement and the corners of his eyes crinkled.

"We are mountain people. Have you forgotten our ways? If we were dissatisfied with you, then we would select a new leader and you would visit your ancestors."

Nguyen Duc nodded thoughtfully. If anyone had wanted to be leader, he would have been killed long ago. It had been so with his people for hundreds of years. *Eeeah.* Since they moved to the mountains at the time of the Great Flood when the Pure One sent the waters to destroy the Dragon-Serpent that was killing the people. It was not such an uncommon thing to happen either. Had not his own great-grandfather dispatched the chief of his time and been selected chief by the elders?

His fingers fondly touched the haft of the old dah at his waist. It was with this very dah that his father had killed Da Thieu when the shares of the fall sale had not been equally divided. He frowned. Now he had no son to whom he could give the dah. Perhaps that was good. It was not good for one family to remain too long in power. They became kings and the mountain people could not be ruled by kings. They had to have their freedom. That was why the old way was best.

"Well?" Loc Thien asked crankily. "Do we sit here until our piles bleed from the cold or are we going to do something?"

Nguyen Duc stood and slung his rifle over his shoulder.

"Do not prattle like an old fool," he said. "We leave for Tay Ninh where the Dai-uy said he would meet us. There we will get more food and ammunition and return and kill the upstarts. But," he added soberly, "if your piles pain you too much to march, we can wait until your old bones are ready."

Loc Thien made a rude noise and stood. He moved down the trail, walking on stiff legs. His knees popped with every other step.

"Old bones! These old bones will walk all here into the ground. They march when you all groan and moan for hot tea and a young woman to rub the ache from your limbs. Oh, you farmers, you boaters! Keep up with one of the mountain people if you can!"

The others grinned and climbed to their feet and moved down the trail after him. Nguyen Duc felt his lips turning at the corners and suddenly he laughed. The others laughed with him and the pain of the ambush slid anonymously into the past, not to be forgotten, for no one could forget such a thing, but to be remembered another time, another place, when hate would be needed or when the gods decided. Perhaps this was the reason for the failure. One did not rush the judgment of the gods.

Sunlight broke through the trees and fell on the trail. Nguyen Duc's bones seemed to warm instantly. It was a good omen. The forest spirits were back with them again.

The old man stopped the others in the tree line and looked carefully at the razed hamlet in front of him. Since the ambush four days ago, they had been traveling through the thickest jungle to avoid detection. The men were exhausted and leaned against trees when they stood. The flesh under their eyes sagged, and more than one had tremors from the cold, sleepless nights high in the mountains. But they did not complain and the old man was proud of the way they followed him, and although he knew they should bypass this hamlet and continue on to Tay Ninh, he also knew that they needed food and rest.

Reluctantly, he motioned the men forward, and the old men

fanned out on either side and moved forward slowly, first one, then the other as the one in front covered him in the ancient pattern of the hill warrior.

Tiny slips of smoke lifted lazily from fire-blackened timbers, and kites and vultures, bellies swollen from feasting on dead bodies, rose awkwardly into the air, ugly beaks crying shrilly at the invaders. The old ones slipped like shadows from cover to cover. They ignored the pile of heads in the center of the hamlet and the bodies, horrible wounds gaping wide from savage machetes, sprawled randomly in doorways and in the dusty street. One was slumped half in the well and a water buffalo stared sightlessly at the pile of heads, an unborn calf hacked from its womb by its side. Chunks of meat had been cut from its haunches, and when the old man found this, he sighed and pursed his lips and trilled. The others moved back to him and stood in a loose circle around him, seemingly careless, but eyes constantly searched the bamboo surrounding the hamlet. They did not need their eyes to hear the old man's words.

"Do not take water from the well," the old man said. "It may be bad. Take what meat you can from the cow and see what you can find in the huts, but be careful. The northerners obviously expect the Americans to find the people in this manner so there will be traps in some of the huts. Do not touch the bodies for they are most certainly hiding grenades."

Vo Moc Thien hawked and spit a red stream of betel juice on the ground. "We are not children," he said. "And the young ones are not with us."

"Sometimes one needs to be reminded of realities when old age makes one forgetful," the old man said. "And cut the meat from deep within the cow. Remember what the Dai-uy showed us with the needles?"

"*Eeeah*," Vo Moc Thien said, and spat again. He looked sheepish. "I had forgotten that." He started to move toward a hut, then stopped as one of the others grunted and dropped to a knee, lifting his rifle to his shoulder.

"What is it?" Vo asked. He rapidly scanned the thicket behind the huts. He brought his rifle ready in front of him.

"Movement," the crouching one said.

"Probably a kite," Vo replied, but he did not relax.

"On the ground. There!" The man pointed at a small bush tucked half into the bamboo, and Vo Moc Thien brought his rifle around and sighted at a patch of darkness against the green leaves.

The others quickly spread themselves in a curve like a water buffalo's horns toward the bush and slowly advanced. Nguyen Duc held the center of the line, and looked just above the bush as he slowly stalked forward. He knew better than to stare too long at the bush, for the eye catches movement at the edge of vision. He moved carefully on the balls of his feet, ready to throw himself to the side at the first sign of danger.

"Vo Moc!" he said sharply. "Watch behind us!"

Obediently, Vo Moc pivoted and dropped to his knee. The others on the right horn readjusted the space between them automatically.

They were almost to the edge of the bamboo when the bush quivered and a woman rose and stared defiantly at them. She held a parang ready in her hand, and Nguyen Duc could see blood spattered on the front of her white blouse. He clicked his tongue against his teeth, and the others stopped and watched her warily. She was squat and thick in the middle with broad shoulders, but she stood easily and her eyes were dark and intent in her moon-shaped face. There was dried blood, too, on her cheek, but it was not hers and the men knew by this that she was dangerous.

"So," she said. Her voice was low and hard in the quiet, not shrill and excited as a woman's should have been. "Now, the scavangers come, the toothless ones, eh? No matter. Come! Kill me, if you can. I'm not afraid of you!"

She swung the parang menacingly and the men could hear the heavy blade moving through the air. Her thick wrist rotated at the top of the swing and the blade flashed brightly as she delivered the backstroke.

"Huh! Why do you wait? There are many of you and one of me. But I'll take—"

"Be quiet, woman," Nguyen Duc said. He shifted his rifle under his arm so that the barrel pointed to the bush. "No one is going to hurt you."

The woman lowered her parang warily and brushed her hair back from her forehead with her free hand. Her hands were thick and stubby, but strong, and Nguyen Duc could see the power in her shoulders as well.

"How did you escape this?" he asked. He gestured at the village. The woman sighed, and the tension dropped from her.

"They came when the cook fires started," she said. "But I was voiding myself in the bush, and they missed me. All except one," she added grimly, and lifted the parang with satisfaction. She bent and fumbled in the heavy grass at her feet and lifted a head by its hair. Ants crawled wildly over it, and she spat into the glazed eyes, then threw it from her. A choked sob came from behind her, and Nguyen Duc lifted the barrel of his rifle.

"What—" he began, and the woman turned and raised a young woman by her hand.

"Do not be afraid," she said gently. "They stink like wet, old men, but they mean us no harm."

The young woman stared at them with terrified eyes and gnawed at her lower lip with sharp, white teeth. She huddled close to the woman who gently stroked her long, glossy hair, lifting it clear from high cheekbones.

"What is your name?" Nguyen Duc asked. She didn't answer, but turned into the woman's heavy breast and hunched her shoulders protectively from anticipated blows.

"She is Dinh Hoa," the woman said. "Her parents were killed there." She pointed to one of the huts. "The one I killed chased her here. He was thinking with his groin and was easy to kill because of his thinking."

Nguyen Duc nodded. That had often happened in the past and there were many stories about the treachery of women. But men were often fools and when their blood was hot, they were even more foolish.

"And how are you called?" he asked politely. He placed the

butt of his rifle on the ground and only then did his men relax and move to find the supplies they needed.

"I am Kai," she said. A wisp of hair touched with gray slipped over her cheek, and she brushed it back.

"Was your man—" he began, and allowed his voice to delicately trail off. He pretended to cough.

"My man died with the chest sickness two years ago," she said. "The gods did not bless us with children. I am alone." She moved toward the village and the young woman stayed close by her side. "I will pack and we will come with you. Here"—she turned to the young woman and pushed her gently to the ground—"rest here, in the shade. I will get your things for you. If there is anything left," she muttered to herself as she turned back to the hamlet.

"Come. What are you called? Where are you going?"

The old man smiled to himself. Her bluntness was annoying, but pleasing.

"Nguyen Duc. Chief of Tan Bien of the Rands," he said. He fell in beside her, and followed her to her hut. He watched with satisfaction as she carefully ran her hands around the timbers of the doorway and gently patted the earth in front with her fingertips. Finding no trip wires, she moved inside the doorway and searched the interior, her eyes noting what had been taken. Satisfied, she pulled a quilt from the pallet on the earthen floor and quickly packed a pan and pot, a butcher knife and boning knife, a small packet wrapped in a piece of red silk with a green dragon embroidered upon it, dried herbs, black blouse and pants, and a comb and stainless steel mirror. Nguyen Duc picked a sewing kit from the floor and handed it to her. Soon, she had the pack neatly tied with another blanket like a sling enclosing it. She slipped it around her forehead and rose easily to her feet. Nguyen Duc nodded in admiration: she was strong, like a cow, and would not hold them back.

"Where are your people from?" he asked as they stepped out of the hut. He looked around; the others were almost through and Vo Moc had already moved to the south end of the hamlet and waited for the others.

"From there." She pointed to the mountains to the north. "Where do we go?"

"To Tay Ninh," Nguyen Duc said. "We go there to meet the Dai-uy."

"Who is he?" she asked. She shifted the load until it was more comfortable and fell in step beside him. She did not take the customary step behind him and, although this was disquieting to Nguyen Duc, he decided not to remind her of her place. The others noticed, too, and watched them curiously.

"The Dai-uy is an American who has brought great honor to my village," Nguyen Duc said. She stopped and stared at him in disbelief.

"An *American*?"

Nguyen Duc nodded, and she spat disgustedly into the dust.

"It is because of the Americans this was done. They came here and stuck tiny needles in the children's arms, and gave us food and asked us to tell them all we knew about the Viet Cong. But we could tell them nothing. I do not think they believed us. They said they would return today, but the Viet Cong came first. If they had stayed away, the Viet Cong would have left us alone. There was nothing here for them. We were a poor village. The young men had already left. No, the Americans caused this to happen to us. My advice to you is to stay away from the Americans or the same thing will happen to your village."

"It already has," the old man said. "But it was one of us who betrayed us, not the Americans. We search for him, but first we must meet with the Dai-uy at Tay Ninh. We will take you with us to the temple there. The Cao Dai will help you."

She snorted and moved away from him. "I do not need the Cao Dai, and you set a great deal of store by this Dai-uy. I would see him."

"He is more Montagnard than American," Nguyen Duc said proudly. "He is more of the mountains."

"We shall see," she said. "We shall see. Now, let us go before the Americans return and force us to go with them. I have no intention of living behind wire, for that, I am told, is where they put the homeless." She moved down the trail toward Vo Moc, then stopped and turned back to him. "Where are your women? Surely some must travel with you."

"Dead," the old man said bitterly. "All dead."

"Ah. Then, you see? You will have need of us. Come!" She crossed to the young woman and pulled her to her feet.

"Follow me." She turned again to the trail. The young woman obediently fell in behind her and treaded on her heels as they walked. The young woman's flanks barely touched the silk of her black longi. Nguyen Duc guessed she was sixteen, but wasn't worried. They were all too old for that to be a problem.

It will be good to have a woman to take care of us. It is too bad about the young one. Now, she must forget about being a child and become a woman. That is a sad thing, to lose one's childhood in this fashion. Very sad.

He motioned to the others and they fell in behind him. The kites watched the bedraggled column leave the hamlet, then with glad cries, swooped back to the feast.

Chapter Twenty

The C-130 transport flew above the scudding clouds heavy with rain. Stephens and Morgan stood at the cockpit entrance and watched for the telltale patches of green that fleetingly appeared. The pilot tapped the compass and turned to Morgan.

"Thirteen minutes," he said loudly above the roar of the engines. "We'll have to go in low under the clouds for verification. Sorry, but there's a heavy front moving in on us. We'll have to drop you quickly."

Morgan nodded, and motioned Stephens back into the bowels of the plane. They moved around the freight cargo to the rear door and began checking their equipment.

"Doesn't look good, does it?" Stephens asked. His fingers trembled as he checked the quick-release of his parachute harness. "The low drop, I mean. Doesn't look good."

Morgran shrugged. "Much better, actually. You want to get down fast. You're pretty helpless in the air."

Stephens wiped the back of his hand across his mouth. "Hell, in that case, maybe we'd better not use any chutes at all."

Morgan laughed at the old joke, and the tension disappeared from around Stephens's eyes. That was good. One had to be in complete control during a low drop. There wasn't enough reaction time to correct any sudden malfunctions if fear or apprehension caused any hesitations.

A red light flashed its warning, and Morgan leaned out and saw the prearranged flares flickering below. Quickly, he hooked the static line of his parachute over a c-ring, checked Stephens's equipment, and stepped into the doorway. The cargomaster grinned and leaned close to Morgan's ear.

"Northeast wind! Ten knots!" he yelled.

Morgan nodded, and tensed as the red light flashed again, then leaped through the door as the green light began to blink urgently.

He felt the wind and cold moisture from the cloud quickly dampen his face, and then his parachute snapped open. Quickly he rolled and craned his neck to make sure it had deployed correctly. Satisfied no panels had ripped, he looked around for Stephens, but the cloud was too thick. He looked down between his dangling feet, but could not see the ground. There was no sensation of falling, no sense of direction. The world seemed a far and distant place as if he had been suspended in a gigantic womb.

This must be what death is like, he thought. Cold, clammy, swirling fog, silky filaments of spider-web gray that cling briefly and melt away. Somehow, there's a mixed metaphor there. It really doesn't matter. The only thing that matters is here and now. Mildew. That's what it smells like: mildew on old army blankets. Is this the waiting period for the Hindu's rebirth? But that is impossible since we know the rebirth can come only at the horn of Gabriel. Will he play "Taps" or charge? And what of evil? Will it awaken as well? No, there is nothing after death. This is only a cloud or fog and it is very good because a smart fighter does not waste ammunition on what he cannot see.

He remembered the banyon trees and the thorns and twisted anxiously in his harness and looked for the ground beneath his dangling feet. He broke through the clouds at about a hundred feet and saw the green smoke immediately in a small clearing to his right. He reached for the riser in front on his right and pulled it down to his chest. He began to drift toward the smoke, and he looked quickly around for Stephens and found him above and to the left. Somehow, Stephens had managed to get turned and was drifting backwards to the smoke. He was hauling frantically upon the risers in an attempt to right himself, and then the treeline flashed in front of Morgan's eyes and he forced himself to relax. The ground rushed up at him and he landed and rolled quickly on his hip and spun on his shoulders to allow the parachute to pull him to his feet. Then, the old men were standing around him and slapping him on the back and grinning.

"*Eeeah*," Nguyen Duc said. He held him by the forearms and smiled and looked closely in his face. "It is good to have you back."

"It is good to be back and see your ugly face again." Morgan said, slipping easily into the hill dialect. The old man laughed and helped Morgan shrug out of his harness.

"Look out!" a voice called frantically from the sky, and they scattered as Stephens fell backwards in a tangle of static lines, risers, and parachute in the middle of them. Quickly, they clustered about him and began to cut him free. Morgan helped him to his feet. He took a couple of steps and winced and rubbed his hip.

"Are you all right?" Morgan asked.

"Think so," he said. "Sore butt is all." He rubbed his face and winced; there was a static line burn across the bridge of his nose and down his left cheek. He spat and ran his tongue over his lip; it was already twice normal size.

"Christ," he began, then jumped sideways as a crate crashed near him. He darted into the trees just behind Morgan and the old men as crates and boxes began to fall into the clearing. Some caught in the trees and the men began to gather them and pile them at the edge of the clearing. Morgan counted seven loads, then nodded at Nugyen Duc.

"That is all," he said. "Gather the supplies quickly."

The old man turned and shouted orders at the others. Knives flashed and the parachutes were quickly rolled into small packages to be divided later. The supplies were broken down into smaller loads while Morgan gazed curiously around the clearing.

"Where are the others?" he asked. "Outposts?"

The old man shook his heads. "No, Dai-uy. There is much to tell."

Morgan sighed and rubbed the back of his neck. "Yes, but later. Gather the equipment and let us move away from here. The smoke can be seen and the Viet Cong have long eyes."

"Are they near?" Stephens asked as he strapped on the harness one of the old men handed him. He staggered, then regained his balance under the unexpected weight. "How can you tell?"

"You don't," Morgan said. "You feel." He checked the action of his Thompson and rammed home a full clip. He eased the straps of his pack harness into the hollows of his shoulders. "When you begin to feel secure, that's when they will strike. When you begin to feel nervous, that's when they will strike. Think of them as always being there. That is the safest."

He settled the black beret onto his head, and knotted the paisley scarf around his throat. The others watched with satisfaction: now the Dai-uy was back and everything would be as it should.

"Then, there is no way to tell?" Stephens said. "Be careful with that!" He took the radio from a man who was already carrying it as if it were explosives. He bent and checked it; it hummed and squawked loudly and the men in the clearing jumped nervously. "It's all right."

"Stay near Nguyen Duc," Morgan said. "Do what he does. That's the quickest way to learn. And the safest," he added. "Soon, you will be able to tell."

"Ready, Dai-uy." Nguyen Duc touched his head respectfully and waited.

"You will take the point, Vo Moc," Morgan said. He turned to the old man. "Is the camp near?"

"It is not far." The old man unslung his rifle and cradled it in his arms. "But it is safe and difficult to find for men used to soft arms and whiskey."

The others laughed behind cupped hands. Morgan nodded solemnly at Nguyen Duc.

"As always," he said, "you have shown great wisdom. Please lead us to this vacation spot for I see it must truly be a bit of paradise with all the fat and lazy men you have brought." He turned to Stephens and motioned him forward. "This is a great warrior who has heard your eyes are dim and your legs weak, and he has consented to accompany you and help you over the difficult parts of our march."

"Your mother's milk must have been truly sour," Nguyen Duc

said. He turned to the others who were stuffing their fingers into their mouths and strangling with laughter. "Offal of monkeys, do you not hear the Dai-uy? Then, why do you waste our time like silly old women? Let us go!"

He shouldered the largest pack and moved rapidly north out of the clearing. The others laughed and shouldered the remaining boxes of ammunition, food, and medical supplies, and followed quickly after him.

"What did you say to him?" Stephens asked Morgan.

"I told him you were here to help him."

"I wish you hadn't said that," Stephens said mournfully. "I think that old man is gonna kill me."

He hurried after the column, and Morgan looked carefully around the clearing. All signs of the air drop had been removed and the ground carefully brushed with branches. Even now the jungle seemed to be erasing all traces and Morgan fancied he could see the trees and shrubs creeping slowly around the clearing.

He smiled to himself and fell in behind the column. He felt warm and comfortable. It was home.

Chapter Twenty-one

The mountain rose majestically, a solo upthrust of granite from the tail of the fractured corderilla that dominated the surrounding plains. But, according to the hill people, the mountain had been planted there by the mountain spirits themselves and upon its summit the gods rested in satorial splendor and haughtily observed the frail humans below. An old temple still stood upon the summit, abandoned now except for the forest that had invaded the stone, upheaving paving blocks and sending tenacious roots into cracks and crevices. The forest had been very patient: patient for so long that no one could remember how the builders of the temple had managed to move the huge, granite monoliths to the top of the mountain through the heavy timber. The large columns were thickly entwined with climbing vines and moss and lichens covered ancient stone terraces, a giant's staircase that still stood in line. The vines looked as if a giant's darning needle had hooked them into the stone. The roof lay in jumbled piles of slate on the floor and the carved faces of the gods showed the strain of time and countless prayers. The names of the gods had been lost. One of the statues resembled the Indian statues of Kali, but no one knew if the Indians had immigrated this far this early. Another statue was so eroded that only huge teeth and a large, protruding stomach remained of the original carving. There were others: one stared stoically over the valley despite a carved snake that curled itself tightly around its body, one wore a headdress seemingly composed of skulls and carried a peacock feather fan in a hand that wasn't so much a hand as a tiger's paw. Still another had two horns curving from a high forehead and wore a wide-mouthed, chilling grin and rose from a shelf that still bore faint, curious, dark stains.

The old man did not like this place, but it was easy to defend and a cold stream sliced quickly through the heavy undergrowth beside the temple walls. The first night he thought he heard voices and the next morning he had climbed to the temple and left a small piece of red cloth at the foot of each god. That night he dreamed about an eagle eating a struggling monkey, and he knew the gods were still there and he was glad that he had left the red cloth even if they did send him a dream he could not understand.

He thought about that dream now as he squatted on his heels across from the Dai-uy and his friend, the young man, Stephens, who slumped tiredly in front of the fire, and thought about asking the Dai-uy if he could explain the dream. But he had just told the Dai-uy about the loss of the young men and the ambush and his own foolishness and now the Dai-uy was stirring the coals in the fire and staring as if he could read the answers there and perhaps he could, Nguyen Duc thought suddenly. Perhaps he could. His face bore the far-away look of Nguyen Duc's grandmother when she would stare into the coals and see what would be. Sometimes, she would shudder and draw her shawl tightly about her and would not eat or drink for days, but would sit and rock and softly sing about strange things.

Perhaps the Dai-uy was like this, he thought, and his breast filled with sadness for the Dai-uy for he remembered how the villagers had shunned his grandmother when they discovered what she could do. No, it was best that he did not ask the Dai-uy now about his dream. Better to wait and see what the Dai-uy decided to do. He sat back on his heels and watched the firelight play on the Dai-uy's face. *Aiyee*, it would be good to smoke his pipe now. He fingered the small pellets and pipe in the sack beside him and tried to remember if he had smoked his pipe the night he had the dream.

Morgan stirred the embers with a long stick as he thought about what the old man had told him. The desertion of the young men was a definite blow to his plans. His fighting force had been halved. Halved? More like sixteenthed! He pulled the sleeves of his old brown cardigan sweater closer about his neck and reached for the bottle of Johnnie Walker resting in the dirt between his heels. He raised it and sipped from the bottle and set it carefully back. The Scotch burned through his throat and warmed his stomach.

This is a miracle, this Scotch, he thought. It warmed the body and made the mind much clearer with its warmth. The taste brought back the quiet evenings and the oaks and ash as they changed their colors for fall. There were cottonwoods and maples, too, and walnuts, and the pleasant smell of the leaves moldering in the creek running down to Bad River from the stock dam below the big house on the ranch or burning in piles raked by the people in Ithaca, and the sounds of the football games from transistor radios playing against the scratch of rakes in the grass. This Scotch is a miracle. It is also an antiseptic and it can keep you awake or put you to sleep.

He sipped again from the bottle, looked at the label reflectively for a moment, then handed it to the old man. The old man held the bottle against the stars of the night, then took a long drink and passed it to Stephens. Stephens drank deeply and handed the bottle back to Morgan. Tears sparkled in his eyes, and Morgan smiled to himself. The tears would be gone by this time next month, and the Scotch would be little more than a quick bite that would cut through the tiredness and frustration. He raised his eyes and looked at the old man.

"This is a bad thing of your son," he said.

Nguyen Duc looked at him bleakly. The flesh of his face hung in folds from the many wrinkles.

"I have no son," he said.

" 'Until the vine is destroyed, the fruit will multiply,' " Morgan quoted. "I grieve for your wife. She was a good woman."

"*Eeeah*," the old man said. "She should have died in her own village."

"I grieve for the others," Morgan said. "This is a terrible thing."

"Yes," the old man said. He watched the Dai-uy closely, keeping his feelings from showing in his eyes.

"The people in Saigon wish us to go north to Mu Gia and Ailao and keep the Viet Cong from using those passes. They bring the white powder from the poppy flower over these routes to people in Saigon," he explained. "This is very bad."

"Yes," the old man said. "This is very bad. But Mu Gia and Ailao are many days' march from here, and there are others in the north who are good at this."

"There are many," Morgan agreed. He drank from the bottle again and passed it to Nguyen Duc. "But it is the time to be considering their fields. You have no fields. But the people in Saigon are promising you this if you go north to the passes of Mu Gia and Ailao: you will have your village again." The old man's eyes sparkled, but he watched impassively as Morgan sketched out the plan that Colonel Black had given him in Saigon. When he finished, Nguyen Duc stared into the fire for a long moment before speaking.

"The people in Saigon have promised us many things but have never kept their word," he said. "For years, the emperor and his people hunted my people in the hills like tigers and jackals. When we tried to speak with the people in Saigon, our leaders were killed or put in prison and made to work the trees on the plantations owned by the French. The people in Hanoi promise us that this will no longer happen, but many of the people in Hanoi were there when the French were there, too. This I remember from what my father told me and from what I saw when my father took me to Haiphong once. The Rands and the Montagnards and the Khans and others of the hills have never been treated with the respect that is given to the people of the lowlands. We have learned to be not only hill people but forest people as well. And now, these people will give us land that they took from us, give us back our village, and give us our own province in the hills to be governed by hill people?" He spat into the flames and listened to the sound hiss. Then he raised his eyes and looked at Morgan. The planes of his face softened.

"What do you think. Dai-uy? Should we trust these people again?"

"If they were only words that fly through the air, no," Morgan said. "But these words have been placed on the paper and agreed to by my people and the people in Saigon, and so I would say that you could trust these people. But," he amended. "I would keep my hand in my pocket and not clasp theirs with both hands." The old man nodded and stared thoughtfully into the fire again. He took the bottle of Scotch and drank deeply and handed it to Stephens.

Movement at the edge of the firelight caught Morgan's eye and the woman, Kai, moved into the circle and silently placed a large pot of thick, gray stew between them. The old man leaned forward and ate three spoonfuls of the stew and handed the long-handled, wooden spoon to Morgan. Morgan followed suit and washed the stew down with another long drink of Scotch. It was monkey stew and well-seasoned, and he nodded appreciatively at the woman.

"Very good," he said. The young woman stepped from behind Kai and looked shyly at him. He had forgotten her name. "How are you called?"

"The stew was to your liking?" Kai asked, ignoring his question.

"Very much," he said.

"It is nothing," she said, and spread the fingers of her hand. "The monkey was very old. Such meat should come from a young monkey. But old men catch only old monkeys. The young ones are too quick for them. This is too bad because old teeth need tender meat."

"Go away, woman," Nguyen Duc said. His face grimaced with disgust. "This is no place for woman's bantering. Men speak in council here."

"Men!" She spat, and placed her hands on her hips and spread her broad, bare feet firmly in the dirt. "More like the babblings of once-greats remembering too many years. This one"—she pointed at Morgan—"this one shows intelligence. You are right; he is of our people and not like the others. The rest of you are little more than chan."

She spat again, and walked out of the firelight. The young woman followed her, pausing to shyly glance at Morgan. Morgan grinned at the old man.

"She is very strong," he said.

"Her tongue is the tongue of a farmer," Nguyen Duc said. He spat into the fire.

"But she cooks well," Morgan said. He took another mouthful of stew.

"Passable," the old man said grudgingly.

"Has she a man?"

"What man beds a viper?" The old man sighed. "A man would have to beat her with a bamboo whip to make her a wife. But"—he spread his hands in dismissal—"I think it would take many beatings and who has that time, now?"

"True," Morgan said. "The war is too much to allow such things to happen." He grinned. "And she might take the bamboo whip from you and beat you with it, instead."

"Ahhh," the old man said disgustedly. He drank again from the bottle. He looked closely at Morgan. "Remember, Dai-uy, when this is over and you mate, you must choose a woman who is strong and tender and speaks softly. Women like this one are much headache."

"You are wise, and I shall remember your words," Morgan said. "But, now, we must talk of the passes."

"Ah, yes," the old man sighed. "This thing of the passes. Cannot the others do this of which you speak?"

"They have their villages to which they must return," Morgan said. "And I do not trust those with whom I have not fought to do such a thing."

"*Eeeah*," the old man said. "I understand. We have nothing and therefore, we lose nothing." He grimaced and stared at Morgan. "You are wise not to trust such people too. But what of our village? We, too, have a village."

"This is true," Morgan said. "It does not take much to make a village." He looked around the clearing, at the others sitting or sleeping beside other fires a respectful distance from them. "But it is a village of old men. Where are the young men who will supply the seed to keep the village alive? This village will die when you die, old man."

"Perhaps," the old man said. "But if we kill he who was once my son and those who went with him the first time, the other young people who have gone with him out of foolishness may see how wrong they were and return to us."

"But could you trust such people?"

"They are Rands," the old man said. "This thing with that man is only a thing of youth. They will return."

"It is this I hope is true for you."

The old man sighed and reached for the bottle of Scotch. He drank deeply from it and placed it on the ground at his feet. He closed his eyes and rubbed his face.

"There are four noble truths," he said. "The noble truth of ill, the noble truth of the origins of ill, the noble truth of the stopping of ill, the noble truth of the way that leads to the stopping of ill. But, you must remember that birth is ill, age is ill, disease is ill, death is ill. And that is why I must kill the man who was my son. To end this illness. To bring the peace back to my village.

"It is true that we have no women and no young people to bring us grandchildren unless the young people return. But we still have a village. Here"—he pounded his chest with his fist—"we have a village. And here"—he touched his forehead—"we remember what our village was, and here"—he touched his eyes—"we see what our village has become. But why has all this happened? Why?" He looked in the direction of Kai. "The old woman believes it to be the fault of the Americans." He shrugged. "I do not know. I know our homes are all gone, and I know the why of that, and I know what must now be done. That is all."

"That is needed," Morgan agreed. "But is there not something of a larger consequence? What of freedom and the evil those of the north bring to the south with the white powder? What of the war?"

"When man is set free, there rises in him the knowledge of

his freedom. It is then that he knows that rebirth has been destroyed and the higher life has been fulfilled. What must be done must be done. That will mean there is no more to rebirth. That is the noble truth about pain. Birth is painful. So is old age. And sickness. And death. Sorrow and despair are also painful. One must get rid of that pain."

"That will be hard to do," Morgan said. The old man shook his head.

"And what of our lives and those that have been lost and those that will never be?" the old man returned. "I have never seen Saigon, and I do not know of these fine words about which the governments argue. I do not know any of this. And I do not know why those of the north hate those of the south. But this I do know: we are old land. Our ways are old and strange to those in Saigon and Hanoi. They do not understand that we must do what must be done in the ways of my grandfather and his grandfather before him. The people of Saigon have forgotten their ancestors. Here, in the hills, we remember."

He drank from the bottle, shook it, and listened to the Scotch slosh, then passed the bottle to Morgan. Morgan took a sip and handed it to Stephens and motioned for him to finish it. Stephens upended the bottle, swallowed twice, and threw the bottle aside. He weaved drunkenly in his seat, then stretched out beside the fire. Within seconds, he was asleep.

Morgan returned to staring into the fire. He wondered if he could explain the old man to Colonel Black and his people in Saigon. Probably not. The old man was beyond their understanding as he refused to be a little red-headed pin on a map moved from west of Dalat and north to the passes of Ma Gia and Ailao by an impersonal thumb and forefinger. How could he explain a thousand-year-old culture to a man limited to twentieth-century warfare?

You can't, he thought. He wouldn't understand. The old man and his people would be taken to a refugee camp where they would be given three nutritious meals a day and talked to like old people and treated like old people and then, when their spirit was properly broken and they began to feel like mindless clumps of flesh, they would die from a sense of shame and humiliation and would be buried in a common plot that would become the site of a factory or apartment building in a few years after the war was over. Or, worse, maybe a golf course.

His eyes blurred as he thought of the old man squatting on his heels in front of a large tent, staring at clumps of mud and dozens of cookfires while white-coated, arrogant young medics and social workers moved efficiently through the camp, hanging metal tags around the necks of the old people so they would be properly numbered and could then receive the rations and medical attention they would need and be dutifully recorded when they died and were buried in large graves where they would be known by numbers only.

How do you explain dignity? he thought. How do you explain honor? How do you explain the responsibility of a chief? You don't. You must feel it. That is the only way.

"Where does the vine sink its roots?" Morgan asked at last.

The old man's eyes glistened, and he stretched out his hand and gripped Morgan's forearm.

"*Toi co mot trai*," he said. "I have a son."

He pulled a dah from his belt. The leather handle was smooth from much use. Two blood-red rubies were set deep on each side of the shaft and the blade was bright and sharp from careful honing.

"This was my father's and his father's before him. It now belongs to you." He handed it to Morgan.

Morgan ran his fingers over the handle. He was touched by the old man's gift and felt a lump grow in his throat. He reached across and wordlessly took the old man's hand. The old man smiled through the tears in his eyes.

"You are a Montagnard. Dai-uy," he said.

"Yes, old man," Morgan said. He gripped the dah tightly. "Yes, old man. And now let us plan for that which must be done."

"We will talk of the passes, then," the old man said.

Morgan reached into the map case at his side and removed another bottle of Scotch and a map. He handed the bottle to Nguyen Duc and spread the map on the ground between them. Across the fire, Stephens began to snore.

Chapter Twenty-two

Bao slept uneasily and shivered as the wind crept through the forest on cat's paws. It was a warm wind, but it whispered bad things in his ear. He moaned and rolled to his side, pillowing his cheek on a lump of moss. His nostrils twitched from the acrid odor of the wet earth, sour and bitter, full of death and decay, an endless cycle of dying leaves and branches and vines and the rotted bloom of dead flowers and grasses.

Bao breathed deeply and began to dream of emaciated specters stretching thin arms toward him from a sea of fog. Slowly, they grew in numbers and his heart began to beat faster and faster. A strange hooded form moved among them, touching them with the hem of its black garment and the specters began to writhe and twist in a nameless dance. They beckoned to him, and he felt something within his breast surge toward them. He crossed his arms over his breast and hugged himself tightly. He began to sweat and he smelled the fear that came with the water to the surface of his skin. The dark form appeared again in the middle of the specters and the dance became more frenzied and they moved closer and closer to him.

A tiger roared its hunting cry and the dark form stretched out its garment to touch him. The hood fell away and he looked into the face of his mother. Flesh fell in decaying folds from her wide cheekbones like dripping tallow, and, although sightless, she stared at him with accusing sockets. The tiger roared again, nearer, and he screamed and awoke. He rolled onto his back and stared up at the sky. The Southern Cross burned whitely against the night and he could feel the blood pounding savagely in his temples. He reached for his canteen and drank rapidly. The water tasted metallic and the odor he had smelled while asleep seemed stronger and he furiously scrubbed the back of his hand across his nose.

Footsteps rushed toward him and he felt a moment's panic and fumbled on the ground beside him for his rifle. Then he relaxed as Bong Dien knelt beside him.

"What is the matter? Is it a viper?" he asked anxiously.

Bao forced himself to laugh and immediately knew he had made a mistake: his laugh was high and cracked. He took another drink from the canteen.

"It was nothing." He tried to keep his voice steady, but there was a faint tremor to it and he hoped Bong Dien did not notice.

"Surely something," Bong Dien insisted.

The tiger roared again and Bao shuddered before he could stop himself.

"The tiger must have startled me. Truly," he lied. "I do not know."

Bong Dien nodded. Bao could see the outline of his head against the white of the Southern Cross. "The night spirits ride the wind tonight."

"I do not believe in the night spirits. They are foolish inventions of the peasants who know no better," Bao said. "I believe in the tiger and the tiger believes in me and that is all. I do not believe in the night spirits."

He saw the flash of Bong Dien's teeth as he smiled. "But do the night spirits believe in you? That is something else."

"I believe in the tiger," Bao repeated stubbornly. "And, I believe in the tiger's hunger, and I believe this makes him angry."

"Yes, of course," Bong Dien said soothingly. "I, too, believe in the tiger. But is that enough to believe in?"

"That is all to believe in," Bao said with authority.

"But what of the kite? And the monkey?"

"I believe in what is here and now," Bao said. "The tiger is here, now, and I believe in him. When the kite is here. I will believe in the kite. And so with the monkey."

Bong Dien shrugged and rose to his feet. The Southern Cross was blocked by his squat, powerful figure. "It is late. I will tell the others it was only the tiger."

"And what will you tell thyself?" Bao asked.

"What is there to tell? It is only a tiger. You said so." He laughed and moved toward the others.

"Better double the watch." Bao called softly after him. "The tiger is close and hungry."

Bong Dien laughed again, and waved his arm in acknowledgement. Bao watched the night swallow him, then lay on his back and looked at the Southern Cross. Something flew across his vision, dipped twice, and disappeared.

It is only a bat, he thought. But are you sure? What else could it be? Peasant superstition? A lost soul? We have no souls. That is an invention by those afraid to die. And are you not afraid to die? Knowing this is the only life thee has to live, you are not afraid to die? We are born to die. Then, surely you must be born again. No. Man is born once and only once. If he is born again, it is only through his children, but he is not born again. Then, are you not afraid to die? No. What happens when you die? Nothing. It is as night. It is as night now. Is it so when you die? Much like this. But can you not feel the wind and see the stars? Of course I can feel the wind and see the stars. I am not dead. What happens to your flesh when you die? And your bones? Do they become as dust? And, if so, what of your thoughts? Dead. All dead. Truly, then, you are a modern man to think thus. Yes, I am, I am. I am not the foolish person of my parents and their parents. Or like those who follow me. They are foolish. They still believe in the old ways. I do not. And why do you not believe in the old ways? I no longer have a need for the old ways. Is that not enough?

Another shape dipped against the Southern Cross and the wind blew colder. He shivered and groped in the dark around him and found four small twigs. He broke them and made eight. Then he carefully laid one across the other to form a cross and placed them around him to the north, south, east, and west. He lay back down between the crosses and looked at the sky. The Southern Cross burned mockingly.

"But I do not believe in you," he whispered. The tiger roared an answer, and he lay awake and listened to the jungle noises around him.

Morgan, too, was listening to the noises of the jungle. He sat on the curious bench in the forgotten temple and the warm wind blew gently across his bare shoulders and chest.

The day had passed swiftly, stealing more time from him and leaving in its wake only shadows. Now, darkness covered him with soothing palms and the ancient stone figures seemed friendlier and more alive in this old holy place than the cold, pious relics of youthful Sunday schools. Sermons spoke from stones, sermons of old promises that had materialized centuries before and fulfilled the dreams and desires of meditators and worshipers asking for crops instead of fire engines and bicycles. Their spirits seemed to move about him now, but he felt no uneasiness about them for whichever way he looked in this country phantoms waited. Phantom soldiers, phantom farmers, warlords, Buddhists, Taoists, Hindus, the Cao Dais, fanatics and monks, phantoms all. But deep in the forests and high in the mountains the phantoms were more than the apparitions that haunted abandoned pagodas in the lowlands and temples in the highlands, they were physical phantoms felt in the early morning fog that caressed the face with clammy palms and the crisp nights that ran cold fingers down the spine.

Why are you here? What purpose do you serve? the phantoms asked in cold whispers that rubbed branches together and kept frightened soldiers awake and guessing in the dark hours before the gray dawn. What do you want here?

Reason vanished at times like this with frightened soldiers on guard against the phantoms and enemy alike while their friends pretended to sleep, but did not sleep and listened to the same branches rub against each other and the scurrying sound of mice that sounded like a soldier creeping through the brush in dead nights and the skeptics who did not believe this way died early with their twentieth-century misanthropisms proving inadequate shields for the bullet in the guts, the garrot around the neck, the knife in the kidneys, or the mortar fire that rained like hail around their ears.

Yet, it was this suspension of reason that Morgan marveled at. It was science falling back on alchemical days and medicine returning to the herbs and poultices of the shaman. It was magic and Wagnerian and dark rings of power that lay hidden in murky woods from time before man counted time. It was a time of simplicity and here, in this temple, Morgan was aware of that simplicity and took comfort in it. He heard the sound of mice scurrying and the whispers of the night air through the branches were soothing and comforting to him and allowed him to reflect back on tiny scenes that were important only now. He breathed deeply and tried to wish himself back into oneness with the ancient ones of the temple, but they were gone and now something padded quietly across the stone floor of the temple toward him. He tensed for a moment, then relaxed as he recognized Kai's chunky frame.

"It is a lonely place where you sit, Dai-uy," she panted as she approached.

"Yes," he answered. He breathed deeply and smelled the odors of the cookfire upon her. "I think on what is to come. Why do you come here?"

"The gods are still here and although forgotten by those who brought them here, they live still and must be honored. Is this not so?"

"It is so." He could barely see her face in the thin light, but he sensed something else behind her words and waited, patiently. Presently, she stirred.

"It is peaceful here, too, is it not, Dai-uy?"

"Yes. It is very peaceful and very lonely, and the gods watch us even now. But this is not why you have climbed to this place. What troubles you?"

Kai chuckled; it sounded like a rumble. "The old one was right; you are different from other Americans."

"You have known many?" he asked innocently, his tone suggesting more.

"Not in that manner," she laughed. "I am too old and too fat and too ugly. But I have known many men in my time before the Americans. And I have had much love and much pleasure. Shall I tell you of them, Dai-uy?"

"It is not necessary," he said quickly. "One can see you have lived richly."

"Richly. Yes, I have lived richly. But only with one man at a time. Do not make the mistake of thinking me a *coong-kenh*, Dai-uy. I do not carry knotted cords beneath my dress, and I have never had the dripping sickness."

"This one can see," he answered, slipping into formal speech with her.

"But I have known many men," she said proudly. "And all stayed with me until death."

"That is the mark of a good woman," Morgan said seriously. "You can be very proud to be able to say so much."

"Yes," she said sadly. "But the first was the best. There never was such a man as he. Strong like the buffalo and tender like the butterfly. There was some goat in him, too, but that is a private matter of which I cannot speak. Ahhh. It was always a pleasure to sleep with him. Even from the first when the pain is supposed to be there I felt no pain."

"You felt nothing?" Morgan asked.

"Yes, I felt the gods' fingers upon me and that happens rarely."

"Which gods? How did you know this?"

"You will know," she said. "There will be no mistake. It is like the big winds from the southeast and gentle like the first soft rains at the end of dusty summer. And then you will feel hollow and empty and your spirit will leave you and you will be aware of all things beautiful, the stars, the flowers, the sun, the moon. All of this you will feel and understand. Have you never felt this, Dai-uy?"

"Yes. I have felt this many times."

She shook her head. "No. You have never felt this. It happens only twice. You have never felt this or you would know."

"Perhaps," he said, trying not to smile. "Perhaps. But maybe the gods visit some more than others."

"No. It happens only twice."

"How will you know the second time? By virtue of the first?"

"By my death. That is how I will know the second time."

"The gods must be very busy this year," he said jokingly.

She grasped him by his knee and shook him roughly. "No, do not joke of it, Dai-uy. This is not a thing one takes lightly by making jokes of it."

"I am sorry," he said. "I did not know it was so important to you. I meant not to offend."

"You do not believe, Dai-uy?"

"No. There is nothing after death but empty blackness. No. I do not believe as you, but that is of no matter. In such things, each must believe as he will. That is the only thing of importance."

"You are a fool, Dai-uy," she said. She clapped her hands together softly. "You have a woman."

"No," he said, then strangely thought of Kate and a sharpness sliced through him. He frowned, wondering where the thought came from. Kai saw the way his eyes slipped for a moment into the past and smiled.

"I think you have a woman. And she waits for you. Is this not so?"

"No."

"She has been waiting long?" she asked stubbornly.

"No one waits for me."

"And you do not go to her?"

"There is no one."

"All things are simple, Dai-uy. It is man who makes them hard."

"There is no one," he repeated.

"Do not confuse love with need, Dai-uy," she said. She pointed toward a bright star in the south. "That star is beautiful and many have suffered much. Many around you have suffered much. Yet, the star is still beautiful and the reason it is beautiful is that none of this suffering has touched it. Do you understand?"

"You are reading much into what is not there," he said. "I have told you that there is no one. That is enough."

"But has her suffering touched her?" she asked. She leaned intently toward him. "Has her suffering touched her? That is the test of love; when the suffering touches her here." She touched her breast. "And here and here." She touched her belly and face.

"How can one know the answers to such questions?" he said. He began to feel annoyed. "Those are questions that never may be answered. Not all feel suffering, and still they love."

"Then, how do they know they love?" she said. She thought a moment, then asked. "Does she give of herself to you?"

"No more," he said firmly. "We will speak no more in this way. There is no one waiting for me. Enough has been said on this."

"But if someone did wait for you, why would she wait?"

He sighed. "Probably for pleasure. But there is no one."

"Which is the greater pleasure? The giving or the receiving?"

"Are they not both the same?"

"No, Dai-uy. They are not. You have much to learn before you can truly love," she said. "Of that, I am sure."

She moved away from him, and he listened as she walked carefully over the dead leaves and down the hill to the camp. The night sounds quieted as she passed, then resumed again, and he took comfort in the familiar sounds. He looked down the slope toward the camp and the flickering fire. He could see the men wrapped like cocoons against the cool air sleeping around the fire, and then the figure of Kai as she moved across the circle of light. He shivered as the breeze began to cool and the fire became warm and friendly as his flesh pebbled in anticipation of its warmth. But he remained in the temple. He felt a distance open between himself and those at the fire, and he wondered why this strange feeling should be with him at this time.

Because of the woman and her strange ways, he thought. To think that one must suffer to know love! Preposterous. One does not have to suffer to love, but rather love and suffer as you are suffering now with this separation. Ahhh! This is crazy thinking. When you remember Kate and Timmy you forget where you are and what you are. You want to remember too much of home, and it is very dangerous to remember too much of home while you are here. But it is very hard not to remember those things this time of year for Christmas at home is listening to Father's Glen Miller records and the Christmas songs of Hank Williams and Dean Martin and Frank Sinatra and listening to those records while it snows outside, and you are making popcorn balls and drinking hot cider or hot buttered rums in the kitchen where it is warm while the wind blows outside. And then at night, up in your room, when you lie beneath the heavy quilts— No, do not think about this. Think about something else. Think about how tomorrow will be a long day. A very long day and you will have to be firm with the old man for he does not think straight in this matter of his son. But who can blame him? The son should have been stillborn rather than do this which he has done to his people. And who's to blame for that? Try a thousand years of tribal warfare and twenty-five or thirty years of watching your land, your crops produce plunder that your sweat pours into a foreign land's coffers. What do you suppose you would do? I wouldn't betray my people. That, I would not do. That comes from confusing the enemy. And who is the enemy? He is and he has become corrupted with empty promises and you will have to kill him to destroy the corruption and then you will be corrupt because one cannot walk away from a killing of this sort. I will not kill him as a soldier but as an avenger and there is no glory or honor in that. There is truth, however, and there is duty, and the truth is in that duty which I owe to the old man. And the truth is also that there is no honor in this death for you, but there is for the old man and this is a thing that must be for the old man must live by his own ways and those ways also predict your life as well. And I will kill him for Billy.

The tiny scratchings of a lizard broke through his thoughts. He looked for the lizard in the darkness, but could not find it. He felt lonely and remembered the bottle of Scotch in his pack and rose and walked down the hill to it.

Chapter Twenty-three

Stephens rested quietly against his pack and watched the firelight dance over the sleeping figures and create a shimmering curtain against the trees. He saw Kai climb to the temple and return. Moments later, Morgan appeared and crossed to his pack and removed a bottle of Scotch. He went to the fire and sat cross-legged in front of it and drank from the bottle. The light from the fire danced over his bare chest and etched cruel lines of power in his face. He seemed to belong to the forest, and an uneasiness came over Stephens at the transformation in Morgan.

He belongs here and you're just visiting, he thought. I wonder how many men he has killed and if it bothers him in the night knowing how many men he has killed. He probably doesn't keep track and why should he? It is his job. But did he ever kill as I have killed? It bothers me. No, be truthful; the only time it bothers you is when you remember how and where and why you killed him and it is the fear that someone will find out that bothers you and not the right or wrong of the death. It is fear and the mistake you made in coming here because you thought it would be safer here than in Saigon, but you forgot about the helicopters that can come and lift you out and take you back to Saigon where they can try you and hang you. But this is silly because you can die just as easily here. Yes, you can die here, but it is the matter of death. The thought of a rope bothers you and the thought of twelve marksmen and the final bullet in the head bothers you. Here, it does not bother you. Perhaps it is the thought of the other death that makes this death one without much fear. He stirred uneasily. This is very dangerous. Think of something else. Do not think of the war and do not think of the dead Vietnamese in the river.

Morgan shifted his position slightly and lifted the bottle and drank from it. Stephens could hear the gurgle of the Scotch over the crackling of the fire.

He is secure. Composure plus knowledge makes us secure and this is why he can live this way. And loss of faith. Yes, that may be the most important thing as he is not concerned with the dreadful insecurity of the hereafter. That allows him to be brave for what fear does death hold for the man who recognizes it? None. But that does not mean that one should actively court it. So, where does he find his sanctuary? Where does he go when he thinks too much upon things man is not supposed to think about? Religion for some, but what of him? Booze? Books? Or, this isolation we have around us now?

He closed his eyes and strained to put himself in Morgan's place, but the warmth of the fire and his blanket plus the long march and Scotch were eager allies and he fell fast into a dreamless sleep.

There was no sun the next morning, just a thick sluggish fog that moved about them and investigated their faces, their bodies, with long, milk-white tentacles that whisked across the skin and left it feeling cold and clammy with a smell of mildew and decay. Morgan moved around the fire and squatted on his heels beside Stephens. He handed him a battered tin cup filled with thick, black coffee, then raised his own cup and sipped. He grunted appreciatively, sipped again, and nodded toward Stephens's pack.

"Ready to go?" he asked. He wore his black beret, stained and worn, cocked rakishly over one eye. His chin was stubbled with morning beard, but he held himself easily and his eyes were bright and clear. Stephens remembered the amount of Scotch he had seen him drink the night before and marveled at his recuperative powers. His own head had a dull ache to it.

"When will we move out?" he asked.

"Soon." Morgan blew on his coffee and sipped it with relish.

"Coffee's good this morning. The weather's responsible. Coffee always tastes better when it's rotten weather. Have you ever noticed that? There's an anesthetic quality to it that makes the outside mellow like the inside. And that's something that can't be freeze-dried." He shuffled closer to the fire without rising. His face hardened as he stared into the coals and ashes of the fire. Stephens noted the change and moved uneasily.

"Do you understand what happened to these people?"

"Some," Stephens said softly. "The old man's son sold him out."

"That's part of it," Morgan said. The problem is that we must do something about it."

"Go after the kid?"

"Yes," Morgan said. "We'll go after Bao."

"I see. And the orders? What about them?"

"They'll have to wait."

"Can I know why?"

"No. Not yet. I'm not sure you're ready."

"And if I refuse?" Stephens bit his lip as he watched Morgan's face soften and become serene, composed. He turned to Stephens, and Stephens looked into his eyes and felt the calm commitment and savage fire that glowed like banked fires beneath the serenity. Powerful forces were at work within him, and Stephens could feel the outer heat of their burning fire. It was a fire both magnetic and all-consuming and he could smell the sickeningly sweet odor of death and a thrill ran through the pit of his stomach, as he recognized it as one he had felt as a child suddenly accosted by foes several years older and knowing he was going to be beaten, and there was nothing he could do about it.

"You don't have a choice in the matter. You can come with us, or stay here. Frankly I'd come with us." He looked around the clearing. "It can become very lonely out here by yourself. Especially at night." He smiled softly. "Of course, there's always the other. I could offer you a field court-martial. But then, you know, there can only be one verdict there, don't you?"

The funny thing is that he will kill me. Stephens thought, and none of the others will even blink an eye because he is the

Dai-uy and whatever the Dai-uy says will be. The others would not stop him, but they would not help him, either. It's sort of like Kipling's wolf pack, something the leader has to do himself. The question is, could you take him? No, I don't think you could. You might hurt him, but you would be very dead by the time it was finished. He swallowed a mouthful of coffee to ease the dryness of his throat and looked at Morgan.

"I don't think that will be necessary," he said. He tried to smile and surprised himself with the effort.

"This isn't Saigon," Morgan cautioned, and Stephens's smile widened. If only he knew he'd said the right thing.

"You might be surprised," Stephens said. "You really might be surprised."

Morgan arched his eyebrow in question, but Stephens pretended not to notice and threw the dregs of his coffee upon the fire. He rose and hitched his pants higher on his hips.

"I've got to take a leak," he said. He took a step toward the brush at the edge of the clearing and stopped as Nguyen Duc hurried up to Morgan.

"Dai-uy," he said, and smiled. His eyes danced with glee and Stephens waited to see what had made the old man so excited.

"Dai-uy! There is one who wishes to speak with you."

"Who is it, old man? Is something wrong?" Morgan placed his cup on the ground and picked up his Thompson.

"No. It is very good. Dai-uy. He has brought others with him." Nguyen Duc could hardly contain his excitement.

"Others?" Morgan's brow furrowed anxiously. "How many? From where?"

"Like us, Dai-uy! They, too, have lost their village to the dogs from the north."

"Get your weapon," Morgan said softly to Stephens. "The old man says that some people have come to join us because their village has been destroyed. This is too convenient. It might be a trap." Stephens nodded and hurried to his pack. Morgan turned back to the old man.

"Bring the one who wishes to speak to me here," Morgan

said. "Watch the others carefully for it is strange that this should happen at this time."

"The gods are smiling upon you, Dai-uy," the old man said. He fidgeted at Morgan's skepticism.

"Yes, but which gods, old man?" Morgan said, then relented. He smiled gently at the old man. "Watch the others carefully until we are certain of why this one has come here. Remember that the gods may smile, but life always ends in death."

"*Eeeah.*" Nguyen Duc slapped himself on his forehead. "Because I am impatient I am careless. It shall be as you say, Dai-uy." He hurried away and Morgan turned to Stephens.

"I don't know about this," he said, and pulled thoughtfully at his earlobe.

"A coincidence?" Stephens asked.

"Coincidences don't happen in the jungle," Morgan said. "Everything is a part of everything. Remember that. It's your first lesson."

Nguyen Duc hurried toward them with a thin, wrinkled old man and Morgan nodded at the opposite side of the fire and said to Stephens, "Sit there and watch all around."

"Anything in particular?" Stephens asked and obediently walked around the fire and knelt on one knee.

"For anything," Morgan said under his breath, then raised his voice to greet the old man. "*Chao ba*! Welcome to our camp. What brings you here?"

The old man stared hungrily at Morgan's cup of coffee on the ground and Morgan bent and handed it to him with a smile. The old man took it and drank greedily, then sighed.

"*Cam on ong*," he said. His voice was thin and reedy. "We have been without food for three days."

"Bring food," Morgan said over his shoulder, keeping his eyes on the old man. Kai silently appeared and handed the old man a bowl of stew. He squatted on his heels beside the fire and began to eat rapidly with his fingers.

"What happened to you?" Morgan asked. He squatted beside the old man, but carefully kept the Thompson between them.

Nguyen Duc moved to the old man's right and squatted also.

"They came at sunrise three days ago," the old man said. "There was a loud explosion in the middle of our village, and then they were among us. Some of the young ones fought back, but they did not have rifles and were easily killed. We ran into the forest and hid. Soon, they tired of looking for us and returned to our village and—" The old man's voice faltered and tears formed in his eyes. "Then we heard the women begin to scream and knew what they were doing to our women, but there was nothing we could do but listen to the women scream and the children cry."

He fell silent and stared at his half-empty plate. Morgan heard Nguyen Duc shift uneasily, sympathetically, beside him, but he did not turn to him.

"And then they killed the women and children?" he said softly.

"Yes. All. And burned our homes."

"And what do you wish me to do?"

The old man wiped the tears from his eyes with the back of his hand and ran his hand over his dirty cotton shirt. "Let us come with you."

"Why?"

"We will fight with you and kill those who have done this thing to us," the old man said fiercely.

"You did not fight before," Morgan said. His voice grew hard and cold. "Why should I believe you would fight now? Go back to your village, old man, and rebuild your homes. Here are only warriors who have much fighting left in them. We do not need those who hide and then speak of bravery."

The old man's eyes flashed, and he rose to his feet. Morgan watched him warily. "We do not have a place to return to," he said. "Our young men and women are dead. We are too old for children, but we are not too old to fight if we have something with which to fight. But we have nothing except ourselves. Everything was taken from us."

"What was the name of your village?" Morgan asked.

"Ban Ho."

"I know of this village, Dai-uy," Nguyen Duc said. "It is north in the Mountains-Like-Elephants near the border. It is not a Rand village, but they are hill people."

"There are refugee camps to the south," Morgan said. "You would be safe there."

The old man drew himself up proudly and stared disdainfully at Morgan. "We are Montagnards, not farmers," he said. "If you do not want us, we shall go elsewhere."

"Dai-uy, the people of this village are not cowards. They fought the Japanese and helped smuggle arms and ammunition over the border during that war. Many times the Japanese tried to stop them, but they could not. They are not cowards, Dai-uy. They have learned the truth of suffering." Nguyen Duc looked at him anxiously. Morgan slowly nodded.

"Your advice has always been good, old man," he said. "And since they are without a village they may come with us who, too, are without a village." He turned to the old man. "How many do you have with you?" he asked.

"Seventeen," the old man said.

"And women?"

"Twelve."

"Bring them to the fire," Morgan said. "They shall eat, and then we travel north. Nguyen Duc shall be above you, but you will not be forgotten in our councils. You understand?"

"Yes, Dai-uy," the old man said. "So shall it be."

"Good. How are you called?"

"Trien Da."

"Bring your people to the fire, Trien Da. And welcome."

He nodded and hurried away and Morgan turned to Nguyen Duc.

"You have enough for them?" he asked.

"Yes, Dai-uy. Some will have to carry the old weapons, but each can be armed."

"Good," Morgan said. "Do not make them carry any packs until tomorrow for they must regain their strength. But tomorrow, they will share alike with the rest."

"It shall be as you say, Dai-uy," Nguyen Duc said. "These

Wanderers may teach us something as well. You would do well to remember that, Dai-uy. Although a man may be a Wanderer, he does exist and in all existence there is knowledge." He turned away to make the arrangements. Stephens stood and walked around the fire to stand next to Morgan. He shook his head.

"Looks like you're leading a gray brigade," he said.

"Don't count them out," Morgan said. "We may be better off this way."

"Why's that?"

"They understand loyalty and not one of them is here for a political reason. They've all lost their homes, and that is all that matters to them," Morgan said. "Better get your things together. We'll move out as soon as they're fed."

Stephens suddenly remembered his swollen bladder and moved to the end of the clearing and turned his back to the fire. Steam rose from his urine, and he thought about how hot it would be by midday, and he would remember how cold it was this morning this high up, and that would make the heat more bearable.

But you will have to be very careful not to think too hard on it for that would be daydreaming with a skill-saw in your hand, he told himself.

"Ready?"

The voice seemed so close to him in the fog that he jumped, then hurriedly finished and returned to his pack. He slipped his arms through the straps and eased the weight so it rested in the middle of his spine. He picked up his rifle and looked around the clearing.

The new men had finished eating and now waited patiently to move out. Some carried crossbows and others rifles, and Stephens marveled how quickly Nguyen Duc had organized them for the march. They seemed to belong, and then he realized with a start that they did belong. They were united through loss, a homeless band.

He saw Morgan heading his way and bent and picked up the radio.

"Have you checked your ammunition?" Morgan asked. He

smiled thinly at Stephens's mystified expression and reached for his rifle. He removed the clip and then worked the bolt and caught the cartridge as it flipped in the air. He placed the cartridge back in the clip, reloaded, and worked the bolt again.

"The brass sometimes swells in this humidity, and that will cause a jam. The bolt will pull the head of the cartridge off when it recoils, and then you'll have the most expensive club in the world," he explained patiently. "But you won't know that because you'll be dead."

"I'll remember," Stephens said. "Anything else?"

"Yes. Stay in the middle of the column in front of Kai and the rest of the women. I don't want anything to happen to that radio." Morgan checked the ammunition in his pistol and Thompson while he talked.

"Where will you be?" Stephens asked, slightly annoyed at being placed in the middle of the column with the women.

"I'll be around," Morgan said, and suddenly grinned. His eyes sparkled and he tightened his garrison belt then jumped lightly to be sure nothing rattled. "I really do need you with the radio. We lose that, and we're in big trouble."

"It's okay," Stephens said. "I can be a hero some other time."

"They're dead," Morgan said. He turned and walked away, rocking lightly from heel-to-toe. He disappeared in the fog. The others rose silently and followed him. Stephens fell in in front of Kai. She gave him a thin smile, but her black eyes were humorless, and Stephens could feel them staring steadily at his back. Then the column began to move rapidly, and he forgot about her as he concentrated on the man's back in front of him and followed him down the mountain and out of the fog. He paused as the sun suddenly appeared and marveled at the green hills that lay before him like Aztec pyramids. Then he groaned as he realized he would soon be climbing them and the weight of the radio seemed to double.

Chapter Twenty-four

Morgan could feel the heavy pack on his back, and the sweat trickling from under his beret down through the five-day stubble on his cheeks and chin. The straps of the pack chafed his shoulders. His bloodshot eyes burned from lack of sleep, but his mind refused to relax as he moved alertly along the tiny game trail curling through heavy undergrowth beside a narrow creekbed. No breeze stirred the thick and muggy air among the heavy leaves as they drooped over the trail and filtered the sun's rays and cast dappled shadows on the forest floor. It was quiet, very quiet, too quiet. The noises had stopped many minutes ago, and Morgan knew it had not been his party that had alarmed the monkeys and the birds. There had been something else. A predator? Probably not. The noises had not returned and the noises always returned after a predator had passed. The danger, Morgan knew, was still here now, and he was a part of the danger. His flesh felt cold despite the heat, and he was aware of the many smells, sweet flowers and rotting leaves. He could hear the tiny scratchings of lizards and mice burrowing themselves deeply into piles of leaves and twigs as he passed. A bee buzzed about him, and he automatically noted the direction of its flight for that would be the direction in which they would find fresh water. But all this took only a second, and then he was concentrating on the dusty trail in front of him, the thick vines trailing from the banyan and teak trees, and the thick branches above the trail.

Ahead, the trail bent around the huge, gnarled roots of a giant banyan tree and Morgan slipped into the shade beneath a cluster of ferns. He studied the bend carefully. Something disturbed him about the trail, the bend, and he did not know what it was. He frowned; it could be anything, a branch bending the wrong way, a misplaced shadow, anything. He was thirsty and the thought of the bee and what the bee meant made him thirstier.

You will ignore this thirst for it is a mark of carelessness and the gods first make careless those they wish to destroy.

The muscles in his legs began to quiver, but he willed them still, and began to quarter the trail and bend with his eyes. Carefully, he examined each branch, each leaf, the path itself. He slowly turned his head and looked at the trail behind him, then quickly to the front. Then he saw it: the trail was too smooth, the dust too even. He narrowed his eyes thoughtfully, and then he saw the tiny brush marks where someone had brushed the trail clean.

He smiled thinly to himself. He checked the Thompson, then stepped out of the shadow and stopped, his muscles taut and quivering with tension. He followed the path of sweepings with his eyes to the roots of the banyan tree and saw where a patch of bark had been carelessly broken by—by what?

Quickly, he looked to the first branches of the tree and found an irregular shadow crouched in the darkness of the heavy branches. Without thinking, he raised the Thompson and reflexively fired a short burst at the shadow. He threw himself flat in the dust beneath the ferns. Something cracked inches above his head and was followed by a strangled cry. The shadow fell through the leaves and branches to the ground. Morgan rose and rushed in a crouch to the side of the shadow.

A young man dressed in camouflage clothing gasped for breath. His face and black hair were gray from the trail's dust. A thin line of blood trickled from his mouth. He opened his eyes and stared at Morgan and grimaced and tried to spit, but the movement made the pain too great and he gasped and his black eyes rolled back in his head until the whites showed.

"No, you don't, you bastard," Morgan muttered, and kicked him sharply on his right elbow. The man hissed like an adder and tried to move, but his legs stayed twisted beneath him, and Morgan knew his lower limbs were paralyzed. He heard a noise behind him and whirled and dropped smoothly to one knee. Thompson ready. He relaxed as Nguyen Duc, followed by Stephens, anxiously appeared. The old man looked around quickly but carefully, then, satisfied there was no imminent danger, walked to Morgan and the man on the ground. He looked at Morgan and Morgan smiled.

"From the tree," he said. "But he was careless when he built his nest."

"We heard two different guns," the old man said.

"I was careless, too," Morgan replied. "But not as careless as he."

"*Eeeah*. It was very bad to be so careless. But you were too long in Saigon, and it is to be expected. Who is this filth?" He gestured contemptuously at the figure on the ground.

"I believe he is one for whom we search," Morgan said.

The old man frowned and said quickly. "He is not from my village."

"No. I did not mean that. I meant those who bring the white powder down from the north. Those for whom we also search."

The old man blinked and looked hard at Morgan. "You have come this way looking for two?" Morgan nodded. The old man's face grew sad. "But you did not tell me this."

"Would you have come if I had told you this?" Morgan asked.

"No. But you should have told me this," the old man said. He shook his head. "The truth makes life beautiful in all of its purity. The gates to life are knowledge. If you hide that, you do not walk through the gates and wander forever in despair."

"We have lost nothing by coming this way," Morgan said patiently. "Had we found he-who-was-your-son, he would by lying here now. But we did not. We found this one first." But even as he spoke he knew he had lost something with the old man for he could see the tension in the old man's shoulders, the deep concern in his eyes.

"This was not right, Dai-uy," the old man said. "I should have been told. Even if the others were not told, you should have told me. So long as brothers gather often and frequently and honor is shown to the elders of experience, then there is delight even in a life of solitude but more so among brothers."

"You are right," Morgan said, sighing. "I should have told you this. But, I did not expect to find this one and the others first."

"You searched for he-who-was-my-son first?" the old man asked anxiously, and Morgan knew it was important that he give the old man the answer that he wanted.

"Yes," he said. "Yes, I searched for him first. I had hoped that we could then look for the dung that lies at my feet. But, the gods have decided that this dung must come first. So, we have him and not the other."

Satisfied, the old man nodded. "But you still should have told me." He squatted next to the young man and stared at him carefully. "But he wears no insignia." He nudged the young man's chin with the barrel of his rifle. "Filth. Defecation of your mother's womb, to whom do you belong?"

The man mumbled something and tried to grin. His teeth were stained red with blood. Morgan moved to his side and found where one of the .45 caliber slugs had entered through his groin and torn off his left buttock when it emerged. He took the dah from its scabbard, knelt, and sliced the man's pants and peeled them back from the wound. His penis had been severed and the testicles blown back into the wound.

"Jesus," Stephens breathed. Morgan looked up at him then at the old man. He shrugged and flipped the pants back over the lost manhood and looked at the man who had stared at him through the examination.

"He will not live long, and he does not understand you," Morgan said to the old man. The black eyes flickered, and Nguyen Duc shook his head.

"He understands, Dai-uy. He is just being foolishly brave." He turned back to the wounded man. "Speak and we will give you medicine that will make the pain go away. Why do you sit in the tree like a vulture? Who owns your black soul?"

The wounded man looked at Nguyen Duc with contempt and hawked and spat. The red-tinged glob struck the old man's face, and Morgan rose and stepped back hurriedly as he tried to spit again.

"American jackal," he whispered. Morgan could barely understand him. "I piss in the milk of your mother, and dogs vomit your father's testicles."

"Strong words, but foolish words," Nguyen Duc said. He wiped the spittle from his face and craned his head to look at the sky. "The day is young yet, and it will get much hotter in this place of no breeze. You will go nowhere, and we are very patient. We will wait in case you should wish to change your mind about the medicine. We are not barbarians."

"I piss in the wombs of your sisters, and they will produce others like you."

"Very foolish," the old man said, and shook his head sadly. "You will be not pissing or having children again. You are like the eunuch. Think on this. But do not think too long as the day grows hotter, and your blood is food for the ants. Look: even now they crawl to feast on your flesh."

He scooped a handful of dust from between the man's legs and dropped it on his chest. Tiny red ants scampered wildly across the wounded man's chest and for the first time fear flickered in his eyes.

"Kill me," he whispered. "Kill me."

"Kill you?" The old man laughed. "You are already dead. The question is how long before the gods take your soul. We will wait."

He moved to the side of the trail and squatted in the shade of the tree's roots and watched the wounded man.

"Dai-uy, I am very thirsty, and my canteen is empty. Would you have some water left?"

"There is some nearby," Morgan said, remembering the bee. He gestured to his right. "Over there, somewhere. I saw a bee fly that way before this one tried to shoot me," he added to the old man's quizzical look.

"I'll take a look," Stephens said. He shrugged off the radio and placed it in the shade beside the old man and took the old man's canteen and Morgan's before hurrying in the direction Morgan had indicated. He was glad to get away from the dying man, but there was a part of him, too, that wanted to stay and watch.

He found the water about fifty meters down the trail, a small stream that bubbled merrily over two moss-covered rocks. He filled the two canteens and returned.

"Ahh." Nguyen Duc gratefully took the canteen from Stephens's hands and sniffed at its mouth. "Fresh, cool water for an old man. Thank you very much!" He raised the canteen and tilted it so the water ran into his mouth.

The wounded man suddenly screamed, and Morgan nearly dropped the canteen as he turned. The figure weakly brushed at the ants clustered around his wound.

"Shit," Stephens said in awe. Tiny muscles clenched and unclenched at his jawline. He looked at Morgan. "We gonna do something?"

Morgan shook his nead and nodded at the old man. "It's his show." He shrugged. "Look at it this way: it could be you lying there."

"And I hope someone would put a bullet in my head," Stephens said. He took a firm grip on his rifle and took a step forward only to be brought up short by Morgan's hand on his arm.

"Stay out of this," Morgan said warningly. "The old man knows what he is doing. We need that information, and we don't have the time to try and talk it out of him."

"So, you're going to let the pain do your work for you?" Stephens shook his head. "That ain't civilized."

"Sir."

"What?" Stephens gave him a blank look.

"Sir. It ain't civilized, sir. Don't forget who you are just because we're out here in the jungle," Morgan said lowly. "Now, take a drink of water and tend to the radio and leave the prisoner to Nguyen Duc."

Stephens stared hard into Morgan's eyes, hot words on the edge of his lips. Then he dropped his eyes and stepped across the trail to sit in the shade beside the radio. He took a drink of water from his canteen, then pretended to examine the radio, dusting off grains of sand.

"The young boy is worried about the offal?" the old man asked Morgan.

Morgan nodded. "Yes."

"It is good that he worries for he will remember what this man looks like and that will not make him as careless as his youth would otherwise," the old man said.

"Perhaps," Morgan answered. "But, why not kill him? He is finished." He glanced at the figure as the man screamed again in pain.

"He has not made the trade I offered him," the old man said loudly for the figure to hear. "I have offered him medicine for information, but he wishes to try and impress us with his foolish bravery when there are none here who care for his bravery."

"But have we not waited long enough?" Morgan said. The man screamed again, the sound echoing through the trees.

"Not much longer, Dai-uy," Nguyen Duc promised. The figure coughed, and his eyes opened, seeking them out.

"I—was—to guard—for those who come," he gasped through clenched teeth.

Nguyen Duc rose and crouched beside his head. He seized the man's hair and rocked his head back and forth.

"When?" he demanded. "When do these you wait for come?" He shook the head again and the man licked his lips and tried to speak. A croak slipped from his throat, and Morgan wiped the sweat from his eyes and watched as Nguyen Duc swore and unscrewed the cap from his canteen and let a few drops dribble onto the wounded man's lips. He poured some water on the man's wound, washing the ants away temporarily.

"See?" he said softly. "We are honorable men. First, the water." He poured a little water into his hand and bathed the man's face. "Later, the medicine." His voice was firm and kind. Morgan watched, amazed as the man opened his eyes and stared gratefully at Nguyen Duc. The arrogance was gone.

Strange how pain can make a man see his enemy as his father, Morgan thought. Is he asking for forgiveness? Perhaps. More likely, though, he is seeking comfort from the pain and it is this desire to be free from pain that makes a man see his enemies as his friends.

"Tomorrow," he gasped. "They come—tomorrow."

"Who?" The old man leaned closer. "Quickly. The medicine is here. Who?"

"I—do not know. I—was told—to guard path—superiors—please—" He closed his eyes against a sudden stab of pain as the ants began to work again in his wound.

The old man sighed, and stood. He looked at Morgan and shrugged his shoulders.

"I do not believe he can tell us anything more, Dai-uy."

"Ask him about his unit. Where it is stationed, how many there are, the arms and supplies." Morgan squatted on his heels and shook a cigarette from a package of Salems. He looked at the bent and dampened cigarette sourly, then lit it and drew the cool smoke into his lungs as he watched Nguyen Duc lean closer to the man to hear the faint whisper. The old man gave his hair a fond jerk and rose to his feet.

"He is from the Thirty-third Regiment," he said. "His unit is at Ha Tinh now for resupplying. They have roughly six hundred men and several field mortars. He was detached from them along with twelve others to guide a party down through the mountains two weeks ago. He and three others moved ahead to guard the trail."

"When will the party arrive?" Morgan asked.

"Tomorrow."

"And there is nothing else to be gained?"

"I do not think so, Dai-uy. He knows not the names or what they carry."

Morgan frowned. "They carry things, then?"

"Yes. Many packages like a brick, Dai-uy." The old man indicated the size with his hands.

"Very good, old man," Morgan said. "Give him the medicine."

Morgan turned to go as Nguyen Duc drew a machete from its scabbard. He glanced at the figure on the ground and noted how its eyes widened as realization hit the numbed brain. Then, he heard the blade descend and the solid chunk! as the blade bit through tendons and sinews and buried itself deep into the dust. He turned back to the old man.

"Stake the head here," he said, and dug a depression with his heel. "Then, move the body down the trail ten paces and place grenades beneath it." He looked at the decaptitated body and shook his head.

"War is a terrible thing, Dai-uy." Nguyen knelt beside the body and went through the pockets and handed Morgan three letters and a picture. Morgan looked at the young, pretty woman, almost a girl, smiling at the camera. She held a young child on her knee. The child looked as if it did not know whether to cry or not. The old man handed him a wristwatch, and Morgan turned it over and read the inscription on the back: "Capt. H. L. Dunlevy. Happy Birthday. Julie."

"Yes, old man," Morgan said. "War is terrible. But necessary. Very necessary. Do you not agree?"

Nguyen Duc rose and took the head by the hair. He carried it to the depression in the dust and laid it there, then shrugged off his pack and dropped it in the shade of the overhanging ferns.

"Yes, Dai-uy, it is necessary. But it is still terrible because it becomes a necessity. When one grows up with the war, then one must always have it." He looked off into the distance and shook his head. "This is what is for me, but it is not what should be for you. You should go home. Dai-uy. Go back to those who love you. You do not want to be like me."

"I must stay," Morgan said. "You know this."

"Yes, I know this. And it is terrible."

"But not terrible that this should die." He nudged the body with his toe.

"Yes, Dai-uy. That is the necessity of war."

"I wish I could believe that," Morgan said in English.

The old man's brow knitted in puzzlement. "I do not understand, Dai-uy."

"I am sorry. Please tend to the business of the pole and grenades. I must use the radio."

"*Eeeah*. It shall be as you say, Dai-uy." He watched fondly as Morgan moved toward Stephens and the radio.

It would be nice to have the Dai-uy for a son, he thought. He is becoming more and more like a son. Soon, there will be nothing left of the American, but only the Dai-uy and that is both good and bad for the Dai-uy will lose all that he is. But think of what he will become. Yes, think of that. At least, he will live an honest life and will no longer forget to tell you what he is thinking. Already he thinks like a Montagnard and soon he will be one of you and then our people will learn and prosper. It will be good to make the Dai-uy the head man. Much good for all.

But, he frowned to himself, he thinks too much on things like this and that is very bad. It will do him no good to think too much on things of this sort. That is the way of madness. There is no reason to think about things that have to be. That has already been written and there is nothing that a man can do to change what has been written. *Eeeah*. You should tell the Dai-uy of this. Yes, tell him tonight. He glanced at Stephens, regarding him thoughtfully. But there is even more of the Dai-uy in the young man. There is more of the Rand in him, I think. The Dai-uy still thinks much of the men in Saigon while this one thinks only of where he is. This is something to think upon.

The old man drew his machete and disappeared into the growth behind the trail. He hummed a half-forgotten song from his childhood while he searched for a pole. For the first time in many weeks, he was happy.

Chapter Twenty-five

Morgan found Stephens hunkered beneath the shade of a thorn bush next to the trail. He hugged his knees as he watched Morgan approach. "That was pretty harsh, sir," he said as Morgan stopped beside him, tugging his canteen out of its pouch. He stood, brushing himself off. "I don't think the Geneva Convention boys would like that."

"The Geneva Convention isn't out here," Morgan said. "It stopped somewhere in Saigon. Probably bogged down with all the pedicab and rickshaw drivers and shoeshine boys who cut your femoral artery when they begin to shine your shoes." He paused to take a sip from his canteen. "What we did was necessary. The same thing would have happened if the roles were reversed, and you were lying there in place of that man."

"Except I wouldn't be hauling drugs up to the north," Stephens said. "Tell me: was it because he was a soldier that you let the old man do that or because he was a drug runner?"

"That's bothering you?"

"It doesn't you?"

"Yes and no. I've seen how the Viet Cong leave the American wounded. Usually, they cut off the American's dick and shove it into his mouth while he's still alive. Then, they use him for bayonet practice. Whatever torture you can think up, these people have already practiced. They like to maim because they believe that they will not enter paradise if parts of their bodies are severed. You don't have to like what we do out here, just accept it."

"It's accepted," Stephens said. He shook his head. "I don't like it, that's for sure, but I accept it. But what scares me is that I understand it."

"Okay," Morgan said. His face softened. "Just remember there is no such thing as the noble enemy. That's an invention of Hollywood." He glanced at his watch. "Set up the radio. I want to send a message at sixteen hundred hours."

"You got it," Stephens said, rising and picking up the radio. He glanced around him. "I don't know about the trees, here. But, we'll give it a shot."

"Just get it," Morgan said.

Stephens tossed him a half-salute and shouldered the radio and climbed up and over the bank, hesitated, then began to work his way back into the jungle, searching for a small clearing.

Morgan turned and saw Kai squatting across from him, watching them with amused, dark eyes. He smiled and stepped to her side and dropped to his heels. He pulled the black beret from his head; it was soggy from his sweat.

"You are amused," he said.

She smiled and spat a bright-red stream of betel juice on the ground. "Americans. Paugh. The young one does not like what was done to that one?" She tossed her head at the body stretched out on the trail.

Morgan shook his head. "No. Nor do I. I do what is necessary. That is all. And, although he is young, he understands what must be done. You do not like Americans?"

She shook her head. "No. It is because of them that the Viet Cong came to my village and destroyed it."

"No," Morgan answered. "They came to your village and destroyed it because it was what they do. If they can make other villages afraid, then they will have won."

"But they chose my village because the Americans had been there," Kai said, shaking her head. "No, I do not like the Americans. They should have stayed in their country and left this one to the Vietnamese. But," she said, softening, "it is good that you are here, Dai-uy." She glanced to where Stephens had disappeared. "And if it is as you say with the young one, then it is very good that he is here, too."

"I too am an American, though," he said mildly.

She shook her head vigorously. "No. You are the Dai-uy. You are more of us than them."

"But still, I am an American, and you speak of Americans as if they were like the eel that hides in the mud," Morgan said. "When you speak like this, I am insulted."

"No, do not take insult, Dai-uy," she said. "But I have seen many Americans, and I have seen how they fight and what is important to them. I tell you they would rather be chasing whores in Saigon than doing that for which they came. They seek too much pleasure to be of any use to us. Except for the young one."

"But they bring supplies and guns and ammunition, and they teach you how to fight," Morgan said. "How then, can you say they do nothing for you?" He was beginning to enjoy the argument. He took off his beret and wiped his face with it and placed it in his lap. He took out the crumpled pack of cigarettes and offered her one. She took it and placed it in her mouth. He lit it for her. She sucked the smoke hungrily into her lungs and blew it out slowly, sighing.

"I will grant you the supplies, Dai-uy," she said grudgingly. "But to teach us to fight? Teach the cobra to strike, the tiger to spring! We have been fighting for hundreds of years! What can you teach us in this? No, Dai-uy, the Americans may bring us supplies, but they do nothing else. They do not know the jungle, they do not know the mountains. They are men of the city, and their blood has gone weak from whores and drink, and their hands are soft and their eyes lazy."

"Why do you speak like this?" Morgan asked.

A sad smile played at her lips. She shook her head and took a deep puff on the cigarette, letting the smoke trickle out through her broad nostrils. "I am fat and old and ugly, Dai-uy, but this does not mean that I am stupid or useless. Only the farmers will win, Dai-uy. Only the farmers. They are of the earth and the only immortals. It is the land that makes them so, Dai-uy. That is what is important. The land. Americans do not think of this but only of thought that flows through empty spaces. They have lost the reason for being and that is the land. You think of things like this, too, Dai-uy. But the young one," she paused, shaking her head, "I do not think he thinks like this, I do not think he has thoughts like this."

"You speak in riddles. This does not answer my question," Morgan said impatiently, but Kai reached out and touched his knee, stopping him.

"Americans do not understand that they cannot defeat that which is not visible," she said. "They do not live and become a part of us, but stay in the safety of their camps and come out for brief battles then retreat back into their camps. They will fight here until they capture a hill, a temple, then go back to the safety of their camps and lick their wounds and beat their breasts and cry about how mighty they are in battle. But the hill, the temple, is lost as soon as they leave, and if there is a village next to the hill, the temple, an example will be made of the people of that village, and the Americans will return and tear their hair and cry, 'What beasts these Viet Cong are!' But no one of the village will hear because they will be all dead, their heads piled in the center of the village and the homes destroyed so no name will live on. But the land will remain, and those that were there will become a part of that land and the horror that made them a part of the land will be forgotten."

"How can you forget piles of heads and babies torn from dying mothers' wombs?" Morgan asked. He shrugged his pack from his shoulders and placed it on the ground behind him, leaning against it. He opened his shirt to cool his chest and pulled the metal flask from a pocket on the side of his trouser leg, "I have seen this, and I cannot forget them."

"I too have seen this, and I will never forget what I have seen," she said. "But I was not meant to see. This was an accident of men and so the horror will live through me and her." She gestured at the young woman squatting silently a few feet away. "It will live through her as well and her children and her children's children, but it will not be the same by then because they will not have seen it and this is the only way such horror will live with us. In stories. And as the stories grow older, the horror becomes less. But, you were meant to see the horror, Dai-uy, because you were meant to carry it with you. And others, too, were meant to see it because such horror is much more to the Americans than it is to us. For us, it is only the matter of the moment. For the Americans, it affects them forever."

"You are a rare woman, Kai," Morgan said. "Perhaps I should sleep with you," he teased.

"Aiee." She laughed with pleasure and hit him hard on the arm like a man. "You are used to weak women of the city. Even now, as old as I am, I would be too much for you. But there was a time, Dai-uy, there was a time."

The old man hurried up to them and looked suspiciously from one to the other. "There was a time for what, old woman? Must you hammer at our senses with what is in the past?"

"I speak for the Dai-uy's ears," Kai said disdainfully. "Must you always listen like a lover of boys where things do not concern you?"

"Your father," he said, and used an epithet Morgan had not heard.

"Your mother," she answered and spat.

"Quiet," Morgan said. They fell silent and glared at each other. "Old one, have you finished that which I asked?"

"Yes, Dai-uy," he held his nose between thumb and forefinger and blew. "I hope many stand around when they move the body. I used five grenades."

"And you never blew yourself up? This is indeed a day of wonder," Kai said. Her voice was heavy with sarcasm, and Nguyen Duc flushed deeply.

"No, but I know where I may place one to do the people and the gods the greatest favor," he said. "Your gate would at last be satisfied."

"As your stalk could never," she answered.

"Stop it," Morgan said. His voice was quiet, but they heard the command in it and obediently turned to him.

"Move back two kilometers to where this trail joins the one that follows the sun," Morgan directed. "There, you will make camp. Leave two men here and two more half back. They will watch for those that come by this trail."

"There is no water there, Dai-uy," the old man objected. "If we are to do this thing that you think of we will need water."

"Take two men with you to the water ahead and fill all canteens and water bottles," Morgan said. "You will sweep their footprints from the trail while they return. Be quick. I do not want any traveling on this trail at night. The forest must be normal so those who come will not be alarmed."

The old man nodded and hurried down the trail, calling for two others to gather the canteens and water bottles and follow him.

"You will kill those who come by this trail?" Kai asked somberly.

"Yes," Morgan squatted on his heels and pulled a map from the battered leather map case and spread it out on the ground. He traced a trail from Dong Hai into the mountains of Laos and down until it recrossed the border above Dak To. His finger stopped where he figured they were and, holding his finger on that spot, he retraced the trail north, carefully studying the topographic lines on either side of the trail. The lines were very close together and showed that the terrain was very steep and allowed few places for a party to leave the trail and follow a different route.

Yes, he thought, they will still be on this trail if the map does not lie. Remember the lieutenant who swore your village was not where it was because the mountains were too steep? That is the problem with these old French maps. Sometimes, they lie and usually at the wrong time and someone dies because a surveyor or cartographer could not trouble himself to take careful measurements. But this time, the map feels correct and even if it is not, the party will probably take the easiest route because they will not be warriors and will trust those warriors who guide them to take care of them. They will be careless by the time they reach here as the trail will have been long and the forest will no longer amuse them as they remember the women and beer and parties they left behind and the women and beer and parties that wait ahead of them. They will be impatient by the time they reach here and those who should know better will not care anymore and will be anxious to be through with this assignment because it has shortened their leave and they, too, will be thinking about what their comrades will be doing and they will resent their superiors who have made them guide this party of complainers. But there may be a professional with them and you must remember that there are those who do not need rest and do not like time away from the fighting and if the commander is a man of wisdom, he will send such a man with the others to keep them believing that they are soldiers and not like those they are guiding.

He folded the map and returned it to the map case and rose to his feet. He looked around carefully and noted the places of concealment.

We will place a claymore mine here to spray down the trail. One man will wait behind that log, another in those vines, and a third in the heavy brush above on that bank to fire down upon them with the machine gun after the mine is exploded. They will turn and run back toward that large banyan tree and I will wait there with Stephens and they will be stopped on the flanks and rear.

He turned and looked behind him where the trail bent around a thicket.

The old man and two others should be able to hold that with hand grenades and rifles, but I think the soldiers will be dead before they get that far. Yes, it will be a fine ambush.

"Dai-uy?" He turned to Kai and, happy with his plans, smiled at her. "It will not distress you to kill these men?"

The smile disappeared from his face. "I have killed many before, and it is not right to talk of these things before they happen."

She hesitated, then shrugged and spoke, "I am sorry, Dai-uy, but is this not that which you said would come last? What of the old man's son and the promise you made to him? Does that not come first before this?" she asked. Concern showed itself in the tiny frown lines between her eyes.

"I have spoken with the old man and told him why this must come first," Morgan said. He sighed. "There are promises that have been made by the people in Saigon who will give a province to the hill people if we do this thing for them, and keep the passes of the north closed to others that may follow them. For doing this which they cannot do, the hill people will be considered equal with the people in Saigon. Besides, I will kill a rabid dog any time I may come upon one."

Kai thought a moment, then said, "But you gave your word as the people in Saigon gave theirs. Cannot they do what you have done?"

"Yes," Morgan said. His lips stretched into a thin line. "But one must do some things with the hope that better follow. This is what I am doing now. I hope for better things. There are things that must be done when the chance to do so presents itself."

"And if something should happen in this perfect ambush you have set, an accident, and the old man or you are killed, what then? Will the promise and the old man's wish be fulfilled?"

"Yes. But there will be no accident," Morgan said. "It is a good ambush and nothing will be lost but time."

"Tell me, Dai-uy," she said. She placed her hands on her hips and stuck out her jaw toward him. "Tell me. Do you do this to kill a rabid dog, or to please those whom you obey?"

"We must go this way," Morgan said. "To avoid those ahead of us we would have to travel many days out of our way. It is much safer for us to wait for them here and kill them when they come. Now go and make camp for I too am very hungry, and there is much to do that does not require your presence."

She held her ground and looked steadily at him. "Why not let them pass? Would that not be safer still? Would that not keep an accident from occuring from your perfect ambush and would we not gain time by not fighting with them?"

"Who can predict the viper who strikes from behind leaves or rocks and who can predict where the assassin may wait? No. This is better and this we shall do. Now, take your pack and do what I say."

She grunted and reached into her pack and withdrew a small packet of polished sticks wrapped in a white band. She thrust the packet into his hands and he looked at them curiously.

Strange hieroglyphics were woven into the cloth and the sticks felt smooth against his fingertips. He looked up at Kai and frowned.

"I do not understand," he said. "What is the meaning of this?" He ran his finger along the figures on the cloth.

"Undo the bundle and throw the sticks into the air," she instructed. "Throw the sticks high so the forest gods may whisper through them."

"And what will they whisper?" he asked. A smile tugged at the corners of his mouth. She clicked her tongue and wagged a broad finger admonishingly.

"Do not take this lightly, Dai-uy," she said. "The gods do not like mockery."

"I am sorry," Morgan said and forced his face to relax. "But what will I discover when I throw these sticks?"

"I do not know," she said soberly. "Perhaps nothing. Perhaps everything. That is for the forest to decide. Who can tell what she wants? There are secrets that no man may know."

"And woman?" Morgan asked innocently, enjoying himself. "What about woman? May she know these secrets?"

Kai shrugged, and stared at him, eyes black and opaque like obsidian, her face a noncommital mask like those carved from teak before the missionaries came. She resettled herself on her haunches, her feet flat on the ground, weight back on her heels, and her hands planted squarely on her hips. She merged into the thicket behind her, and Morgan blinked rapidly to bring her figure back into focus. A strange, green glow began to emit from her, soft, but there nevertheless, and a powerful force seemed to tug at his mind. His face became numb.

"Throw the sticks, Dai-uy," she said softly. "Throw the sticks."

The words floated dimly to him through a sudden roaring in his ears. He tried to speak, but his lips had become rubbery and would not form the words.

"Throw the sticks," she said gently, and a thickness built in Morgan's throat. With wooden fingers, he fumbled the cloth open, then threw the sticks high in the air and watched them float lazily end-over-end to the ground between them. They landed in a jumbled maze, and Kai bent forward eagerly to pore over them. The spell was broken, and Morgan placed his hands in the small of his back and stretched. He felt foolish and amused at himself. A trickle of sweat ran down the side of his face and he raised his hand to wipe it away and felt his fingers slide over the stubble of his beard and the grit on his face.

Dog would like this, he thought. It is much the same way that Dog looks into the soul of the world when the fire coals do not give him the vision he seeks. And you are tired, very tired. It is very lucky for you that the northerners do not come while you are playing silly games with this woman. This is what Professor Nordstrum would call primitive hypnotism and write a monograph on it.

"Throw them again," she commanded suddenly. He paused and blinked at her as her words broke through his thoughts.

"Huh?" he grunted stupidly. She gestured toward the sticks.

"Again," she said impatiently. "Throw the sticks again."

Automatically, he reached for the sticks and gathered them in, then paused.

"Why?"

"Do not ask questions. Throw them!"

Feeling foolish, he tossed them high, flicking his wrist so they spun rapidly like tiny pinwheels. Again, she leaned forward and stared over them. She pursed her lips then frowned and gathered them and carefully wrapped the cloth around them.

"What did you see?" he asked curiously.

"Nothing," she said indifferently, and thrust the sticks back into her pack. She made tiny, unnecessary adjustments to the sling on her pack and hefted the burden experimentally.

"I do not believe you," he said lightly. "Tell me. It does not matter."

"No," she said thoughtfully and looked him in the eye. "No, you are right. It does not matter."

"Then, tell me. I wish to know."

"Nothing," she said calmly. "I saw nothing. Sometimes, the forest does not give its secrets readily."

"Then, we have wasted enough time with these silly games

of children," he said, half angry at her refusal. "Take your pack and make the camp in the place of which I spoke. There is much work for men to do and when we have finished we shall be hungry and tired."

He stared deeply into her eyes until she shrugged and bent and collected her pack. She swung its bulk with ease across her broad shoulders.

"As you wish, Dai-uy," she said. "But this seems great foolishness to me to risk yourself when a greater responsibility lies ahead."

"It is also foolishness to look away from evil," Morgan said.

She shook her head stubbornly, but moved back along the trail. She paused and said something in a low voice to the young woman. The young woman looked from under her long hair at Morgan. He was struck by the sudden boldness of her stare. She gave him a tiny smile and hurried after Kai.

What the hell was that all about? he wondered. Better watch yourself. This could become a bit sticky.

"Sir?"

He shook himself from his reverie and turned to Stephens. "Yes, what is it?"

"The radio is ready," Stephens said. "Did you want me to send alone?"

Morgan considered, then shook his head. "No. But you be there as well. In case something happens to me, you'll know what is going on."

Stephens frowned. "You expecting something you're not telling me?"

"You know," Morgan said, miffed at Stephens's tone, "you are getting to be a bit lax with military courtesy."

"Yes, sir," Stephens said, straight-faced. "Would the Dai-uy like to tell this poor serf just what is going on in case the poor serf unfortunately finds himself in a position where he cannot ask the Dai-uy for wisdom and guidance, sir?"

"Ah, nuts," Morgan said, rising. He slapped his beret back on his head. "Come on. Let's send that damn message and let

Colonel Black know that we have found the group that came across the border. I think," he added, moving up out of the creek bed and following Stephens to the small clearing where the radio waited.

Chapter Twenty-six

Stephens sat back away from the fire in the early dusk and watched Morgan and the old man ceremoniously pass a bottle of Johnnie Walker back and forth. Morgan was naked to the waist and Stephens, in conscious imitation, had also removed his shirt. He slapped irritably at the mosquitoes that zeroed in on him in delight and wondered with envy why Morgan and the old man didn't seem to be bothered by them. Neither talked and both stared quietly into the flames as if they could read the future in the burning embers. Stephens looked from one face to the other; they seemed to belong to each other, and he felt uncomfortable and knew he did not belong there.

Why does he spend so much time with that old man? Why do they sit and drink like that together? Always at night. That's what Mother would do—always drink at night. Never during the day. Always at night like all whores. Then, it was like you weren't even there when she started drinking. Hell, it's like you don't even exist. But what did you expect? A boy scout camp-out? Hot dogs and roasted marshmallows over a comfortable fire and scary stories from big brother? Remember where you are!

Furious with himself, he grabbed the bottle from between his legs and drank deeply. Morgan caught the sudden movement out of the corner of his eye and glanced at Stephens. He raised his eyebrow and Stephens shook his head, rose, and walked out of the firelight into the darkness. He carried the bottle with him. They could hear him slapping at the mosquitoes as he went.

"The young one is upset, Dai-uy," Nguyen Duc said. He chuckled and lifted the bottle, drank deeply, paused, and drank again. He smacked his lips and wiped the back of his hand across his eyes. He shuddered and handed the bottle back to Morgan.

Morgan took it absently, drank, and placed it on the ground within easy reach of the old man.

"It is his first battle," Morgan said, thinking, and I hope it isn't his last. Hubris isn't a virtue, and there's a moment when a man lives through his first combat and thinks he has magic. I hope Stephens doesn't fall into that. That is a very dangerous time. Lips pursed thoughtfully, he stared after Stephens and back to the fire. The heat from the fire was warm on his eyebrows and cheeks and he watched the yellow heat coil like tiny snakes around the cherry-red and gray-black coals.

"What do you see there, Dai-uy?" Nguyen Duc asked. He, too, could feel the heat from the fire and it felt good on his knees and hips and hands, and as he inched closer, the heat made the ache go away from his joints and the warm Scotch inside made him thoughtful and pensive.

"I see many things, old man," Morgan answered. "I see you and me and this bottle of whisky that will soon be empty, and I see many dead Viet Cong in the morning."

"Do you not see anything else, Dai-uy?" The old man threw a small stick onto the coals and they watched it smolder briefly then burst into quick flames. "Can you not see yourself? Or any of us?"

"I can see you surrounded by many fat grandchildren," Morgan said soberly and the other laughed appreciatively.

"*Eeeah*. And does the fire say who will be their grandmother and who their mother? Uhhh." His mood changed, and he reached for the bottle of Scotch and drank again from it. "She was a fine woman. The finest in the entire village, was she not, Dai-uy?"

"The entire mountains," Morgan said. "She was the forest and the sea as well."

"Yes. Thank you for the truth," the old man said. He looked into the fire again and a tear ran down his leathery cheek, but he did not notice it and Morgan watched its path and how it changed from a sparkling diamond to a blood-red ruby from the reflected light of the fire.

"She did not deserve to end that way. We shall take many heads for that and the forest will be filled with new souls crying in pain with their blind wanderings."

"Many heads," Morgan said. "And tomorrow we will stake them along the trail as a warning for those who will come after that this is our land and we will patrol it and kill all who misuse it."

"Yes. We will do all of this. But this is not a good land, Dai-uy. This is a bad land. There are no farms here, and the air smells like rotting carcasses. It is better higher up." He raised his head and looked to the north. "Children must grow like the rice—where it is best for them."

"Then, we will keep this place and live elsewhere," Morgan said recklessly. He drank from the bottle and handed it to Nguyen Duc. His back felt cold and he turned sideways to the fire and faced the old man. "Your village will be the most admired in the mountains, for it will be the richest and the largest and other headmen will admire you and hold the name of Nguyen Duc in reverence."

The old man didn't answer and his eyes grew distant and faraway as he stared into the fire. Slowly, his muscles relaxed, and he began to look like the old statues in the crumbling temple where they had made their first camp. His face was a mask of carved sternness with lines of cruel determination, revenge lines, curving down at the corners of thin lips. His arms rested over his knees and heavily-corded hands dangled, almost touched, the ground in front of him. Firelight flickered against his face and shoulders, and Morgan thrilled to a sense of primitivism that swept through him and his eyes and heart filled with happiness as he realized that he belonged here and now, drinking Scotch with this fierce old man who called him Dai-uy and followed him without question. He did not feel like an American, but a part of the whole—the forest, the mountains, the cats that prowled at night. He belonged to all of this and the feeling made him proud and the thought of what he was going to do tomorrow seemed familiar and natural as if he had been doing it for his entire life.

But you can no longer think about only yourself, now that Billy is dead. You have other responsibilities. What about Kate and Timmy? he thought as the dim memory flashed on his mind. Where do they fit in this newfound wisdom of yours? Do they now belong to you as well? Yes, but that is another world. That is a world for your other self. The self that once was but will probably never be able to become again. And why won't you be able to become that again? Because you have learned too much about this world. And you really are one son-of-a-bitch. Billy's death was your fault and now you think about his wife. What kind of sick bastard are you?

Kai and the young woman moved into the circle of firelight and squatted beside the old man. The old man sensed Kai and turned his head slightly toward her. Their eyes met and Morgan watched as Kai touched his knee gently and the old man's lips turned upward in the briefest of smiles. The old man rose and followed Kai away from the fire. They disappeared into the darkness beyond the fire.

Morgan listened and followed them through the night to the old man's pallet. He heard the familiar rustling, then closed his ears to the noise of their lovemaking and smiled and reached for the bottle of Scotch. He raised it to his mouth and drank as his eyes caught those of the young woman. The light danced across the high planes of her face and touched her eyes, black and luminous. Her long black hair fell softly across one shoulder and touched her waist. He saw the outline of her young breast and firm buttocks where the material of her blouse was black trousers pulled tightly. Brown and bare peasant's feet clutched the bare earth around the fire, and Morgan felt the beating of his heart in his temples and swallowed heavily and lowered the bottle of Scotch to the ground between his feet. His nostrils flared, and he smelled the wood smoke, the damp night air, the musk of sweated man, and the faint hint of woman. He felt warm and flushed and closed his eyes and tried to think about home, but the flickering fire and the dancing flames formed a wavering red curtain through which he could not see.

Kai laughed, and he opened his eyes quickly, but he was still alone with the young woman and then he remembered Kai's words to him from the night at the temple:

"Man was not made for one woman, Dai-uy. You would not enjoy a flower if all the flowers were the same nor the sun if there was no rain. How, then, can you enjoy one woman only?"

He moistened his lips with the tip of his tongue and spoke to the young woman.

"It is late. You should sleep and rest for you will need your strength tomorrow."

"And you," she said lowly. Her young, vibrant voice carried promises to him. "Do you not need sleep?"

He swallowed and turned back to the fire and threw a small stick into the heart of the coals. The flames flickered and danced in and out of the shadows and Morgan breathed deeply, nostrils flaring at the smell of the burning sandalwood.

"I have talked to Kai," the young woman said.

Morgan looked at her. She had not moved and the shadows of the fire writhed sensuously like Salome's veils over her high, brown cheekbones.

"And what did that old cow tell you?" he asked. His throat felt dry and raspy, yet his mouth filled with saliva as the girl shrugged and her nipples hardened and thrust like bullets against the fabric of her blouse.

A log broke in the heat of the fire and sparks floated up and disappeared, but her eyes did not follow the sparks and widened into dark, luminescent pools from whose depths gleamed a desire and need that wrenched and tugged at his soul. She had become a woman of the earth and forest, and Morgan felt the fierce intensity of the thousands like her that came before. He rose and walked around the fire and squatted beside her. She turned her head and watched him. Her eyes were softer now and her lips full and red from berry juice, and he could smell the clean, womanly scent of her, like fresh apples, and he knew she had been to the spring. He touched her hair and its silky softness caressed his fingers. She did not move and he took her hand and felt the hard callouses on the palm just beneath the fingers and the softness of the skin beneath the callouses. He squeezed the mound of flesh by her thumb and watched the pulse quicken beneath the dawny soft, brown skin in the hollow of her throat.

Still holding her hand, he rose and brought her to him. Her almond-shaped eyes widened and the combination of woman and innocence and promise started drums beating in his temples. He released her hand and stepped away from the fire. She came with him and pretended to stumble and he caught her and felt her young breasts against his chest and thin shanks against his groin. His throat thickened, and he tried to speak, but she laid her cheek against his bare chest where it burnt like a brand. He slid his hand beneath her knees and lifted her and carried her to his bed away from the fire. He lowered her to it and gently bared her body to the night. His breath quickened as her small breasts rose against the cold. The Scotch left his head and the raw power of her innocence pulled him to her. He kissed her and felt her lips quiver uncertainly, then boldly, beneath his. He tasted the berries on her tongue and felt the womanly strength of her thin arms and legs, and then she became a woman, a savage priestess of the forest, and the vast gulf between himself and her closed, and they merged together on the floor of the jungle and became one.

Morgan pulled the poncho liner over them as a blanket, and the young woman snuggled tightly against him and twined her legs around his. She turned her face up to him expectantly, and he gently kissed her eyes and mouth. Her lips looked puffy in the moonlight, and he touched them gently with his fingers.

"*Ong bao nhieu tuoi*?" He asked. "How many years are you?"

"Do my years matter?" she sighed, and hugged him tightly.

"No," he said after a moment's reflection. "No, they don't. Only the moment matters." He tried to feel guilty, something told him he should, but strangely there was no shame, only a sense of having been purified, exorcised from the guilt he knew about but could not feel and a thankfulness and tenderness to the young woman for giving him the release from that guilt overpowered him and made him grateful.

"This disturbs you, Dai-uy?" she asked softly. Tiny worry lines appeared between her brows. "I was promised for after the rains. My father was to make his choice after the first market day."

Morgan smiled gently, reassuringly, at her and erased the lines from between her eyes with his thumb.

"No, I'm not disturbed," he lied. "I was taught to be so, but I am not." He kissed her again, and she rested her chin on his chest and stared at him. He could not see her eyes for they were lost in the shadow of her hair, but he knew she was staring at him for he could feel the tension in her body, and he ran his hand down her back to her narrow hips and delighted in the way she shivered beneath his touch.

"Why were you taught this, Dai-uy?" she asked. "This is a strange thing for the teaching of."

"My people would think this is wrong," he said. "We are not married."

She reared back from him, and he could feel the indignation vibrate through her like a harpsichord. She grabbed his hand and placed it on her breast. "Is this wrong?" she demanded.

"No," he said mildly. "But would a woman behave like this?"

Chastened, she hastily dropped his hand and lay back beside him and again rested her chin on his chest. Her breath was quick and moved through the hairs of his chest, and he could smell its sweetness and the musk beneath the sweetness and he felt the beginning of tumescense.

"I spoke wrongly," she said. "I should not have done this thing or spoken harshly."

Her pagan mouth fastened urgently against his and in that moment he felt reborn and the sweat from their bodies merged and baptized each as one entity and they danced the dance more ancient than religion.

The forest was gray and quiet, and the men squatted around the dying coals of last night's fires and silently waited. Tall baobab trees stood around them, huge and columned with thick ridges.

Gnarled roots the size of men's thighs curved out of the ground and back in. Thick clumps of fern spilled down over the trail and liana vines crawled up young trees. They did not eat for empty bellies made men more aware and contented themselves with cups of water. They did not throw wood on the coals for the wood would be wet from the heavy dew and the smoke from wet wood in the early morning could be seen far off as the heavy air held it close and grudgingly sent it up as a column. The women, too, were silent and moved around the men and left them with their own thoughts of what was about to happen.

Kai nodded in satisfaction at Morgan and the girl who squatted close beside each other. Only their eyes and thoughts touched and Kai felt the closeness between them. She looked up at the old man as he squatted beside her.

"The girl and the Dai-uy?" he asked softly.

"Yes," Kai said. "They were very close with each other, now. It is good."

"Maybe." The old man reached for a bamboo cup of water, sipped and shivered. He glanced over at Stephens, sitting silently, staring into the ground. "I hope we have chosen the right one," he muttered.

Kai raised her eyebrows, staring at him. "Do you think it should have been the young one? But the Dai-uy is the stronger."

"No," the old man said. "He is only the older. There is strength in the young one that has not shown itself yet." He frowned and tugged at his earlobe. "Much has changed in the Dai-uy since he came back from Saigon. He is not the same. There is a darkness to him."

"Because of his brother," Kai said. The old man stared quickly at her.

"You know this?"

"I saw this in the sticks," she said soberly.

The old man's face tightened. "What else did you see?"

She shook her head. "I do not know. The rest I must think upon."

"Perhaps we were wrong. Perhaps the young woman should have been sent to the young warrior."

"We did what we thought was right at the time. No one can ask any more of themselves."

"I wish I knew," the old man said, brooding. "It is not good for a man's thoughts to wander at a time like this."

"And what of you?" she asked him roguishly. "Will not your thoughts wander? Or will you be like the monkey and forget everything?"

"Shame, woman," he said severely. "Do not talk like this. Of course I will remember, but I am old and know that I cannot think of things like that at the wrong time. And, it is because I am old that I will remember when I wish to remember."

"The Dai-uy may be like that," she said unconvincingly. She stared back at them. Perhaps she had been wrong in sending the girl to him. But when would the time have been better?

"No." The old man shook his head. "No. He is young, and he still has the foolishness of the young with him. But there is nothing wrong with that for that is what the young are for. The old ones must protect them from their dreams."

"They are happy with each other for the time," Kai said. "That is very important. Perhaps more important than the isolation you speak of. They belong together, now."

But she did not sound sure of herself, and the old man saw the worry in her eyes and softened. He patted her arm and said, "It is good to belong. Perhaps I am too cautious. He has something to return to here now. This may make him careful. Yes, this may have been wisely done as he is now a part of us as surely as if his mother had come from our village."

Kai grunted, pleased with herself, and poured Nguyen Duc another cup of water and handed it to him.

"They are watching us," Morgan said. He sipped from his water cup and smiled at her with his eyes. "What are they thinking?"

"The same as I am thinking," the young woman replied. She smiled shyly at him, and he was amused at the daylight change in her.

"And what are you thinking?" he asked.

She blushed and dropped her head. Her hair fell forward like a curtain over her face, and he reached out and moved it back over her shoulder.

"It is not right for me to say what I am thinking," she said. "Those thoughts are for the dark and not the light of the day."

"No," he said. "The night is good, but the light is much better for then you can see if what you think is true."

"I—care," the girl said, and a soft pink appeared beneath the brown of her cheek. He touched her cheek gently and she pressed it against the palm of his hand.

"I am afraid for you," she said. "There is a coldness this morning that I feel in my stomach."

"That is the fault of the water," he said, and smiled at her. "I too feel the coldness, but it is nothing to fear."

"I do not want to lose you," she said. "May I not go with you?"

"No." He shook his head and pulled his hand away and wrapped it around his cup of water. "You must stay here. I will not have time to worry about you."

"I will be very careful," she begged.

"You will stay here," he said. "But I will remember you and that will be the same as having you with me only better for I will know that nothing will happen to you and this will help me do what I must do."

"You care? There is not other?" she asked.

"I care," he said, and rose and checked his equipment. The others rose with him and silently began moving down the trail.

"I care and there is no one," he said, and turned from her so she could not see the pain and the lie in his eyes as the memory of Kate and Billy flooded accusingly back. He felt Billy's eyes, watching from the darkness of his soul. You are the one responsible for Billy being gone. No, he came on his own to the village. You couldn't help that. But he wouldn't have come if you had gone to him. You could have flown out to Ton Son Nuht and taken a quick hop over to Bien Hoa to see him. But you didn't. You stayed away from him. Deliberately. And you know why you didn't go to him. But he didn't know that. And because he loved you like a brother should love a brother, he came to you. And you betrayed him. And killed him.

Kai watched the men move down the trail and then called the girl to her. She came, slowly, and Kai waited patiently, knowing the thoughts and feelings running through her.

"Do not worry," she told the girl. "The Dai-uy is a strong and careful warrior, and this ambush of his is a good one."

"I do not feel right about this," the young woman said. She watched Morgan disappear down the trail. She turned to Kai. Worry clouded her eyes, and she frowned and shook her head in confusion. "I do not understand these feelings. It is as if an evil one has entered my soul. I think dark thoughts, now, only dark thoughts."

Kai patted her gently on the shoulder and affectionately pinched her chin with thumb and forefinger. "That is a woman speaking now," she said. "That is all that is wrong. You are no longer a child."

"Perhaps you are right," she said, and tried a smile.

"Of course, I am right," Kai said crossly. "I am always right. Now, help me pack. We must be ready to leave when the others return, for we have lost much time on this foolishness of men. That is something all women have to bear—this foolish game of men, *Aieee*." She sighed. "But what else is there for men to do?"

Stephens winced as his head pounded when he lifted the radio from the ground. He paused, shaking his head, closing his eyes and digging his thumbs into the hollow of his temples, trying to squeeze the pounding away. Someone nudged him, and he opened his eyes. The young woman held a cup of water out to him. He smiled at her and took it. A soft blush covered her cheeks, and he drank the water and handed it back to her.

"It's all right," he said softly, and hurried after the others waiting impatiently on the trail ahead of him.

Kai looked thoughtfully at the young woman and Stephens, then frowned. She turned to her pack and took the bundle of sticks from it, untied the bundle and tossed the sticks into the air. She leaned over them, studying them for a long moment, then shook her head and gathered them, carefully tying the cloth around them.

Who could understand the gods?

She sat back on her haunches, looking at the ground in front of her. She stretched out a forefinger and began drawing in the dust.

The young girl came up and squatted beside her. "What are you doing?"

Kai shook her head, concentrating on the drawing. "This is not a time for talking, now. Now, we must wait. Listen and wait."

"What are we listening for?"

"The sounds the men will make when the others come."

"Are you listening, too?"

Kai sighed and raised her head, studying the young girl. She smiled, but it was a small smile and she shook her head. "Do not care for the Dai-uy too much."

"Why do you say this?" the young woman asked curiously.

"There is a darkness in men like the Dai-uy."

"I do not see such a darkness."

"You entered into the darkness with the killing of your mother and father and brothers," Kai said. "I had thought you and the Dai-uy would bring each other out of the darkness. But now—" She shook her head. "Perhaps I was wrong to send you to the Dai-uy at this time. Perhaps I should have sent you to the young warrior instead."

The young woman shook her head vigorously in denial. "No! This is not true. I care very much for the Dai-uy!" Then she paused and glanced at where Stephens had slept. "But the young one is almost like the Dai-uy."

"We shall see," Kai said. She turned back to her drawing. "We shall see. Now, be quiet and listen."

Dutifully, the young woman sat back away from her and watched the strange hieroglyphics emerge in the dust beneath the old woman's finger as she tried to understand the strange words of Kai.

Chapter Twenty-seven

Carefully, Morgan set the claymore mine into position and stretched the detonating wire across the trail and covered the wire with dirt. He placed Nguyen Duc behind the log and handed him the wire.

"Do not trip this, old man, until I give the signal," he said. "And be sure you do not fall asleep. The sun will be hot, and I know how old men like to nap in the heat."

The old man made a rude noise through his nose and carefully pulled the wire snug and anchored it with the butt of his rifle.

"Your father surely mated with a monkey," he said. He leaned back against the log and pretended to sleep. "Go back to the women and leave this business to the true men."

The others laughed. This was going to be a fine ambush. Did not the Dai-uy joke with the old man? Yes, he was one of them for he did not worry about that which was coming.

Morgan placed the other claymores and took Stephens with him to the tree, walking backwards down the trail, carefully covering his path with dead leaves. He eased into position behind the thick trunk of the banyan tree and looked at Stephens.

"Do you know what you are supposed to do?" he asked.

Stephens nodded and stared at the trail. His knuckles gleamed whitely where he gripped his rifle. His mouth was tastelessly dry as though he had been inhaling dust. He scrubbed his tongue back and forth against the top of his mouth, trying to work up saliva. But when he swallowed, it tasted brackish, bitter as if he had sipped salt water. He felt as though his spirit had winged its way back into the past.

"Don't fire until I give the word," Morgan said. "We want them to come running back this way, and when we fire, the confusion will be great."

"Yes, you told me that," Stephens said. He looked over his shoulder at Morgan and tried to grin. "Strange, isn't it?"

"What's that?" Morgan asked. He took the radio from beside Stephens and placed it firmly behind the tree.

"Why does a man's hands get wet and his mouth dry at times like this," Stephens said. He wiped his hands across his jungle blouse. "You'd think it would be the other way around."

"It's the anticipation," Morgan said. He removed the flask from his pocket and unscrewed the cap. He offered it to Stephens.

"No, thanks," Stephens said. "I had more than enough of that last night."

"Probably a good thing," Morgan said. He took a small sip and held it in his mouth until the burning stopped, then spat it out. He took his canteen from his belt and drank deeply. He handed it to Stephens. He shook his head. "Go ahead," Morgan insisted. "It will be the last time you move until it begins. From now on, we have to sit and wait."

Stephens took the canteen and drank. "How long do we have to wait?"

Morgan shrugged. "The scouts said no one was coming down the trail during the night. So, we have to assume that the one we killed yesterday was a day scout. Could be any time. Could be not until late this afternoon. But, this will be the last drink you have until then just in case."

Stephens took another long drink, then handed it back. He wiggled into a more comfortable position. "Then, I guess we'd better begin waiting."

"Yes," Morgan said. He took another long drink of water, capped the canteen, and placed it back on his belt. He settled down and stared back at the trail, waiting.

Hours passed, but it was only noon when they moved silently around the bend of the trail, five wearing camouflage suits leading three others dressed in bush clothes followed by three peasants with loads, headbands laced around their foreheads to keep the sweat from their eyes as they strained under the heavy loads, their sullen faces fixed with smoldering resignation on the ground in front of them. Morgan lay still behind the roots of the tree and ignored the sweat that prickled his flesh and dripped onto the ground. The rear guard had yet to appear, and he waited patiently as he had many times before for the guard to appear. Beside him, Stephens breathed rapidly in quick puffs, and his fingernails scratched nervously against his gunstock. Morgan knew the sudden burst of fear, like bile, was in his mouth. He reached out cautiously and pressed his palm against Stephens's shoulder. The scratching stopped.

The rear guard strolled around the bend of the trail. He wore a camouflage uniform, but he carried his carbine under his arm as he cracked seeds and spat the hulls out to the side of the trail.

Beside Morgan, Stephens took a deep breath and let it out slowly.

Good, Morgan thought. The fear was fear only for the first time. You should have recognized it for that, but it has been so long since the first time that you had forgotten what it was like to be frightened.

The guard moved past them, and Morgan watched as the leader came to the bend in the trail ahead and stopped suddenly, staring with confusion at the head on the pole in front of him. He disappeared around the bend and Morgan counted to five, giving him time to reach the corpse, then whistled loudly, a high, piercing cry like a kite, and brought the Thompson up firmly against his shoulder and anchored it against one of the thick roots of the banyan tree.

The explosion came hard on his whistle, and he took up the slack in the trigger and waited. The cough of the machine gun and the stuttering of the rifles punctuated the echoing roar of the mine and cut off startled cries from the men on the trail. They turned and started running back toward Morgan. Beside him, Stephens began to hum tunelessly, and Morgan waited until the Viet Cong were almost upon them and Stephens's hum became a high-pitched keening before he locked the trigger back hard against the guard and moved the bucking barrel across the trail quickly in three-second bursts. Stephens fired rapidly, covering the gap between Morgan's bursts, and the fleeing figures fell like rice stalks before the wind. One knelt in the middle of the trail and leveled a Soviet AK-47 assault rifle and fired a quick burst toward Morgan's position. A bullet from Stephens's rifle split his skull but not before a bullet from the AK-47 smashed into Morgan's shoulder and drove him backwards.

Dazed, Morgan reached with his left hand for the Thompson, but his fingers would not close. Puzzled, he frowned and tried again, then saw blood dripping from his fingertips. Dimly, he realized the firing had stopped. He craned his head and looked up at Stephens. Stephens's lips twisted in a half-smile. The pupils of his eyes looked like tiny pin-pricks. Then, he saw Morgan's shoulder, swore, and cast a quick glance down the trail as a shot echoed when one of the old men applied a coup de grace to a wounded man.

Stephens nodded in satisfaction and lay his weapon down. He pulled a knife from his pocket and pressed a button. The blade snicked out, and he reached for Morgan's jungle blouse, neatly cutting it away from the wound. He smiled at the pain in Morgan's eyes.

"Looks like you forgot to duck in time," he said. He took a first aid packet from the pouch on Morgan's belt. He pulled a canteen from his belt and washed the blood from the wound. He shook his head. "It's a good one," he said. He pressed the packet against the wound and Morgan gasped in pain. "Sorry," he said.

"Don't be," Morgan said. He leaned forward from the tree trunk so Stephens could pull the rest of his jungle blouse off. He held the packet as Stephens tightened the strips over his shoulder and around his chest, knotting them. "It's my own damn fault."

A rustling of leaves came, and Morgan drew his .45, cocking it. Stephens looked over his shoulder.

"It's only the old man," he said. He glanced down at the pistol in Morgan's hand. "You don't leave much to faith, do you?" he said.

"Faith gets you killed," Morgan said. He felt faint and gritted his teeth as he slumped back against the tree trunk. The small clearing swam in front of his eyes, and he rested his head against a large root and fumbled the battered flask from his side pocket. He drank deeply and gagged.

"You probably shouldn't drink that," Stephens said. He took the flask from Morgan's fingers, drank, then handed it back. "But, what the hell do I know?" He said arrogantly, and Morgan knew he was still in the grip of the killing spirit. He had killed, and now he was a god, and Morgan knew how very dangerous that could be when one felt like a god.

"You're probably right," he said. He handed it back to Stephens. "Save me and have another."

"Obliged," Stephens said. He drank deeply, handed the flask back, shuddered and sighed. "Man, that is good."

"It gets better each time," Morgan said. He sipped this time. Stephens stood and shook his head, and Morgan knew that the uncertainty of his own mortality was beginning to return to him as he quickly grabbed his rifle and looked out over the trail.

If he is lucky, he will realize how lucky he is to be alive, Morgan thought. But that will disappear as soon as he drinks enough Scotch. If he is really lucky, he will forget the fear and remember only that he had killed today as a necessity. But if he is not lucky, the fear will remain with him and the next time he is in battle, the fear will freeze him when he needs to be quick and deadly.

"I'd better check on things," Stephens said. He looked down at Morgan. "You'll be all right for a minute or two?"

Morgan nodded. "Make sure that the others are all right, then place the call to Colonel Black."

Stephens looked around at the trees and shook his head. "We'll never get a chopper in here for a dust-off," he said.

"I know," Morgan said. "We'll have to think of something. Meanwhile, check the men. When you return, I might have thought of something."

Stephens nodded and stepped lightly over the roots of the tree and moved carefully down the trail toward the old man. He paused to check each figure carefully before moving on.

He'll be all right, Morgan thought. He lifted the Scotch and took another sip. And this Scotch is all right, too, and this root is a fine pillow. I am lucky to feel its roughness and to taste the Scotch.

He heard Stephens talking to the old man and the stunned silence before the rush to the tree trunk. The old man's face looked closely into his as he prodded the wound gently with a bent forefinger. Morgan gasped.

"This wound, Dai-uy, it is not bad?" Nguyen Duc asked anxiously. He looked closely at the bandage and tried to peek under the edges.

Morgan smiled and handed the flask to the old man.

"It is a good wound," he said. "I will not have to look at your ugly face for a while."

The men laughed and joked among themselves about how the Dai-uy had stepped in the way of the bullet as it was better to be shot than be forced to look at the old man who looked like an old, toothless monkey and smelled worse. But each man felt a certain pride about the Dai-uy's wound for the wound belonged to each of them and made them part of that secret fraternity of men who have fought and bled together. They had shed blood for the Dai-uy in the past and now he had shed it for them. They could see it seeping from his shoulder.

"Are the others all right?" Morgan asked.

"You are the only one who is hurt," the old man said. "It was a fine ambush. Your wound, it does not pain you? We know how tender your skin is. Even the sun's softest rays fry it like spoiled meat."

"Should I make the call?" Stephens asked. He picked up the radio and looked questionly at Morgan.

Morgan nodded and Stephens shouldered the radio and stepped up out of the creek bed and disappeared into the thicket across from them. Morgan looked poker-faced at the old man and said, "Your face pains me more than this bite of the insect."

Satisfied, the old man nodded and rose to his feet.

"Now, we shall have to do all the work as usual," he said to the others. They covered their smiles with their hands. "This is so true of the Americans. They promise us much help but it is we who must do the work." He drew a machete from his belt and tested its edge with his thumb.

"Even then, you must be shown," Morgan said. Gritting his teeth, he rose to his feet, held tightly to the tree until the dizziness passed, then took the machete from the old man and staggered to the first body. He raised his arm and swung the blade at the neck. It took him three swings to cut the head from the body. He fell beside it and willing hands picked him up and carried him to the cool shade of the bank and placed him on a bank of ferns.

"Rest," the old man said softly, affectionately. "You have done well."

Morgan leaned back gratefully against the ferns. He handed the old man the flask and pulled the old man's canteen from his belt. He uncapped the canteen and took a long drink of water and sighed. The old man drank deeply from the flask, capped it, and placed it in Morgan's lap. He turned back to the others and spoke quickly, giving directions. The men drew their machetes, some moving toward the bodies, others moving off into the thicket to select poles.

"Search the bodies well," he said to the old man. "Especially those who are not soldiers. Bring everything to me."

The old man nodded. "And as to that which they were carrying?"

"Destroy it," Morgan said. "It must not leave here."

The old man moved away and Morgan took a deep breath. A tiny shower of dirt and leaves fell down upon him as Stephens dropped lightly from the bank and squatted beside him. He set the radio carefully beside Morgan and took Morgan's flask, opening it.

"Well?" Morgan said. "What did you find out?"

Stephens took a long drink, capped the flask, and handed it back before speaking. "There's a MAC-V camp about ten kilometers from here. We're to take you there and a chopper will lift you out. You're to bring any papers out with you and destroy the junk."

"We've already started on that," Morgan said, nodding at the old men squatting beside the packs and carefully cutting them open. "What else?"

"I'm to stay with them for now," Stephens said. "We're to wait at the MAC-V camp for further orders. I think that means until they find out how badly you're hurt. Gee, my first command."

"Enjoy it," Morgan said. "It ain't what it's cracked up to be."

"Yeah," Stephens said. "It sure would be nice, though, if I knew what the hell I was doing."

"You'll do all right," Morgan said. He nodded at the old man. "Pay attention to him. He's fought more battles than we'll ever know. And remember that there is a great difference between what happens in Saigon and what happens out here."

"Yeah, I can see that," Stephens said dryly, nodding at the men cutting the heads from the bodies.

"That's just what I mean," Morgan said. "Most of our soldiers go home without once having seen a Viet Cong and not knowing why they were here in the first place. In the Korean War and World War Two they knew why they were fighting. But here"—he shook his head—"it's different. There's no sense of glory to what we are doing. It's just a job. That's what you have to remember: it's just a job. But it's a job that has to be done very carefully. A man doesn't control his destiny; that is decided for him by the actions of others. One more thing," he said, fighting to keep his eyes open. "Colonel Black is twice the headhunter I am. Be very careful when you are dealing with him. And make sure that you keep our people together."

"Our people?" Stephens said. He glanced down at Morgan, but he had passed out. Stephens sighed and shook his head. He glanced down the trail and saw the young woman running down the trail with Kai lumbering in pursuit. He took Morgan's flask. "Yes, maybe you're right," he said, standing and moving out of the way as the young woman fell beside Morgan.

"He'll be all right," he said, and staggered as Kai rudely pushed him away.

"Bring water," she said bruskly, and pushed the young woman away. She untied the knot and carefully peeled the bandage back from the wound. She sniffed it, then looked closely at it and felt behind Morgan's shoulder. She shook her head.

"The bullet did not go through," she said. "Get water!" She shoved the young girl away and took her pack off her shoulders. She opened her pack and removed a small bundle wrapped in plain white cloth. She opened it and took out several small packets, setting them aside. The young girl returned with a small pot of water and Kai took a small piece of cloth and scrubbed the dried blood away from the wound. She took another square of cloth and placed a handful of dried leaves and powdered root on it. She soaked the poultice with water and held it up for Stephens's inspection. He sniffed it and shuddered.

"Christ, that stinks!" he said. Kai nodded and laughed, then looked at the young woman.

"Watch closely! You must learn this as you will need to do this many times. There is nothing unusual in being wounded and our men will have need of our skills many times before this is over."

She placed a green paste over the wound and tied the poultice tightly over the wound. Then, she took a small bamboo cup from the sack, dropped a dried gray powder into it and filled it with water. She pinched Morgan's ears until he shook himself awake.

"Drink!" she said, holding the bamboo cup to his lips. He opened his mouth and drank and spat.

"Ugh," he said. "Hemlock!"

"Drink!" Kai commanded, holding the cup again to his lips. Resigned, Morgan opened his mouth and swallowed.

"Good," Kai said. "You will rest now. Then, we will remove the bullet while you rest."

"Later," Morgan said, the word slurring. His tongue felt thick, and his eyes heavy, but his body felt like a balloon filled with helium gas that floated away from the ferns beneath him. He watched Nguyen Duc approach, and his voice seemed distant when he spoke.

"The Dai-uy sleeps?" the old man asked. Morgan felt him poke at the wound, and he tensed in anticipation, but felt no pain. "You have done well."

"He will sleep, and when he sleeps, I will remove the bullet," Kai said.

"You have done this before?" The old man placed a bulging knapsack beside Morgan and squatted beside him. His knees popped like faint gunshots.

"Many times," Kai said resignedly. "Men have always been foolish and have given me many opportunities to do this."

"It was a fine ambush," the old man said, ignoring her. He beamed and rubbed his hands together gleefully. "A fine ambush, and we have killed many of the enemy."

"A fine ambush," Kai said scornfully. "See what your fine ambush has done. Now, we will have to wait and already he moves far to the north."

"This makes no difference," the old man said. He craned his head looking up at the sky. "The rains will come and he will not go far. We will find him. How long will the Dai-uy sleep? I have that of which he asked." He patted the sack beside Morgan.

"Until night," she said. She felt his forehead and spoke to the young girl. "Boil water. Soon, it will be time."

Morgan tried to speak and tell them about the helicopter, but his lips felt frozen and lifeless. His eyes closed, and he watched thick darkness approach.

"A pipe would have been much better," the old man said. Morgan strained to hear him as his voice cut thinly through the darkness.

"This is more certain," Kai answered, and he heard the old man's words flutter away like flies, and then hands moved him gently and removed the poultice and a cool breeze sprang from nowhere and then he felt nothing.

Chapter Twenty-eight

"Share it, Putman, or wear it up your ass."

"Roll your own. This ain't a community stick."

Friendly banter bunted gently against Morgan's ears. Slowly, he woke from the drugged sleep. Something odd about the voices troubled him slightly, and then he felt the rough nubbin of the wool blanket covering him from his chest down and realized he had heard American voices.

He opened his eyes and stared at the top of a tent stretched tightly over heavy, rough-hewn timbers. There was a breed of familiarity in that and in the medicinal smell that prickled his nostrils and he felt cool, but not uncomfortable, and realized he was in an American compound somewhere.

"Hello. He's back with us."

A friendly face floated over him and smiled. Deep clefts showed in the narrow cheeks, and the eyes crinkled merrily at the corners. His hair was cropped so close that the scalp showed through the stubble. The faint twang to his voice automatically registered Missouri.

"How are you feeling? Don't know what that woman gave you, but I'd give fifty dollars for a six-pack."

"Where—" His mouth was dry and his voice cracked painfully. He tried to swallow, but his tongue felt sealed in cement.

"Wait a minute."

The face disappeared and returned. An arm slipped beneath his head and raised it and a cup pressed on his lips. He swallowed the cold water, coughed, then drank deeply.

"Enough?"

Morgan nodded, and the cup was taken away.

"Where am I?"

He turned his head and saw the others staring curiously at him. A sword stood out on a field of red on their shoulder patches, and he knew he was at a MAC-V camp. They lolled lazily on rumpled cots and passed a hand-rolled cigarette back and forth.

"A few miles from Dak To," his nurse said. "But it might as well be a hundred. Helicopter's the only way in and out unless you want to get your arse shot off as you well know. I'm Harry." He held out his hand and Morgan took it.

"Morgan," he said. "Henry Morgan."

"Hungry?"

Morgan nodded, and Harry moved to a cupboard, opened it and removed a can of Spam.

"Sorry, but there's no fresh meat. Refrigeration's a problem. The bastard Cong keep destroying our generators, and we have to keep the searchlights juiced. How'd you get hit?" He cut the Spam into tiny chunks.

"Ambush," Morgan said. His mouth watered at the sight of the Spam and he raised himself to eat the plate of food Harry brought to him. He was surprised to feel little pain.

"Fill your little mothers," one of the others said. Harry pointed to him then to the others as he named them:

"Jack, Jim, Billy, Teddy the Toad," he said. "They're not so bad when they take a shower. Which should be today, by the way, it's Saturday." The others booed and rained pillows at him. He grinned and ducked behind Morgan's cot. "Easy. Easy. You want to hurt our patient?"

"Where're you from?" Harry asked as the others returned to passing around the cigarette.

"North of Dalat," Morgan answered. "Small village there." He chewed slowly, enjoying each bite.

"I mean the States. Man, you've been here too long if you think of this as home. How long have you been here?"

"Four years." It hurt a little to swallow, and he grimaced and asked for a glass of water.

"Four years? Who'd you kill?" Jack brought him a glass of

water and offered him the cigarette. Morgan sniffed cautiously. It smelled like burning leaves.

"Marijuana?"

"Thai grass. The best," Jack said proudly. "Want a hit?"

Morgan shook his head and handed his empty plate to Jack. He shrugged, drew deeply on the cigarette and moved back to the others.

"You never said what your unit was," one of the others (John?) said. Jack handed him the cigarette, and he drew on it until his eyes bulged and his face turned red with the effort.

"No, I didn't," Morgan said. The others exchanged quick glances and looked at him strangely. He sipped the water and cautiously moved his shoulder. It was stiff, but not painfully so. Harry watched his inspection.

"She took the bullet out," he said. "I tried to change the dressing, but that old battle-axe wouldn't let me. I was afraid she'd cut my ballocks off if I did. But the wound seems to be closing all right, and I don't think there is any infection. I gave you a hundred cc's of penicillin, and you'll probably get another hundred when you get back to Saigon. Precautionary, you know. Never really know what the hell kind of bugs in this lousy place.

"Where's my gear?" Morgan asked, looking around.

"On the floor," Harry said. "Say! You're a real walking arsenal."

"There should be a knapsack," Morgan said, as he tried to look over the side of the cot.

"Here," Harry said, and rose and picked it up from the foot of the bed. "That fellow of yours, Stephens? He's a real spook, isn't he? Is he jungle?"

"Just private," Morgan answered. "Crowds bother him."

Harry nodded. "Well, he left this sack with you, too, and told us to stay the hell out of it. A real winner." He handed Morgan the map case. "He said you'd know what it was."

Morgan took it. "Where is he?"

Harry shrugged. "With the 'yards' I expect. He stays with them. Him and that old man sit out on the north bunker together all the time. Damn if I know what they talk about." He shook his head. "Sometimes, they don't even talk. Just sit there and stare north. Damnedest thing." He watched Morgan open the sack and begin sorting through the papers. "You said you were ambushed?"

"No," Morgan said absently, his attention on the papers. "I was the ambush."

"What the hell did you want to do that for?" Jack asked from his cot. Billy and John seemed to have fallen asleep and Teddy the Toad was having trouble finding his mouth with the cigarette. Jack reached out and took it from him and he sighed as if a great weight had been lifted from him and fell asleep immediately.

Morgan raised his head and stared at him. He seemed blurred around the edges, and his eyes slid like oil bearings from their focus.

"Why do you do that?" He nodded at the cigarette.

"You mean grass?" He drew deeply on the cigarette until the coal threatened to burst into flames. He exhaled insolently. "Because it gets me the bloody hell away from this."

"Does it?" Morgan asked. "Or is that just an excuse for you? And why try a constant escape? Reality will still be there when you come out of it, but you will be less able to cope with it than before."

"Bleeding heart," Jack groaned. "Fuckin' phil—phil—" His head rolled and he jerked it back and fell flat on the cot. He giggled once and fell asleep. Harry sighed, rose, and crossed to the cot and removed the cigarette from betwixt his fingers. He pinched it out and laid the butt on the footlocker beneath the cot. He turned and looked at Morgan.

"They really don't mean any harm," he said defensively. "They just don't like it here."

Morgan grunted noncommittaly and turned back to the papers.

"You've got to understand them," Harry said. He crossed to a camp chair and sank into it.

"Why?" Morgan asked curiously. "Why should I? Do they want my understanding? Is there any reason why I should try to understand them?"

"They don't know you," Harry said defensively. "Why did you set that ambush? Do you believe in this war?"

"A matter of pride," Morgan said defensively. He shuffled the papers together and placed them neatly on his blanket-covered lap and turned his attention to Harry.

"I guess you could say it was also a point of honor," he added. "The war really had nothing to do with it. Do you have a cigarette? A real one, I mean, not those funny ones?"

"A Chesterfield okay?" Harry asked, and held the pack out to him. Morgan took one, and Harry spun the wheel of his Zippo and lit it for him. Morgan nodded his thanks and exhaled a long, thin stream of smoke.

Harry shook his head and crossed to a pop cooler "liberated" from a destroyed Shell Oil service station. He lifted the lid, hesitated, then shrugged his shoulders and removed two beers. He pried the tops off the bottles and handed one to Morgan and returned to his seat.

"I don't think this will hurt you," he said.

"No," Morgan agreed, and drank.

"What happens," Harry asked softly, "after a man has been here too long? What happens when he becomes inured to all the killing and uncertainty and has nothing to go back for? What happens when he simply doesn't care anymore?"

"He may become a part of the country," Morgan said, and stopped himself before he finished. Or, he may become fanatic about his work and that would be dangerous for fanaticism is a younger brother to madness and evil. Mercenary. He becomes a mercenary. Was this where he was?

"Or?" Harry prompted, and startled him.

"A professional soldier," Morgan said. "For anyone. Preferably, the highest bidder."

He finished his beer and dropped the bottle on the floor. Light grew dim and Harry rose and lit the lantern on the portable desk at the head of Morgan's cot. He lifted a pistol belt from the desk and strapped it around his waist.

"I have to make the rounds," he said. "We always have to

check the generators before it gets too dark. Those little bastards are tricky."

He crossed to the tent door, paused, and turned back to Morgan. "War is still war. Fighting in it is evil as well."

"So are thoughts like those," Morgan said automatically. He picked up the papers again. Harry hesitated, started to speak, then thought better of it and left.

Insects buzzed and slapped against the lantern's glass. A snore bubbled briefly from one of the figures on the cot and stopped as he grunted in his sleep and rolled over.

A soft scratching came from the doorway, and he quickly folded the letter and slipped it into his pack. He stuffed the rest of the papers back into the sack.

"Dai-uy?"

He recognized the young woman's voice and called out: "Come in."

The tent flap moved aside and she slipped inside and slid against the wall. She looked quickly, nervously, at the figures on the cots, then rushed on silent toes to his side. She knelt beside the cot and spoke softly.

"Are you better? Does your shoulder hurt?" Her eyes were luminous in the lantern light and Morgan felt a great tenderness within him and smiled at her.

"It is fine," he said. "Lay your head upon it."

"I do not wish to pain you," she said.

"You won't," he said, but winced when she gently did his bidding.

"I am sorry," she said. Concern edged her words, and Morgan hastened to reassure her.

"Lay your head here, instead," he instructed, and pulled her head gently onto his chest. He could see the pulse move in her throat, and he touched it gently with his fingers.

"Tomorrow a helicopter will come, and you will be taken to Saigon," she said. "Will you return?"

"Yes," he said, and smiled lightly in the dark. What else was there to do? And suddenly, he realized he wanted to return and the thought of not returning made his throat feel swollen and his eyes stung.

"You will not find another woman and forget me?"

He thought guiltily of Kate and Billy, but it all seemed strange and foreign as if everything between the three of them had happened in another life, but he knew that it had not been in another life but much too much had happened since then. Her body stiffened beneath his hands as he did not readily answer and he looked down at her.

"I will not forget you," he said quickly.

She smiled radiantly at him, and he felt a weakness in his stomach and wondered if it was the smile that caused it or the guilt building in his mind about what he had to do.

"I will not forget you," he said again, firmly, and she raised her head and kissed him gently on the lips and laid her head back on his chest. He stroked her hair fondly, feeling its softness between his fingers and smelling the juice from the mangos she had rubbed over her skin.

Chapter Twenty-nine

Morgan lay naked on the cool and crisp hospital sheets and sipped cold 7-UP from a tall glass with a straw. The doctor had disdainfully ripped Kai's bandage from his shoulder, mumbling something about beggars and superstitious mumbo-jumbo, and affixed a gauze bandage over the bullet wound in his shoulder after reopening the wound for irrigation. Now, the wound ached, and Morgan thought wryly that he would have been better off under Kai's crude care. The pain had almost disappeared before his arrival in the hospital, but now even his buttocks ached from the units of penicillin and gamma globulin shots he had been given.

He thumbed through an old copy of *Playboy* that featured Playmate Jo Collins's triumphant visit to the fighting man in Vietnam the year before. She was stepping into a helicopter to ride to a firebase camp, and he thought about his own helicopter ride. Stephens had listened to Morgan's instructions carefully as he reflectively chewed a cold cigar.

"Make sure that none of these people bother our people," Morgan said lowly to him as the helicopter made its cautious descent.

Stephens shook his head. "Our people? Sounds like I've just been initiated into the tribe."

"In a way, you have," Morgan said. "You fought with them. That's enough." He studied the young man carefully. "And you seem to care for them. The old man tells me that you're filled with questions. That's good. Work on the language, though."

Stephens nodded. "I will, boss."

The old man stepped forward and touched Stephens on the

shoulder, speaking to Morgan. "Do not worry, Dai-uy. The young one is learning very quickly. Already he knows Kai to be a water buffalo!" Morgan nodded as they lifted him and slid him into the helicopter.

"Do not do anything foolish!" he called to the old man. "We will hunt together upon my return."

The old man nodded and the helicopter rose rapidly and turned toward Ton Son Nhut. The ride was anticlimatic except when the pilot made a low strafing run over the Michelin Plantation and the door gunners fired long bursts from their .30-caliber machine guns at the helpless rubber trees. Morgan criticized the young pilot for his recklessness, and the rest of the ride was made in sulky silence.

He turned the page and looked at another picture of Collins. She had nice legs, he thought, and would probably be very good in bed. But he did not care for the layout as it was really a cheap advertising campaign using the war for sales promotion.

But, he thought, that is the way of all things—to make the best use of the worst. It is too bad, he thought, that they did not take Collins through the worst wards where she could see the patients with their manhood blown off from the Bouncing Betty mines or those blinded from grenade fragments or minus limbs from machine gun bullets. Instead, they took her through the wards where those with brave, Hollywood wounds in the shoulders and legs were kept and the nurses moved around with their bright, porcelain death smiles and tucked blankets with false tenderness around clean-cut, whole American boys.

The door to his room opened and the floor nurse walked in. He pulled the sheet over his lower body. She stared at Morgan's bare torso and looked with distaste at the *Playboy*.

"You're supposed to be wearing your hospital gown," she said accusingly. She bent and retrieved it from the floor and held it out to him.

"Too hot," he said, and grinned at her as the color mounted in her face.

"There's a hospital rule about indecency," she said. "We do have lady nurses."

Morgan smiled broadly at her, and she flushed deeply and motioned for him to get out of bed so she could make it. He slipped into his robe and stood up.

"How long am I to be here?" he asked, as she moved efficiently around the bed. He tossed the *Playboy* onto the table and picked up his glass of 7-UP. He crossed to the window and stared out at the garden.

"What's your hurry?" she said. "The food isn't that bad, is it?"

"Terrible," he grinned. "I just don't like hospitals. People die in them. That's very depressing."

"People get well, too," she said defensively. She tucked the corners of the new sheets in and smoothed the wrinkles out with an economy of motion.

"That's true, but while they are here, they are sick, and that's depressing. I prefer to be around well people who know they're alive and are planning to stay that way."

She sniffed, tossed her head, and went out, carrying the soiled sheets with her. The door hissed shut behind her. Morgan felt the blackness begin to drape itself over him again. He turned back to the window and moodily stared out at the garden.

I wonder what the old man and Stephens are doing now. I hope the old man listens to him and does not go off on his own. No, he won't do that. He remembers what happened the last time he did that. Still—

The door opened behind him and he turned to face Colonel Black. He nodded at Morgan and plodded heavily, tiredly, to the chair and settled his thick body in it. He stared coldly at Morgan from pouchy folds, and pulled a dark cigar from his shirt pocket and wallowed it around in his cheek until he had it familiarly settled.

"How you feel?" he asked. He took a bundle of papers from his bulging briefcase and laid them on his lap and stared unblinking at Morgan.

"Fine." Morgan flexed his shoulder and ignored the tiny stab of pain. "Doctors are just playing games. None of them are happy unless they have forty patients each."

Black nodded and chewed thoughtfully on his cigar. "A

couple more days for observation, then I'll see what I can do."

"How about now if I promise to be a good boy and stay in bed?"

"No." Black placed his hand on the pile of papers. "Did you read these?"

"I glanced at them. When do I get out of here?" Morgan asked again.

"Like I said: in a couple of days," Black answered. "There's the usual check for sepsis and tests. You know, befuddled bureaucracy."

There was his mind too, Black wanted to add, but stood instead and shuffled the papers back into his briefcase.

"I'll leave you now. We'll go over these papers later. You want anything?"

"A bottle of Scotch?" Morgan said, and turned back to the window. He thrust his hands deep into the pockets of his robe.

"I'll see what I can do," Black said. "Anything else?"

"No. Yes. A copy of *Moby-Dick* if you can find one."

"*Moby-Dick*? Why *Moby-Dick*?"

Morgan shrugged. "Just came into my mind. You asked if there was anything."

"Uh-huh. Take care of yourself," he said to Morgan's back.

"Sure," Morgan said without turning.

Black hesitated. Either the man was stronger than he thought, or there was something dreadfully wrong with him, he thought. Black did not want to think about the latter. He needed Morgan now more than he had before.

He moved silently to the door and let himself out. He paused outside the door, fished a cigar out of his pocket, and asked a passing orderly where he could find the psychiatric wing. The orderly pointed and Black, ignoring the NO SMOKING signs, lit his cigar and walked rapidly through the green-tiled halls, his brow furrowed like corrugated tin. He'd be damned and sizzled in hell if he was going to lose Morgan.

Morgan waited until the door clicked shut behind Black, then turned back to the room and leaned against the window. The warmth from the glass soaked through the thin hospital robe, and he slumped against it like a lethargic lizard and willed the images of the jungle from his mind.

He began to laugh quietly, and he staggered to the bed and fell flat upon it and muffled his laughter with his pillow. He saw pictures of what he had become and what he would always be, and they were pictures that would only disappear, he thought, when he died.

The sun filtered through the venetian blinds, casting bar shadows over Morgan's bed. He thumbed absently through the battered copy of *Moby-Dick* that Black had sent over, reading scattered phrases here and there, instantly recalling the rest. It was the tired game of boredom practiced by those familiar with the only work available to pass the time. He felt the restlessness of an active man and the boredom was the boredom of a spirit harnessed, and his thoughts returned constantly to his people growing dull and lethargic at the firebase camp, and he worried about Stephens, and, lastly, the girl.

The door opened and he looked up as Maurice entered the room. He carried a hamper covered by a gay red-and-white checked cloth and moved to Morgan's side. His eyes crinkled as he smiled, and Morgan closed the book gratefully and placed it on the small table by his bed.

"So how does my malingering friend feel?" Maurice asked. He placed the hamper on the bed by Morgan's side and rested his hands casually upon it.

"Bored," Morgan replied. "And how does old age treat you?"

"As can be expected." He smiled and gently touched Morgan's shoulder. "There is no pain?"

"No. It was an accident," Morgan said. "A freak accident."

"But it is an honorable wound," Maurice said. "And as such, deserves to be honored." He reached inside the hamper and removed a bottle of Mumm's. He pulled a snow-white linen napkin from the hamper and wrapped it carefully around the bottle, then hesitated.

"It is all right to do this?" he asked. His eyes reflected concern and Morgan laughed.

"Not only all right, but needed," he said.

Maurice nodded in satisfaction, drew the cork expertly, and removed two fluted glasses from the hamper. He filled both, handed one to Morgan, and lifted his in salute. They drank and Maurice refilled the glasses, then set the bottle on the table within easy reach of Morgan and crossed to the room's only chair and comfortably settled himself.

"I was distressed to hear of your injury," he said formally.

Morgan drank and reached for the bottle of champagne. He held it suggestively toward Maurice who smiled faintly and shook his head. He filled his own glass and replaced the bottle.

"A stray wound. Fortunes of war."

"This sounds more like carelessness to me, my friend," Maurice said. He sipped from his glass.

"Perhaps," Morgan said. "But these things do happen, are bound to happen. No names are written on bullets except for the careless. Those are the only certainties. The others are accidents, freak chances of nature."

"And now what do you plan?" Maurice asked.

Morgan shrugged. "To go back. What else? How is your wife?"

"Fine. Thank you. I think I have changed my mind: may I have another glass?" He held his glass out, and Morgan leaned forward and carefully filled it. The champagne was cold and heavy; he already felt it, and he made a mental note to slow down.

"She sent pickled mackerel and a fine paté to you. And her best wishes, of course."

"Thank her, please," Morgan said, and he peeked under the checkered napkin. Another bottle of Mumm's rested inside along with a variety of cheeses and crackers.

"A veritable feast," he observed. "Compared to the tasteless pap fed to the inmates here."

"No one recovers on bland food such as this pureed nonsense," Maurice agreed. "How long before you have to go back?"

"The sooner, the better," Morgan said. "There is much to do, and they have need of me."

"The natives?" Maurice's eyebrows shot upward. "I really do not see their importance for you. Were they not the reason for you being shot?"

"I don't think I can explain it to you," Morgan said slowly. "I'm not sure that I want to."

"Ah," Maurcie said. "One of the mysteries of man, eh? Tell me, then: what were you doing when you had this 'accident'?" He exaggerated the word and Morgan smiled.

"A small ambush. We received information that a band of smugglers would be bringing heroin down from the north." He shrugged. "We stopped them."

"Heroin?" Maurice's eyes widened. "But how did you receive this information?"

"The advance guard," Morgan said. "Just before he died."

Maurice grimaced. "Be careful, my friend, or you will become like them. Where was this heroin coming?"

"To Saigon, I think," he replied. He laughed and drained his glass of champagne.

"I see," Maurice said. He studied his glass casually. "Did you find out to whom the heroin was going?" He swirled the champagne in his glass idly.

"No," Morgan said. A nagging worry touched him slightly. He frowned. Why do you ask these questions? "All we found was the heroin. Word of what happened must have leaked back to Saigon by now. Have you heard anything?"

Maurcie shrugged, then smiled and raised his glass. "I'll look around for you. But right now, I must get back to the club," he said. He emptied his glass and rose. "Please finish the champagne." He placed his glass on the table and carefully set his straw skimmer at a rakish angle popularized by Maurice Chevalier in the fifties. He tapped the flat crown jauntily.

"And you must come and stay with us when you are free from this, this tomb. Please. We count on you as our guest."

"Thank you," Morgan said. "I accept."

Maurice gave him a sunny smile, squeezed his forearm

affectionately, and left. The door shut softly behind him, and Morgan reached for the bottle.

You were very foolish to think even for a moment that Maurice was prying, he told himself. Heroin is a dirty business and not for one like him. He may cut a few corners in the business sense, but he most certainly would not be involved in heroin. It is too bad he is prejudiced toward the Vietnamese, but he is a member of the old class and remembers how things were before Dien Bien Phu. You cannot expect men like that to change their feelings once their world is uprooted. It will be nice to visit Maurice and his wife, but not for long. No, not for long. Too much provincialism and regency mannerisms become stifling.

He laughed and raised his glass in a toast to himself.

Face it, Morgan. You're no gentleman. This champagne is good, but Scotch is better. You can trust the Scotch while champagne is too tricky as it will slowly dissolve your will when you do not know it and will make a greater fool of you for that. Scotch is sudden and because of this, you can catch yourself before you become too much the fool. But, now, you have been drinking champagne, so why not act the fool? Is that not a gentleman? One who confuses life with art by relating life to the importance of literature and painting?

The door opened and broke his thoughts. He turned to it, defiantly holding his glass of champagne in plain sight. He felt a mild shock as a white-suited figure, wearing a clerical collar and carrying a briefcase, stepped in and nodded at him.

"Hello," he said pleasantly. "I'm Father Gilhooey."

"Impossible," Morgan said, shaking his head. "Nobody's named Gilhooey."

"That's what my first bishop said," he answered. He smiled and his gray eyes crinkled merrily at the corners. He crossed to the chair beside the bed and sat, placing his briefcase at his feet. "You'd be surprised, actually, to know how many times I've heard that. Often I've thought about changing my name to something more probable like 'McGillicuddy,' but this is my cross to bear and what was good enough for Father and Mother must be good enough for me, don't you think? That wine looks delicious."

Morgan laughed delightedly and quickly decided that he liked this white-haired man with the roly-poly manner and paunch. He picked up the glass Maurice had left behind and filled it without waiting for an answer.

"Will you have a glass with me?"

"If you insist." The priest drank the wine appreciatively and sighed. "I was right: it was delicious." He looked pointedly at the bottle. Morgan smiled and held it out.

"Another?"

The priest eyed the contents critically, then shook his head regretfully. "I never take a man's last drink," he said sorrowfully.

Morgan pulled the other bottle from the hamper and held it up. The priest's eyes brightened, and he stretched out his glass.

"In that case, I would be delighted." He sipped the champagne this time and sighed again. "I wish there were more patients like you."

"What brings you here, Father?" Morgan asked. He carefully twisted the cork from the second bottle and eased it free. A soft *pop!* sounded and the champagne rose in the bottle. Quickly, he covered the top of the bottle with his thumb. "You must know I'm Protestant."

"I know," Father Gilhooey said. He smiled. "But I never give up hope. Actually, I'm here as a favor."

"To whom?" Morgan asked. He pulled a jar of paté from the hamper and opened it. "Join me?" He placed a box of crackers beside it.

"Yes, I think I will," Father Gilhooey said pleasureably. "You wouldn't have a jar of Major Grey in there, would you?" He pulled the chair close to the table.

"I'll see," Morgan said. He placed a jar of Capitaine Cooke's Pickled Mackerel beside the paté. Then he found the chutney and lifted it in triumph from the basket.

"The horn of plenty!" the priest exclaimed. He reached for the jar and twisted the cap free. "You have worthy friends, indeed."

Lavishly, he spread the chutney on a cracker and paté and bit into it. He chewed slowly, then swallowed and rinsed his mouth with champagne and sighed.

"Heaven must be endless bottles of Mumm's, good paté, and Major Grey," he said. A piece of chutney clung to the corner of his mouth, and Morgan laughed and spread paté on a cracker and washed it down with champagne.

"And good friends to share it with," he said. "If, of course, there is a heaven."

"Oh there is," the priest said hastily. He eyed the pickled mackerel. "Is that Capitaine Cook? I haven't seen Capitaine Cook Mackerel since before the war."

Morgan handed him the jar and watched with amusement as he greedily opened it, speared a chunk, and stuffed it into his mouth. He masticated slowly and an expression of delight spread over his face.

"You are the strangest priest," Morgan said. "Now what brings a person like you to a person like me?"

"And what might a person like you be?" the priest asked. He smacked his lips over the mackerel and spread paté over another cracker, piling it high with chutney. It threatened to spill over onto his lap, and he cautiously raised it to his lips, one hand poised in anticipation beneath it.

"Not an atheist, if that's what you mean," Morgan said, and smiled at the priest as he cautiously stuffed the heavily laden cracker into his mouth. "Despite my question about heaven, I do know there is a god, somebody's god. But why me? Surely many of your flock could use your guidance through this, the worst of times. Perhaps even now someone may be shuffling off this mortal coil without absolution."

The priest shook his head. A piece of cracker slipped out the corner of his mouth, and he quickly caught it with his tongue before it dropped down his chin.

"No, I think not. I hope not. But there is a priest here at the hospital to take care of those. I'm here to see you."

"Why?" Morgan sipped his champagne. "More mackerel? Help yourself."

The priest snatched greedily at the jar, then looked apologetically at Morgan.

"This really is very good. You don't mind, do you? It is very hard to come by these days."

Morgan waved his hand and said. "Who? Or is that a secret?"

"No secret," the priest said. "At least, I don't think so, I mean, he never really said anything about it one way or the other so I don't think it matters, do you?"

"That's all right," Morgan said. "I can guess. Black really can be a bastard at times."

"I suppose he can," the priest said. He washed down another piece of mackerel with a swallow of champagne. "But then, he's in that type of position. And he does worry about you."

"Perhaps," Morgan said. His mood shifted and he stared gloomily at the wall. "You know, at times I really hate the good colonel."

"And why is that?" the priest asked gently. He twirled his glass of champagne carefully between thumb and forefinger. His hands, Morgan noticed, were large and square, the nails carefully trimmed straight across and highly buffed. Except for the thumbnail on the right hand which was broken and jagged. The backs of his hands were heavily corded, a picture of power in repose. They were carpenter's hands that should have turned lathes and raised roof beams and not the hands that fumbled their way through worn-out rosary beads.

The priest cleared his throat and sipped at his wine. Morgan started and raised his glass.

"I beg your pardon. I was wool-gathering. You asked?"

"Why do you hate the colonel? I thought you two worked closely together."

"You don't have to love a woman to sleep with her," Morgan said, and grinned as the priest's eyebrows raised quizzically.

"A sensual attachment? Oh, come now! Even Freud wouldn't be that obvious."

"Sorry." Morgan placed his glass on the table and laced his fingers behind his head and stared at the ceiling.

"It's really not all that complicated. At times, a part of me is like him and yet a part of me is also repelled by what he stands for."

"What does he stand for?"

"Ruthlessness. Cruelty. Barbarism."

"Natural repulsion. But why do you see a part of yourself in him?"

"Because these traits make a powerful person."

"And you want power?"

"No, I have power. Therefore, I have those traits. They are necessary and because they are necessary, I hate them."

"What else?"

Morgan looked from the ceiling to the priest. "What else what?"

"What else do you hate?"

"No, Father," he said firmly. "We've played enough of these games."

"I'm sorry if I upset you," the priest said smoothly. His brow furrowed.

"This has gone on long enough," Morgan said. He laughed. "No disrespect, Father, but I think you had better go. I'm becoming rather tired."

"Your wound?" The priest leaned forward sympathetically. "I'm sorry. I would not have troubled you had I known."

"Actually," Morgan said, forcing a grin, "I believe it is a combination of the mackerel, wine, and paté. I'm afraid my constitution isn't up to such luxuries."

"I'm sorry. Let me know if there is something I can do for you," he said.

"Go back and tell Black I'm sane and quite capable of resuming my job."

"I'll tell him what you said," the priest said, and rose.

"What? No more questions?" Morgan smiled and held out his hand. The priest took it, then turned to the door.

"Not much sense in asking questions when I'm answered with questions," he said. "I'll remember you at Mass. Even if you don't want it."

"Just be sure no one hears it," Morgan said. He laughed. "I have my reputation to consider."

"I'll whisper," Father Gilhooey grinned. "Oh, just one more thing."

"I knew it," Morgan groaned, and pretended weariness. "What is it?"

"If we were to have one of those ethereal discussions, how would you define truth?"

"Good lord," he said. He sighed and looked up at the ceiling for a moment to prepare his thoughts.

"The truth is what you want to believe and can forget and forgive. When I first came over here, I was very frightened so of course, I had to be very brave. And worldly. I drank endless puddles of booze to be worldly, but that wasn't the truth. I had to forget to be frightened, and I could only do that by forgiving myself for being frightened. Understand?"

"A bit," the priest said. He grinned pleasantly. "By the way, have you seen this?"

He handed Morgan a magazine. The cover showed a long-haired, bearded youth with flowers in his hair, trying to pin a small bunch of flowers to the uniform of a policeman. The policeman's face mirrored loathing, disgust, and a little fear. He was surrounded by other youths, identically long-haired and flowered.

Morgan looked questioningly at the priest.

"The new beatnik," the priest said. "But more outspoken. The anti–Vietnam War movement is gaining momentum."

"Why?" Morgan asked.

"Why? Oh you mean why against the war? I'm not sure they even know. They claim it isn't a just war—"

"No war is just," Morgan interrupted.

The priest scratched his head. "Yeah. I don't like that Nietzsche crap either. Look inside."

Morgan opened the magazine and stared at the pictures of young women wearing leather skirts that halted scant inches from their groins. He tossed the magazine aside and laughed. "Why did you show me that?"

"I thought you might like to see what has happened to your world," the priest said.

"It's not my world," Morgan said. "It's their world."

"It's the same world."

"No, you're wrong. I don't belong there."

"Where do you belong?"

"I'm not sure."

"Here?"

Morgan smiled. "Very clever, Father. But you can tell Black that I'm all right. He can't expect the government to inquire into the state of a man's soul. I just need to get back to my people."

"Your people? The Montagnards?"

"Yes." He looked away. "I belong out there. Not in here." He gestured at the magazine. "Nor there."

"Why out there?"

"It's primitive and barbaric, but all men are advancing steadily to the same beat. Our civilization is crumbling and there is nothing we can do to stop it. People no longer believe in the better tomorrow."

"It has nothing to do with your brother?"

The question caught him by surprise and Morgan pushed his head down in his pillow and stared at the priest.

"Is this why you are here?" he asked softly. "To see if I'm becoming tracked?"

The priest shrugged and spread his hands apologetically. "It is a possibility. Revenge is a natural emotion that unfortunately settles upon people when it shouldn't. They lose their perspective."

Morgan shook his head and closed his eyes. "All life is revenge, Father. For being born."

"Rather gloomy," Father Gilhooey said.

"Perhaps. But it is the nature of existence. The Montagnards exist with the forest. There's a primitivism there that is salvation. The forest gives them life and will ultimately take it. They know that and so they live their lives in harmony with it. As much harmony as they can get. Yet, at times, they must go out and kill, raid, to revenge themselves against what may come after they are dead. And no, Father, they don't believe in your type of divine recycling. Now was there anything else?"

"I hope to see you again when you are well," Father Gilhooey said. "I'm at St. Peter's. Why don't you stop by and see me?"

"You're not with the military?"

"Less sticky this way," the priest said. "Stop by and see me and if you can find some more of that Capitaine Cooke—"

"I'll try," Morgan laughed. "But remember: I'm not Catholic."

"Would you like to be?" The priest grinned impishly.

"Not yet."

"God be with you anyway." He made the sign of the cross, nodded pleasantly, and opened the door. It closed softly behind him, and Morgan lifted his glass to the door, toasting it.

"Words, words, words," he said. His lips twisted, and he laughed and drained his glass and placed it upside down on the table.

Chapter Thirty

Colonel Black looked up in irritation as his office door clicked open. His face cleared as he recognized Father Gilhooey. He closed the file he had been reading and gestured to the priest to enter.

"Come in, come in, Father," he said. He gestured toward the chair across the desk from him. "How did things go?"

The priest shook his head. "Did Notre Dame win?"

"No. Southern California beat them. That's another five you owe me. Drink?"

"Yes, thank you. I think you might have a problem."

Black rose and went to the filing cabinet next to the huge wall map. He removed a bottle of Bushmill's and two glasses.

"Might? Then I might not as well?" Black filled the glasses half-full and handed one to the priest.

Father Gilhooey sighed as he took the glass. "You always find the loophole, don't you, Colonel Black?"

"The day I don't a lot of people will be after my butt. Happy days."

They drank and Black crossed behind his desk and sat.

"Ahh," he sighed, and swung his feet on top of the desk. He leaned back and pinched the bridge of his nose between his eyes. He sipped slowly, with relish. "So what happened? Where's my problem?"

"I'm not sure you can call it a problem, yet," Father Gilhooey said. He sipped thoughtfully from his glass, then slid down in his chair so his neck lay on the back of it. He balanced the glass on his chest and frowned.

"But there is something," Black pressed.

"Oh, yes. There is something, but I'm not sure it's what you think?"

"You're talking in riddles," Black said. "What about the lack of concern?"

"Perhaps there was never anything there to be concerned about," the priest answered. "It's quite common for men to confuse motion with action and convince themselves that they are, for the moment, invincible. He was very evasive about a few things. Too insistent about getting back to the jungle. I would be a bit worried about that." He hesitated. "I think his brother's death is mixed up in this somehow."

"Revenge can be good." He frowned. "As long as it doesn't interfere with other plans. As to the other, somehow I can't see Morgan going jungle on me." Black snorted in dismissal and drank. "I just need to know if he has suddenly become aware of his own mortality. That is what often happens when a person is wounded. Then they refuse to take those chances that they need to take and that is when they become dead."

"What about innocence, though?" the priest mused. "What if he found innocence out there?"

"In a war zone? Wait a minute." Black swung his feet down and stared at the priest. "What the hell are you talking about?"

"He may feel he's found his niche, his utopia, his place for belonging. There is comfort in the thought of revenge, you know. Need, too, but that need is satisfied only by the action, and that makes the action a comfort."

"Jesus." Black drank absently from his glass and stared at the map. "You mean he has gone jungle."

"I think so," Father Gilhooey said. He set his drink on the desk and leaned forward, placing his elbows on his knees and allowing his hands to dangle. "The basic concern I see is his preoccupation with what he has found or thinks he has found in the jungle: a sort of noble purpose in primitivism, a denial of civilized order. He has become an atavist and, consequently, he's lost his preparation for death." He paused to take a drink, emptying his glass. "You know what you are creating with him? Another Kurtz. He has his own plans now and all intentions of carrying them out. Right now, you fit in with his plans, but as soon as he finds that you are interfering with them, he'll leave you. You can forbid him to go back out there, but he will return to it." He frowned. "He thinks the government has failed him and when your government fails you, your whole world—the world that took care of you and sustained you—fails you. Then, your soul seems to float in limbo. I think he sees something profound, now, in what he is doing. Redemption for his brother's death, perhaps, but there is also the sense of honor, of some fixed standard of conduct that drives him on to what he is doing. He isn't afraid of death. I think he is quite resigned to that."

"That's not so good," Black said.

"No, a certain readiness to die is not so rare. You seldom meet one, however, whose soul is ready to fight a losing battle. I think that has happened to Henry. His desire for peace grew stronger and stronger as the war became longer and longer until it conquered the basic desire for life itself."

He glanced at his empty glass, and Black rose and went back to the filing cabinet to retrieve the bottle of Bushmill's. "I'm afraid I don't quite follow your train of thought," he said. "What is this 'death preparation' you're talking about?"

"Simple," Father Gilhooey held his glass out for a refill, then rolled the glass between his hands. "You are carefully groomed all through your childhood and young adult years on the inevitability of death. You are usually taught that a better place awaits you, a nirvana, heaven, paradise, whatever, but you have this firmly in mind as protection against the uncertainty of death. You have been prepared for death. Maybe you're not ready for death when it comes—who ever is?—but at the core of all your fears you are convinced that a better world is waiting for you to cross over. Most people are prepared in this matter through the church and school. Although education may create questions in a person's mind, it is basically an intellectual question. His faith still remains. He has a need for this faith because all minds are orderly. Different degrees of order, perhaps, but order just the same. We call that 'faith.' Morgan no longer has this. At least, not so it's recognizable." He frowned. "His brother's death may be behind this—revelation, I guess you could call it. I don't know what else—but whatever it is, it cannot help but affect his performance. If it is revenge, then it is consuming him. His own life will become secondary to his fulfilling what he sees as his purpose."

"Strange words for a priest, Father," Black said. He pulled at his lower lip with a hairy thumb and forefinger and crossed back to his desk and sat. He took a file from a drawer, flipped it open, and stared at it for a moment, then leaned back again in his chair. He steepled his fingers and rested his chin on them.

"What happens if he has lost his faith, Father? This death preparation, will that affect his performance?"

The priest shook his head. "No, not at first, anyway. Then there could be a sense of apprehension as he becomes more and more aware of death and if that happens, fear. And then his usefulness will be over. More important, however," he added softly, "his usefulness to himself will be over, and he will become aware how far he has sunk in the order of the world, his world, and he will come to loathe himself and others."

"But this is speculation, isn't it? Couldn't he remain totally impassive, apathetic about his situation?"

"He could." Father Gilhooey said doubtfully. He drained his glass and held his hand over its top when Black made a motion to refill it. "But I doubt it. He is an educated man. Highly educated. He has been trained to question, to challenge. He won't be able to stop himself. I don't really understand how he ended up in this situation at all."

Black ignored the priest's gentle prod and said. "But couldn't he also rationalize his way back to this sense of order?"

"He could." The priest looked at him closely. "I'd say, Ray, that you'd already made up your mind before you sent for me."

Black rubbed his hands hard across his face. They felt gritty and sweaty to him, and he grimaced and pulled a handkerchief from his pocket, soaked the handkerchief with water from the bottle on his desk, and scrubbed his hands with the handkerchief.

"You're right. I need him, but I also wanted him to get over feeling sorry for himself. That nobility you spoke of earlier. I don't need nobility out there. I need assholes, bastards who won't play philosophical games with what they are told. He needed to talk to someone and a psychiatrist was out. So I thought of you."

"I thought so," Father Gilhooey said. He rose and pulled the seat of his pants away from his buttocks. "Be careful about playing too many games, Ray. They often backfire when you least expect it."

"I've had that man for four years." Black said. He shook hands with the priest and walked him to the door.

"And he, you," the priest said. "Besides, I believe he's beginning to think again. I just wonder which of you will win."

"One more thing." The priest paused, looking at him questioningly. "What can we do to help him?"

"You could send him home. Time would help," the priest said.

Black shook his head. "That's out. I need him now."

"Then, take his mind off it," the priest said. "You have to change his mind slant. Get him preoccupied with something else. Think of the mind as being a series of rooms and each room is filled with a memory. You cannot force him into another room, but you can provide a situation that would let him build another room. This might be Morgan's road to Emmaus."

"What?" Black furrowed his brow, glowering at the priest. The priest laughed.

"It's from the writings of Matteo Ricci, a sixteenth-century Jesuit priest who experimented philosophically with memory. The road to Emmaus was his awareness of how memory works." He shrugged. "It's worth a shot, that's all."

"And what could such a thing be?" Black asked.

The priest frowned. "Who knows? It differs from individual to individual. Sometimes, the rooms are similar enough that we can guess what is in them. Other times, we simply have to take a shot. Morgan has been caught up in the war for so long, maybe he needs to experience pleasure that is distant from the war. If one spends too much time in unpleasant surroundings, depriving oneself of pleasure, sometimes the individual will satisfy the need for pleasure by aligning pleasure with the unpleasantness that is around him."

"It isn't fear in Morgan's case?"

The priest shrugged. "Difficult to say. I doubt it. One doesn't die of fear; one dies because of fear. Still," he added thoughtfully, "it's always there. There is a point for the best when one has to let go of everything. Given a certain combinaton of circumstances, fear will always come. Anything can bring it on—disappointment, bad food, a fallen comrade—there are things we simply cannot understand or comprehend about the dark powers loose in the world that are always on the verge of triumphing over the souls of men."

"The death of a brother?"

The priest pursed his lips. "Yes," he said slowly. "Yes, the death of a brother will certainly be a consideration. But death is only a moment. A man's honor is forever. Even after he dies. And that, I think, is what you are up against with Morgan. He's a man of honor in a world that has forgotten the meaning of the word."

"I see," Black said. "Pleasure. What kind of pleasure?"

The priest grimaced. "I'll leave that to you. I don't know the man well enough to suggest something."

Black watched him go and crossed to the bottle of Bushmill's. He poured himself another drink, then firmly corked the bottle and replaced it in the filing cabinet.

Pleasure. Well, there was one pleasure that all men knew and enjoyed. The trick was in getting the right person for the right job.

Women. Wasn't that the common denominator? There is always one basic thing that stimulates a progression of other things. Now, to change what is happening with Morgan, what?

He pondered the problem a moment, then smiled, finished his drink, and went back to his desk. The leather creaked as he settled his frame and flipped the file open to the back. He removed two sheets of green flimsy, read them carefully, and smiled again. He jabbed a square finger hard against the intercom and listened to the faint buzz.

"Yes, sir?" The voice was mechanical, nervous.

"Send Lieutenant Holmes in," he said, and lifted his finger from the switch. He leaned back in his chair and drummed his fingers on his desk top, humming softly to himself. He picked up the damp handkerchief from his desk and again began to methodically wipe his hands.

Chapter Thirty-one

Morgan was packing to leave the hospital when the door to his room opened and closed behind him and he heard her voice.

"It looks like I almost missed you," she said.

He slowly turned to her, a crisp, new khaki shirt in his hands. She looked very pretty in her summer dress. The white set off the golden tan of her arms and legs and the blue polka dots matched her eyes. Her hair was pulled back so tightly in a bun that it seemed to screech.

"Lucky I came when I did," she added. There was an awkward silence. "How are you?"

"Fine." He half-turned and dropped the shirt into the open canvas bag on the bed. "It's almost healed."

"I'm glad," she said. They stared at each other. "I was sorry to hear that you had been wounded."

"Were you?"

She dropped her eyes from his stare and awkwardly smoothed the front of her dress. "Yes. Well. I guess I shouldn't have come." She turned to go.

"Wait," he said. She stopped, but did not turn back to him. "Why did you come?"

"I was worried," she said lamely. "Where are you going? Back to the jungle?"

"No. Not yet, at least. I have a week and Maurice has asked me to spend it at his place. It's quiet," he added.

"I see."

"Rachel, why don't you look at me?"

She turned and threw her head back and stared at him. She wore no makeup, and the look of vulnerability he remembered from the last time he had seen her was gone, replaced instead with a quiet certainty that was fresh and appealing. He looked down at her hands and saw that the nails were no longer bitten and ragged, but smooth and squarely cut. A breath of freshness hung about her, as of frangipani just after a soft rain.

"I have to be truthful. Colonel Black sent me," she said.

Morgan nodded slowly and sat on the edge of the bed. He lit a cigarette, exhaled, and said, "You didn't want to come?"

"I did," she said. "But I wasn't sure."

"About me?" Her eyes disturbed him with their directness, and he felt uncomfortable and warm.

"Yes. And myself." She stood still, appraising him. He rose nervously and crossed to the table and poured himself a glass of water from the pitcher there. He drank thirstily and turned back to her. She hadn't moved.

"What did Black want?"

"He thought I might be able to help you." She smiled wryly. "No sacrifice too great, or something like that."

"That's Black all right. You can tell him that I don't need womanly comfort right now. That'll get you off the hook."

"How about just a friend?" she said calmly. Her eyes widened fractionally, almost hypnotically, and he heard a dull roaring like the sea in his ears.

"I think I'd like that," he said. "I don't have any here, you know. Outside of Maurice, that is." He laughed. "I've been here long enough that all of the others have been killed or gone home."

She smiled and her shoulders rolled forward slightly, and he became aware for the first time of the tension that had been within her and then his own nervousness revealed itself in his sweaty palms. He laughed and wiped them on the bed. She looked at him, puzzled for a moment, then laughed as he showed her his palms.

The door swung open and Maurice stepped into the room. He was cool and meticulous in his white suit and raised an eyebrow at the sight of Rachel. Then, he smiled.

"Always, my friend, I find you surrounded by beautiful

women." He clicked his tongue and shook his head in mock resignation. "The gallantry of the wound. I suppose, or the mytstery of youth. Which is it?"

"The need for friends," Morgan said. He smiled at Rachel. She smiled and nodded back.

Maurice crossed to the canvas bag and looked at its contents and grimaced. Gingerly, he poked around inside the bag and sighed. "Are you ready?"

"Almost," Morgan said. He zipped his shaving kit shut and dropped it into the bag and closed it. Maurice lifted it from the bed and crossed to the door.

"I shall wait for you downstairs," he said tactfully.

"Maurice," Morgan said. He stopped and turned back questioningly. "Do you think—that is, do you have room?"

Maurice looked quickly from Rachel to Morgan. "Of course," he said graciously. "It is a very large house and my wife and I have been quite alone for some time, now. Too alone. A bit of youth in the house would refresh us."

"Thank you," Morgan said. He turned back to Rachel. "How about coming with us?"

"Why—Oh, no! I couldn't. Colonel Black wouldn't allow that," she said.

"Why not?" They both spoke at once and she laughed.

"I couldn't impose," she said. "Maurice has made plans—"

"Which can easily be changed," Maurice interrupted. "Besides, nothing is more boring than the reminiscences of old people and another young one around would keep that from getting out of hand."

"It is a large house," Morgan said.

"Very large," Maurice agreed.

"And, we will be chaperoned," Morgan added.

"Very chaperoned," Maurice emphasized.

She threw her hands into the air in mock surrender. "All right! You've convinced me. Now, all we have to do is convince Colonel Black." She grinned at Maurice. "Very chaperoned? In this day and age?"

"You will find, my dear, that I have never been one to defend progress," Maurice said firmly. "I prefer to be an observer from the side. When it comes to politics and women, then one must savor them as fine food, tasting all the sauces, but one must avoid allowing either to give one indigestion."

"I'm not certain Colonel Black would agree," she laughed.

"Let me handle that," Morgan said firmly. "After all, he did send you here, did he not? I believe, then, that you are assigned to me for the duration, Lieutenant."

She laughed and took his arm. Maurice opened the door for them and they left, leaving the awkwardness behind in the room. They moved with a fresh lightness that caused others to stop and stare after them with envy and wonder at the cheerfulness they had discovered in a place of sickness.

Chapter Thirty-two

Her disheveled hair was the color of golden wet sand. One lock fell over her forehead, giving her the look of a gamin in the hot afternoon sun after their return from a walk in Maurice's vineyard. The vines had clustered thickly on both sides of the path they had chosen, leaving the narrow gap between the rows hot and humid. Her high cheekbones had the tinge of a rosy flush to them and her fine upper lip was dotted with perspiration. Beneath her white cotton blouse he could see the dark outline of her bra, soaked with her perspiration. She was stockingless, her fine calves shiny with sweat, her feet dusty in her Spanish sandals. She caught his stare and laughed, lifting her hand to touch her hair in such a manner that a sharp pang went through him.

"I must look terrible," she said. "The heat—"

"Compliments you," he said, interrupting her. She glanced at him and laughed, her mouth curving up into deep dimples. Her laughter gave her a delicate haze of sensuality.

"I doubt that. But it was good of you to say it anyway." She glanced around. They were alone among the vines with the heat and the silence. She shook her head and used both hands to sweep perspiration from her cheeks and forehead. "I think we had better get in out of the sun."

Obediently, he turned and led her around the end of the row, heading back toward the villa a short distance away. She stepped close beside him, her hip unconsciously bumping his.

"Did you sleep well last night?" she asked.

"Yes," he lied. It was their third night at Maurice's villa. Only the first night had he slept soundly, then he had caught the outline of her breast when she bent to pet one of Maurice's dogs in the courtyard. A brief flash, nothing more, but he could not get rid of the image of her laughing and petting the dog, crooning nonsense to it.

"Good," she said. "You need your rest."

He looked at her and caught her eyes. In that instant, they glowed slightly with an empty gray brilliance, and he knew that it wasn't simply the heat of the day that had made them glow like that, but suffering and fear as well. Or was it? He also knew that fatigue often dulled the mind enough to make the eyes look like they were afraid.

Bewilderment. That's what it is—bewilderment. She is as uneasy here as you.

"I hope Maurice's man has filled the ice bucket," she said, stumbling and turning her attention back to the hard, packed earth between the rows. He reached out and caught her arm, steadying her. His fingers burnt like a brand, and he hurriedly dropped her arm. She looked at him quizzically. "What's wrong?"

"Nothing," he said curtly. She frowned, then shook her head, smiling.

"Something, I think."

"No," he said. "It is nothing. He better had." She looked at him blankly. "Maurice's man? Filled the ice bucket. I could use a cold gin-tonic."

They passed under the arbor and stepped up onto the terrace, pausing to pant in the heat. Then she crossed to the French windows and stepped into the dark coolness of the library. The sudden change in light made her head ache, and she dropped gratefully onto a small divan while Morgan crossed to the small bar tucked in an alcove in the far corner of the room.

"A miracle. Ice. Would you care for one?" he asked.

"Please," she said.

He made the drinks and brought them to the divan, handing one to her. She took it and drank deeply, then sighed and leaned back against the divan. She sat up abruptly, shivering from the cool leather.

"I'm all sweaty," she complained. She laughed and stood. "I

think I'll change out of these." She drained the gin-tonic and handed the glass back to him. "Why don't you make another?"

"All right," he said, standing. She walked to the door.

"I'll only be a minute."

She disappeared through the doorway. He stood for a moment in the room, all rock and wooden beams and crammed bookshelves, then crossed back to the bar. He heard the wind rising and glanced out the french windows at the tops of the palm trees beginning to shiver and shake. Then a sudden gust of wind whipped through the treetops and a black cloud rolled over, sending hot rain to splatter against the terrace. He watched as the wind whipsawed through the bushes, ripping leaves away and spiralling them upward in a tiny whirlwind.

And then he found himself in the stubblefield, shotgun held across his chest while a black thundercloud rolled toward him. The fenceline curved sharply up away from him to the black, creosoted timbers of a railroad trestle. Beneath the trestle bright-red sumac danced and shimmered as clouds slipped rapidly over the sun.

Looks like a storm.

He turned to his left, seeing his father standing four rows away, shotgun tucked carelessly under one arm. In the distance, their border collie, Teddy, quartered the field, searching for pheasants.

Should we head back?

No, this is where the pheasants will sit. His father whistled sharply, and Teddy stopped, sitting on his haunches, head cocked in their direction. That is, his father amended, they will sit if Teddy doesn't run up on them. I'm thinking they'll be in that milo patch we left in the corner there.

They walked slowly toward it. Teddy slipped in behind his father's heels, head up, alert. They were nearly to the patch when five pheasants lifted up out of the ground so fast he caught his breath and raised his shotgun, firing before he was aware of firing. Dimly he heard his father's shotgun exploding beside him, Teddy barking, then he swung the barrel and dropped two in quick succession. He heard the bolt click on an empty chamber and stood for a moment, wondering why he hadn't felt the recoil of the shotgun, then wondered when he had worked the pump, shucking the shells as he fired.

You did good, Henry, his father said.

He glanced up as Teddy bounced over the stubble field in front of them and slipped through the milo patch, returning with the heavy body of a pheasant, limp in his jaws.

We got three of them, his father said. He looked warmly at Henry. That was as fine a double as I've ever seen. Usually only see that in a duck blind. With pheasants—he clicked his tongue. That's damn fine shooting.

A hard whick of lightning flashed followed hard by a loud boom of thunder. He blinked, staring out into the storm. He glanced down at the bottle of Gordon's in his hand.

Now, why the hell would you think about that at a time like this?

"Wicked isn't it?" He turned and saw her standing close beside him. He had not heard her coming into the room. She had changed into a white blouse and gray flannel slacks, her feet bare in tasselled moccasins. He caught the slight hint of cologne that she had used to cool her wrists and forehead. He handed her the gin-tonic.

"Yes, I think we are in for it," he said. He crossed to the French windows and pushed them slightly closed to keep the rain from blowing in upon the slate floor.

"Do you think Maurice would mind if we played some music?" she asked, moving over to the huge record player. She opened the doors and knelt, steadying the albums standing stiffly in their jackets.

"No," he said. "He won't mind. We're pretty much alone anyway. I don't see the Renault. I think he took Judith shopping."

"Yes, I had forgotten," she said. She selected a record and placed it on the turntable. The strains of Lizt's "Hungarian Rhapsody No. 4" came through the speakers, merging in counterpoint to the rain and the thunder.

"Who is Nuguyen Duc?" she asked, settling herself back on the couch.

"Nguyen Duc?" he corrected automatically. "An old man. A remarkable old man. How did you hear about him? Oh. Dispatches." He laughed and gestured with his hand holding his glass, nearly spilling it. "I had forgotten for a moment that we weren't alone here."

"We are," she said quietly.

"The war, I meant," he said. "I had forgotten the war."

"That's good," she answered, smiling. "That's what needs to be done. You need to forget occasionally."

"One shouldn't forget," he said. "That's when mistakes are made."

"Not necessarily. Sometimes, one needs to take a break to regroup one's thoughts. All work and no play, you know."

He remembered the way her breast had been outlined in the morning light when she bent to play with the dog, and again among the vines when she had been soaked with perspiration and the golden curl had lain dankly over her forehead. A hollowness settled in his stomach, followed by a flash of irritation.

"Is that what the colonel said? Are we supposed to be at play?" he asked, his voice hard with innuendo. She flushed and took a long drink, shuddering.

"No," she said, her eyes bright. Her voice sounded brittle. "No, that's not what the colonel told me. Why are you so defensive?"

"I'm not—"

"Oh, you are." She finished the drink and rose, carrying it back to the bar. She placed it on the zinc top and turned.

"Rachel—"

"I'm going up to my room," she said, interrupting him.

She left, and he turned again to stare out at the rain now lashing the ground so hard that droplets seemed to bounce from the earth.

Well, you certainly were a fool about that. She was only trying to be friendly and you slapped her in her face with it. Why?

But he knew why although he did not want to know why. A half-hour passed before he convinced himself that he had been sufficently the fool and that an apology was needed. He rose and went to the bar, finding a bottle of burgundy on the rack under the bar. He opened it, placing the cork back in the bottle, then picked up two glasses by their stems, twining them through his fingers, and left, climbing the stairs to the second floor.

He knocked on the door of her room, calling her name. When there was no answer, he edged the door open and called again. Her voice came, muffled.

"What is it?"

"I want to apologize."

"Go away."

"I'm sorry. I didn't mean what I said. I was being stupid."

"Yes, you were."

"May I come in?"

A long moment followed his question, and he was afraid she was going to refuse. Then she told him to come in, and he traced her voice through her room to a door opposite. He opened the door without thinking and walked in. She was in the tub.

"Sorry," he said, turning quickly.

"Sit down," she said. He glanced at her, and she motioned to a wicker chair opposite the tub. He held up the wine and glasses. A tiny smile touched her face.

"You think of everything, don't you, when you apologize?" she said.

"A peace offering," he said, trying to ignore her fine breasts and freckled shoulders wet and shiny in the dim light. She rubbed milled soap on a washcloth and scrubbed her neck. He knew his eyes were betraying his thoughts, and then a familiar ache grew in his groin. He sat hastily to keep it from showing. "Would you care for a glass?"

She eyed him appraisingly for a moment as she rinsed the soap from her neck and breasts. She smiled tightly at him and slid down into the tub, her arms resting on the sides so that only her shoulders were above the water.

Remarkably clear water for being soapy—

"A glass of wine would be nice," she said.

He poured hurriedly, slopping over the rim of the glass and

swearing silently to himself as he stretched to hand the glass to her.

"Thank you," she said, and he could hear the mockery in her voice. He rose.

"I'll just wait, uh, downstairs for you?" he said, making it a question.

"All right," she said.

He rose and without thinking, took a quick look at her, then turned away and left. He was halfway across the bedroom when he heard water splash and her voice from the doorway stopped him.

"You took the bottle with you."

He turned. She held her glass, empty, toward him. Her other hand held a towel over her breasts. He looked stupidly at the bottle in his hand, then felt himself growing scarlet. Why are you behaving like a schoolboy? he asked himself fiercely. It's not as if you hadn't seen naked women before.

He placed the bottle on a small table beside the bed and started to go, then stopped. He turned. She waited for him while he crossed and put his hands gently upon her naked shoulders. She shivered. He bent and kissed her firmly but not hard on the mouth. He leaned back and looked into her eyes, narrow, smoky.

"It doesn't have to mean a thing," she said, her voice husky. The towel dropped.

Chapter Thirty-three

The storm knocked the power out at eight that night and still the rain came down, flooding the highways. For three days, the rain fell, keeping Maurice and his wife away from their home. For three days, they made love, sometimes in her bedroom, sometimes in his, again in the library where he made a fire in the fireplace against the sudden cold brought by the rain. They drank wine and played music by the firelight. He told her about the mountains, and asked her to tell him about herself. But she refused, saying that in order for a woman to preserve some attraction she had to surround herself with a little mystery. Later, she relented and told him about college in Boston and how a man had approached her after her defense of her thesis and how she had decided to go into intelligence work. When he persisted, telling her that she was being unfair with him, she laughed and said that a woman could never be too unfair with men. And although he wanted to ask her again about herself, he sensed a strange attraction coming from her, sweetly, dangerous, and when she asked him about himself, he felt forced to tell her what she wanted to know. He told her about the ranch and finally his brother and Kate and Timmy, but even then, he held back, refusing to tell her everything about Kate and Timmy, telling himself that those lives were their lives and theirs only to tell if they wanted. She called him a traditionalist. When later she tried to talk again about his brother, he refused to add anything more other than to say that dying a proper death was becoming increasingly difficult to do. She pouted, then, accusing him of being a rogue, a lonely man, and he told her that was the egotistical inner grace of a man. And she laughed at that and things were again all right between them. Then they walked naked outside together to let the rain wash over them, cleansing them, and they stood in the thunder and the lightning and the rain, listening to the wind roar through the trees, smelling the wet earth and suddenly knowing together the world without end.

"My friend," Maurice said, moving out onto the terrace where Morgan sat on a chaise lounge, taking in the sun. "There is someone here to see you."

"Hello, boss," Stephens drawled. "Doesn't look like you're suffering to me."

Morgan opened his eyes. "What in the world are you doing here?"

"Pulled back for a little R and R," Stephens replied. "So I thought I'd slip out and tell you what's happening. I didn't mean to intrude." He looked at Maurice apologetically.

"Nonsense. You are not intruding. Will you stay for lunch?" Maurice replied.

"Well," Stephens began, but Maurice interrupted.

"Good. Good. I shall tell the cook that there will be five for lunch. Meanwhile, you two can talk your business." He nodded and smiled and walked into the house. Morgan frowned.

"Black pulled you back for R and R? You've only been out there six months."

"Yeah, I know," Stephens said. He glanced around. "Where's Lieutenant Holmes? Colonel Black said she was out here, too."

"Visiting with Judith, Maurice's wife," Morgan said. "What's up?"

Stephens pulled a chair close to Morgan and leaned in. "There's something else, but I'm not sure what it is. Anyway, I'm supposed to tell you about an old Sûreté file on Maurice that Black dug up. It seems like your good friend has his fingers in quite a few pots. Prostitution, gambling, suspected smuggling—"

"Smuggling?" Morgan's pulse quickened. He sat up, frowning. "What kind of smuggling?"

"Cigarettes and booze," Stephens said. "He didn't mention

drugs. 'Course that don't mean he ain't dealing, now. The market's changed a bit since the fifties, I'm told."

Morgan blew out a long, slow breath and leaned back against the chaise lounge. "Well, that's that, isn't it? We have our Saigon link."

"It would seem so," Stephens said. He glanced toward the house.

"What is Black going to do?"

Stephens shook his head. "Nothing," he said lowly, leaning toward Morgan. Morgan's eyebrows went up in surprise. "He has decided to use Maurice as a gathering point. Black says to tell you to leave him alone. They are going to let him stay because they want the shipments to continue coming to him. Meanwhile, they'll get someone inside to work with him. Now that they have a toe in the door, they are going to edge it open. They'll let some of the shipments trickle through to keep suspicion from him, but the big ones they'll take and try to trace back to shut down the lines one by one." He grinned. "Since they know the central destination in Saigon, they can work backwards and forwards to shut down the rest of the operation."

"So," Morgan breathed, frowning. "They're going to use another old man to do their dirty work."

Stephens moved uneasily in his chair. "Looks that way. But I don't think you can compare Maurice to Nguyen Duc."

"Can't you?" Morgan murmured. "I wonder." He rose and walked up the terrace and entered the French windows. He paused inside the room to let his eyes adjust from the bright sunlight. Prostitution and gambling and probably drug-running as well. What else has he hidden from you? And why did he go to such pains to disguise his other businesses? You really are a fool, you know. You should have realized the Club Eve wouldn't pay for all this, even with today's war economy.

He touched the rich brocade of the curtains beside the French windows and turned slowly to look at the room's furnishings with a new eye. A small Matisse rested in a gilt-edged frame above a high mahogany dresser to his left. He turned again and noticed two long, thin Chinese paintings in gold frames flanking the door on either side. The one to the right of the door was a series of peacocks painted in different shades of blue and contrasted nicely with the cherry blossoms of the one on the left. Although he did not know the artist or the period, they were obviously very expensive. Too rich for a café owner.

"Hello, darling," Rachel said, entering. She wore a light blue dress that lay softly against her golden tan. She paused, surprised at finding Stephens in the room. "Hello, Stephens. When did you arrive?"

"Ah, just a few minutes ago, ma'am," he replied. "The colonel pulled me out for a little R and R. I was gonna stop by the hospital to see the captain, but I heard that he was out here, so I asked for a couple of directions and, well . . . "

"Is everything all right?" Rachel asked, tiny frown lines appearing between her eyes.

"Sure," Morgan said. "The Montagnards are still camped but Nguyen Duc is getting a bit impatient for me to return. That's all." He nodded at Stephens. "Maurice asked him to stay for lunch."

"I see." She looked from one to the other. "What else?"

Morgan shrugged. "I don't know what you mean. What else?"

"You two look like the cat that swallowed the canary," she said. "What else brings you out here, Stephens?"

Stephens shrugged. "That's about it. I thought Captain Morgan would like to know that his people are doing all right in the base camp, but they're getting pretty restless. The old man wants to get back out into the forest."

"Really." Rachel shook her head. "You'd think that he'd like the base camp with all the amenities there."

"They're Montagnards, ma'am," Stephens said. "They don't belong there. They belong in the mountains. There ain't nothing about civilization that they will miss. In fact, they really think of us as the barbarians. Maybe they're right, you know?"

Morgan gave him a strange look. "Well, I see the old man's been giving you a bit of instruction. *Ông se duroc thurong.*"

"*Câm on ông,*" Stephens said. "Yes, he has been trying to teach me. I don't think I'm a very good student, though."

"It seems to be coming all right to me," Morgan said. "What do you think?" he asked Rachel.

"I think I'll see if lunch is ready," she replied, tossing her head. She left and Morgan glanced at Stephens.

"You played that pretty well."

Stephens shook his head. "No. I don't think so. She knows something else is up."

"You might be right," Morgan said. He led Stephens into the sitting room. Judith looked up from her place on the couch and marked her place in the book she was reading with her forefinger.

"Yes?" she asked, raising an eyebrow at Stephens's entrance. "I do not believe I have met this young man."

"This is Sergeant Stephens. He works with me, Judith. He just came in to give me a report on my people, and Maurice asked him to lunch. In fact, we were just looking for Maurice."

"How nice," she murmured and raised her hand. Stephens crossed the room and awkwardly took it. Unsure what to do, he pressed it gently then released it. She smiled. "I hope you enjoy your lunch, young man. I'm afraid it will not be very much. In the heat of the day, we do with very little, I'm afraid. It is an old person's fancy."

"I'm sure it will be fine, ma'am," Stephens said. He cleared his throat and glanced over at Morgan.

"You will find Maurice in the library, dear," she said to Morgan. "He said he had a few telephone calls to make before lunch."

"Thank you, Judith. Enjoy your book," Morgan said.

"I always enjoy Colette, my dear. She reminds me of—better times."

"Excuse me, ma'am," Stephens stuttered, and turned to follow Morgan from the room.

"Of course," Judith murmured. She frowned at their exit, then sighed and returned to her reading.

Maurice looked up in surprise from his desk as Morgan slid the library doors open. He hastily replaced the telephone and rose. "Ah. Are you finished, then? Good," he said, smiling. "I think there is just time enough for a glass of sherry before lunch.

Unless," he said, suddenly conscious of Stephens, "you would prefer something else? A beer, perhaps?"

"Sherry will be fine, sir," Stephens said.

Maurice beamed at Morgan. "Well. Sir. I may have to revise my opinion of Americans. Manners aren't thrown by the wayside, I see." He moved to a small table in front of the fireplace. He carefully poured three glasses of sherry from a crystal decanter and handed one to each of the others. "I would offer you a cigar—I have Banderillos—but I believe the cigar would be more enjoyable after lunch. What do you think, my friend?" he asked, looking at Stephens.

"I'm afraid I don't know that much about proprieties one way or the other," Stephens confessed. "But I think a cigar would go better after one eats than before. Common sense."

"You see? Common sense. Is that so hard for people to remember? Bon," he said delightedly. "Now, sherry," he paused to take a sip, "that is one of the small things that really makes life pleasurable." He crossed to a chair and motioned the others to a seat on the small sofa. "Please." He sat. "Man does not really take much pleasure in the large things, but in the small. Don't you agree? The drink to celebrate the end of a business deal, the bottle of wine with a beautiful woman, the cocktail at the end of a successful day, these things are the true pleasures in life."

"Perhaps," Morgan said. "There are others, though. Certain smiles at certain times and the mornings at quiet pools when the animals come down to drink and the flowers that bloom after the first gentle rains before the monsoon."

"You see," Maurice said. "We are in agreement."

"About the small things in life?" Morgan smiled. "Perhaps. But life cannot be lived for simple pleasures. There must be a responsibility, too."

Maurice laughed silently. "Spoken like a Frenchman! You do not belong in the military, my friend. You belong in business like me."

"I have been giving some thought to that lately, especially since this," he touched his wound. "But," Morgan smiled, "it is so difficult to find the backing to get started."

"Hmm," Maurice said, sipping. "Of course, that could be easily overcome between friends, you know."

"Perhaps," Morgan answered. He shrugged and leaned back against the sofa. "I suppose, however, that would depend upon one's friends, wouldn't it? What do you think, Stephens?"

"I don't know," Stephens said, shaking his head. "I'm afraid I don't know much about business." He rubbed his nose with the heel of his palm and grinned. "I'm more the worker than the boss, you see. I'll leave that end of it to you, sir." He finished his sherry.

"Another?" Maurice asked, making to rise. Stephens shook his head.

"No, thanks," he said. He rose and crossed to the small table and placed his glass beside the decanter. "You have some interesting books here," he said, pausing to look at the titles.

"Oh?" Maurice raised an eyebrow at Morgan. "Are you a reader, then?"

"When I can get the chance," Stephens said. "Mostly mysteries, that sort of thing."

"Then, you have never read Marcel Proust?"

"Who? No."

"You should try him. You'll find his work to your right, second shelf," Maurice said. He looked at Morgan. "It used to be that one had to have a friend in the banks." He shrugged. "*C'était la coutume alors.* But, times have changed. Now, one can sometimes arrange a business with a friend or two. You have one friend here, *mon ami.* What is it you would wish to do?"

"Would I not need another friend?" Morgan said.

"That would depend upon the business," Maurice said. "Certainly one needs many friends these days in order to get supplies for one's business, but money, well, that simply depends upon *une amitié solide.*" He gave a wry smile. "Sometimes, one must do business with the enemy, you know."

"Oh?" Morgan said. "What do you mean?"

Maurice sighed. "Let me see if I can explain. In March 1945, the Japanese removed the Vichy authorities and the Americans, through the OSS, began to supply arms and instructors to Ho

Chi Minh who was by then in command of the Viet Minh. But Ho Chi Minh was clever and knew the Japanese would not last long. Soon, they would be defeated. Meanwhile, he eagerly accepted the supplies being given to him to fight the Japanese which he had no intention of doing. Instead, he cleverly played a waiting game and built an army. When the Japanese surrendered in August 1945, Ho Chi Minh seized Hanoi and declared an independent Democratic Republic of Vietnam. This, of course, would have meant we, the French, would have lost everything we had. In all actuality, though, we were not French, but Vietnamese. I was born here. My family goes back to 1872. Yet, according to Ho Chi Minh, we were French and therefore, had no right to own Vietnamese land."

His eyes became distant and he rose and crossed to the French windows and threw them open. "Our land once stretched for miles along the river," he said softly. He rubbed his hand across his eyes and turned back to Morgan. "Naturally, we could not allow that to happen. We tried to negotiate with Ho Chi Minh, but he refused and we did the only thing we could. We seized the Viet Minh headquarters in Saigon. Perhaps that was a mistake. Who knows? But it seemed the only thing we had left. But we were still too weak and we were almost beaten before General Jean de Lattre de Tassigny was appointed the High Commissioner and Commander-in-Chief of Indochina with full freedom to do as he wished.

"He promptly defeated the Viet Minh at Vinh Yen, but," Maurice shrugged, and ran his hand helplessly through his hair. Morgan noted the perspiration on his upper lip. "But, de Tassigny died of cancer in 1952 and General Raoul Salan was named to succeed him. He overextended his forces and was almost totally defeated until General Henri Navarre replaced him. He knew the only thing that could save his army from defeat was help from the Americans. He needed money, materials, but more importantly, he needed men. France could only send him ten battalions. The Americans gave him a few token supplies, but that was all. Tell me, my friend, what good are guns if you have no one to shoot them?"

He paused, shuddered, and crossed to the small table. He removed a bottle of cognac and poured a glass, drinking it. He shuddered again. "My son was fresh from St. Cyr and was one of the officers of those battalions. Yes," he said at Morgan's reaction. "Judith and I had a son. Our only child. There were complications at birth and—we could have no other. In November 1953 he jumped with his men into Dien Bien Phu. He was killed on May seventh when the Viet Minh 308th Division broke through the defenses."

He fell silent and stared out into the bright sunlight. "He didn't have to die," he said softly. "The Americans could have sent the necessary forces before Dien Bien Phu as requested earlier by General Navarre, but the Americans preferred to wait and see what happened. They knew money and supplies would be needed to rebuild the country. No matter who won, the country would have to be rebuilt. The Americans had the money and supplies and for collateral, there were the rubber and sugar plantations. Very shrewd businessmen, the Americans. Our resources would have gone very cheaply had it not been for Ho Chi Minh."

He paused and refilled his glass with brandy. Deep lines of pain crossed his face. He smiled bitterly at Morgan and continued.

"You see, my friend, Ho Chi Minh knew the United States wanted the rubber and sugar of Vietnam, but more importantly, the harbors. Haiphong was a natural port for the United States merchant vessels. All of Vietnam, for that matter, would have provided the United States with several ports for trade and refueling. Instead of complying with the American wishes for a free election to be conducted under the watchful eyes of the United States and its allies, Ho Chi Minh used the two-year waiting period before the elections were to be held to establish several administrative zones which undermined the influence of the United States. He made one mistake, however, when he alienated two religious groups, the Cao Dai and the Hoa Hao. That gave the United States the opening it needed."

"You forgot the Binh Xuyen," Morgan said mildly. "Ho Chi Minh also alienated them."

"My friend, do you not know about the Binh Xuyen?" He laughed. "They flow with the tide. They control the opium distribution, the gambling and prostitution, and gold and ivory smuggling. They will support anyone who does not interfere with them. Bao Dai had allowed their leader, Van Le Vien, to control the police, but Colonel Edward Lansdale knew this gave the Binh Xuyen too much power and he convinced Ngo Dinh Diem to cancel the—er, arrangement with Van Le Vien.

"Of course, Van Le Vien chose to ignore Diem's orders and Diem ordered his paratroopers to drive the Binh Xuyen from Saigon. Following his victory there, Diem promptly removed the Cao Dai and Hoa Hoa leaders from his government. This gave him control over the election offices and he severely defeated Bao Dai in the promised election by over ninety percent, but the counting of the ballots was made by Diem's officers. That election, my friend, had the sanction of your government. But, Diem made one mistake: he forgot about the Binh Xuyen. He thought they were totally defeated, but they were not. They are still here, my friend, only secretly."

Morgan clasped his hands behind his back and looked at him thoughtfully.

"And what of communism, my friend?" he asked quietly. "Do you seriously believe you could survive like this under Ho Chi Minh's rule?" He indicated the room.

Maurice shrugged his shoulders. "What is government to a people who have known many? I do not care for one more than another. I am a businessman, an old businessman. I have enough to live my years as a gentleman. Ho Chi Minh may have the rest if he wishes."

"Excuse me," Rachel said, entering the room. "But Judith says that lunch is ready."

"Ah," Maurice said, beaming. He gestured toward the door. "And now, my friends, enough of this talk of politics. I am afraid that it is really much beyond me. So, let us enjoy ourselves as we can. Time is so short."

"Yes," Morgan said absently. "Time is so short."

Rachel gave him a strange look as she linked arms with him,

but he pretended not to notice. The lunch was a success in small talk. They joked with each other. Maurice gently insulting the United States, Morgan and Stephens insulting France, both insulting the South Vietnamese government. Rachel tactfully engaged Judith in discussion about the changing fashions and promised to send the newest American magazines to her when she got back to Saigon.

Later, when they were alone in her room, Morgan almost asked her to marry him. But then, he remembered her reluctance to tell him about herself. She sensed something disturbing him, and later, when they rested in bed, she asked him what was wrong.

"Are you afraid something's going to happen?" she said, propping herself up on her elbows. Her naked breasts swung near his lips. He kissed them, grinning as her breath caught in her throat.

"Something always happens," he said.

She sensed the change in his mood and quickly changed the subject. She looked out through the open French windows and sighed.

"This reminds me of Florida," she said. "Have you ever been to Florida?"

"No," he said.

"But"—she frowned, nibbling on her lower lip—"Florida lacks something this place has. I can't quite place it, but—"

"Danger?" he suggested.

"No." She frowned, concentrating. "I just can't say it."

"Maybe it is us," he said. She sat up, looking soberly down at him.

"Have you ever thought about what will happen to us when this is over?" she asked.

"We'll go back home," he said. "We'll go back home. Together."

"Will we?" A sadness came into her eyes, and for a moment, he thought he saw a small tear trickle down. Then, she laughed.

"Why are we getting so serious about all of this?"

"Because it is serious. For the moment, anyway," he said.

The smile slipped from her face. She fell across him, her head tucked into his shoulder.

"Yes," she said, her voice muffled. "For the moment."

Later, when she slept deeply, he rose and made his way downstairs to the library. He poured a drink in the darkness and sipped it, listening. The ticking of the clock on the mantel seemed to fill the room in her absence, and Morgan stepped through the windows to the outside. He sat in a chair on the terrace and watched the sun slowly come up. The sun beat warmly upon him. Across the river, a dog barked, and then it was quiet. A cool breeze caressed his cheek, and he thought about the old man waiting for him.

You are the only one who is true to himself. You, old man, in your search for your son who has wronged you for that is your way. That is the difference between you and Maurice and it is myself who has done this terrible thing to both of you. No, I'm wrong, aren't I? You both have been true to something greater.

"All right," he whispered. "All right. I'm coming."

Slowly he turned and left the sun.

Chapter Thirty-four

"*Aiee,* but it is good to see the Dai-uy again!" Nguyen Duc beamed and pumped Morgan's hand.

"And your ugly face again, old man," Morgan said. He returned the handshake and clapped Nguyen Duc on the shoulder. "You have grown fat and lazy in my absence. Kai has been taking very good care of you."

"And I her," the old man said slyly, and made an obscene gesture. "It is good you are back. And the Trung-sĩ," he added. "It is good you have returned as well. You had us worried."

Morgan's eyebrows lifted. "The Trung-sĩ? Promotion? You didn't tell me," he said to Stephens.

Stephens grinned, embarrassed. "Well, it's sort of new."

"Good," Morgan said. He smiled. "Real good. I'm pleased." He turned back to the old man and reached into the thigh pocket of his jungle trousers and produced the battered silver flask.

"Here, old man, drink." He handed the flask to Nguyen Duc, but the old man shook his head. "The Dai-uy and the Trung-sĩ must drink first."

Morgan hesitated, then shrugged and took a swallow of the Scotch and handed the flask to Stephens who took a cautious sip. Morgan was amused at the change that Stephens had undergone over the past months. The arrogance of the young man he had known in Saigon was gone, leaving in its place a thoughtful and introspective young man who was rapidly becoming assimilated into the Montagnard ways.

Stephens handed the flask to Nguyen Duc, the old man eagerly seized the flask, tilted it high, and swallowed deeply. He brought it down, sighed heavily in satisfaction, and handed it back to Morgan. He wiped his mouth with the back of his hand and sighed again.

"Good," he said. "The old woman has been cooking a monkey stew. You are hungry?"

"Eeeah," Morgan said gravely. "It has been long since I ate as a man should eat. They feed a man as a baby eats in the hospital and then wonder why he does not get better." He spat on the ground and the old man grinned delightedly.

"Tonight, we feast and dance and then tomorrow, we hunt," he said. He looked at Stephens. "And you. Trung-sĩ, you will join us?"

"I am honored," Stephens said gravely, haltingly. "You are good to make me welcome on this joyous occasion."

"Yes," Morgan said, clapping Stephens on his shoulder. "Tomorrow, we hunt. The young one, she is still with Kai?"

The old man glanced quickly at Stephens, then back to Morgan. "Yes, she is still with Kai."

They began to walk from the landing pad toward the cookfires just inside the sandbag wall. Nguyen Duc grunted and shook his head in mock dismay.

"That one! Young men follow her around like moonstruck dogs, but never does she smile or talk to them. They are like forest ghosts to her. Every day she asks when the Dai-uy shall return, and every day I tell her when the wound is better. And since the Trung-sĩ left, she asks about you, too. And I tell her that such things I do not know. And every day she burns the stew and ruins the meat. It is a good thing you are back, Dai-uy for it is not good for a man to eat in this manner."

Morgan smiled, and said, "Perhaps tonight the food will be right."

"Perhaps." The old man scowled ferociously. "If not, you must cut a length of green bamboo and beat her to teach her duty and respect."

"It shall be so," Morgan said solemnly, repressing his laughter. "She will learn to cook better if I beat her." Stephens made a strangled sound, and he glanced at him. He looked solemnly back at Morgan, but Morgan could see tiny lights dancing in his eyes and knew that he had caught the joke.

"And you. Everything is all right with you?" the old man asked. He touched Morgan's shoulder. Morgan nodded, but his eyes lifted and stared out over the wall of the compound to the green hills in the distance. A cloud seemed to pass over him and he shivered and looked up, expecting to see the sun covered, but the sky was cloudless, a startling blue that hurt the eyes to look at. It was the sun of the prairies on the rim of the Badlands of South Dakota, and for a moment, he smelled the rich green of the prairie grasses and the bitter saltgrasses and dropseed that lived on the edge of the Badlands and then he thought of Dog and a great sadness filled his spirit and he blinked against the sudden tears that seemed to collect in his eyes and he squeezed his eyes shut and wiped them with his thumb and forefinger.

"You okay?" Stephens asked, concerned, looking at him. He forced a laugh.

"Yes, yes. Dust."

Ahh, Dai-uy, the old man thought. There is much sadness within you, and I do not know what this sadness is, but you had better rid yourself from the sadness before we hunt or the sadness will consume you.

They had drawn close to the cookfires. One of the figures turned and stared at them, then leaped to its feet. "Trung-sĩ!" The young woman ran around the fire and rushed to him and threw her arms around him.

Morgan frowned, then the young woman stepped closer to him and hugged him. He held her tightly against himself, imagining that he held Rachel in his arms. But it was not Rachel and he knew it was not Rachel and although for the moment he could pretend it was Rachel, he knew that moment would not last. She took herself away from him and stepped closer to Stephens.

"Long have I waited for you to return!" she said. She thrust her chin at Nguyen Duc. "And this one says tomorrow, perhaps, and if not then, the next day, and tomorrow comes and the next, and again he says tomorrow, perhaps, and if not then, then next day!"

Her voice softened, and she looked into his eyes, then drew back a little and frowned, pursing her lips. "But you have not forgotten and you have returned. You have both returned. This is so?" The last was a question, and Morgan knew she could sense the hesitation in him, but he forced a smile.

"Yes," he said. His voice sounded strange to his ears. "Yes, I have returned."

"Dai-uy," the old man said uncomfortably. "There is much that needs to be said."

"No," Morgan said. He smiled at Stephens and the young woman. "There is nothing that needs to be said. Enough has been said already."

"You are not angry?" the young woman asked him anxiously.

He smiled gently at her and touched her face with the tips of his fingers, tracing the outline. "No, I am not angry. I am pleased. Very pleased," he added, looking at the old man.

Relief shined from the old man's face. She took his hand and led him around the fire and pushed on his shoulders until he sat on the ground in front of the fire. The old man followed, his joints making tiny popping sounds as he lowered himself to the ground. Stephens dropped effortlessly on the other side of the old man.

"Fix the stew!" the old man grumbled. "Kai, bring the fermented goat's milk. We have guests!"

"Fix the stew," the young woman mimicked, then squatted on her heels beside Stephens. Her hair smelled fresh and clean and hung in a glossy black mantle over her shoulders. Her eyes shined brightly and a rosy bloom highlighted the brown of her cheeks. The gaunt hollows had filled, and she seemed almost womanly now, instead of the frightened young girl he had first known. She smiled anxiously at him. "You were lonely for me?" An anxious note crept into her voice, and Morgan thought of Rachel. He felt the old man's eyes upon him, but refused to look.

"Very much," Stephens said, smiling at her. "Every day more than the first."

She blinked, then clapped her hands excitedly. Morgan grinned and cleared his throat, but the old man growled at her.

"Enough! Ready our stew, then find Kai. Cannot you see how hungry we are?"

She stood and placed her hands on her hips and glared at him.

"And you, what do you do but sit around the cookfire and demand this and demand that? Get food! Get beer! Aiee!" She spat into the fire. "It is good the Dai-uy and the Trung-sĩ have returned. Now, you will have to be like a man and not an old woman!" She flounced away as Nguyen Duc began to splutter angrily.

"Kai has taught her well," Stephens observed solemnly. "She is almost a woman."

"Badly," the old man disagreed, shaking his head. "She has become a witch." He looked shrewdly at Morgan and hunched his shoulders. "And you have changed, also, Dai-uy."

"How so, old man?" He pulled his flask from his pocket, drank, and passed it to the old man. Nguyen Duc took it but did not drink and passed it to Stephens beside him.

"In the eyes," the old man said. "They have become older in such a short while. It is not the wound, but something else, I think."

Morgan laughed. "The young one is right: you have become an old woman from too much time around the fire."

"No," Nguyen Duc said slowly. "I have not changed. Have you had second thoughts about doing that which must be done?"

"What must be done, must be done," Morgan said. He heard the women hurrying to the fire and turned his head to watch their approach.

"Yes," he heard the old man say softly. "What must be done, must be done."

Kai bustled up to the fire, bellowing his name, her arms outstretched in greeting, and Morgan rose to his feet to meet her. Stephens rose as well, politely, but his eyes were soft on the young woman who pretended not to notice, but Morgan caught the slight red to her cheeks before Kai seized him and hugged him roughly to her broad breast and a sudden contentedness filled him and he did not know if it came from Kai or the relief he felt with what he read in their expressions.

Chapter Thirty-five

The night was clear with the last hint of rains still in the air. Morgan rested comfortably on a poncho liner, his fingers laced behind his head supported by his pack. Many stars were out and glistened like dots of ice and he listened to the singing and the arguments among those still at the campfire and the hillbilly twanging of a guitar, badly out of tune, from the American barracks at the far end of the compound. He could still taste the hot curry from the monkey stew on his tongue and his belly rolled and gasped contentedly. A faint hint of opium wafted across on the night breeze, and he knew Nguyen Duc had used one of the carefully hoarded brown pellets and would be sleeping contentedly, safe once again in his dreams beside the fire. He smiled as he remembered Nguyen Duc's patient explanation when he had tried to talk the old man from using the opium.

"A man lives many lives," he had said. "And, if he is fortunate, he may live them many times over. An old man needs to be reminded of those many lives before he dies so he will be able to answer truthfully when the gods judge him."

"Many lives? Most men would be satisfied if they can live one true life," Morgan had answered.

"Then, they have lived sorrowful and empty lives," the old man answered. "For a man has many lives he must lead to be a man. First, there is the life to himself which is very private and of those things he must keep within himself. Second, the life he leads with his woman and third, that which he leads with his children. A fourth life is the one he leads with his people and a fifth he leads with his friends. And, if a man has many wives and many friends, he may have need of many lives to satisfy them."

"And his god," Morgan said. "You have forgotten his god. A man must have a life for him."

"The gods," the old man said gently, but stressing the plural, "are always there and with him in each of his lives, so he does not need a separate life for them. But he does owe a life to the forest and those that live in the forest for they are as much a part of him as his hands and feet. But, I think you know this, Dai-uy, for I think you have been told this before."

"Yes, old man, I have been told this before, but it is good to be told this again, for I had forgotten it until you spoke. But, tell me, does not the opium make you also remember the unpleasant and sad lives as well?"

"No, Dai-uy, that is forgotten by remembering the happiness. Those who do remember the sad times and unhappiness are those who have lived but one life and that one very badly. They do not allow the bad times to disappear and thus they lose the other lives they may have had."

But some things, old man, can never disappear. Or is that why you hunt so desperately for your son who is your son no more? And what will happen when you kill him or he kills you? Will those many lives you visit tonight disappear? With one death like this, you kill all or a part of yourself for he is a part of yourself, your flesh, your blood, as surely as your soul is part of yourself.

The guitar stopped and a glass broke in the American barracks followed by a loud argument, and Morgan knew the soldiers were either drunk or high on marijuana, and he raised himself on one elbow to satisfy himself that the watchtowers were still manned. He was thankful for the bright night that allowed him to see the sentries still posted and the clear fields of fire his Montagnards had made by cutting the brush back a hundred meters past the concertina wire that enclosed the compound fifty meters outside the wall. If the sentries had left their posts, he would have had to place Montagnards in the towers and although he did not believe the Viet Cong would be so foolish as to launch an attack on so bright a night, guerilla bands, led by foolish men still secure in their belief of their own vulnerability, roamed the area.

He relaxed back on his poncho and stared again at the sky and wondered at the weakness of the American soldiers who allowed themselves the luxury of getting drunk in the middle of such danger.

One day, you will do this one time too many, and then you'll be dead, he thought. But you won't know you are dead because you will be too drunk or high to feel the bullet in your belly or the knife across your throat. Then, the whole business will be started again and MAC-V will send another group out here and soon the jungle will press on them, too, and they will become afraid and begin to drink and smoke and a third group will come out when they are dead and the jungle will drive them mad as well.

It is too much civilization that causes this. We are taught to hate, but we are not prepared for hate. A man must learn how to control his hate and learn not to be afraid of the night and the darkness of the jungle. We have been away from the jungle too long. We do not understand her ways and she is not a patient teacher. That is the true killer out here, those who come out into the jungle from Saigon and Hanoi. They try to live in the jungle, the forests and mountains and keep the ways of their cities with them, but they do not know how the jungle, the forest and mountains, will not forgive them for what they try to do. Even the ones who are trained to fight here, the killers, will be killed by the jungle because they do not understand her and that is another reason why we will still lose this war.

Unless, he corrected himself, you do what Black has told you to do and bring an army together from all the tribes of the Montagnards, the Rands, the Mois, the Brus, the Cuas, Pachos, Katus, Sedangs, all of them, along with the Jarai and the Rhade. And then, there will come an end to everything for the people of the jungle will become the people of the city and they will change their ways and destroy that which they have learned from living in the jungle, the forest and mountains, until that, too, dies, and that will bring about the death of the jungle, and the forest and mountains just as surely as the prairie back home died when the Indian was forced to change his ways. And with the death of the prairie came the death of the animals and the death of the land and with it, a death of that which lived in the animals and the land.

Soft footsteps approached, and he silently eased his hands from behind his head and lifted the pistol beside his body. The young woman stopped beside him, and he lowered the pistol and slipped it beside his pack. She knelt beside him and he felt her fingers move gently across his chest.

"Dai-uy?" she whispered quietly.

"I do not sleep," he said, and saw her teeth flash whitely in the dark of her face. She sat cross-legged beside him. He breathed deeply and smelled the mango oil she had rubbed on her skin and the jasmine from her hair. The guitar began again, and he recognized the Hank Williams song through the slurred lyrics of the singer and then the Montagnards began their drumming and the singer stopped abruptly as the drumming swelled and consumed the night. The Montagnards began to chant, and he recognized the words about the man who was changed to a tiger and sired a new clan of warriors to fight the Dacoits and these warriors became the Montagnards, one with the mountains and the jungle and the forest.

"You are not angry? This is true what you said? About the Trung-si and myself?"

"No," he said. He smiled in the darkness. "I am not angry. It is what was meant to be. I hope you are happy together."

"I do not want you to be angry," she said.

"I am not angry," he reassured her. He reached up and gently touched her cheek. She took his hand and held it tightly. Tears glittered in the moonlight in her eyes. "It is better that you be with the Trung-si for he is much younger and will be better for you."

"This has been much on my mind," she said.

"And mine," he said quickly. "I did not know how to tell you."

"You have found someone back in Saigon?"

"Yes," he said. He smiled. "You see, I, too, had a secret that I did not know how to share with you."

"You feel strongly for her?"

"I do not know. Not yet. Perhaps later."

"But you do feel something for her?"

"Yes."

"Then, that is enough," she said. She released his hand. "I am glad that this did not become *mat cua muop dang*—sawdust and bitter melon, Dai-uy."

> "All things are fixed by Heaven, first and last.
> Heaven appoints each creature to a place.
> If we are marked for grief, we'll come to grief.
> We'll sit on high when destined for high seats.
> And Heaven with an even hand will give
> Talent to some, to others happiness."

She walked away from him. He lay, remembering the old poem—*The Tale of Kieu*—and listened to the drums and the song of the Montagnards. The drumming came inside him, then, and began to explode along his frame, and he felt the mountains and the forest once again seize his soul and merge with it, the soul of the universe.

Chapter Thirty-six

Strange shapes moved through the fog in Bao's mind as he slept and, although he did not dream they were speaking, the sounds of the night forest crept stealthily through his unprotected ears and leaped from the mouths of the shapes. It was a bad dream, a nightmare of ponderous proportions that brought beads of sweat to his forehead, his upper lip, and caused him to tense the muscles in his stomach and legs until they cramped painfully and he woke to their agony and cried out against the fear he had felt.

He opened his eyes and stared at the palm fronds lashed hastily together for a temporary shelter above him. His mouth felt dry and caked, and the ground was cold and clammy against his outstretched hands as he lay crucified on his bed of ferns. His heart hammered heavily in his ears, and he heard the rain dripping on the palm fronds and the rustling of the young woman beside him as she turned, half-awake, quizzically, toward him. He rolled weakly away from her questioning hands, and she grumbled and rolled to the back of the bed, yawned, and was still. Soon, she began to snore softly against the patter of the rain on the palm fronds.

Bao felt the palm fronds pressing in on him and turned his face to stare out into the rain and blackness. A small puddle had formed where the rain dripped off the roof over his head and he watched the heavy drops strike the puddle and form circles that moved on tiny waves to the edge of the puddle. He lifted his arm and dropped his fingers weakly into the puddle and brought them to his dry lips. He rubbed the wetness over them. The water was cool, and he dabbled his fingers again and again in the puddle and brought them repeatedly to his lips until he felt his arms and legs grow stronger. He rolled to the puddle and drank deeply, slurping the water like a rabid dog, his throat constricting with every swallow, until his lips brushed the mud at the bottom of the puddle. He rolled onto his back and let the rain wash over his eyes and cheeks and cleanse his mouth.

Refreshed, he sat up and spun around and sat cross-legged under the palm fronds and stared out into the blackness. Although he had been sweating earlier, he was cold now, and he pulled a blanket from the bed of ferns and draped it over his shoulders. The woman grunted once in complaint and curled tightly into a fetal position.

Bao ignored her and watched the rain refill the puddle he had just emptied and an image of himself as a small boy inside the large, airy hut that denoted the importance of his father flashed across his mind, and he saw himself standing on top of his soft bed, staring out into the night at the violent cracks of forked lightning as they danced a god's dance along the rim of the gorge by the hanging bride and played tag with the smooth, gray granite walls of the gorge. He laughed and clapped chubby hands delightedly as the lightning forked and danced for him and then there was a sudden flash so near and so bright that he saw only darkness and dancing balls of color, red and green, and dark shapes beyond that leaped threateningly at him. He knew he was screaming for he could feel the tautness at the corners of his mouth, but he could not hear his scream, only the roaring echo of a large explosion, and his nose burned from brimstone, and his urine ran down his leg. Then, arms wrapped soothingly around him, and he felt his mother's warmth and turned himself in to the warmth, her breast a soft pillow against his cheek, her hands stroking the back of his head, cunning fingers kneading the terror from his back. Slowly, her voice came to him, first as a pleasant rattle in her chest and throat, then slowly separating into familiar words that fell in the night like raindrops and melted his fears and halted his tears.

"Mother," he whispered to the night. But there was no answer. Softly, he hummed the tune of the song to himself, cautiously because it was a child's song, a comforting song, and he tried to imagine her face as she sang, her lips forming the words. He closed his eyes and pressed his lips together in concentration, but nothing appeared save a scant outline that could have been anyone or even a willow bush. She was gone.

He pulled the blanket over his head like a shawl and hunched his shoulders inside its thin warmth. He closed his eyes and searched for a memory to quiet the tremor of terror that built slowly within him. But there was only darkness, and the sounds of the forest, once familiar sounds, now the sounds of the alien dark that cause wild speculation of their origin and painted terrifying pictures in his mind. That cough, was it a tiger? But there were no tigers in the rain and what was that crackling in the underbrush?

He opened his eyes and stared at the growth of bushes ten feet away. A streak of lightning flashed through the gloom and there, against a tree, rain sluicing off his body, stood the Dai-uy.

"No," he whispered. "No. No." He threw the blanket off his shoulders and fumbled for his carbine. But it was lost in the bedclothes, and he scrambled wildly in the darkness for it. Another flash of lightning, and he turned back to the tree and the Dai-uy was gone. He rubbed his eyes again and stared wildly around in the darkness in search of him, but found nothing.

"You are here," he whispered to the dark. He felt the trembling begin in his tightly tense muscles. His hands quivered, and he clasped them tightly between his legs. "I know you are here." But no sound came and suddenly he had to urinate and he cringed from the idea of stepping out into the rain. He rose and moved cautiously to a corner pole and leaned against it and urinated. Shame burned through him, but he knew if he stepped out into the darkness, the Dai-uy would be there and there would be only the Dai-uy and him in the darkness in the forest, for now, even the forest had left him and he was all alone.

Chapter Thirty-seven

Morgan watched the old man move slowly and carefully from sleep. He blinked at the gray light of morning and dug gnarled knuckles into his eyes and worked the gummy matter free. He ran his tongue around his teeth and spat into the coals of the fire. Then he sighed and slowly sat up, his joints popping in protest. He saw Morgan watching him with amusement, and he vigorously scrubbed the heels of his hands across his face, held his nose delicately between thumb and forefinger and blew the night mucus onto the ground.

"Good dreams, old man?" Morgan asked. He felt Stephens move up silently beside him and squat. He handed Morgan a cup of coffee and blew on his own, sipping.

Nguyen Duc yawned and pressed his hands hard against his temples. "Aiee! My head!" he rasped, hawked, and spat again. Morgan took a sip from his tin cup filled with thick, dark coffee and handed it to the old man. The old man sipped noisily, gratefully. He yawned and contentedly scratched his groin.

"I dreamed about the tigers and the one that killed a woman of my village," he said. "I hunted two days for that one and finally killed him north of Plei Mrong. But not before he gave me this." He pulled his baggy trousers back from his right leg and proudly displayed the ancient scars, four parallel white ridges running down the outside of thick muscle and stopping at the swelling of the calf.

"A good omen, that dream, do you not think so?"

"A very good dream," Morgan said gravely. "It is an omen for our success."

"As I think." The old man hawked and spat into the coals.

He glanced around at the quiet figures huddled around the fire. He smiled at the young girl still asleep on Stephens's pallet, then glanced at Stephens.

"You slept well, Trung-sĩ?"

"Very well," Stephens said gravely. "I did not dream of tigers, but I thought I heard them in the night."

The old man beamed and pointed a gnarled forefinger at him. "See?" he said to Morgan. "The Trung-sĩ has become one of us. Already he hears the forest in his dreams." He smiled at Stephens. "There is much inside of you that is inside of us," he said. Stephens looked startled for a moment, then slowly nodded.

"Yes," he said. He looked at Morgan. "There isn't really that much difference from the Blackfoot," he said in English, then switched back to the old man's language. "My grandmother was very much like your woman."

"My woman?" The old man looked with horror at Kai. "Truly there was a demon loose in the world to make two like her!"

"Perhaps," Morgan said, grinning. He pointed to the map folded out on the ground before him. "I have been looking for Bao. I think he will be going north, now that the rains are over. Here"—his finger stabbed where Laos and Cambodia merged and formed a corner with Vietnam—"We will find him here, I believe. What do you think, old man?"

Nguyen Duc stared at the map and slowly traced the contours with his finger. He could not read the strange words on the map, but he understood the area and knew the names of the towns and hamlets.

"Yes," he said at last. "He will be running north to the river, and he will be here, north of Kontum and south of Dak To where the mountains become like elephants, but the forest is thick. There is a way through the mountains here, Dai-uy, where one can cross without too much difficulty. It is a way for an impatient man, and he has had to wait a long time." He grunted in disgust. "He has many women with him, now, and the women have made him lazy. He believes that we are finished, and the village is no more. But, he still will wish to cross to the mountains by Muong Tat for he knows the Americans cannot go over the border. Foolishness!" He glared at Kai's sleeping form and his stomach growled. "He-who-was-my-son has forgotten the manhood of his father."

"A dangerous thing to forget," Stephens said somberly. "The old ones should always be remembered for what they were."

"You see?" Nguyen Duc said. He spat and looked warmly at Stephens. "You should have been my son, Trung-sĩ. You are more of our people than the other one. As much as the Dai-uy." He nodded. "Yes, as I have told you. He will not have moved north because the rains made the way very difficult for the women and children with him. With just the man, he would have already crossed, Dai-uy, but not with the numbers he has now. He has become very proud, Dai-uy. He will not leave the others behind. He thinks of himself as the headman of a village, and he will wish to take the village with him."

Morgan pursed his lips and carefully studied the map. The contour lines lay almost on top of each other, and he knew it would be very difficult to travel rapidly through the mountains into Cambodia where the mountains gave way to the Moi plateaus that ran north to the Dangrek Mountains. Here were only hills, and travel would be much easier as long as the Jarai and Rhade bands were not encountered. They could race north along the Moi plateaus through the hardwood forests to the Dangrek Mountains and come upon Bao from the west where he would not be expecting them.

"Look, old man," he said, and he explained his plan to Nguyen Duc, tracing the proposed route with his index finger. Stephens looked over his shoulder, while the old man watched and listened and when Morgan had finished, he nodded.

"Sounds good to me, boss," he said.

The old man slapped his knee in delight. "Gods' eyes, but it is a good plan, Dai-uy! He-who-was-my-son will never have thought of this for he has never seen the land and does not know that such a way is possible. But I have seen this, and I know this land for my father travelled this way once after the Jarai who had stolen our cattle. *Eeeah,* but it is good!"

"Then, let us start," Morgan said, and carefully folded the map and slid it into his map case.

"I will wake the others," Nguyen Duc said. "We will eat and go." He moved toward Kai, drawing his foot back to gently kick her awake, but Morgan stopped him.

"No, do not wake the women," he said quickly. "They will wish to go, and we must travel fast. How many men have you, now?"

"Thirty," the old man said. "Not many, but they have many years of such things behind them, Dai-uy."

"Wake them. We will eat as we march. Do not take any who do not have good legs, but leave one who will be able to bring the women after us. They must join us after this is over."

The old man looked at him strangely, then shook his head and sighed. "Dai-uy, I must tell you that I have been thinking that perhaps you should not do this."

Morgan stared steadily at him. "Why is that, old man?"

The old man sighed again and scrubbed his hand over his leathery face. "This is not something anymore for you," he said quietly. "I have been telling myself that you are doing this because you are one of us, but you are not one of us, Dai-uy. You should return home. Otherwise"—he looked away, then thumped himself on his chest—"you will become like me. This is all I know, Dai-uy. If it were not for the man-who-was-my-son, it would be for someone else or something else that I would go fight. It has always been this way for me and those who are with me. You are not meant for this."

"And," Morgan said, "what about the Trung-sĭ? Is he not the same as me?"

The old man shook his head. "No, Dai-uy. He is not. The Trung-sĭ is different. He goes with us because he wishes to. You are going because the man-who-was-my-son killed your brother. You cannot kill the world for your brother's death. The fight for you is not out there. The fight for you is inside of you. There, you must find your victory before you will know the peace that you think you want. I have never said this to you, but I do now, and this is what I have to say: Go home, Dai-uy. Go home. You cannot find what you are looking for here."

"And your wife," Morgan said. "Have you forgotten her? Is that not why you are going after him?"

"Partly," the old man said. "But that is our nature. It is not your nature. And I would go after him despite this. It is duty for me. For you, it is different."

"I will go with you, old man," Morgan said slowly. "Know this. We will speak of the other later."

The old man did not say anything and turned and walked from fire to fire, quietly shaking the men awake and demanding silence from them.

"What's going on?" Stephens said quietly.

Morgan stared at him and shook his head. "After this is over," he said. "We have to do this if we want the old man to agree to help us bring the other tribes together."

Stephens spat and finished his coffee, swirling the last swallow around in the cup to clean it of grounds before quickly throwing it away. He glanced at Morgan and shook his head. "Somehow," he said slowly, "I don't think that's what you have in mind. But," he added, rising to his feet, "I'm with you."

He walked away, and Morgan rose and crossed to Stephens's pallet and stared down at the sleeping girl. She had curled herself into a ball against the cool morning. Even in sleep there was a proud beauty to her face, a savage splendor in her high cheekbones and the black hair that curled around them, and he felt a sadness move within him. She muttered crossly in her sleep and drew the blanket tighter about her and sighed contentedly.

He turned and walked back to his pallet and picked up his pack, slipping into it. Then he bent and retrieved his Thompson and moved silently away. He checked the action of the Thompson and wiped the dew from the barrel with an oiled cloth and slipped the weapon over his shoulder. He crossed to the compound gate and waited impatiently for the men.

Nguyen Duc hurried toward him, checking his rifle as he came. A short, bow-legged man, wrinkled like a monkey, came with him. They paused in front of Morgan.

"Tran will stay with the women and bring them when they awaken," he said. The bow-legged man nodded at Nguyen Duc's words. "He is familiar with that area for his people once raided the Mois up there. And, he is a good tracker and will be able to follow our trail. They will come as fast as the women can march. Dai-uy, but they will have to bear their burdens. Still, I do not think they will be that far behind. They are," he finished proudly, "Montagnards."

"This is good," Morgan said. "Do you need a map for this?" he asked Tran.

Tran spat and tapped his temple with a stubby forefinger. "The map is in here, Dai-uy. That is all that I need."

Morgan nodded as the other men came up behind the old man. All carried rifles and some had slung crossbows over their shoulders. Heavy parangs hung on straps across their bodies and several had dahs stuck in thin belts from which hand grenades hung like goiters.

"We are ready, Dai-uy," Stephens said, as he came up to Morgan.

"Good," Morgan said. "You will bring up the rear. The old man and I will take the point together. Do not crowd us, but let us work ahead of you and the others so that we will not be surprised in this we do once we reach the Moi territory. But do not lag too far behind that you will not be able to come to us if we have need of you. Understand?"

Stephens nodded and the old man grinned. "This is good," he said with relish. "We are ready."

Morgan turned and led the ragged band through the gate. He stretched his stride and moved rapidly through the roll of concertina wire, across the field of fire, and plunged into the forest. When the thick trees closed above them like a canopy, he felt a wild pleasure race through him. He turned abruptly and moved west, the feeling growing stronger with each step.

Chapter Thirty-eight

They moved rapidly across the mountains to Cambodia and the Moi plateaus. None of the men moaned about the forced march, but moved with a singleness of purpose molded to the intensity that drove Nguyen Duc. They moved through the dense forests of the plateaus as avenging ghosts, slipping through the stands of mango and palm, climbing slowly to the forests of teak, and from there, to the foothills of the Dangrek Mountains that looked like elephants and where the teak trees gave way to their cousins of kapok and oak and maple and the isolated pine.

Several times they saw roving bands of the Jarai, but the old man and Morgan were far enough ahead that they could give the others enough warning to let them conceal themselves in the heavy growth of the forest as the Jarai passed. Twice they encountered tigers and once a band of small hog deer that fled as they slipped by. They lived on the rations they carried with them and avoided the temptation to shoot one of the roaming gaurs, the wild ox, for fear the sound of the gunshot would give their position away. But there were mangoes and other fruit, and they quenched their thirst with coconuts and fresh-water springs that still trickled through granite rocks.

They moved rapidly through the days and far into the nights before they rested, and many of the older men rested fitfully then because they never stopped in time to allow the men to weave hoops and crosses from twigs and grasses to protect their sleep from the evil forest spirits. But, strangely, even the older ones rose fresh in the early morning, eager to travel, the fever of purpose proving a strong stimulant to carry them through another hard march.

Finally, the old man led the party onto a high ridge that ran across the tops of the mountains, and they marched quickly along the ridge line until it suddenly fell away into a deep, narrow valley barely a kilometer across at its widest point and buttressed on each side by high mountains. The valley was a green carpet and small pockets of steam or mist rose from its floor. A small stream boiled savagely through the middle of the valley and tiny rainbows leaped from the spray thrown high where the stream tried to smash its way through heavy blocks of granite that had fallen from the cliffs into its bed. It was wild and beautiful and savage, and Morgan felt as if he was staring into the soul of the earth. The old man turned and looked at him and smiled and a thrill of expectation ran an icy finger up Morgan's spine. They had arrived.

Chapter Thirty-nine

Morgan leaned against a granite outcrop, his knees drawn up and the Thompson balanced carefully over them as he methodically cleaned the dust from the action. Beside him, Stephens rested as well and both anxiously watched the trail that twisted down the face of the cliff to the floor of the valley. It wasn't much of a trail. Any traveler had to be half mountain goat to travel over the thick, twisted roots that jutted out over the trail and the liana vines that climbed like spider filaments around and over the roots, but it was the only trail down to the floor of the valley where the old man had taken a small group to search for Bao's party.

Morgan's flask rested on the ground beside a package of Salems and a small heap of cigarette butts. Behind them, the men huddled together in small groups and shared cigarettes and the small talk common among seasoned warriors. They told each other about their wives and children and the homes they had had before the war, but said nothing of the battles they had fought for to speak of the past was to invite failure in the future. After they had fought, though, their past bravery would be recounted again and again, and they would quarrel among themselves to affix the portion of bravery each felt entitled to. But not now. Only a foolish man boasted of his bravery before fighting, for the gods could easily take his bravery from him and leave him an object of scorn and ridicule.

"The old man has been gone a long time," Stephens said.

Morgan unscrewed the top of the flask and sipped the Scotch, holding it in his mouth until he almost gagged, then spat it out and inhaled. He did not drink the Scotch to be drinking Scotch, but to keep his mind from gearing down since their sudden stop and long wait.

"Not so long," Morgan said. He grinned and handed the flask to Stephens.

"Perhaps we should send out more scouts," Stephens said. He drank and handed the flask back to Morgan. "Maybe they got lost? No, that ain't possible. Maybe we're just too impatient."

"Perhaps," Morgan said. He slid the action of his Thompson back and forth noiselessly and stared down the trail. It had been very sunny and hot when they first settled here and now they were in the shade. It was still hot, though, and a small pool of sweat had formed in the seat of his pants.

"Perhaps we have missed them," he said, but he said it only to make conversation. There was no indication of a large party having passed.

Stephens shook his head. "I don't think so. If they had passed through here, the scouts would have been back long ago."

Morgan grunted and reloaded the Thompson and rested it back on his knees. He lit another cigarette and continued to stare down the trail to the valley.

You may be pretty, he thought about the trail, but you will be one son-of-a-bitch to move down. You are a deathtrap for there is no way off you until we reach the valley. If Bao is not a complete idiot, he would go around this pass to the north. It is longer, but safer. I would go to the north, but then I have no place to go to. That is the difference between us, Bao, you have a place to go to where you can sit out this war and fight when you wish and with whom you wish. But that will also be your downfall for a man who has a destination is an impatient man and now your impatience will kill you. I hope I kill you or one of the others. I do not think your father should kill you though he wants to very much. He would hesistate and then you would kill him for you do not have the dignity and respect he has or the feeling for your own child that all fathers have despite what they say.

He looked involuntarily at the sky and remembered Dog's words: "Remember that you have four souls: *niya, na°gi, na°gila,* and *sicun.*"

"What's that?" Stephens said, and Morgan realized that he had spoken aloud.

"Oh, just something that an old man told me once," he said. He grinned. "The Lakota believe that a man has four souls: the first is "life breath" that ties his body to the innermost, the second soul is like the typical ghost, the third is the "little ghost" which causes all things to move, and the fourth soul is that which is the sacred power that can be received from a vision quest." He shrugged.

"Sounds like a wise man," Stephens said.

"He is," Morgan answered. He nodded. "Here come the scouts."

They turned back to the trail and watched as the men cautiously emerged from the trees, their weapons held high and ready. Carefully, they looked around before climbing the trail, leaning into the slope to take the strain off their calves and stepping nimbly and quickly over the roots and vines, anxious to get up the trail and back undercover.

"Four," Stephens said with relief. "They've all returned."

"What did you find?" Morgan asked as the old man came over the lip of the rim and squatted beside him, breathing deeply.

"The dogs have camped at the start of the pass," Nguyen Duc replied. "There are many with him. Many women; children, too."

"Damn," Morgan said. The women and children made things more difficult for although they were just as deadly as the men, he was always reluctant to kill them and one did not always have time to pick his targets in an ambush. "How many men?"

The old man flashed his fingers rapidly and Morgan counted. Eighty-three.

"All men?" he asked. Nguyen Duc nodded. "All with rifles?" He nodded again.

"There was a mortar, too, Dai-uy," one of the others ventured.

"You saw this?" Morgan asked.

"Yes. And a machine gun. The kind with a trigger and not the leaves one pushes with his thumbs."

"A thirty-caliber. Well, that bitches it," he said to Stephens. "They'll be able to reach us wherever we set up. Shit morou. This is getting worse by the minute." He turned back to the others. "Rest. You have done well. Now, the old goat, the Trung-sĭ, and myself will have to think on what you have told us."

They smiled wearily at the praise and moved back to the others who had respectfully kept their distance, but were eager to hear what the others had found.

"Gods' blood, but I am thirsty! Who has water?" A canvas bag was quickly produced. The first drank and passed the water back to the others, sighed, and moaned softly, "*Aiee*, but this is a steep mountain."

"Mountain? It is nothing but a hill," one of the scouts scoffed. "You are too old for such work as this."

Dimly, Morgan heard the banter and smiled at Nguyen Duc. He raised the flask, drank, and handed it to the old man who drank and handed it to Stephens. He drank and passed it to Morgan who carefully screwed the cap on the flask and placed it in his pocket. Then he squatted and pulled the dah from his belt and drew a rough sketch of the pass in the dust with its point. He hugged his knee and stared at the outline. His mind felt like sludge, nothing suggested itself.

"Do either of you have any ideas?" he asked.

Nguyen Duc stared at the outline of the pass. The cliffs sloped out over the pass at the west end of the valley where huge slabs of granite had broken free and tumbled to the floor of the pass. If they placed the ambush here, Bao could take shelter among the rocks where the sides of the pass sloped away from the floor and formed a rough canopy that would keep them from firing down upon him. If he reached this place he would be safe from fire above and could wait until they ran out of ammunition and then make his escape. It would not be a pleasant wait, but there was no doubt in the old man's mind that Bao could and would wait.

He traced the outline with his finger to the widest point and drew a small circle in the dust.

"Here," he said. "It will have to be here."

"I think so, too, old man," Morgan said softly.

Together they turned and stared at the point in the pass. The stream curved sharply to the south here and formed a sharp bend before it ran against the south side of the cliffs and then turned back to the east. Bao would have to cross the stream at this point and travel along it to the north wall and then recross it. It was a natural place for an ambush as he would be vulnerable once he had crossed the stream. He would have his back to the stream and would be cut to pieces if he tried to recross it once the ambush was sprung. Likewise, if he ran to the north and tried to recross it there he would be vulnerable. It was the best spot, lots of trees and heavy brush for hiding, but the same held true for Nguyen Duc and Morgan. They would be in the same situation, and Bao had more men. Surprise would be an advantage for them, but once the initial attack was over, Bao would have the edge since he had more men. Unless they could kill enough of them in the first firing, and that was very risky for where there was enough cover for them, there was an equal amount for Bao and his men. And Bao had the mortar and machine gun while they had traveled lightly with rifles and crossbows.

"That may be the best place," Stephens said, "but I do not like it. We could be caught in our own ambush. If he has time to set up the mortar and machine gun, we will not be able to get away from them."

"It is too bad we do not have time to dig punjis," Nguyen Duc said.

Morgan looked at him curiously. "What do you mean, old man?"

"Once, my grandfather chased a band of Jarai who had raided our village. He dug punji pits along the trail they were following and when some fell into them, my grandfather and his men killed those that did not. But we do not have time to dig punjis," he said. He spat in disgust. "Why could that dung-eater not be a day late?"

"No," Morgan said slowly. "You are right, old man. We do not have time for punjis, but we do have the forest, and we do have hand grenades."

"I do not understand your meaning," the old man said.

"Look." Morgan turned back to the outline of the pass in the dust. "He will follow this path, and we can place hand grenades here and here like so." He drew a small box over the trail in the dirt. "When he is in the middle of this, we will set off the hand grenades on the sides. He will try to retreat, and we will set those off behind him. He will turn and try to run forward and then we set those off. He will be very confused, and at the time when he is confused, we will fire upon him. But we must not fire upon him until the third group of hand grenades goes off for he will know our positions, and he will attack us at those points.

"We will fire only a short time, old man, and then we will allow him to chase us here." Morgan drew another small box indicating about two hundred yards north to where the stream cut back against the north wall. "Here, we will have set punjis on tree limbs and bent them back so they will spring and strike them in their bellies. We will leave half the men here, and they will bend the branches back on both sides after we have passed. Then, they will move back toward the first ambush and wait with the rest of the hand grenades to keep him from retreating. We will be in front of him with the rifles. The pass narrows here, and he will not be able to go around us. The punjis and hand grenades will force him forward into our rifles."

Nguyen Duc stared at the plan for a minute, then slowly nodded. "It is good, Dai-uy. But you have forgotten the mortar. He could set up the mortar, and we would be trapped ourselves because the stream and cliff will be at our backs, and we will not be able to escape."

Morgan shook his head. "Time, old man, he will run after us after the first ambush for he will think we are much weaker than we are, since we will not use all of them in the first ambush. By the time his confusion clears from the second ambush, we should be equal in strength for we will have killed many in the meantime. It also will take time for him to decide where to set the mortar, and we will have killed even more."

"But once the mortar is set, Dai-uy," the old man insisted, "then, his strength will be tripled."

"Leave the mortar to me and two men," Stephens said. They looked at him. He grinned bleakly. "We will concentrate only on the mortar. After the second group of hand grenades goes off, we will try to slip in among them and kill those carrying the mortar. Either that, or shoot them from ambush. We can find someplace nearby and wait until the second group of hand grenades goes off before we make ourselves known when they run by. They will have to run past us at one time or another. In the confusion, we'll slip away."

"It is very dangerous, Trung-sĭ," the old man said. "But it is a good plan. You will have to be very careful of the machine gun."

"Maybe we will get lucky and get the machine gun too," Stephens said. The old man shook his head.

"Do not think about luck," he said. "If you think about luck, the gods will take it away from you. Do not think about luck."

"And maybe Bao will be killed in the first ambush and that will make him even weaker. But I do not think we should count on this either," Morgan said.

"No. I do not think so either, Dai-uy. He has the luck of a Hon Bo gambler. He is very lucky. But I will kill him. The gods will give him to me for I gave him life. This, I believe, Dai-uy," Nguyen Duc said.

"Perhaps, old man," Morgan said. "We shall see. You will have the second group and will set the second trap. I will take the first. Stephens, take two of the men and set yours where you wish." He turned back to Nguyen Duc. "Remember not to bend the branches until we are passed."

They rose and moved back to the waiting men. The men nervously ran their palms over their crossbows and rifles and lightly touched the razor-edged dahs and parangs as they carefully explained what had to be done in the night.

Chapter Forty

The wind moaned through the trees, and Bao awoke and stared uneasily at the coals of the campfire in front of him. A few stars glittered, but clouds covered most of them like a shroud. The muscles of his leg trembled, and the girl beside him stirred restlessly. He rose carefully and moved away from her toward the fire. His bowels tightened, and he shivered. He did not want to go into the woods for the woods were full of evil night spirits that fed on human dung and absorbed a part of his being, but he had eaten much of the stew and peacock, and now his belly protested, and he walked slowly, silently, into the trees and squatted by a large bush.

It is only the superstitions of my father and his fathers, stupid people, he thought, but I will cover my dung with the leaves of this bush anyway. A good soldier must never leave any trace of where he has been for his enemies to find and follow. But I do not do this for the spirits for they are only the fears of my father whose mind is like this dung I leave on the ground beneath me.

He heard something move in the bush and froze and remembered that he had not brought a pistol or knife with him. He listened intently to the rustling of the leaves and cursed himself for his carelessness. The noise stopped. An eerie silence followed.

It is only a rat. He comforted himself with the thought. Or a snake. But it is not an evil spirit for I do not believe in evil spirits and therefore, they do not exist because I do not believe in them.

He finished and stood and heard it again in front of him. He turned and walked quickly to his left to detour around it. Another rustle. He stopped and his flesh pebbled on his arms and back. He stood immobile and strained his eyes to see through the darkness. A dim outline crouched in front of him. A shiver ran through him as he saw its front quarters hunched low on the ground and the back quarters bunched and ready to spring.

Once, while he was hunting in the forest with his father, his father had suddenly gripped his arm tightly. He had turned; puzzled at the strength of his father's grip, and then had looked to where his father pointed. A tiger crouched, ready to spring on a peacock unconcernedly strutting in a small clearing. He remembered the sudden spring, now, and the gutteral hunting roar of the tiger and the frightened, shrill cry of the peacock as it knew it was killed.

He wanted to run, but couldn't and knew if he moved away it would spring. He swallowed and forced himself to move slowly toward it. His heart thumped in his chest, and he heard the blood rushing through his ears. Still, it did not leap, and he moved closer, and the outline began to break apart and formed a bush with a dead limb lying across it. He touched the bush and felt the thorns and shuddered and moved rapidly away from it back to the camp. He crossed the small clearing to his pallet and quickly lay down and pressed close to the young girl. She muttered sleepily, threw an arm over his shoulders, and went back to sleep. Slowly, his muscles relaxed against her warmth, and he squeezed her tighter and tried not to remember that he had not covered his dung with leaves to keep the Night-Eater from it.

Chapter Forty-one

Morgan lay flat on the jungle floor and pressed his chin hard against the sour earth and watched the scout move cautiously up the trail through the early morning fog. His hands were slippery with sweat, and his mouth dry, and his nostrils filled with the smell of decaying leaves and vegetation.

Strange it should be this way, he thought. I wonder why nature made the hands wet and the mouth dry? Is it to remind us of our own vulnerability, that we may be killed even as we plan to kill?

He wrenched his mind back to the present and fervently prayed that the old man had had time to prepare the punjis and that the old men would not throw their hand grenades too soon before all were in the trap.

The scout moved slowly past him. Once, he stared straight at Morgan's hiding place, and Morgan could see his sharp black eyes and the tense muscles in his neck. Then he was past him and moving slowly down the game trail, eyes constantly search-ing either side and the tree limbs overhead. The second scout appeared, moving as cautiously, but with less fear, Morgan knew, for there was a man in front of him and knowing that gave him more confidence. Morgan watched him pass and waited.

I wish the birds would sing, he fretted. It would be better for us if the birds would sing for that would make the men less nervous and they would not be as suspicious. It is too quiet. If Bao thinks like this, perhaps he will send flankers out around the trail, but I do not think he will do this for he knows he is near the border and we have not bothered him for many weeks. But I would not do this. I would send the men around both sides of the trail just to be sure and he may remember this is how I did it when he was with me.

The thought bothered him, and he decided that he had better check for flankers. He started to rise, then froze as the front of the column moved into view. Slowly they moved down the trail, five men and two women.

Smart, he thought as he sank back to the floor. He knows the women can make a man hesitate. He is very careful and smart, but he is not that smart because he did not send out the flankers for they would be ahead of these. But I wish he had not sent the women with the men. That is very bad.

Then Morgan saw the rifles in the hands of the women and forgot about them as women. He gripped the hand grenade harder as more appeared, three men, a woman, then five men, and then Bao.

He will be in the front quarter, and you must let twenty more pass before you throw the grenade. It would be nice if the mortar or machine gun was among them, but it will not be, for you trained him very well and the mortar and the machine gun will be in the last third of the column. You cannot wait that long, but maybe Stephens will be able to get them. Thirteen. Fourteen. Wait for twenty. You must wait for twenty and then you must wait for the kite whistle, for that will mean that the last of the column will have passed and the men are in position. But it is very hard to wait. Very hard.

Bao moved closer to his position and Morgan's hand tightened over the grenade until the skin of his knuckles hurt, and he forced himself to relax before his hand cramped.

You could kill him now and that would be the end of it unless he has trained his men thoroughly. But if he has trained his men, those in the front and back will not know he is dead and those in back will fan out and come upon you from all sides and encircle you and then you and your men will be trapped.

He watched regretfully as Bao moved up the trail and disappeared from view. He continued his count. The twentieth man passed, and then five more and a moment's panic tightened his stomach muscles. The kite whistle sounded clear and sharp, and heads snapped up and shoulders stiffened in surprise. He took a deep breath and threw the grenade high. It dropped in the center of the column, bounced once, and exploded.

Fragments whistled in the air and tore into soft flesh. A woman began screaming. Then the air was filled with explosions and fragments and the column milled in confusion and Morgan heard Bao roaring like a wounded bull: "Back! Back!"

The column seemed to gather itself and hurtled down the trail, leaping over the broken and bleeding bodies lying in the trail like twisted tree roots. A series of explosions, muffled by the trees, came from the rear of the column, and then it was hurtling back up the trail and again Morgan saw Bao and resisted the impulse to spray him with bullets from the Thompson. A young woman clutched her belly with both hands and fell. A fountain of blood gushed from her mouth. Her hands slipped from her belly and her insides rolled out like thick worms, and she convulsed and died.

More muffled explosions from up the trail sounded, and then the front of the column came racing back and charged into those following. They milled in confusion like cattle, and Morgan settled the sights of the Thompson on the back of a young man with long black hair and squeezed the trigger. Blood spurted from neat holes across his back, and Morgan fought the bucking barrel and moved it rapidly back and forth in a large arc. Dimly, he heard the others begin to fire, and bodies twisted and fell as his men began to pour round after round into the column.

The bolt of the Thompson clicked open, and he rammed a fresh clip home. He pulled a whistle from around his neck and blew three short, shrill blasts, then turned and ran through the woods as stray bullets began to whine through the leaves above his head. He ducked his head automatically and ran harder and heard his men following. A figure stood suddenly, and he brought the Thompson in front of him, then recognized the man as one he had left at the front of the ambush. He stopped.

"Everything is all right?" he panted. The man nodded as the rest hurried past them. Morgan counted. Fourteen. Miraculously, all were unhurt.

"Come," he said, and turned and ran past the others and led them onto the trail. A stitch began to form in his side, and his lungs burned from the humid air. Far behind, he could hear shouting and knew they were being followed. He threw his head back and gritted his teeth and forced himself to run faster. His heart thudded in his chest, and then he saw Nguyen Duc standing in the middle of the trail and stopped and hung his head, fighting for air.

"All—here," he gasped. "No—one—hurt."

The old man clapped him on the shoulder and shouted at those behind Morgan. Morgan waited as they staggered past, drew a deep breath, and forced himself to straighten.

"Remember: do not fire until we do, they will try to get off the trail and will discover the punjis too late. They are ready?" The old man nodded. "Good. They will turn and try to run back down the trail, and that is when you must throw the grenades. They will turn again and then you will fire upon them. We will close when we hear your rifles and then we will have them."

"Did you see the mortar and machine gun?" Nguyen Duc asked worriedly. The shouting came closer.

"No," Morgan said, and turned and ran up the trail.

He found his men, and they quickly flopped down behind trees and rocks. Above and to the right of them the cliff loomed as a huge barrier. They appeared trapped, and Morgan listened to the stream crashing angrily over the rocks and hoped that Bao would not realize this too soon and make the necessary adjustments. He threw himself behind a large, dead log, wiped the sweat from his face, and laid the barrel of the Thompson across the log. He pulled four clips from his ammunition pouch and laid them close to his left hand. He took the .45 from its holster and laid it by his right hand behind the log and slipped the dah from its sheath and placed it by his left. He reached over his shoulder and loosened his pack and shrugged out of it and pushed it aside. Then he took a deep breath and waited.

The brush crackled and a band led by a young man dressed in black appeared and ran toward him. The young man's cone-shaped rice hat hung down his back from a strap around his neck. Two belts of ammunition crossed over his chest and Morgan settled himself and sighted carefully on the point where the belts crossed and squeezed the trigger.

Bullets thudded into the young man, and a bullet on one of the belts exploded. He slammed backwards onto the ground and lay still. Surprise flashed across the face of the one behind him, and he tried to stop but another bullet smashed into his face, and his skull exploded and he fell over the first.

The others began firing, and Morgan emptied his clip into the band, rammed home another, and emptied it into the young men as they turned and tried to run back down the trail.

"Cease fire!" Morgan yelled, and the firing stopped as quickly as it started. A brief moment of silence fell, then he heard the thudding of the grenades and the cries of pain and anger and high-pitched screams, and he knew the punjis had been discovered.

A figure burst into view, and Morgan fired and saw the young woman fly back from the force of the .45-caliber bullets. He fired again as more tried to come up the trail and emptied the Thompson into them as they ran back down the trail. He pushed the fourth clip into the Thompson and slipped it over his shoulder. The hot barrel burned his ear, and he cursed as he picked up the dah and pistol.

Firing erupted down the trail, and he knew Bao's men had run into the old man and his men the second time. He leaped to his feet and ran down the trail. He could hear his men on either side and he slowed to a trot. The brush rattled to his left, and he turned as a figure ran at him, screaming and whirling a parang over his head. Morgan shot him in the belly and decapitated him with one swing of the dah and continued down the trail.

He rounded a bend of the trail and found four men trying to set up the machine gun. He fired, then saw Stephens hurtle toward them, firing as he came. Three dropped, and the fourth leaped up and rushed him. They crashed to the ground, and Stephens's hand clutched the man's throat, and then his knife glittered in the air, a tiny rainbow sweeping across the man's throat. Lips curled back from greenish-yellow teeth, then blood boiled from his throat, and Stephens threw him from him and rose. He stood, panting for a moment in the clearing, his eyes wild, blood matting his shirt and streaking down his face. Another man threw himself at Stephens, but Stephens stepped aside and threw his forearm across the man's face and throat. The man fell to the ground, gagging, then he stiffened and died as Stephens dropped his knee upon the man's chest and slipped the knife up and under his chin.

"What about the mortar?" Morgan croaked. He slipped the pistol back into its holster and sheathed the dah.

"We got it," Stephens panted. "In the first rush."

"Good job," Morgan said. A young woman ran screaming toward him, and he saw the whites of her eyes rolling madly in her head. Morgan slipped the Thompson from his shoulder and fired twice. Then he saw Bao.

He pulled the trigger of the Thompson, and Bao grabbed his hip and spun to the ground. Movement flitted in the corner of his eye, and Morgan whirled, fired again and the Thompson jammed, the bullet missing. He dropped to a knee and threw himself to the side and rolled. A bullet smashed the earth near his face, and he twisted and rose, pulling the dah from his belt as he did. The man ran toward him, then stiffened and fell backwards as a bullet slammed into his forehead. Morgan glanced at Stephens and saw him shift toward Bao, bringing the pistol to bear.

"No!" he shouted.

Stephens hesitated, then threw himself to the ground and rolled desperately behind a tree as a bullet whined over him. Morgan dived for another tree, pulling the .45 from its holster, and cautiously peeked around its trunk. Bao grinned, and raised his rifle at Morgan, but Morgan lifted the pistol, firing twice rapidly. Bao fell backwards, the rifle flying from his hands. He grabbed his belly and writhed in agony on the ground. He raised his head, and Morgan registered briefly the shock on his face, then his lips twisted with hate as he spoke.

"Father—"

Nguyen Duc slipped into Morgan's line of sight. Morgan took a step to the side and fired again. The bullet tore into Bao's chest and knocked him back to the ground. He coughed once, then died as the old man knelt beside him. Nguyen Duc lowered his rifle and stared at his son. Morgan slipped the .45 back into its holster and crossed to the Thompson and picked it up. He cleared the jam as he walked to the old man. The firing had stopped except for the random shots as the old men moved among the bodies. Then the moaning and screams stopped as well, and Morgan knew it was over.

He sighed, and squatted on his heels beside the old man. He touched him on the shoulder, and Nguyen Duc raised his head to look at him. Tears streamed from his eyes and ran through heavy wrinkles across leathery cheeks.

"It is finished, old man," Morgan said gently. A wave of tiredness swept over him, and he felt a sting in his cheek where sweat dripped into a cut he didn't remember receiving.

"Yes," the old man said. He sighed. "It is over. All over."

The old man's shoulders sagged with weariness, and he looked tiredly around the clearing. The light that had shone so fiercely over the past days was gone. Flesh hung slackly from his face, and his fingers trembled when he raised his hand to brush the tears from his cheeks. He dropped his hand and stared at Morgan.

"What is left?" he asked.

"It is over," Morgan said quietly.

"What is left?" the old man repeated softly. "What must we do now?"

Morgan sat back on his heels and took a packet of cigarettes from his pocket. He took one and handed the packet to the old man who automatically selected one. Stephens came up and squatted beside them, and the old man handed him the packet.

"Go north." Morgan said quietly. The old man looked up at him, blinking. "Go north." Morgan repeated. "Go far away from here up into the mountains until you find the place where you belong. There, make your village again."

"What about this plan you said?" the old man asked. A wry

grin touched his lips. "This thing of the Montagnards?"

Morgan spread his hands and shook his head. "Like all things from the men in Saigon. I do not believe they will keep their word."

"And the war is lost," Stephens added. They looked at him in surprise. He lit his cigarette, drawing deeply. "I do not think this should involve us anymore. This war," he added. He gestured around the clearing and said, "You see we are now killing each other. What is left for us here? It would be better if we left."

Morgan drew a long breath and pulled the beret from his head and stared at it. He had worn it for the first time when he and the old man had set their first ambush. He tried to count how many there had been over the years and in counting, he remembered Bao laughing and running with the boys of the village and growing into the warrior who had accompanied them on other ambushes and learned what Morgan and the old man could teach him, the many ways to kill, the careful setting of traps. It seemed a small step from that young boy to the young man he had trained to the dead one lying on the ground in front of him.

"Yes," he said, quietly. "It would be a good thing to go north. Wait here for the women to join you, then go north. Far north."

"Will you come with us, Dai-uy?" the old man said.

Morgan shook his head. He nodded at the figure of Bao on the ground. "No, you know there is no place in your village for one who does this."

The old man nodded. "Yes, it is so. And this is why you killed him, is it not?"

Morgan nodded. "Yes. Your people need you. Not me. Everything has been lost by this I have done, old man. Empty deeds spawned by empty words. You say you have failed, old man, because your son has failed you. But I was the one who failed you and your son and so it should have been I who killed him, not you. And because of this, I cannot go with you."

"So, you will return to Saigon," the old man said.

"Yes."

"And you will return to your land and the one who waits for you?"

"It is too soon for me to know that."

"It will be lonely without you, Dai-uy."

"It will be lonely without you, old man."

"But, in truth, Dai-uy, you are not one of us. I thought you were one of us, but you are not. There is too much of other places in you. And you are needed at home. I know about these things." He glanced at the dead Bao. "My son is dead," he said softly. Your guilt is over. Your time here is done."

Nguyen Duc looked at Stephens. "Will the Trung-sĭ return, also?"

A bitter grin twisted Stephens's lips. He shook his head and looked at Morgan. "No, I do not think so. I will go north with you."

"Are you certain of this?" Morgan asked.

"Yes. There is nothing back there for me. You know it," he said, falling into English. "You know what is back there for me, don't you?"

"I have a pretty good idea," Morgan said. He smiled at Stephens and the other returned his smile, relief shining cautiously in his eyes. "It doesn't have to be said. But, are you certain? There are other ways of getting around difficulties like that." He paused, looking at Stephens. "I didn't tell you before, but Black said that he would purge your record if anything came up."

Stephens nodded. "Still risky. We've seen how much we can trust him, haven't we?" He glanced at the others and shook his head. "This way is better. I don't have any family to go back to. And this war doesn't seem as important as it did."

"What's different?"

"These people. They have a dignity of living that appeals to me. At least, it's better than what I left back in the States." He took a deep breath. "Of course, you could force me to go back with you."

Morgan shook his head and held out his hand. "Give me your dog tags."

Stephens hesitated, then pulled the dog tags from his head and slowly handed them over, his eyes questioning. Morgan took them and placed them in his pocket.

"As far as anyone else knows, you have died here in the ambush."

"Thank you."

"It's the girl, too, isn't it?" Morgan asked. Stephens gave him a quick look then nodded, the red slowly mounting in his cheeks.

"A part of it is," he said.

"I wish you well," Morgan said, slipping back into the old man's tongue. He took the dah the old man had given him and handed it to Stephens.

"I think you will be needing this," he said. Then he slipped the flask from his pocket and unscrewed it. "Let us drink, then, to what we have."

He handed the flask to the old man who took it solemnly and lifted it high. He poured a small amount from it onto the ground.

"For the gods," he said, and drank.

Morgan felt a lump move in his throat as he took the flask from the old man. He poured a drop onto the ground. "For the gods," he repeated, and drank. But the Scotch had no taste for him, now. A vague emptiness settled over him, and suddenly, he could feel the world he had known fall away from him and in the dry-rot of the world, his soul disintegrated and fell apart, leaving him barren.

Dog

And so Henry left them there and made his way back to Saigon. But his heart was no longer a warrior's heart. This happens at times to those who have been chosen to be warriors by Sacred Woman. Their spirit becomes tired, and they wish to be like the others, but they cannot be like the others. They must follow the Warrior's Path and that is a lonely path, a very lonely path. Perhaps I should have explained this to Henry when I took him to the Badlands and gave him his warrior's name, but I did not. It is something that each warrior must face and defeat for it is as much of an enemy as those a warrior can see. But it is much more dangerous, too, for it hides in the darkness of a man's spirit and when a man feels sorrow, it comes out upon him and makes him wish for that which he cannot become no matter how hard he tries. And Henry tried. He tried very hard. But he could not become that which he wanted to become. And because the world would not let him become what he wanted, he withdrew from the world. This a warrior does also, but it does not matter how much he fools himself into believing that he has become what he has been trying to become. Those who have need of a warrior always will find a warrior, a protector. He discovered that in several places during his wanderings.

It was time for another warrior to find his way back home. And return to Ithaca.

The
Return

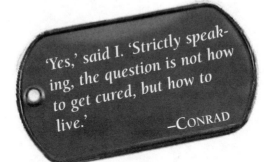

'Yes,' said I. 'Strictly speaking, the question is not how to get cured, but how to live.'

—Conrad

Chapter Forty-two

Timmy stared long and hard as Henry sat quietly, hands folded on top of the table, across from him. "I'm a bit slow," he said quietly. "Others came home after Vietnam. Sure, some of them were traumatized—what the hell do they call it?" He drummed his fingers on the tabletop. "Oh yeah. Delayed Stress Syndrome. Something like that. Sounds like a fancy name to excuse those who don't want to get on with their lives to me." He eyed his uncle narrowly. "Is that like you? Is that you?"

Henry shrugged. "Perhaps. Once. Maybe. I don't know. I just know that the time wasn't right. Those men who returned home are the ghosts of people who could have been and weren't."

"Did you want to go along with the old man and his people?" Timmy asked. Morgan nodded slowly. "Because of the girl?" Timmy asked, his voice harsh and accusing.

"Partly," Henry said softly. He looked away, his eyes on a distant memory. "And there was a purity there. A chance to be reborn, I guess. Have you read *Beowulf*?" he said suddenly.

"Uh, yeah. In school. Sure," Timmy said, frowning.

Henry nodded. "The Fire-breathing Dragon. Remember? Beowulf's last battle. That was a spiritual fulfillment for him. If I could have gone with the Montagnards, that would have been a spiritual fulfillment for me. But"—his eyes grew dull with memory—"that couldn't be after Bao's death. There is no going back after a death and"—he hesitated, his lips compressing into a thin line—"the Montagnards have strict laws. They may seem harsh, but their life was—is," he corrected, "harsh. They need laws to reflect the harshness of their existence. Much the same way that our laws reflect our society—permissiveness is just another word for decadence. Murder, among the Montagnards, is punished by immediate execution; self-defense is exile. Although I suppose Bao's death could have been seen as an execution, in my hands it became something else. The old man would have been excused as the executor, but he would have had to live with his son's death on his conscience. I couldn't have that. And so, I took exile."

He fell silent, thinking. And that was a difficult time for me. I went back to Saigon and Colonel Black and his people. They didn't know what to do with me, and I didn't give them many options. They didn't dare send me to a line company or leave me in operations for I was a security risk—I had already proven that I was independent, and they didn't understand that type of person. Undying loyalty was the only criterion, and I had violated that by helping the old man's people escape. So, a line company command was out. Operations was out. The only feasible outlet left for them was to accept my resignation. Or kill me.

The debriefing was a sham. They wanted me to come back into the fold, so to speak, but I knew what that meant. I would be placed in one impossible situation after another until I was killed. But I became friends with a *Times* reporter—Con Edwards—who was willing to help me. He printed a couple of columns about the deceitfulness of the U.S. and Saigon governments, how they had rejected the idea of giving the Montagnards a voice in the Saigon government. Of course, he attributed the information to an anonymous source, but those columns, along with my veiled hints of other information left with him to be used in the event of my death, decided the issue for Colonel Black's people—I was to be discharged.

He stared for a long time into the past. Finally, Timmy cleared his throat and Henry blinked and looked at him, seeming startled for a moment as if wondering what he was doing there, then he grinned.

"What about that lieutenant?" Timmy frowned. "Rachel?"

"Yes, that was her name." A wry smile twisted his lips. "She was Black's lever. At least, I think so. Women like that have their own drums to march to. Do you remember when I tried to find out about her, and she said that women had to always remain a mystery to be attractive?" Timmy nodded. "She was right. When I discovered that Black had sent her to me and that she had come willingly for Black, things changed between us. Oh, we tried, but we drifted apart. Different values. Funny. Last I heard, she had taken up with Con Edwards. That reporter who wrote for the *Times*? I wonder what ever became of that? I wonder if she betrayed him as well?"

"Why didn't you try and stay with her?"

He cleared his throat and fixed Timmy with a steady stare. "I will not serve anything that I no longer believe in," he said. "Whether it is my country or . . . my home."

"What," Timmy said deliberately, "did your home have to do with all this? I would have thought that you would be more than willing to come home after all this."

Henry shook his head, again looking away. "I was, but then again, there were . . . events," he said lamely.

"Events." Timmy shook his head. "All I'm hearing are excuses. What happened?"

"It took a while to separate me from the services," Henry said. "You have to remember that I was involved in something that was very . . . delicate. I guess you would call it. A lot of people were very reticent about letting me go in the first place. I was detained for a while in Saigon. Again in the Philippines. Again at Oakland and yet again at the Presidio while I was told again and again—brainwashed, I guess you would say—with the importance of my remaining silent about what I did in Vietnam.

"I no longer wore my uniform. In San Francisco, uniforms were beacons to the war protestors who had become fashionably rabid about anything having to do with the war. But there was a certain falseness to their protest. I don't think many even had the slightest idea of where Vietnam was or why they were protesting. Our country had progressed far enough in its civilization that it had become too secure. Pseudo-intellectualism had given birth to causes where causes did not exist. There is something about comfort that awakens the predator in man. Our young had begun to prey upon their elders.

"In a way, I supposed the U.S. should have expected it, but unfortunately, our country is not led by philosophers. And about the same time, the death toll began to mount in Vietnam which added fuel to the protestors' fires." His eyes turned inward for a moment. "You would not think that so many had died. But in that, too, there was mystery, one common to all. So common, in fact, that there no longer seemed a need for blame or praise. The entire world seemed to have become . . . a wasteland that needed a new king to sacrifice to make the land whole again. The small man's dream of a perfect world—house, car, wife and family— became meaningless mechanics. The world of Vietnam had become an exact parallel for our world—each had become desolate and sterile, ruled by impotent kings.

"Once in Vietnam I saw a monk pour a can of gasoline over himself and strike a match. For a long time I wondered about the futility of his protest, then I realized that he had exhausted all human experience and, having walked among the living dead of Saigon's streets long enough, he knew exactly what he would find at each turn and twist of Rue Catinet that had become Tu-Do Street. He knew what each newspaper article and broadcast on the war would say and everything would be a familiar lie. He had learned how to read the leaves of Sibyl. Like Tiresias, he had sat below the wall of Thebes, and like his Buddha, he had seen the world as an arid conflagration. His soul had become haunted by the music coming from the jukeboxes on Tu-Do Street, the air stifling with the dust of futility floating from open windows over bars where the girls took their momentary dates. I realized, then, that I too was that monk. And what I had thought and believed in had become a wasteland.

"I began to drink rather heavily. Then, one day in the Officer's Club, I punched out a colonel, his aide, and a couple of other officers before I was, ah, 'subdued,' by others. That was exactly what Black's people were looking for." His lips tightened from the memory. "I was declared dysfunctional by a team of the outfit's psychiatrists and placed in a special hospital for 'corrective therapy.' " He grinned mirthlessly. "Another term that gave them freedom to do what they wished with me—as long as they didn't kill me. I don't remember much about the treatment—I do remember electrical shocks, drugs—the rest pretty much became a haze and a series of nightmares. I lived in darkness for a long time."

His brow furrowed with pain as murky memory began to swirl like dirty fog. For a brief moment he remembered the bitter taste of hard rubber being forced between his teeth, the sudden searing white light followed by the darkness through which murky shadows crept, the bright blots of lights—balls of greens and blues and oranges and reds, brilliant colors flashing and dancing crazily through his mind—the darkness of his dreams through which his primordial howls of terror and pain echoed again and again. Broken images, fear in a handful of dust. He shook his head.

"I would like to think that I became, in Jung's terms, 'individuated' during that time, but I didn't really know how to put on and off the masks of my life. There had become too many masks and I had to try and live out of my own center. But I had become too involved in the many masquerades to even know what my life was, let alone where the center of my life was. Do you understand? No," he said without giving Timmy a chance to respond. "No, you do not. I can see that. When I was finally released from the hospital, I bought a used car—a 1969 Ford Mustang." He smiled faintly at Timmy's look of surprise. "Yes, over three years had passed since I was brought back from Vietnam. Your grandfather was first told that I had been sent back to Vietnam. Then, that I was missing in action. Finally, that I had been 'rescued' but that I had become violent and, for the sake of security, was being held in a special hospital for those with high security clearances who needed 'special attention' due to the delicacies of their jobs but who had also slipped away from reality. Seven Palms." He shuddered, closing his eyes against the memory. "A delicate sobriquet for Hell, for Seven Palms was Hell, and I was in it along with others. I remember—silence. Until the keepers opened my door, then the wails and cries of lost men echoed down the halls and into my room. You don't ever want to hear those cries, Timmy," he said. "Not ever. The men who screamed weren't human. Not anymore."

Timmy gently tapped the table between them as he stared at his uncle. He shook his head, sighed, and rose, stretching. He crossed to the window and looked out. Late afternoon shadows of tall oaks stretched across the parking lot. He felt tired, drained, from his uncle's story. Suddenly he realized that it was pity he felt.

He turned and looked at Henry, waiting quietly, watching him anxiously, waiting to see the impact his words would have upon his nephew. "And so, you came here to ask God's forgiveness?" Timmy asked.

"No," Morgan said gently. "No, I came here so—"

"To withdraw from life, then?" Timmy interrupted. "What do you find here that you couldn't have found at the ranch?"

Morgan's forehead twitched. "Nothing. It's not what I find here: it's what I don't find here."

"And what's that?" Timmy demanded. The skin tightened perceptively over his face. "What is it?"

"Hatred. I don't find hatred here. And"—he hesitated—"and, perhaps unconsciously, I thought I would find something that would redeem me, a merciful explanation of creation. I knew a man once who was never afraid, who never made a mistake, who won a chestful of medals over there. One day, he went into the bathroom of the Officer's Club at Ton Son Nuht and put a bullet in his brain. You see, we never really know what a man's made of."

"Uh-huh," Timmy said. He shook his head. "I'm not sure that I understand that. I don't even think I want to understand that." Morgan shrugged. "Don't do that."

"I'm sorry," Morgan said gently.

"Sorry don't shut the barn door after the horse is gone," Timmy said.

Morgan smiled. "You've been listening to your grandfather."

"Well, I sure as hell couldn't listen to you or Dad, could I?" Timmy demanded. He picked up his coffee cup and sipped. The coffee was cold, but this time it felt rancid on his tongue. Suddenly he hurled the cup from him. It struck the wall and shattered, and Morgan leaned back watchfully in his chair. Timmy shook his head and drew a deep breath, then turned and looked back out into the gloaming. A crow landed on a small birdbath at the end of the parking lot and preened itself. Silence filled the room. He felt as if musty words began to collect silently around him.

"Do you pray?" he asked suddenly.

"Sometimes," Morgan said quietly, waiting.

"Then, you're not a monk?" Timmy said. He turned and looked at his uncle, meeting his eyes. "You can come and go as you wish?"

"Yes," Morgan said. "I've taken no vows."

"Then there's no reason why you can't come back to the ranch with me, is there?" Timmy demanded.

"I told you why," Morgan replied gently. He ran his palm along the gleaming surface of the table, avoiding Timmy's eyes. "I came here to escape hatred. If I go back to the ranch, now, I go back into the hatred. I have had enough of hatred." He frowned and leaned back in his chair. "I don't make any apologies for what I've done. I can apologize for what I haven't done, and for that I'm sorry. But I do not apologize for what I've done. It's something that I don't want to have to do anymore. That's why I came here. Life is physically hard here. There is no need to become a monk to find a refuge here and for that. I repay them with work. You ask me if I pray. Yes, I find it very difficult to pray. When I try to pray, my words seem like dust motes floating in a sun ray. Only that and nothing more. I am here because I cannot find the answers I need anywhere else."

"So you continue to withdraw from us?"

"No," Morgan said, looking away from Timmy, unwilling to meet his eyes. "I withdraw from myself."

"I see," Timmy said quietly. "Then I can tell Mother that you aren't coming back, that we're alone as usual?"

Morgan shook his head, remaining silent. Timmy waited a long moment for him to speak, to deny Timmy's words, but

Morgan sat silently as the shadows crept from the walls to gather around him in the center of the room. And Morgan wanted to tell him what the boy wanted to hear, but he could not. He knew that going home would bring the walls tighter in upon him. He thought about telling the boy that he thought constantly of home and never more than he did at this moment but that to go home now, with Timmy, would only mean that he would think again of the jungle and what he could do in the jungle.

"I'd better go," Timmy said. Morgan made to rise but Timmy stopped him with a raised hand. "No, don't follow me. I want this to be left here." He shook his head. "For a moment, I thought that there might still be something in you that would make you come with me. Reynolds is no different from your Colonel Black. And the government ain't changed none, either. What they did in Vietnam, they're doing here. I suppose I thought about that all the way down here, hoping that you'd come back and help us do away with that. But I was wrong. As far as I can see, you are really dead here, aren't you?" He walked to the door, paused, and turned back. "Please don't misunderstand me when I say that it would have been better for you to have died in Vietnam instead of Father, than to carry it with you all this time. One year, two years, even four years is a long time from a man's life, and it was a long time from Mother's life and Grandpa's and mine. But I can understand that. It's hard, yes, but I can understand that. But the rest of the time I cannot. You are not a victim of the war, Uncle Henry. You are a victim of yourself."

He left, and Morgan remained seated for a long time, staring into the growing blackness of the room, letting Timmy's words linger in his mind, feeling the hurt behind them, feeling the hurt in his breast. He rose and went to the window to catch sight of Timmy as he emerged from the front door of the monastery, but he had waited too long. He thought he could catch movement as someone walked down the road to the front gate, but couldn't be sure if it was Timmy moving away from him or just shadows in the night.

He heard the door open behind him and lights click on and turned to look as the thin figure of Father Lawrence moved into the room. The priest paused for a moment, staring at him, then crossed to the table and slipped into the chair Morgan had occupied.

"He has gone," Father Lawrence said gently.

"Yes," Morgan said. His throat ached, and he swallowed against the soreness.

"And you wish you had gone with him," the priest said.

"Part of me does," Morgan said. He turned back to stare into the night. "Part of me does just as part of me does every morning. It is only after the day grows long, and I grow busy that the thoughts of home disappear."

"You miss your father?"

"Yes," Morgan said.

"You can always go and return if it doesn't work out," the priest said. "You are not bound to us by any vows."

"I know that," Morgan said. "And that is what I am afraid of. That it won't work out, and I will have to return. It is much better not to go and keep the hope than to go and have the hope shattered."

"That is only life," the priest said. "You must remember that that is something that man must do. We don't have any guarantees given to us. We are what we become and nothing more. Everybody lives with disappointments, but those are disappointments that must be met and overcome. I think you had better go. You have been with us long enough, Henry. There are no expectations that life puts on us; there is only life. If you were meant to be with us and knew that in your soul, you would have taken the vows many years ago." He smiled gently. "Go home, Henry. You are needed there. It does not matter what you search for here. You will not find it if you haven't found it by now."

Morgan's head jerked up. He stared long and hard at the priest. "You are telling me to go?" The priest nodded. Panic rose and, for a moment, locked hard on his throat. Perspiration dotted his forehead despite the coolness of the room. "But, why?"

"Man wanders over the face of the earth, both the illustrious and the obscure, seeking his fame, but then eventually, he must return home to face those he left behind. It is the only way that he can meet the spirit that dwells within the land, in its valleys, in its fields, in the very heavens. And you must return with a clear consciousness. That is your reward. But you must touch your reward with clean hands or it will turn to dead leaves and thorns in your grasp. Your family has come for you. That is their forgiveness. Now you must forgive yourself. It is time for you to go back home. You have paid the debt to your conscience long enough." He smiled gently. "There comes a time when illusions can no longer be used to see the world. That's when suffering becomes only pain and not a means to the end."

"Do you know what waits for me back there?" Morgan demanded. "There is a man who wants my family's ranch and will stop at nothing to get it. If I go back, there's a good chance I could end up what I was when I came here."

Father Lawrence stared at him for a long moment, then sighed. "Henry, we are what we are and nothing more than that. There is a place for each of us in this world as long as we do not deny peace to others. The God of peace is never glorified by human violence. But we recognize that God must have men of violence in His services. This is awkward for me to say as I do not believe in violence—that is more for the Jesuits than we Cistercians—but I know that there is a need for people like you. And that need isn't here. That need is out there"—he gestured toward the windows—"where people live and breathe and fight and die. The storm must come to cleanse the air, to allow fresh seeds to grow and ripen into whatever they can become. The violence of grace is really order and peace. You see, violence in your case is the voice and power of God speaking in your soul. Sometimes, even God has need of the Archangel Michael. He had need of him before, and He will have need of him again. Are we so much more than God that we too do not have need of our warriors as well?"

"You have waited here long enough, Henry. You are a good man, please do not forget that, but it is time for you to go back to your world." He rose and smiled fondly at Morgan. "I shall miss our little talks, Henry, but the silence of the monastery is meant for people whose withdrawal from the world affects only them. You do not belong to us, Henry. You belong to those out-side these walls. They are the ones who have a need for you. We do not."

"You are throwing me out of here? I thought that this was a place of sanctuary, someplace where I could find the light that I need," Morgan said desperately.

"It is true that some of us find light here," Father Lawrence said. "But here, you have found only darkness. When you pray, what do you hear?"

"I don't understand," Morgan said.

"Do you hear the voice of God? Do you feel a lightness within your body? Do you feel His hand come down and touch you? What do you feel?"

Morgan shrugged. "I have tried," he said lowly. "God knows, I have tried."

"Yes," Father Lawrence said gently. "He does. But He is hold-ing His light back from you because your light is not here. It is out in the other world. The meaning to your life is not here. Henry. The silence of God tells you that. *Alter alterius onera portate.* It is time for you to take up your burden again, my friend. You have rested long enough. You are needed. The presence of your nephew here tells you that. You must resume your journey. Your vacation is over. Go home. That is where the soul lives."

"I'm not certain I know where that is," Morgan said quietly.

"Yes, you do," Father Lawrence said. "Home is where there are people you love and where people love you. That is back in Ithaca. That is where you belong. That is where your soul be-longs. It is not the world who remembers Vietnam, Henry. It is you. Go with peace."

He turned and left the room, the hem of his robe brushing against the floor seeming as loud as the rasp of a saw. Morgan turned and looked out into the night and felt uncertainty brush cold fingers gently across his skin. He shivered.

Dog

I dreamed of a lodge as high up as the clouds and inside the lodge I saw myself sitting, naked, my body painted blue and black and on the blue side I was dotted with hailstones and on the black side a streak of lightning blazed from my hair through my groin to my feet. Red-painted men entered, bearing a man with a gaping wound in his body and from his mouth leaked blood. They placed the wounded man between me and the fire in the center of the lodge. The man looked up at me, and I thought I recognized Henry, but I could not be certain. I reached out my hands and placed them over the wound and felt the pain of the wound move up my arms and enter into my body. I shook from the harshness of the pain, but the blood slowly stopped leaking from the man's mouth. When I took my hands away, the wound had closed and left a huge scar in its place. I sprinkled dust made by the Bone People upon the scar for a voice spoke within my head saying, "He bleeds because he no longer knows the love of the People. He has fogotten the ways of animals and of the prairie. Give him this stone and he will again remember the ways of the world." And suddenly within my hand was a plain brown pebble with tiny black spots upon its surface. I stared at the pebble for a long time, but I could only see a pebble. That is when I knew that it was not given for me to see what was in the pebble but to Henry had that gift been given and when he returned, I was to give him the pebble so he could once again learn the magic of living.

My heart swelled as this was revealed to me, for I knew, then, that Henry was on his way home. I did not know that Henry was coming home, but I felt that he was beginning his journey again after having rested his spirit for many years and with that knowledge, I knew a great fear, too, for I did not know what he would be bringing with him.

I have never told this to anyone before, but it is true that a man's mind, *tawacin*, and soul, *wicana°ga*, is all around man and reaches a great way. When a man is not using all of his mind, then it leaves him and goes away on a far journey. But the man is not dead, he is just traveling in the Otherworld. It was this that I had found in my dream. I knew other dreams would come and that this dream would become clearer with those dreams.

It is like being in the dark and having pictures float lazily across your mind. You can dwell on those pictures for a moment, but no matter how fascinating they are, they will disappear. At first, they will seem to be natural pictures and familiar to you, then you will wonder why they are so familiar. But later, those pictures will become familiar to you.

Henry's period of grace was over, and although he did not find the peace he sought while he was in that holy place, he realized finally that no grace is isolation and that he had to return home to find that peace that had been missing in his life. I do not fault him for this, and it is not something that I could have told him or his father or his wife. It was something that he had to find for himself.

And so I waited for him to come and went to the Ring of Stones high on the hill and built a fire out of sage and bathed myself in the smoke of the sage to purify myself and sat and prayed there, waiting for a vision to come instead of a dream so that I could ask my protectors, my Grandfathers, the meaning of the strangeness that had settled in my breast.

Chapter Forty-three

Kate sighed as she looked out over the window above the sink onto the prairie. Slowly, gently, she rubbed her temples, trying to ease the throbbing there. The migraines had been coming with more frequency lately, despite the medicine Doctor Adams had given her. But she did not like taking the medicine for it made her feel foggy and lethargic for the entire day.

"It's nothing but a bout of allergies," the Widow Wilson had told her firmly. "Never you mind what that old quack told you. Men," she sniffed, "know nothing of the woman, yet they think that they have an inner eye into ourselves. Alfalfa tea, dear," she said soothingly, handing her a jar of thick, brownish-black fluid that rolled sluggishly in the jar. "Alfalfa tea. It'll take a little while, but it'll soon set you straight." She sniffed. "And never you mind those little green and ivory capsules that Adams is trying to push down your throat."

Funny thing, though, was that the alfalfa tea did work. Temporarily, at least, but lately, the noxious stuff that would gag a pig was having little effect upon the stabs of pain that came with the day and morning sun that brought the heat from the prairie in shimmering waves.

"Imagination only, old girl," she told herself, yet she still looked across the prairie while she sipped a cup of strong coffee that seemed to have more effect upon the headaches than the tea although she still took the tea as well upon rising in order not to tempt fate.

Movement far out on the prairie caught her eye. She swallowed the mouthful of hot coffee and strained her eyes, staring hard at the movement, trying to make it out.

"Somebody, that's for sure," she decided, muttering out loud. "Now, who could that be, coming across the field instead of using the road. Another tramp, likely enough, looking for a handout." Maybe, she thought suddenly, he hasn't heard about our difficulties and we'll be able to get another hand for haying.

She turned from the window and took a mixing bowl, pouring Bisquick into it, adding eggs and milk, to make a quick coffee cake. She poured the batter into a ten-inch pan and thrust it into the oven. She checked the level of the coffee and, satisfied that there was enough for a cup or two, glanced again out the window.

A wave of dizziness swept over her, black dots appearing in front of her eyes. She grabbed the sink to keep from falling, blinked her eyes and focused again on the figure standing on the brow of the hill above the stock tank.

"Henry," she whispered.

She felt the blood rush to her face, and her eyes misted. She wiped them hurriedly on the sleeve of her black-and-white checked flannel shirt and drew a deep shaky breath. Behind her, she heard Tom's boot heels stomping heavily on the floorboards.

"Still staring, woman," he said crankily as he came into the kitchen. "What is it now?"

"Henry," she said. A strange click sounded in her voice. She felt his hesitation behind her, then four quick steps as he crossed to stand beside her.

"You certain?" he asked huskily.

She nodded. "Out there above the stock tank. By the old cottonwood."

"By God," Tom said softly. "He did come home." His eyes glowed with wonder and pleasure and the harsh lines in his brown leather face softened. He sniffed and wiped a gnarled finger under his nose and along the side of his faded blue jeans.

"Maybe," she said. She turned away from the sink, her hands fluttering around her hair, tucking wisps up into the bun where they had worked loose. Then she pulled hurriedly at the pins holding the bun in place and shook her hair free, combing it back with trembling fingers. She frowned at her image in the window, wishing she would have touched her lips with a lipstick. She pinched her cheeks, though the flush rising from her throat would have dyed them scarlet without any help.

"I'll go get him," Old Tom said excitedly. She stopped him as he turned, tugging hard on his elbow.

"Don't be expecting too much," she said.

Tom looked uncertainly at her then back to the window. "We can't just let him stay there without saying nothing," he objected.

"Why not?" Kate said. She held up her hand as he opened his mouth to protest. "I know. I know. But I remember all the time he's been away. Why come back now?"

"Because we need him, woman," Tom said garrulously. "Hell's bells! Aren't you ever going to forgive him for Billy's death?"

"Forgive him?" She gave a short ugly laugh. "Oh I think I could probably forgive him if he would forgive me."

"For what?" He gave her a puzzled look.

She closed her eyes and leaned wearily back against the sink. "Go out and see him, if you want. But don't push him if you want him back."

Old Tom chewed at his lower lip and tugged at his nose. He ducked his head and studied the scuffed toes of his boots. She patted his arm reassuringly.

"Go ahead," she said. "I'm not the only one here. You and Timmy both got a voice in this too."

"I dunno," Tom muttered. "I dunno." He looked out the window. "He just stands there. Why doesn't he come on to the house?" Nervously he unbuttoned and rebuttoned the left pocket of his denim workshirt.

She shrugged. "I don't know," she said. "This is something that he has to do himself. And that's a bona fide."

He nodded and opened the door and left, pulling it strongly against the jamb. He paused and looked up at the figure standing on the crest of the hill beside the old lightning-struck cottonwood. He stood quietly, but Tom knew Henry had seen him, and his eyes were following Tom's movements. He felt the land whispering to him and crossed the yard and stepped over the fence. The dry grass powdered beneath his steps and an acrid odor of burnt grama drifted up faintly to him. Lights rippled off the water in the tank. Around the edges of the water, the dried gumbo mud stood like a cracked cookie sheet except where the cattle had stepped in its wetness to drink from the receding waters. In places the earth looked white like salt, but he knew it was only because the water had been leached from it by the drought.

Tom stopped in front of him, noting his thinness, the graying of his blond hair, the steady burn of his gray eyes. Tight lines drew his lips down, and his nose had a new bend to it that hadn't been there the last time he had seen him. Yet, there was also a calmness about him that hadn't been there when he had last seen him. He tried a smile and knew it looked false upon his face, stretched tightly across the flesh.

"Dad," he said softly.

"You're looking well, Henry," he said gruffly. "Where you coming from? How'd you get here?"

A smile touched his lips. "Hitchhiked."

"From Kentucky?"

Henry nodded. "Old Man Ferris picked me up on Bad River Road just out of Fort Pierre. He dropped me off at the section road. I walked the rest of the way across country."

"If you needed money, you should have let us know," Tom said gruffly. "I would've sent it."

"I know you would have. But I needed to think about a few things. This way gave me a little time."

"You've been gone a long time."

"Yes, but that doesn't mean that I haven't been thinking about you and Timmy and this place. And Kate. How is she?" He raised his eyes to look around the land. He smiled, but Tom saw the bitterness behind the smile.

"Fine. Fine," he said hastily. Henry shook his head.

"You don't think so? It's true." He looked away and pain flickered across his face.

"It's just that—" He stopped and stood staring out across the valley toward the far hills where the sun touched their tops, painting them red. Tom held his breath, afraid that the slightest movement would send him away again.

"You know," Henry said softly. "You know that nothing belonged to me anymore when we came back from the war. The sun no longer warmed me. At night, I had no place to go. I didn't even recognize the songs of the birds anymore," he said quietly.

Tom felt his eyes burn and blinked away tears.

"We love you," Tom said gruffly. Tom turned to look at him. "I know I didn't say it as much as I probably should have. Maybe I never did. I told you that many other ways. But the words—I just ain't good with the words. If that was what you were looking for, I'm sorry. But there it is."

Henry shook his head. "No, you loved the man who left. You would have hated the one who returned."

"You never gave us a chance," Tom said.

Henry stared away into the distance for a long moment. "Maybe," he said. "Maybe I did owe you that. But there was a loneliness and fear. A fear that forgives—nothing."

"Then why did you come back now?" he asked.

His lips drew down in a bitter smile. "Because I hear you need the man who returned," he said.

"I reckon we do," Tom said. "Come on to the house then."

For a moment Henry hesitated, then his shoulders slumped, and he nodded. He took a deep breath, bent and picked up the small pack lying on the ground by his feet and slung it over his shoulder. Together, they walked slowly down the hill toward the house.

Dog

I did not know that Henry had arrived until he came out to the West Place to see me. It was then I gave him the roan horse and told him how it was a dream horse and what it probably meant. I gave him the pebble too but I do not know if it spoke to him or not. I am old, now, and sometimes I think the wrong thoughts about my dreams. They still come, though, so I know that the Sacred Woman has not left me. This happens at times when men like me get old. But I have never married and so I do not worry if she does not come.

This dream disturbed me greatly for I dreamed of six Grandfathers sitting around the Circle of Stones. They looked as old as the stars which have been here forever.

"It is time for you to teach him," the oldest said. I knew he spoke of Henry, for I had tried to teach him before he went away. But he was not ready for my teaching. He was still too much a part of the *wasicu* world and believed too strongly in their lies as my people had when the *wasicu* were stealing their land from them.

A strange fear came through me, and I began to shake at this Grandfather's words for I knew what the teaching meant and what the teaching would do to Henry. But it was time and when it is time for a thing to happen then it must happen.

"These," the Old One said, indicating the other five Grandfathers, "are the Powers-That-Are: East, North, West, South, and Earth." He did not name himself, but there was no need to name himself for I knew that he was the most powerful, the Sky.

"We will give you our power which you must give to He-Who-Comes. Give him these gifts and tell him their uses. Tell him to use them wisely. We shall be with him then."

I blinked and found that he held a plain wooden bowl in one hand and an old bow wrapped in white deerskin in the other. I looked into the bowl and found it full of water and knew that was the most powerful, for it came from the Sky and brought life. The bow came from Earth and with it came the power to destroy.

"He-Who-Comes knows the power of the bow," the Old One said. "He has used it many times before. You must tell him that he must use it again for he will not wish to use it again. But he must. It is time. Only then will the water come."

"Then, and only then," said Earth. "Do not think that this will bring the end of the wasicu. It will not. They will destroy themselves when the time comes. But it is not ready yet. Soon."

And two young men appeared on the East and West sides of the circle and each young man carried a spear in one hand and held a black leather strap that stretched across the circle. I knew it to be the terrible road that stretches from the Thunder Beings in the West to the Sun in the East.

"This is the road that some must travel," the Old One said. "It is the road that is given to man. A road of troubles and war. Few can walk it and those who are made to walk it must walk it as they are the Guardians. He-Who-Comes is one of the Guardians."

"Look," Earth said, and pointed to North and South. Two young men appeared, holding in one hand a pipe and in the other a red leather strap that stretched across the circle. I knew it to be the road from where the giant lives to where the healing seasons come.

"This is the road that He-Who-Comes wishes to travel. But that will not be his road. He may pretend that this is his road for he may weary of the black road, but it is a road that is meant for others." He pointed to where the straps crossed in the center of the circle. "This is the greening day when he will know peace. Perhaps it will be after this time. I do not know. But the waters will come for him and he will know rest until it is time for him to walk the black road again."

A white mist came up around them and they disappeared and I heard a wind blowing from the west and with it the moaning and mourning for the dead. Then I awoke and stared at the cold stars above me. They no longer looked friendly.

And I wept.

When Henry came the next day, I knew the Grandfathers had sent him. I knew too when I looked into his eyes that he had already seen the sadness. I saw the dead lying upon the ground like fallen leaves. I saw the scars upon him and I felt happy that he was home. And sad. One cannot happen without the other.

When I told him about the dream, he stared long into the past. Then he smiled and rose and thanked me for telling him my dream.

"There are always those who must tilt at windmills," he said.

I did not know what he meant and told him this. He told me that it was an ancient dream written down by a man many years before. I do not know this man. I do not know why one would want to attack a windmill. But when Henry told me that the man thought it was a giant, I could understand. We all attack our giants.

Chapter Forty-four

Tom Morgan stood quietly on the hill by the lightning-struck cottonwood, staring contentedly east over his land toward the old Stone place. He enjoyed evening and the warm breeze blowing gently over the burnt grass just before the last mourning doves called and the whippoorwill answered. Sometimes a burrowing owl would startle him with its nearness and once a rattlesnake crawled lazily in front of him before coiling suddenly and buzzing a warning when it sensed him, but Tom held his place, watching quietly until the rattlesnake decided he meant no harm. He watched it slither away to a prairie dog hole and flow down into it, the mottled back disappearing into the darkness like liquid shadows. He marked the hole mentally and reminded himself to bring a pistol up the next time. Bullsnakes he had no quarrel with, but he had lost too many cattle over the past years to rattlesnakes not to kill them when he discovered them. A coyote barked, then lifted its voice in a long, ululating howl. The wind shifted, bringing with it a hint of sour-smelling prairie dogweed. He reached into his pocket and took out a Union Leader tin of tobacco mixed with curlycup gumweed. He smiled as he remembered his father telling him to always mix the herb with his tobacco as a cure against the cough. He still wasn't sure if it worked, but he did it automatically these days anyway. He rolled a cigarette and lit it, letting it hang in the corner of his mouth as he frowned at the clumps of buffalobur growing on the sparse hillside. He'd have to get Timmy out with a corn knife to cut them away before they went to seed. That, and the clumps of sourdock, he amended.

Slowly the twilight turned, the sunset pinks deepening into

purples. Then the swift October dusk came tumbling clownishly, and he felt a thrill at the gloomy secret night appearing. The moon came up harvest orange—a hunter's moon, he thought, then sighed deeply and started down the hill toward the house where the yellow lamps appeared, the pale light spilling from the windows like pumpkin eyes. He stepped around a clump of iron-plant and goldenweed. He shook his head; it was bad when these plants came out. That meant the dry season would only get worse.

The cedar posts and poles of the corrals seemed silver in the moonlight and the shingles on the barn glowed a soft gray patina. White moths flitted up from the silver grass in front of him, disappearing high in the night among their twinkling sisters. A cow moaned softly in the darkness, looking for her calf and Old Buck whinnied for him from the corral when he smelled Tom's approach. Tom smiled as he heard the buckskin's hoofs tamping impatiently on the corral's dust. He put his hand into his shirt pocket and removed two lumps of sugar and held them out to the old horse. His calloused palm welcomed the velvet nose and the bristles of stray hair as the buckskin carefully lipped the sugar. He stood quietly, rubbing the buckskin between the eyes. The horse grunted with pleasure and ducked his head under Tom's arm. He slipped his hand affectionately down its neck.

"Well, Buck, he's home," Tom said softly. "Don't know for how long, but we'll take what we can get." The horse grunted again and stood closer to the corral rail and dropped his head over Tom's shoulder. "I don't pretend to understand it. Maybe I ain't meant to. I wish—" He sighed and looked up at the house. Faintly, he could hear music playing, straining to identify the tune. Then he smiled as the words came to him.

"Building castles in the sand—"

"Well, it ain't Hank or Roy or Gene, but it'll do. I reckon," he added. He laughed suddenly and the horse jerked its head in surprise and snorted, dancing a little.

A coyote howled in the distance and the horse swung its big head, looking off toward the sound. Tom frowned. The coyotes had been coming closer as the land became dryer and dryer. He remembered the thirties when they became so bold they ran under the heifers, ripping the milk bag so the calves would get weaker until they could move in and pull them down. Sometimes, they'd just run through a herd, snapping at everything like they were crazy. Maybe they were. Crazy with the heat and crazy with the thirst. Those were bad times. And he remembered the many times he had sat on a hill above the home meadow where they'd put the heifers with the fall calves, his old .308 Winchester with him and boxes of cartridges. He sat on the reins to his horse to keep it from wandering off. He'd taped a flashlight to the rifle and when he saw the movement as the coyotes slunk in downwind of the herd, belly low to the grama grass, he'd shoulder the Winchester, snap on the light and shoot as many as he could before they scattered. Sometimes, he'd get as many as four. Then he'd mount his horse and ride around and around the herd singing Christmas songs and feeling foolish for singing Christmas songs, but "Silent Night" soothed the cattle and kept them still. So he balanced the Winchester on the pommel of his saddle and rode around and around the herd, singing, feeling foolish, and listening to the grama grass crackle as his horse stepped on it, but his eyes worried the sumac brush along the gully, watching for shadows that flitted among other shadows.

"Those were hard times. I remember once Dog collected those seeds from the sumac, pounded them into flour and made gruel from them. It took a while to get used to it, but it filled a void. Been a long time since we put in days like those," he said aloud to his horse. The buckskin jerked his head, nodding as if he understood, and Tom laughed again. "Sure hope we don't have to do that again. I'm a might old for those all-nighters, and I think the old pipes would spook the cattle more than soothe them."

He gave a final pat to Buck's neck, then turned toward the house, hitched up his pants, thought a minute, then broke out into song "You are my sunshine, my only sunshine——" His voice cracked as it wavered and rose through the old familiar notes, and Teddy, the border collie they used for herding the milk cows, howled from his house by the woodshed, but Tom ignored him.

"You make me happy, when skies are gray—"

In the house, the tape stopped, and Tom's voice floated in the silence. Kate lifted her eyes from sewing a button on a blue work-shirt and looked across the room to Henry sitting awkwardly in an old armchair, a mug of coffee clasped between the palms of his hands. Her lips pressed hard into a tight line. A smile flitted across his face and disappeared. She looked down at the work in her hands.

"That's the first time I've heard him sing in a couple of years," she said, jerking her head toward the door. Henry's eyes flickered to the door then back to hers. He raised the mug, sipping.

"He never could carry a tune," Henry said. He slid down in the armchair, the cracked brown leather protesting at the shift in his weight. He glanced around the room. The lamplight glowed warmly from the walls covered with well-varnished, knotty pine, and the room smelled fresh like Pine-Sol. The walls were covered with old prints of Remington and Russell. In the corner stood a combination secretary and glass-fronted cabinet. The cabinet was filled with flint arrowheads and stone beads; stiff and cracked parfleche colorfully beaded in red, blue and yellow beads; an old arrow made from dried willow and fletched with owl feathers; an old stone axe head with a groove worn in the middle; a bridle made from braided sweet grass; a turtle rattle; a bone whistle made from a crow's wing; an ankle bracelet with rattlesnake rattles dangling from it; and a fletching knife with wooden handle. On top of the secretary stood several baskets woven from skunk-bush sumac and stained red from the berries. Over the secretary hung a buffalo lance and above it a bleached buffalo skull with the horns still attached. A ceremonial bow wrapped in tanned and painted deerhide lay across the horns. His eyes travelled around the room to the upright piano with old sheet music ("She's Too Fat For Me" and "Glowworm") still on the stand and to the old horsehair sofa covered with Indian blankets used as throws. The huge stone fireplace at the far end of the room had a huge, polished pine mantel stretched across the front with a hearth that marched out a good eight feet into the room. An old duck decoy, its colors faded, perched on one end while thirty years of collected bric-a-brac strewed from it to the other end, swerving around an old, wooden clock, its hands stopped at 2:04 the afternoon his mother had died and never rewound. Two leather-covered, high-backed easy chairs stood in front of the fireplace with a magazine-strewn table between them. At the right of the fireplace a bookcase ran the rest of the way to the corner, wrapped around the corner, and, heavy with books, lumbered to the hallway. At the other end of the huge room stood a long, dark mahogany dinner table surrounded by lyre-backed wooden chairs. A chandelier made from a wagon wheel and lantern glasses hung from the ceiling. Two floor fans blew gently through the room.

"No," she said, and bowed her head again to her sewing. A tiny throbbing began behind her eyes and she paused, closing her eyes and pinching the bridge of her nose hard.

"Headache?" he asked politely. She nodded, trying to will the throbbing away. The coffee mug made a heavy thump, and she heard the leather of the chair creak as he rose. Then his fingers were massaging the back of her neck, stretching up the side to the hollow in front of her ears, pressing gently. Slowly, the throbbing began to cease.

"You—don't have—to do that," she said, hoping that he wouldn't stop.

"I know," he said softly. She suddenly became conscious of the grandfather clock ticking in the corner of the room.

"Do you remember the hunting cabin Dad had in the Black Hills near Hill City?"

"Still has," she said. "We went out this spring before it got too hot or was still too cold to put it back into shape. Your father and I went, that is; Timmy stayed around the ranch to keep it running. We spent three days varnishing the cabin. I had to work the ladder heights because your father kept complaining that he got dizzy on the ladder, but I don't believe him. He just didn't want to climb up and down that ladder." She paused. "That was the first time I'd been there in ten years."

"Remember how you and Billy and I used to drive down to Custer for dinner then swing over to Harney Peak and watch the moon rise?"

"It was better in the Needles," she said. Then she bit her lip and shrugged his hands away from her neck. He stepped away, pretending not to notice the sudden tension in her.

"Yes," he said. "Then we went down to Sylvan Lake, and Billy and I went skinny-dipping below the lodge, and you kept fretting that someone would come out on the terrace and see us. Remember?"

"Is there a purpose to this?" she asked.

"Do you remember?" he asked again softly.

She sighed. "You were reading Yeats at the time and kept reciting one of his poems. I can't remember which."

"I will a-rise and go now, and go to Innisfree."

"Yes," she said. "That's the one."

"And a small cabin build there,
of clay and wattles made;
Nine bean rows will I have there,
a hive for the honey bee,
And live alone in the bee-loud glade.
And I shall have some peace there—"

"But that was it, wasn't it?" she asked, breaking in upon his recitation. "That was the last of our peace together. The war came." Her voice clicked in her throat, and he moved around her, going toward the fireplace. He paused in front of the bookshelf and glanced at the titles.

"I suppose we have to talk about it sometime, don't we?" he murmured.

Before she could answer, the door banged open, and Tom stomped in, spreading his arms wide, bellowing the last line of his song: "Please don't take my sunshine awaaay!"

He looked at them expectedly, and they broke into laughter.

He looked pleased and slapped his hands together and rubbed them briskly.

"Well, now," he said, winking at Henry. "I think a little nip might be in order. What do you think?"

"You know what the doctor said." Kate answered admonishingly. She moved her sewing to the table next to the couch and rose, arching her back to ease the stiffness from it.

"What the hell do those damn doctors know?" he demanded. "Pa had a toddy every night. Sometimes two or three, and he lived to be eighty."

"And you're how old?" she said acidly. "Seventy-one?"

"It ain't the age, it's the mileage," he said stubbornly.

"Uh-huh. And on you the odometer's gone around twice. I'll pour," she said, rising and moving toward the kitchen.

Tom's mouth dropped open as he stared at her disappearing. "Well, I'll be damned!"

"Probably." Henry said dryly. "You want to tell me what's going on?"

Tom shook his head and lowered himself gingerly onto the sofa, wincing as his muscles pulled across his rib cage. "Don't heal as quickly as I usta," he muttered darkly. He looked up at Henry and shook his head.

"It's ugly and gonna get uglier," he said. "We've gone longer without water than ever I can remember, and folks are beginning to feel the pinch. Those along the Bad River are doing okay— although they might come up a bit short on grazing before this is over. We might come up short, too, but I did sow a little alfalfa this spring that should give us an extra cutting, maybe two, although I don't expect it."

Kate returned and silently handed a glass filled with bourbon and soda to Tom, handed a bourbon and 7-UP to Henry, and sat beside Tom, sipping what appeared to be a glass of Coca-Cola. Tom took a long swallow, then sighed and scrubbed his hand across his hair.

"It's Reynolds that's got the folks stirred up around here. You see, when cattle prices jumped last spring, he bought a couple of herds and brought them into his place. Combined with his cattle he already had there, he was stocking his range at about three, maybe four per acre. Grass can't handle that even if we got the best rain season ever. But he was counting on the corn price staying down so he could fatten them and make a bundle on fall sales.

"But the drought has brought the corn price up as well. When there's a shortage, everybody wants something, you know." Henry nodded and sipped from his drink. "Yeah, sure. You'd remember. We had a small one back in the fifties. There ain't no shortage of cattle 'cause everyone's cutting back on stock, trying to preserve what grass they got. Prices right now are incredibly low. I think they're going even lower before the drought breaks. Reynolds paid a dime below premium price on those cattle he bought. Price of feed is up, too, which means he's gonna have to put out a hell of a lot of salt licks to try and get water weight up. But he can't get water weight up without water, and that's where we come in. We've got the only water close to him, and he can't drive to the river 'cause we own the lease on the Old Stone place too."

"You could let him cut through the Old Stone place, couldn't you? That'd solve a lot of the problem," Henry murmured.

Tom's eyes flared at the idea. He took another long swallow from his drink, and glared at Henry. "Of course, I could. But then, that'd open up grazing land for him too and we might need the Stone land for grazing 'fore this is over. No. I don't think there's a whole hell of a lot we can do for poor Reynolds. Not," he added, "that I'm gonna lose any sleep over that."

"But Reynolds is stirring up the rest of the county against us," Kate put in. "Gene Hardy hasn't said anything, but I can tell that he's thinking he would like to run irrigation pipe from the creek across to his fields. He's lost his oats and his wheat, and I don't think that corn he planted is going to make, either. And then, there's Fred Bloch on the south side who's already plowed his sorghum under. I heard he's thinking about trying for a late planting of oats, now."

"Oats? Now?" Tom snorted. "Hell, he's a damn fool for that.

If the drought doesn't kill the oats, the first frost will. I heard a locust singing a week or so ago. First freeze is on its way. Planting oats in the fall? Never been done. 'Course, this is a strange year. If he's that desperate—"

"So what are you going to do?" Henry asked, sipping.

"Me?" Tom snorted and shook his shaggy head. "Hell, I've already done it. Told them all to go to hell. Now that you're here, we can make a damn fine fight of it all."

Henry bit his lip and looked away into the corner of the room. A great sadness seemed to fall over him like a heavy mantle. He placed his glass on a doily on the small end table next to him. He rose and stretched.

"What time's Timmy getting home?" he asked her. She glanced at her watch.

"Probably another couple hours or so," she said. "The movie should be getting over about now, and it's a sixty-mile trip once he's dropped Betty Rhodes off. He'll be surprised to see you."

Henry grinned. "Yes. I should imagine." He looked at his father, and the grin slipped off his lips. "All right," he said softly. "That's what I'm home for. But we aren't going to start it, you hear, Dad? We're going to try and avoid this if possible. We don't antagonize them. We just mind our own business."

"Damnit!" Tom growled. "And if they cut our wire?"

"We'll repair it and ask them nicely not to do it again." Henry said. "Listen to me!" he said, holding up a warning finger as the old man bristled. "I mean this. If you're right, it's going to get very bad before it gets any better, and we want to be able to say that we were only protecting ourselves if this whole thing ends up in court. If things are as bad as you're telling me"—he glanced at Kate who hesitated, then nodded—"then we won't find the courts very friendly toward us, either. But if we are protecting our land and that's all, why, then, we've got a defense if worst comes to shove."

"And what if they cut our wire again after you ask them please not to do it?" Tom said sarcastically.

"Then I'll tell them not to do it again," Henry said. Strange shadows began to moil and coil in his eyes, and Tom felt a sudden chill invade the room, then disappear. He gulped the remainder of his drink and held out his glass to Kate.

"I reckon we can stand another on that," Tom said.

"No," Kate said firmly. "One, and that's all."

"Aw, hell!" Tom said. He slapped his hands upon his knees and pushed himself erect. "Well, reckon then we might as well get some sleep. Got a long day tomorrow. What're you going to do?"

Henry shrugged. "Go for a ride, I think, and look the place over. See Dog again if he's around."

"Uh-huh. Well. I think we'll put Timmy to work cutting out some of that weed up on the hill," Tom said, nodding toward the west. "That'll keep him out of mischief and let him work off some of that Saturday night in town."

"No, better have him check stock," Henry said, shaking his head. "I want a full count by tomorrow night. And, we'd better think about doing a little night riding for a while."

The old man blinked owlishly, then slowly nodded. "Uh-huh. You think something's gonna come up soon, don't you?"

"Better to be safe than sorry," Henry said. "Once Reynolds hears I'm home, who knows what he'll do."

"I think we've got a day or two before someone tells him," Kate said. "We don't get very many callers anymore."

"I'm riding over tomorrow and tell him," Henry said.

"You think that's smart?" Tom asked, suddenly alarmed.

"I don't know. Maybe we'll get lucky once he knows the prodigal son has returned."

"I don't think so," Kate said, shaking her head.

"I don't either," Henry answered. "But it's worth a shot."

"Well," Tom said, standing and stretching. "I'm bushed. Think I'll turn in." He headed for the stairs, then paused and looked back at them. "It's good to have you home, son," he said. He turned and stumped off upstairs.

They sat awkwardly for a moment, then Kate rose and took their glasses out into the kitchen. When she returned to the living room. Henry stood and started for the door.

"I think I'll take a look around before I turn in," he said. He smiled at her, and she felt a moment's softening, then straightened and lifted her chin. Anger flashed through her, and she turned away from him.

"You could at least tell me why," she said. "Was there a woman?"

He didn't answer and she turned to face him. "There was, wasn't there? There had to be a woman."

"No," he said. "There didn't have to be."

"I don't really think I want to know any more," she said dully. She turned to go upstairs, then stopped as he spoke.

"It was entirely different than here," he said gently. "A different life. A different time. And I had become a different man from what you knew." He looked away. "And there was Billy." He looked back at her. "When he was killed. I felt . . . as if I was responsible for his death."

"Why?"

"He wouldn't have been there if it hadn't been for my letters."

"But you wrote them nevertheless," she said. "That's a long time to carry that burden. I think you've worn that part about out. You didn't make Billy join you in the mountains, Henry. He was just being a fool. Like you." She jerked her chin, looking up the stairs. "Like Tom."

"And there was us."

She suddenly felt cold and wrapped her arms around her, staring at him. "Henry—"

"And Billy."

She turned half away, wanting to go upstairs and away from the pain that was suddenly between them, but something held her back.

"I feel like Cain at times, Kate."

"I know," she said in a small voice.

"We betrayed him. We and the war."

"The war," she said bitterly. "Always blaming the war. When are you people going to forget the war and get on with your life?"

"Who knows?" he said. "When it lets us."

"And Billy. He was dead. You—"

"He wasn't dead before," Henry said softly.

Her shoulders slumped and tears came again to her eyes. "Yes," she said softly. "He wasn't before."

"Kate—"

"Timmy will have to be told sometime, won't he?"

Henry nodded.

"I thought so," she said dully. "But not now."

"No, not now."

She left him then and went upstairs, hiding the rest of her tears from him with a straight back.

Chapter Forty-five

The ranch house was dark when Timmy pulled up in the old Buick and slid to a stop in back of the house, parking by the side porch. He yawned, and licked his lips, enjoying the faint taste of Betty Rhodes's lipstick. He felt warm and sated and sat for a moment, remembering how the moonlight glinted off the water drops clinging to her naked skin after they went swimming on the way back from the movie at Pierre.

"Ah, well," he sighed and opened the door. A large moth flew in and began knocking against the dome light. He gently brushed it out into the night, then stood and hurriedly closed the door before it could fly back in. He yawned and stretched and looked up at the sky. The Milky Way stood like a faint band across the sky and the Big Dipper (Great Bear, he remembered Dog calling it) stood with its tail swinging to the east, pouring water from it.

"And that's why we don't have rain, Tim" (an old man told him while he whittled on a stick of pine on a bench in front of the Court House in Fort Pierre), "the water's poured out of the dipper, and there ain't nothing left to wet the earth. Not even a drop. No sir. Won't have another rain till the handle swings around again, and that will be quite a few turnings of the earth. Most likely a year. Maybe more."

"Maybe the old fart was right," Timmy said aloud. He craned his head around and looked up the side of the house to his windows. Kate had left the windows open, and the white curtains were fluttering against the screen in the night breeze. He sighed and walked up on the porch and into the house, singing softly to himself.

"Then I noticed the stranger with the ghost-white hair—"

"Hello, Timmy," a voice said from the darkness.

He whirled, crouching slightly, facing the sound, his heart hammering. A light snapped on, and he saw Henry sitting in the cracked leather armchair, wearing a blue denim workshirt half-buttoned to the waist, a pair of jeans, his bare feet resting flat on the floor.

"So you came after all," Timmy said quietly, straightening from his crouch. He tucked his thumbs in his belt and stood hip-cocked, eyes narrowed, a sardonic smile tipping his lips.

"As you can see," Henry said. "Pretty late, isn't it?"

Timmy flushed and his eyes narrowed. "Are you counting hours on me now? I don't think you have that right. Besides, I'm old enough to mind my own business."

"It was only an observation, not a criticism," Henry said. "Have a good time? Movie any good?"

Timmy shrugged. "I don't know. I guess so."

Henry's eyebrows lifted, a tiny smile coming to his lips. "And your date? Is she someone I should meet?"

"No, don't 'xpect so," Timmy said, his face growing warm. He rubbed his nose with the heel of his hand. "Sorta the girl you ask out for, well, a good time. Know what I mean?"

And in a flickerflash of memory he remembered Bernadette Banks seeing him step down from the truck in Phillip and she came up to him, smiling, her eyes shining black, saying, Is that you, Henry Morgan? I'll be damned! Didn't think you'd ever come home again!

Hello, Bernadette. You're looking well. And she did, her skin tawny from the sun, her long black hair thick as a raven's wing, the tiny mole a beauty mark left of her chin. Lipstick caked thickly on the end of the cigarette she waved at him.

I should smile, she said. She winked saucily at him. Say, do you remember how we used to play after school?

And he remembered when in the late afternoon after school they met in the field behind the schoolhouse and fought Indian battles. Butch Henson always played Red Cloud raiding the ranches, killing the men and carrying away the women for rape and rapine. Of course, he smiled, they didn't know what rape and rapine were, but the principle was there, and Butch did his best until he tried to carry off Jenny Harper by throwing her over his shoulder. But Jenny Harper weighed close to two hundred pounds and knocked him flat to the ground, landing on top of him, legs a-spraddle and her skirt flying up over her head. She squawked and farted and Butch let out a gasping, Shit! and we all convulsed on the ground, laughing while Butch's hands flapped weakly like the wings of a skulled bird and Jenny hollered and scissored her fat white thighs, whapping Butch in the head each time he tried to push himself up.

Miller's Pond? she said slyly and looked up at him from under her plucked and repainted eyebrows, tossing her thick black hair saucily.

And he wrenched his mind back from its reverie and tried to remember the soft white of her dimpled belly and her heavy breasts bouncing like basketballs with puckered nipples as thick as wild plums starting from moon-shaped aureoles, and how she posed, thick thighs spraddled—

"Sorry," he said. He grinned tiredly. "Wool-gathering."

"Where's Mom?" Timmy said.

"Asleep. So's your grandfather," Henry said.

"And you?"

"Thought I'd wait up and talk with you when you came in," Henry said. He held up his hand as Timmy's face tightened. "I didn't mean anything about it. I just thought I'd say hello."

"Well, hello," Timmy said mockingly. He gave a short bow from the waist. "I thought you weren't coming. Leastways, that's the impression I got last time we talked a few weeks ago."

"Yes, well, your impression was right. I wasn't going to come."

"So"—Timmy frowned, puzzled—"why are you here?"

Henry shrugged. "It was time. And you were right. Vietnam's followed me here."

"Well, I'm glad you're here."

Henry watched him climb the stairs, a lump in his throat. Time burns away the troubled spirit. But the whirligig of time can also bring its revenges. And this is mine.

Dog

He told me the story of the years he was away from home and I sat quietly and let him tell me for I knew that he was cleansing his spirit with the telling and once it was away from him, then he would be what he had to become. I did not like all of the story, but it was that story which had to be told. A terrible story of what happens to a man in war when the man is betrayed by his own people. I wanted to tell Henry that it was too bad he had not been born an Indian for the Indians are full aware of betrayal and most have learned how to live with that betrayal. But I did not say this because then it would be my story and not Henry's story.

Henry had tried to come back home after the war, but those who lived here had seen too much of the war on their televisions and so they thought they knew everything that Henry could tell them and wanted to hear no more. And because the college students were protesting the war at the time, some of them thought about the war as a thing to talk about at parties and pretend that they really knew what should be done.

It was at one party when one woman asked Henry why he had left the army. Because of the children. Henry said. In the end, it was because of the children meeting the bullets. There is something obscene about children being killed by bullets. And the woman said that she couldn't understand why he went in the first place. Henry tried to tell her that he went because he was ordered to go, and the woman said something about that being a fool's reply. Then Henry said that if that was what she truly believed, then she could go to hell, and he left with Kate and came home and they fought about what Henry had said because both of them had drunk enough to make them reckless and the next morning, Henry left again.

And that was the beginning of Henry and his wanderings around the country that was supposed to be home. He worked on a Greek fishing boat for a while but the owner of the boat refused to work with the union and some of the men had caught him and made him not a man. Henry got some dynamite from a construction site and blew up the men that did this to his friend.

He tried to live for a while in El Paso, staying with a man called Alfonso Gonzales and his family in the Lower Valley. I knew about this, but said nothing as Henry talked, because he had forgotten that he had written a letter to me about that place. One of four letters that he wrote to me. He wrote others to Kate and Tom, but they became fewer and fewer in time until the letters stopped altogether. That was when I received my last one before he went into the monastery.

Henry went next to North Carolina, where he got into a difficulty with a fishing union and some fishermen.

After North Carolina Henry went to Memphis and went to work cleaning streets. He became good friends with a black man there and often went home with the man who lived near a place called Beale Street. It is here, now, that Henry had trouble. The black man had a young daughter who did not respect her father's ways. She liked to dance and go to the clubs with her friends. Her father did not approve of this, but he knew that life for the daughter of a street cleaner was the life that needed to be escaped from at times and so he let his daughter go dancing at the clubs. One night, she did not come home and when the day came and the black man did not come to work, Henry went to the black man's house and was told that the black man was in the hospital. He had gone to the club where his daughter went and when he found she was not there, he went to the house where he was told she had gone. The house belonged to the man who owned many clubs on Beale Street and when the black man tried to bring his daughter home, the other men there laughed at him and beat him badly. The black man's wife told Henry this while she cried for the family that she had lost. Henry went that night to the house where the daughter had been taken. I do not know what Henry did at that house, but he brought the daughter home.

But the worst happened in New Orleans.

Chapter Forty-six

Morgan blinked as harsh light stabbed against his eyelids. He looked, confused, into a shaft of bright white light that shot through a break in the venetian blinds. An orange haze seemed to permeate the rest of the room. He smelled spice incense (patchouli?) and beneath that, a dank musty smell that reminded him of graveyard north of Bien Hoa where he and the old man had once hidden from the Viet Cong in a running battle. For a brief moment, he returned to that place, his senses confused and distraught: He smelled decay and the fear in his own stale sweat and tasted it, brassy like holding pennies in his mouth. He felt the ground beneath his belly and against the flesh of his hands and cheek and his heart began to pound and then a shadow moved between him and the light and he looked up in confusion at a young woman, her hair pulled back and held with a rubber band, her cheekbones high, eyes clear and free from mascara and eyeliner. She wore a black turtleneck and black pants. But he didn't recognize her until she spoke.

"You're awake."

"Yes." His throat felt caked and he gagged and coughed. She reached hurriedly for a glass and held a straw to his lips. He sucked, swallowing painfully, then winced as pain pushed through the torpor given by sleep.

"Hurt?" she asked. He nodded. Her hand reached again past his eyes and reappeared with a white tablet between two fingers. She slipped it between his lips and placed the straw again between his lips. "Swallow," she said.

He obeyed and twisted his head to look down at himself. His arm had been neatly set in plaster. He could only breathe in shallow gasps and knew his ribs had been taped. He swallowed. The hurt was beginning to lessen.

"How bad?" he croaked.

"Your arm is broken," she said. Her voice was rich and low. "A cracked rib or two and a lot of bruises. They stamped you well," she said.

"Doctor?" His tongue felt caked and he scraped it across his teeth, licking.

A tiny smile touched her lips. Her eyebrow twitched. "After a fashion," she said. "Doctor John lost his license. Abortions. He was lucky that he didn't go to prison. But," she shrugged. "His cousin was the judge and blood is thicker than dry words spoken in air. At least in New Orleans," she added. "And so, Doctor John spends his time in the Quarter and lucky for some of us he does, too. He patches up the odd hurt, sews up knife wounds, and drinks a lot of bourbon. He lives over on Chartres Street up at the end. An old house that belonged to his family. The judge lets him stay there. Keeps him out of mischief. Well, away from those who would think of him as a mischief maker."

"What happened?"

"Well, you came along at the right time for me. Rather the wrong time for you. I'd say." She smiled mirthlessly. "Dupree was about to teach me a lesson."

"Dupree?"

" 'Black Johnny' Dupree. From Algiers. Across the river. He has a place on Powder Street."

"I don't understand," he whispered.

"I danced in one of his clubs," she said. "The night before last the bartender told me that a customer wanted me to visit him in his hotel room after my set. I didn't go. Dupree came over from Algiers to teach me a lesson. But, you got in his way. So you got the lesson." She shrugged. "Either way, it was a lesson for me. The next time will be worse."

"What is Algiers?"

She hesitated, then said, "It's a place where you don't want to go. Algiers Point. It used to have a slave corral there. Later when slavery was illegal, those who lived there found other ways to make a living. Smuggling. Dope. You name it. Sometimes it was called Slaughterhouse Point. The Creoles who ran the smuggling in from the bayous moved in and now it's where people like Dupree live. You go there, you don't go at night. Unless you know someone like Dupree. Then you're safe enough unless Dupree gets a whim. And no one knows when he gets a whim. Like he did with me."

"Why don't you go to the police?" he said.

"In the Quarter?" She smiled and shook her head. "You live here long enough you won't have to answer that question. Is there anyone I should call?"

For a moment he was confused, then realized she was asking who she should notify about his injuries.

"No," he said, looking away from her. "No, there's no one. I was staying at the Place des Armes. I'm Henry Morgan. How long have I been here?"

"Three days. And I'm Jane Seymour," she said. He glanced around the room. A plain room. A framed print of a flamingo hung on one wall next to a dark painting of a bayou. A worn armchair stood next to a floor lamp. A book rested on the arm of the chair and he realized that she had been watching over him while he was unconscious.

"You can stay here if you like," she said. "I'll send around for your things at your hotel. Of course," she added, "we can take you back there. But it won't be as comfortable. And," she hesitated, "you are safe here."

"Safe? From what?"

"Dupree. Who knows what he might do next?" She shook her head and the muscles in her face went lax and he realized from the tiny lines that appeared at the corners of her eyes and faint lines across her forehead that she was older than he thought. "Another arrangement will be made for me. And if I don't go this time, he'll kill me."

"Do you want to go?" he asked.

She gave him a long look, then sighed and shook her head.

"You can always tell, can't you, when a girl's been in the trade. No matter how hard a person tries, you can't get rid of it. How did you know?"

"I didn't," he said. "But I guessed. The bartender wouldn't have made a case out of your refusal if he hadn't known about your past. What was it?"

"Drugs," she said matter-of-factly. "Put it down to an impetuous youth. I don't know. Rebellion, I guess, against my parents. But, well, it got kind of kinky, you know? Parties, rock-and-roll. The day I woke up with three men in bed with me I knew I was over the line and it was time to pull back."

"Why the bar? Why dancing?"

She shrugged. "There's only so many openings for a girl with a past. No education. Hell. I'd been fucking my way across New Orleans since I was sixteen. Nearly ten years. The cops had my address, my phone number. Dime bags were easy to get. I tried waitressing, but all it took was for one customer to recognize me and I was out. Finally I just put an act together. It didn't cost as much as waitressing either. All I needed was a pair of stiletto heels for a costume. The rest was all Mother Nature."

"There are other cities," he said. "Why not go there? Up to Memphis, maybe? Shreveport? Hell, leave the South and head up north to Chicago. It's there if you want it."

She sat back on the edge of the bed and crossed her legs under her. She stared at the picture of the bayou on the wall across from her for a long moment, then shook her head again. "No. This is home. I was born here. Up on Basin Street. A studio apartment. Mother modeled for a painter. You can see her pictures all over. I'll bet a thousand tourists have an 'original' "— she hooked her index fingers in the air—"painting of her hanging in their houses. I've always lived here. The Quarter is all I know. It's a continuous party. Never stops. Just rolls from one end of the Quarter to the other. You can tell the tourists—jaysters, we call them—they walk and gawk and stare at the people of the Quarter as if we're aliens." She laughed. "We are what they think they want to be. And so we laugh and charge five dollars for watered whiskey and overprice our beer and demand a cover charge before they enter the clubs and after the last one staggers out drunk as a hoot owl and positive that he has lived a wild life, we get together and smoke a little dope and drink a little booze and laugh at them and the stories they'll tell to their friends in Peoria. But we aren't what they think we are. We are what they are. It's just a difference in place, that's all. Doctor John lives a long ways away, but I know he'll come when I call and won't try to grope me or charge me anything and it's because he's part of the Quarter. Benny, the blind guitar player in the Absinthe House, once gave me his last dollar when I needed it. Cherry, who makes a great living modeling, has me over to meet her parents when they come down from up north and I help her pretend that we are roommates and she is working her way through college even though she hasn't been taking any courses for a couple of years now. I know that I can walk into Tasso's grocery store and get credit for food if I want it, and Kingko, the tap dancer on Royal Street, sat me through the cold sweats when I decided to leave drugs. I can't leave here. They are family and the Quarter is home."

"I understand home," Morgan said.

She waited for him to say more, but he turned his head and stared at the pictures on the wall. Suddenly she reached out and rested the palm of her hand on his forehead. He rolled his head around and stared at her.

"You can't be left alone. Not until you heal," she said. "You want, I can get your stuff from your hotel. You can stay here." She bit her lip and looked away. "I mean, I owe you and I don't like being beholden."

"That would be nice," Morgan said.

Dog

They did not become lovers until many days had passed. When Henry told this to me I think he meant weeks. But I could be wrong. A golden eagle flew high overhead and we watched him land in a large nest in the high, dead branches of a cottonwood down along Bad River. The sunlight glinted off the tips of his wings and seemed to reflect a strange part of Henry. Something dark. And when we looked down from the hill across the river, the gold leaves seemed to soften and as we watched, the colors began to fade into the gray of the evening. I could feel the heat from the ground rise up from the shale through the burnt grass and escape into the air around us. Yet, the earth seemed to stay warm, too, and down along the creek the burdock and sumac lost their colors and merged into the berry thickets until the river looked like a silver thread running through a rolled black blanket.

It was then that he told me what had happened those last weeks when he lived in New Orleans with Jane Seymour. There was no love between them. This I could understand. It was need between them that brought them together in the end and filled the ache that each held privately. Together they could put that ache aside. But such a thing is only temporary at best and cannot last.

I do not know how long this thing between Henry and Jane would have lasted. It did not last long enough. This much I do know. Had it lasted as long as it should have, perhaps Henry would have been able to lay his demons aside and return to Ithaca. But this was not written upon the medicine path that Henry was to follow.

For a while, Jane Seymour was good for Henry. The woman is the life of the flowering tree and it is the woman who has the power of life hidden in the roots of the flowering tree. I do not think that woman herself knows this or if she does why it is so. But it is there and that is all there is to it. It is hidden from the power of man. Sometimes such a thing can be revealed in the Dog Vision but this is not done very often anymore. I have never done this but I was there once when I was a youth and a holy man came to the reservation from Montana and did the Dog Vision for my people in a heyoka ceremony. They killed a dog by breaking its neck. Then they singed the dog in a sage fire and then took the heart from the dog before the holy man put the dog into the pot and boiled it. Then the holy man took the heart of the dog and covered it with herbs and baked it in the coals of the fire and when it was finished, we ate it. Then we ate the dog. And then the vision came and Sacred Woman came and sat with us and spoke to us and told us many things. It was then that I learned the power of woman. But Henry never learned this power because the chance was taken from him.

Henry took a job working at the Absinthe House in New Orleans. This was the place that had belonged to Pierre Lafitte— the brother of Jean Lafitte, the pirate who had helped Andrew Jackson during 1812, Henry said. I think it was a blacksmith shop, then. Jane Seymour danced at another place where men who had come to New Orleans to do business went to watch naked women dance and pretend to be what they were not. This is in some men's nature, too, and it is a very private thing that they keep to themselves so that they can have a secret from their wives who keep the secret of the flowering tree from their husbands. It makes the man feel less unimportant, I think.

One night Henry was late returning to the apartment he shared with Jane Seymour. When he opened the door, he felt death and knew she was dead before he found her in their bedroom. Dupree had sent his men back to her. Perhaps on a whim. And they had tied her hands and feet to the four corners of the bed she had shared with Henry and beaten her. And raped her. And when they were finished with her, they had killed her by cutting her bowels from her and leaving her alone to die. Before leaving they nailed a spread-eagled cat above the bed, and it was by this that Henry learned that it was Dupree who had sent the men. I think it had something to do with the old ways of the slaves.

This was when the darkness fell upon Henry, a terrible darkness in which he saw demons dancing in the darkness of his mind. He saw Jane Seymour in her coffin, and when he slept at night in the place that they had shared, he heard her screams in the darkness, and he felt the pain of her spirit and the pain of her flesh, and when he went deeper into his sleep, he saw her as he had found her, and finally, he spoke with her spirit in his dreams, and she told him what the men Dupree sent had done to her. When he awoke in the morning, his pillow was covered with tears, but he did not know if the tears were his or hers.

And the dreams continued, and Henry quit working at the Absinthe House and began drinking. The more he drank, however, the deeper into the darkness his spirit walked when he slept until finally, he knew that the darkness had become his world.

I think it was then that the Black Chief rode upon him with his black horse, and he became mad. This I have heard about before and in that darkness, he talked with Benny, the blind guitar player who was a friend of Jane Seymour, and Benny told him about a man in the Quarter who could get anything for Henry that Henry might want. Henry went to this man and got two pistols, a cane knife, and a hand grenade. Then Henry took the old ferry across the Mississippi to Algiers and went hunting.

He found the man who Dupree had sent and left him on his bed in the same manner that he had left Jane Seymour. But not before the man told him who the others were. There were four of them. Henry killed two of them the next night. He watched them come out of a nightclub and when they got into a car, Henry came up behind the car and rolled the hand grenade under the gas tank of the car. They burned to death when the gas tank exploded.

It took Henry two weeks to find the third man. He found him down at the waterfront in a warehouse and cut his throat with the cane knife and left him behind a packing crate of rebuilt generators for the rats. The fourth man he found in a hotel room with a woman. The woman tried to stop Henry, and Henry shot her, then shot the man when he tried to jump from the window. The man was fat and got stuck in the window and Henry placed the barrel of his pistol against the man's naked ass and shot him that way. It was an ugly death.

Henry found Dupree in an old hotel that had been made into apartments. He had to kill three other men that Dupree had as bodyguards before he could get Dupree. He took Dupree from his apartment to an abandoned building. It took Dupree three days to die. Then, Henry set the building on fire. It was an old building, and when the fire department came, they did not try very hard to keep it from burning. They worried more about the other buildings near it. Henry watched the fire burn until the roof fell in, then he threw the cane knife and the pistols into the river.

Two weeks later, he found himself outside the monastery. Or, one of the men who lived in the monastery found him. I do not know which it was. It does not matter. The next ten years, Henry lived in the monastery.

I do not know what he expected to find at the monastery. But it was a place where he could rest and perhaps his spirit healed a little there, too. I do not know this to be true, but I do not know it to be false, either. Perhaps Henry had forgotten the lessons I taught him when he was young at the place where the heart of Crazy Horse lies buried. Perhaps he had not. But the monastery is a place for men of peace, not warriors, men like Henry, who have ridden in the embrace of the season of rain and death.

Chapter Forty-seven

Tom Morgan stepped out into the yard and drew a deep breath. He frowned. The air had an old-time drouthy smell to it like scorched grass. He could already feel the heat of the day, and the sun hadn't been up long enough to dry the dew. Only there wasn't any dew; just a bit of dampness down in the low spots where a ground fog might have stood for a while. The air smelled like the earth was dying and that worried him. He had heard about the droughts of 1918 and knew about the Dirty Thirties when the earth shifted itself from the Great Plains to somewhere else. He glanced down at the tank and noticed how low it had fallen and wondered if the drought would reach deep enough into the earth to dry up the spring down there and turn the creek to dust. Then he shook his head. No, that probably wouldn't happen. Even during the thirties they'd had water. The Morgans had always had water. Some years not as much as others, but water had been there just the same.

But he remembered well those bad years when the west wind would sweep in as hot as a steelman's furnace, pulling the scant moisture from the grass before it could drink the dew. Many times he had watched the grass burn a golden brown, then fade into dust-gray, and finally into dust as the animals' hoofs ground it to powder.

There had been times when the Morgans had been forced to cut back on stock as the range couldn't support as many cattle, but they had never had to sell the breeders. And nature had a way of helping even there. When drought hit, the cattle suffered the most for those white-faced herefords had been bred for the green pastures of England, not the wasteland that could come in

a year in the Dakotas. Nature kept the birth rate down among
the wild animals, though that wasn't always a blessing for the
coyotes would begin to move in on the stock as winter came
closer.

He sighed and rubbed his thick-knuckled hand over his griz-
zled hair. He was happy that he hadn't put in any winter wheat
like some had. There wasn't enough moisture now to do much.
The wisps of wheat were drought-stunted and very few had
bearded out. He was glad that he'd sowed a bit of alfalfa to help
with winter feed, but he'd be lucky to get one cutting from that
field, and one cutting wouldn't be enough to carry the cattle over
to spring if a heavy snow fell. Of course, a heavy snow would
give a little ground water for the spring, so there would be some
good from it, but if they had a regular snowfall, there would still
be some forage available and one cutting might be enough then.

He turned and critically eyed the cattle standing down at the
tank. They had yet to show signs of the drought, but feed was
beginning to become critical. Common sense told him that he
should market some of his stock to tide him over until spring.
But others had the same idea, now, and the market was glutted
with stock as others vainly tried to salvage something from ruin.
Cattle prices had dropped below parity—way below parity—and
feed cost had skyrocketed. If things continued the way they were,
why a man could lose almost fifty cents for every pound the
cattle put on. Bankruptcy lay in that direction.

Reynolds must be feeling the pinch about now. There's not
enough water left on the Rafter R to keep a bumblebee alive.
He'll have to truck in water too, soon. And that will double,
maybe triple his production costs.

He bent and plucked a clump of gramma grass and squeezed
it between his palms. The leaves of grass rolled and powdered
into dust instead of balling as they should have. He tossed the
powder high in the air and watched it settle slowly to the earth.

Has it coming, the damn fool! We tried to tell him not to
overstock his range, but when did he ever listen to anybody?

He frowned as he saw a dust tail rise along the rubboard
graded road leading past the ranch gate. Company coming, and

these days one never knew if company would be good or bad. The drought had stretched everybody's tempers to the breaking point.

A dusty Dodge station wagon, its sides marred by deep scratches and gouges from gravel, slowed as it came to the gate leading into the ranch. Tom recognized the county seal and knew Bill Padgett, the extension agent, was coming to call. He moved down from the lawn to greet him as the station wagon slid to a halt.

"Mornin', Tom!" Padgett called as he stepped out of the station wagon. He stomped his feet to settle them in his high-heeled boots and winced. Tom suppressed a smile. Padgett had been complaining about his bunions for ten years, but he still insisted on wearing cowboy boots instead of shoes to ease the pain. He pulled a handkerchief from a back pocket, removed his Stetson, and mopped his red forehead. "Hot enough for you?"

"Gonna get hotter," Tom said. He looked over the top of the station wagon as the passenger door opened and a neatly dressed man in a white shirt and tie stepped out. He looked cool and fit. He came around the station wagon, smiling, but his lips were too thin to hold the smile and Tom looked back at Padgett questioningly.

"Like you to meet the new director of the federal land office," Padgett said quickly. His eyes shifted away from Tom's stare, then back again. He cleared his throat. "Uh, Dick Prapp."

"Richard," the man said annoyed. His lips thinned in what approximated a smile, but there was no friendship behind the gesture. He extended his hand: Tom took it. It felt like dry straw against his palm. Padgett's tanned face grew redder at the admonition.

"Uh-huh," Tom said. "I'm Tom Morgan. Tom," he added. Prapp gave him a hard look, but Tom's washed-blue eyes met his steadily.

"Yes," Prapp said. He turned and stared over the ranch, shading his eyes with a manila folder he held as he stared down at the stock tank and the creek threading silvery through the burnt grass. "You've got a nice little place here, Mr. Morgan."

"Thanks," Tom said noncommittally. He watched Prapp carefully as he turned slowly, inspecting his ranch.

"I see that you are fixed for water. That spring-fed?" he asked, pointing at the stock tank.

"Has been for seventy-five years or more," Tom said. "My grandfather and father dug it out. Mostly by hand, working a few hours at night. Then, Pa had Heine Koch finish grading it back in the fifties with his Big Cat. We've had sweet water ever since, 'cept back in 'fifty-six when the drought hit hard, then it had a touch alkali to it, but none so's the cattle couldn't drink. I don't think you were around, yet, Richard. Government still had the idea back then that a soil bank was all the farmers and cattlemen needed." He shrugged. "We got along pretty well, considering."

"I'll bet you did, since you had all the water," Prapp said. Tom bristled at the man's tone, but held his silence as Prapp turned to him. "Well, tell you what we want to do, Mr. Morgan. We'd like to trench off through your west pasture to give a little irrigation help to your neighbors and then down the creek a ways, come out to the east with another ditch. I think a little back-hoe is all we need—just a little something to dig a trench, really. Then the others can splice off with irrigation pipe and—"

"No," Tom said quietly.

Prapp turned and looked at him, frowning. "I beg your pardon?"

"No ditch or trench is gonna be dug through my land," Tom said quietly.

Prapp flashed a quick, wintery smile, then said, "Perhaps I didn't make myself clear, Mr. Morgan. We propose to make water available to everyone to help through this drought."

"And I don't think you understand," Morgan answered. "The answer is no. If you know as much about the land as you should, Mr. Prapp, then you'd realize that my water ain't enough for everyone. You trench off'n it, then you might have enough water for a month. Maybe two if the others use it sparingly, which I don't think they would. Especially Reynolds who overstocked his range to take advantage of the cattle market. Sorry, but I ain't bailing a man out for doing something stupid like that. Especially since he knows better. No sir. You ain't taking my water."

"I see," Prapp said softly. He turned and looked back at the stock tank. "You know, Mr. Morgan, that the government could seize your land as you have encroached upon the water rights of the others by building that stock dam, don't you?"

"What are you talking about?" Morgan asked. Padgett moved uneasily beside him at his tone, edging back toward the station wagon. Prapp held his ground, a tight grin fixed upon his thin lips. He pointed down at the stock tank.

"You needed government approval before you built that dam," he said quietly. "There are laws against keeping water from other people to the extent of interfering with its natural flow. Now, I've looked into your records"—he waved the manila folder at Tom—"and I don't see where you or your father or anybody filed an application for permission to redirect the natural flow of that creek. Or," he emphasized, "to build a dam that restricts the natural flow. In short, Mr. Morgan, I believe that you are in violation of federal law, here. Under which, I can seize your property, have a fine levied against you, freeze your assets, in short, halt all work on this ranch until the courts have time to work out this mess." He shook his head. "That would be very expensive for you, Mr. Morgan."

"I think you'd better look at that law again, Mr. Prapp. I think you might find that we come under the grandfathering clause. You see, we started improvement on this land before you people got around to doing anything about the watershed. You try to ditch my land, and you won't need a court to end it. I'll end it. Now, get the hell off my land!" Morgan said tightly.

"I don't think you really want to take this to court, do you, Mr. Morgan?" Prapp asked quietly. His eyes looked stoney and a slight flush had begun creeping up his narrow neck. "There's not a court in this part of the country that would be sympathetic to you. Not now."

"You're trespassing, Mr. Prapp," Morgan said quietly. He

could feel the anger working through him, making his legs tremble. "And I know what the court would say about that. In fact, we still have old homestead laws on the books that give me the right to throw you off the land unless you have a writ of approach. You got that, Mr. Prapp?"

The flush consumed Prapp's face. He stared long and hard at Morgan before answering. "You are making a big mistake, Mr. Morgan."

"No," a voice came from behind them. They turned, startled to see Henry standing hip-shot, staring at them, his eyes expressionless beneath his stained hat. His blue denim shirt faded into the sky over his shoulder. His boots were well-worn and scuffed. A pair of wire gloves were tucked under the plain-buckled brown belt around his waist.

"You are making the mistake," he said softly.

"Henry—" Tom began, but his son cut him off with a tiny gesture.

"You forgot to mention that there is a time limit on the right of appeal to channel changing," Henry continued. "Since the improvements began back in the thirties, that time is way past. According to law, Mr. Prapp, your law, the existing channel is now the accepted channel. Check it out, but do it on your own time. Meanwhile, get off our land."

"This is Henry Morgan," Padgett said hesitantly.

"My son," Tom added. He grinned at the government man. "Was there anything else you wanted?"

"You'll be hearing from us," Prapp said, stepping around the station wagon. Padgett opened his door and plopped down on the seat behind the steering wheel. He pulled the door shut while he started the engine. Henry came over to the station wagon, folded his arms on the roof of the car, and bent down to face Prapp.

"By letter," Henry said quietly. "Leave us alone."

"Are you threatening me?" Prapp snapped.

"Yes," Henry said. "I am. Stay off our property unless you have a court order." His eyes raised to Padgett's. "You're welcome,

Mr. Padgett. Kate still makes the best apple pie in the county."
His eyes fell back to Prapp's. "You're not," he said simply. He
stepped back away from the station wagon.

Padgett put the station wagon in gear, gave Tom a weak smile
and turned in a tight circle, heading down the lane and out the
front gate. They watched as a dust plume grew like an ostrich
feather behind them.

"Goddamnit, I had things in control," Tom snapped.

"Yeah, I could see that," Henry said. A faint smile touched
the corners of his lips.

He turned and started toward the corral. Tom fell in beside
him.

"What if they don't listen to you?" Tom said.

"They will," Henry answered. He stopped at the corral and
looked over the horses milling around. "I want to ride out and
look around. Okay?"

"What the hell you asking me for," Tom said grouchily. "You
just told those government men who was in charge here. Lemme
get my rifle, and I'll come along."

"Kate says we need a few groceries," Henry said. "One of us
has to go into town. Timmy's slipping over to the west pasture
to check the cattle there, then to get started cutting the hay in
the north. That leaves you to get the groceries."

"Well, goddamn all to hell if you ain't the bossy one. Is it all
right with you if I take the pickup? Or, do you want me to walk
into Ithaca?"

"Take the truck," Henry said, grinning. "I wouldn't want you
to tire yourself." He walked into the barn to get a rope. Tom
glared at his back for a moment, then turned and stumped away.
"Take the buckskin," he called back over his shoulder. "He's got
more bottom than any of the others, including that roan. Just
thought I'd better let you know 'cause I ain't sure you remember
how to tell horseflesh."

Henry grinned and took a lariat from a hook inside the barn
door and slipped back into the corral. He let the rope slip
through his fingers, slowly building a loop as he walked toward
the horses bunching nervously together at the far end of the

corral. He smiled as he watched his father stalk toward the pickup, get in and slam the door. The starter ground, then grated. The pickup leaped forward in a cloud of dust and roared down the lane to the gate.

Henry pursed his lips, then recoiled the rope and turned, walking back to the house. He entered quietly and peeked in through the kitchen. Seeing no one, he went to the telephone and dialed a number. He drummed his fingers, waiting for the operator. When she came on, he requested directory service for Washington, D.C., and got the number for the Pentagon.

"Hello? Pentagon? I would like to speak with Rachel Holmes. Army Special Projects, I should think. Sorry, but I don't know the extension." He waited patiently, then heard several clicks, then a cool, crisp voice that brought memory crashing down upon him.

"This is Major Holmes. How may I help you?"

"*Major* Holmes? My, you have come up the ladder, haven't you, Rachel?"

There was a long pause, then her voice tightened. "Who is this?"

"Do you remember Maurice? And drinks on the Continental terrace? The Club Eve?"

"Henry Morgan," she said quietly.

"Yes. How have you been?"

"All right. Where are you?"

"Home. In South Dakota," he added hastily. "At the ranch."

"Well. You finally made it. Taken you long enough."

"Were you checking up on me?"

"What do you think?"

"I think you were checking up on me."

She laughed quietly. "We lost you somewhere in North Carolina. Where'd you go from there?"

"New Orleans. I was in a monastery for a long time."

"A monastery? Henry Morgan? And the roof never collapsed! Miracle upon miracle."

"It was a close one," he said. "Rachel, I need some help."

"You're out of the loop, Henry. Way out."

"For old times' sake?"

"Henry—"

"I need you to call the local sheriff and warn him to stay out of things involving the Morgans. That's all. Just a quick *official* telephone call. I'll do all the rest."

A long silence came on the line. Then, she sighed. "You never told me how you've been, Henry," she said softly.

"A bit on, a bit off," he said.

"I missed you when you left. You never even said good-bye."

"Why did you come to me in the hospital, Rachel? It was Black, wasn't it?"

Another silence, shorter this time, came, then she said, "At first. But I stayed because I wanted to, Henry."

"You should have told me, first, Rachel," he said quietly. "You should have been truthful."

"In our business, Henry? Truth?" she said bitterly. "All right. I owe you. I'll make the call. But that's as far as it's going, Henry. A quiet threat, but threat only. I can't follow up on it."

"Good enough, Rachel." He opened the telephone directory and read the number off to her. "Thanks."

"Henry," she said. He waited. "Do you think you'll ever get to Washington?"

"I don't know," he said.

"You'll let me know?"

"It wouldn't be awkward?"

"I'm a career girl, Henry," she said. "I'll leave word at this number to forward your call any time."

He hung up the telephone and stared at it for a long moment, feeling the pain of the passing years. Then, he turned and left, making his way back down to the corral.

Chapter Forty-eight

Tom Morgan placed the last sack of groceries in the back of the pickup and leaned against its side, panting in the heat. He pulled a red-and-white bandana from his pocket and took off his hat, mopping the perspiration from his face. He glanced up at the cloudless sky and shook his head. Again, no rain, and according to the weather report he'd listened to on the radio after the farm news on the way into Ithaca, there would be no rain again today or tonight. That made it an even hundred and twenty-five days without rain. Worst drought since 'fifty-two, Barney Johnson had said when he found him by the frozen foods in the grocery store.

"Wanna fudgecicle?" Barney had asked.

Tom had made a face and shook his head. "Don't see how you can eat that kid stuff."

"Ain't no different from the Zesto Shop in Pierre," Barney had said defensively. He had pulled a fudgecicle from the freezer and slammed the door. He had peeled the wrapper off and tossed it into his grocery basket. "Ain't seen you pass that any time you're in Pierre."

"That's different," Tom had said. "You can have it made to your specs and it's real ice cream."

"Soft serve," Barney had scoffed. He had taken a bite from the fudgecicle and had wallowed it around in his mouth before swallowing. "Ain't real ice cream. That's gotta be cranked and by hand, by God, or it ain't real ice cream."

"There's that," Tom had acknowledged. He had pushed his hat back with a forefinger, exposing the white band on his forehead where his hat protected it from the sun. He had lounged against the side of the freezer and had watched as Barney took another mouthful of the fudgecicle. His eye had traveled down the old man's neatly pressed denim workshirt to his jean-covered bowed legs and had tightened his jaws reflexively as he remembered how Barney had been pinned against a loading chute by an angry bull. His pelvis had been cracked in three places, the big bone in his right leg snapped, and his insides jellied. Since then, he'd lived with his daughter and her husband, Lonnie Brown, the manager of the feed store in town. Barney earned his walk-around money by running his little errands for his daughter and son-in-law and pretended that he liked it, but Tom knew that his dependency on their generousity rankled him deeply.

"Don't look like we're gonna get any relief," Tom had said.

Barney had shaken his head. "Nope. Some say that this is the worse one since the 'fifty-two."

"Don't know about that," Tom had said "Seems to me that we only went seventy-some days without rain in that one. But it's the worst one that I can remember."

"You still got water?" Barney had asked casually. He looked away from Tom, pretending interest in the bread shelf opposite them.

What the hell? "Yes," Tom had answered dryly. "You forget we got a spring on our place? Water's always good 'cause it comes from down deep. Might have a touch alkali in it at times, depending on how dry it gets, but always got water. Good enough for the cattle, that's for sure."

"Guess you're the lucky one, aincha?" Barney had said. He had lifted a loaf of Wonder Bread down from the shelf and tossed it into his basket. He had pulled a list from his denim shirt pocket and pretended to read it.

"What's this about, Barney?" Tom had said quietly.

"What's what about, Tom?" He had refused to meet Tom's eyes.

"You know. This business about water."

"I don't know what you're talking about. It's good that you have water," Barney had said.

"But?" Tom had pressed gently.

Barney had turned and glanced into his eyes then away.

"Don't seem right that your neighbors will do without while you go with. That's all," he had mumbled. "Don't seem neighborly."

"Barney," he had said gratingly. He looked at the wizened figure in front of him. Suddenly, he felt very tired. "I didn't expect this of you, Barney," he said.

He had pushed his basket away and tromped down the aisle to the register.

"What the hell," he said, hitching up his jeans. He opened the door to get into the cab of the pickup, then paused, staring at the gun rack hanging above the seat. The .308 Winchester was missing. For a moment, he wondered if he had placed it in the rack before leaving the ranch, then remembered that he had. He glanced up and down the street and noticed a small group of Rafter cowboys grouped around a pickup parked at the door to Shorty's Barbershop three doors down. One of them held a rifle he pretended to wipe with a feed sack.

Tom drew a deep breath and eased the door closed, then hitched up his jeans and clumped down to the barbershop. He paused in front of the cowboy with the rifle and nodded at it. "Nice lookin' rifle you got there."

"Thanks," the cowboy said. He smiled and looked up at the cowboy standing next to him. The cowboy snickered, and Tom felt his face flush hotly.

"Uh-huh," Tom said, swallowing his anger. ".308 Winchester, I don't miss my guess."

The cowboy peered at the barrel, pretending to read the worn lettering on the side. "By golly, if I don't think you're right. It is a .308. Hey, Tubby," he said, looking at the other cowboy. "You know that this was a .308?" Tubby shook his head and he looked over at the other one. "You know that, Jimmy?"

"Naw. You sure, Bill? I thought you was shootin' thirty-thirty ammo through it a couple of weeks ago when we were coyote hunting."

"I dunno," Bill said, shaking his head. The others grinned at each other, enjoying the game. "Somebody must've changed the ammo on me when I wasn't looking."

"Well," Tom said, "it was a .308 last I saw it hanging on the gun rack in my truck."

"Now, what you trying to say, old man?" Bill said. "You trying to suggest something to me?"

"Yeah," Tom said. He took a deep breath and stepped closer, smelling the whiskey on the cowboy's breath, noticing the brightness of his eyes. "Yeah, I'm saying that you took that rifle from my truck while I was in the grocery store."

"You calling me a thief?" Bill asked. Twin lumps of flesh appeared high on his cheeks as he smiled. "Now, that ain't a right thing to say to another man."

"I wouldn't say it to a man," Tom said hotly. "A man'd know better than to take something that don't belong to him. Unless," he added, "he was a scurvy thief."

"Better watch your mouth, old man," Tubby said. "Talk like that can get you in trouble."

"There's already trouble here," Tom said. He held out his hand. "Gimme the rifle."

"Or?" Bill said. He slowly wiped the feedsack along the gun's barrel again. "Or what?"

"I'll report you to the sheriff," Tom said.

Bill laughed and leaned back against the barbershop wall. "You really think the sheriff will listen to you?" He nodded at his friends. "Why, these boys will swear that I bought this here rifle off'n you two days ago. Gave you fifty dollars for it. Didn't I, boys?"

"As I recollect," Jimmy said. "Happened over at the west fence line, didn't it, Tubby?"

"Yeah. That's the way I remember it," Tubby answered. He spat into the street. "Run along, old man. You're off'n your patch, here."

Tom reached out suddenly and snatched the rifle, yanking it away from Bill. The barrel tilted in, gouging the cowboy on the shoulder as Tom raked it away.

"Ow! You son-of-a-bitch!" Bill howled, grabbing his shoulder. Then he stepped in toward Tom, backhanding him away. Tom staggered backwards, his heels catching on the curb, then sprawled onto the street. Within seconds, the others were on him. He tried to rise, but a boot suddenly appeared in his vision. Bright lights burst in his brain, then he slumped unconscious into the street.

Chapter Forty-nine

Bill moved restlessly on his bed in the bunkhouse, trying to find sleep. He glanced for the hundredth time at the floor where moonlight slanted in through a dirty window, throwing dim light into the room. His fingers gingerly touched the scab on his shoulder where the sight of Morgan's rifle had raked it. Goddamn old fart! he cursed silently. Got what he had comin', that's for sure. Maybe now those Morgans will let up on the Rafter R. Sumbitches! Since when do people hold back water?

He glanced down at the foot of the bed where he had leaned Morgan's Winchester against the frame and the wall. He smirked. Wonder when or even if they'll come after that rifle? Sure will be interesting.

He closed his eyes again, trying to will himself asleep, but his mind kept wandering, replaying the scene as he and Tubby stomped the shit out of that crusty old man to teach him some manners. Images flashed and flickered in his mind and his muscles tensed and relaxed and his legs twitched from the memory.

A hand slapped across his mouth, and a sharp point pressed against his throat. His eyes flew open, and his hands moved up on their own accord then froze as a whisper slipped out of the shadow bending over him.

"Don't! Not one word! Understand?" The point pressed hard against his throat. The skin broke, and he could feel a trickle of blood begin to slide down his throat. He nodded slightly, and the pressure against his throat eased. The hand slipped away from his mouth. He tried to breathe through his mouth, but realized only then that tape had been pressed across his lips, sealing them.

"Get up! Quietly! Slowly!" the whisper ordered. A hand slipped down and lifted the rifle from where he had leaned it.

Slowly he swung his legs over the side of the bed and stood. His bladder felt full, and he willed himself not to urinate. The close air of the bunkhouse felt hot and muggy against his naked flesh.

"Outside!"

Obediently, he turned and gingerly walked across the floor. He eased the door open and stepped outside, wincing as his bare feet encountered tiny pebbles on the hard earth. He started to turn, but a hard jab from the rifle pushed him forward.

"To the barn."

His legs began to tremble, but he turned and stepped gingerly across the yard to the barn. He wanted to raise his hands and rip the tape from his mouth, but he knew he did not dare to do that. He strained, trying to hear the man moving behind him, but he could not. Yet, he knew that the man was behind him and that he carried the rifle. But even if he did not have the rifle, he knew the knife was there and suddenly, he didn't know which he feared more. His mouth filled with saliva, and he swallowed painfully, his lips pushing against the adhesive of the tape.

The barn door stood open just enough to let a man slip inside. He wondered if he was supposed to go into the barn and hoped that he wasn't. It was very important that he not be forced to go into the barn. He had been inside the barn a hundred, no, two or three hundred times, and knew it as well as he knew anything, and he knew he did not want to go into that barn at this moment. No light shone from it, and in his imagination, it became a dark and forbidding cave.

"Inside," the whisperer ordered.

He waited, though, until the rifle barrel jabbed against him, driving him forward. He staggered, trying to keep from falling, and stumbled through a pile of fresh manure as he bumbled his way through the barn door. A pale light stretched from the open door straight forward into the darkness. He could make out the black beams of the stalls, silver straw, a rope hanging down from a rafter.

"God! No!" he mumbled, but the words were indistinct behind the tape, and he tried to turn, but something crashed against his head, stunning him, knocking him to the ground. He felt the rope roughly looped around his wrists, then suddenly he was pulled painfully through the manure and dirt, splinters from the wooden floor stabbing themselves into his flesh, and then he screamed as his shoulders took his full weight as he was hoisted into the air, but the scream, too, came out a high, thin keening that failed to travel to the door.

And then the beating began.

Tubby yawned and stretched and scratched his scalp with dirty fingernails. He glanced over at Bill's cot and noticed it was empty. He frowned, then shrugged. He looked at the window; early light showed gray. He sighed and sat up and swung his legs over the side of his cot, standing. He yawned and stretched again. His mouth felt gummy, and a slight headache already rose behind his eyes from the heat coming fast behind the day. He pulled on his jeans and sat down on the edge of his cot to work his feet into his boots. He stood and stamped hard to settle his feet into the boots, then took a fresh denim workshirt from the metal locker at the head of his bunk.

Feed line again! he thought sourly as he pulled the shirt on and buttoned it. For the third day in the week he had been assigned to shovel feed into the bunkers, balancing himself on the wagon as Bill drove the tractor slowly down the lines. Hell of a job to do. Shit! With all his money, why don't Reynolds hire a kid to shovel that crap?

He sighed and ran his fingers over his chin, debating whether he should shave or not, then decided he'd feel better if he didn't have sweat running through beard stubble as the day got hotter. And there's plenty of heat in the day already, he thought resignedly. He collected a dirty towel, his razor, and a tube of shaving cream and went outside, heading down toward the pump to shave outside rather than use the sink. At least outside, he'd be cool.

He caught sight of the barn door standing open and frowned. Jesus Christ! Is Bill getting ready before breakfast? What the hell's wrong with that man? He turned his steps toward the barn, ready to accuse his friend of showy ambition. He stepped into the barn and froze, his eyes widening at the sight of his friend, naked, his body a mass of welts and bruises, swinging gently from a rope knotted around his wrists.

"Shit! Help! Help! In the barn!" he hollered and ran forward to loosen the knot and lower his friend to the floor of the barn.

Dog

And so it began. Kate sent Timmy out to get us when the doctor called from Ithaca and said that they had taken Henry's father in to Pierre to the hospital in an ambulance. He did not tell them that the Rafter R cowboys had beaten Tom Morgan half to death, stomping his ribs in with the high heels of their cowboy boots. At first, we thought that Tom had had a heart attack or a stroke. We did not know about the beating until we got into Pierre. Kate knew, though, and Timmy. But they did not tell Henry because they were afraid of his anger. And they were right to be afraid of that anger, but it still came when Henry saw his father lying in the hospital bed with tape wrapped around him like a corpse. I saw the anger come upon him like a north wind, and I shivered and stood away from him so the anger would be his alone.

The doctor told us that Tom Morgan would be all right, but Kate said she would stay with him while the three of us returned home. Timmy drove us back in the old Buick, and I sat in the back and watched as the anger worked deeper into Henry, filling him with its bitterness. Timmy tried to talk to him, but Henry only grunted and finally, when we passed through Hays City, Timmy gave up and we drove the rest of the way in silence.

When we arrived at the ranch, Henry did not go up to the house, but went down to the corral and saddled the roan horse that I had given him earlier that day when he had come out to the hill. Timmy wanted to go with him, but I made him stay with me while Henry rode off into the night.

The next morning, I found him on the hill sitting in the

warrior ring. He had the old man's rifle with him. He looked up
as I came to him.

"We are going to need more people," he said.

I nodded.

"But no one will come to work for us. I think," he said. He
looked at me. "Do you have any ideas?"

"Yes. Tom Standing Bear and Billy Spotted Horse will come.
They have helped before in branding season."

He frowned and stared down at the rifle in his lap. "I don't
know them."

I shrugged. "It doesn't matter. They do not know you either.
But they are good men."

"Where are they?"

"In jail. In Gordon."

He laughed. "These are your good men?"

"It is complicated," I said. "They beat up a white man who
beat up their cousin and killed his cattle and ruined his corn."

"Then why wasn't the white man put in jail?" he asked.

I shrugged. "He is white. They are Indian. It is the way of
things."

"All right," Henry said. "Go down and bail them out. We'll
hire them."

"It is not that simple," I said. "I am Indian too. I will not be
welcome in Gordon."

Henry nodded. "I didn't think of that. So, the two of us will
go down and bring them back to the ranch." He rose, brushing
off his jeans. "We'd better do that now. I don't think Reynolds is
going to be patient much longer."

We drove down to Gordon and brought back Billy Spotted Horse
and Tom Standing Bear. The sheriff was not happy to let them
out of jail, but Henry convinced him that it was better if we took
them away instead of letting them be killed in his custody. He
did not like it either when Henry told him he would call the
Federal Bureau of Intimidation unless the sheriff released them
into our custody.

Henry left two hundred dollars for their bond. Their car had been burned while they were in jail, so we drove them back to Martin so they could gather their things and then brought them to the ranch. Kate was relieved to know that we had two more men to help out. We always left one man at the ranch while the others took care of the stock and gathering what hay we could from the land around the creek.

When Tom Morgan heard about what we had done, he pretended to be angry. But I knew that he was glad to see Billy and Tom. Once again, we were a working ranch and not soldiers guarding our land.

Chapter Fifty

Bob Reynolds cocked a booted foot on the porch railing and leaned back in his chair. Sweat trickled down his back, soaking into the waistband of his blue denim shirt and jeans. He rocked his chair back and forth on its hind legs and rubbed his hands across his face. He looked down toward the gate and shook his head, remembering Tubby and the other men gently moving Bill into the bunkhouse and putting him on the long table so they could wash the dirt and manure from him. The man had been savagely beaten, but beaten in a methodical manner. Whoever had done that had known how to administer a beating.

He shook his head, wondering how a man like Bill could have been taken from the bunkhouse in the dead of night without anybody the wiser, stretched up on a rope, and beaten like that. And now, he reflected, as if he didn't have enough troubles, he was two men short as Tubby had had to drive Bill into Pierre to the hospital.

He sighed and took a long drink from a glass of bourbon so strong it looked like tea and cocked a pale blue eye at the burning sun baking the prairie. A hundred and eighty days without rain, he thought sourly and took another drink and frowned painfully as the bourbon hammered hard behind his eyes. Damn long time.

He shifted his gaze and stared out over the stock pens and corrals, down the hill from the ranch house, and over the Dutch-gabled barn to the pastures where the cattle bunched together, bawling and trying to push each other out of the way in order to get a mouthful of dank water from the tank. The water was so low that he could walk across it and wet his jeans only to the knees.

And by this time next week, there'll only be mud and the cattle will begin to die, he thought. He raised his eyes to the hills glowing softly in the distance like the white humps of charlois bulls. Illusion. Only illusion. No nourishment in those wisps of grass. Damn! When the short days of fall came there would be frost, he told himself. Yes, there would be frost and that would put some moisture back in the ground. But it wouldn't be enough. No, not nearly enough since the grass was going too and although the space of the sky above would begin to turn ever-changing violet and the cold air snap against his cheeks, and the lanes down from the house would still be dry and dusty in the morning and the cattle would begin to die again, slowly from the thirst.

He wrinkled his brow and took another long pull of bourbon. He took a deep breath and held it until the pounding stopped behind his eyes. He tried to blink away the ache, couldn't, and felt the anger at the Morgans simmer.

"Goddamn, them! Goddamn those Morgans!" he smoldered. "The only water west of Pierre, and I can't get to it! And these cattle are dying now. Slowly. Dying. And the stupid brutes don't even know they are dying or they would break through the Morgan fence and help themselves to the water. Jesus!"

He sighed and wiped his mouth, scrubbing his hand over his blue denim shirt. He sighed. Where could he get water? Too expensive to truck in the amount he needed, and if he let the cattle go at current market prices, then he would be broke. Yet, everything had been right for the move. He had waited long for the money, borrowed more on short term against future profits, and plunged. The market had been right. Everything had been right. Except the weather. The goddamned weather. Who would have thought a drought would begin in May? That was the time for thinking about bringing in the hay, raking and baling and stacking it against the winter months. But this year, there would be no hay for winter. He had planned for that too though: he had turned the cattle out onto the grass and now he ruled over barren plains. A supreme folly, as it turned out! Grass gone, water gone, and soon, cattle gone! Nothing.

He took another long drink against the anger building up inside him. His eyes caught movement at the end of the lane, and he frowned as he watched a man on a roan horse pick his way gingerly over the cattle guard and begin climbing the hill toward the house. The rider pulled to a stop in front of the house, and Henry stepped down from the saddle, holding the reins in his hand. He stood for a moment staring at Reynolds.

"Hello, Bob," Morgan said softly.

Reynolds studied him carefully for a moment, noting the faded jeans, the workshirt, the scuffed boots. His eyes flickered to the saddle where the stock of a Winchester stood up from a scabbard beside the saddlehorn. Morgan waited for him, his lips smiling slightly.

"Been a while, Henry," he said. He nodded at the Winchester. "Going hunting?"

"You never know," Morgan said softly. "Coyotes are moving down out of the back hills, what with the drought."

"Uh-huh," Reynolds grunted. He hawked and spat. "We had a little trouble here last night."

"You did?"

"One of my men got beaten pretty badly. Might have some internal damage."

"That's too bad," Morgan said. His eyes looked sadly into Reynolds. "Somebody must've had a good reason for that."

"Uh-huh. Probably." Deliberately Reynolds lifted his glass and drank slowly, watching Morgan. He lowered the glass. "So, when did you get home?"

"Couple days ago," Morgan answered.

"And you came to see me today? I'm flattered," Reynolds said. "What do you want?"

"Just thought I'd let you know that I'll be running the ranch from now on," Morgan said.

"Get all your running around done, then?" Reynolds grinned

wolfishly. "How convenient. But is that suposed to mean some-thing to me?"

Morgan smiled and removed his hat, deliberately wiping the leather sweatband with a red bandana he took from a hip pocket. He smiled gently at Reynolds before carefully resettling the hat on his head, pulling the brim down to shade his eyes.

"Just being neighborly," Morgan said.

"You want to be neighborly, let down your fences so my cattle can get to water!" Reynolds snapped.

Morgan shook his head regretfully. "Can't do that. Way it's going, we'll be lucky to save our herd. The grass is going and"—he paused and looked up at the cloudless sky, squinting against the bright blue—"I don't think it will rain soon. Can't take the chance. Sorry."

"Sorry?" Reynolds puffed his cheeks and blew out a steady stream of air. "Sorry doesn't save my cattle!"

"You have too many head for your range," Morgan said pa-tiently. "Far too many. If I let the fence down, and your cattle come over to our water, we'll both go down if it doesn't rain. That doesn't make any sense."

"Then, sell me your range, and let me take my chances," Reynolds said. "I'll give you top dollar. Hell," he said, warming to his task, "tell you what I'll do: I'll give you a hundred an acre over my last offer to your old man. I'll be taking a beating, but I always was a sucker for land."

Morgan smiled and shook his head. "Land's worth twice your last offer, Bob," he said gently. "Especially now that I've got the only water around."

"You have the only water around?" Reynolds swung his feet down from the porch railing and stood. He tossed his drink aside into the dust and placed the glass on the railing. His belly pushed heavy as a full feed sack against his belt. He hitched his pants and stomped to the stairs. Morgan watched calmly as he stood, spraddle-legged in front of him.

"But it makes sense for me to go down, is that it? Well, let me tell you something, you young peckerhead! I have no intention of going down. None at all. I asked you to let down your fence only as a courtesy." He lifted his head and nodded at the cattle. "In a week, maybe less, they'll be out of water. I'll be coming then whether you let your fence down or not."

Morgan nodded and turned to go.

"No warning? No threat?" Reynolds said mockingly. "I thought you'd make something of that. Your father would have."

"I already have," Morgan said quietly.

His eyes held Reynold's for a long moment. Reynolds suddenly felt himself being drawn deep into them. Tiny fires burned and a dull pounding of war drums began in his head and for a moment, fear knotted in his belly. Sweat popped out on his face, and the bourbon tasted stale and strong on his tongue. Then, Morgan nodded, and stepped up into the saddle again. He settled himself in the saddle and turned the horse, nodding to Reynolds. Reynolds blinked and found himself back on his porch, his chest heaving as he fought to draw breath.

"You know, Bob, you're no different from some of those people I worked with in Vietnam. They used people too. I wouldn't play the game then, and I have no intention of playing that game now. You're like them. I thought when I came home that I'd be away from that war. But I was wrong. They came home too. Little autocrats who were used to using people. It stops here, now, Bob," he said quietly.

"Why, you little shit!" Reynolds said thickly. He stepped down off the porch, shouting. "Get the hell off my land! I'm coming, goddamn you! I'm coming! And you get in my way, and I'll put the cattle over you!" He bent and picked up a stone and threw it at the horse, striking it on the rump. Startled, the horse leaped, then stamped its feet nervously as Morgan held its head high, soothing it.

"I'd be careful, Bob," Henry said. "I put in a call to a couple of friends of mine. The type you wouldn't know. You don't want to mess with a congressional investigation, now, do you?"

"I know one thing," Reynolds said gratingly. "You're trespassing."

Morgan gave him a sad smile over his shoulder, then nudged

the roan with his heels and lifted the horse into a trot down the lane, away from the house, leaving a small trail of dust hanging in the air behind him. Reynolds stood, panting, watching until the horse disappeared over the hill back toward the Morgan ranch. The heat of the sun drummed against his head, and he turned and climbed back up into the cool shade of the porch and hung on tightly to the newel post as he took a long, deep, shuddering breath, trying to still the beating of his heart thundering like a bass drum in his chest.

Dog

One evening a dark cloud came up over the horizon. Lightning streaked from it and for a few hours everybody thought that it would rain and that would make everything right. I knew it would not rain and even if it did rain things would not be made right. Too much had happened for that. They do not understand the depth of time. Such people have spent too much time with themselves among others. They no longer have the humility to say that it is over.

Henry tried to tell me about a man named Thomas Merton who lived alone. Each day, one of the monks from the monastery where Henry lived would bring this Thomas Merton his dinner and wait patiently while the one who lived alone ate his meal in quiet contemplation. One day, a monk asked him a question. How do we know when the devil is tempting us? And this Thomas Merton swallowed his bread and answered, The devils are very pleased with a soul that comes out of its dry house and shivers in the rain for no other reason than that the house is dry.

The monk went away, pretending to understand this, but I do not think that he understood it at all. I do not think that Henry understood it, either, although he thought about it greatly. The souls came out of the people that day, hoping that they would be able to dance in the rain. But there was no rain and no dancing and when the souls tried to move back into the bodies, they could no longer find their way and the men became hollow men because of this.

Chapter Fifty-one

A trickle of sweat crept from under Stumpy Watson's hatband and curled down around his eye and over his cheek. He wiped it away with the back of his hand and stared intently around the sun-baked prairie. Behind him, he could hear the cattle coming, lowing painfully. Dust blew from them over him, and he smelled the dryness in the air. He placed a hand on the barbed wire in front of him. The heat in the wire burned his hand. He jerked his hand away and again looked at the hills. Twin frown lines appeared between his eyes, and he pulled his lower lip between his front teeth, nibbling. He studied the hill line carefully, intently, but saw nothing. Then he remembered that he heard nothing but the cattle coming behind him, and he looked again at the hill line, searching hard for what he couldn't see.

This is wrong. Dead wrong. Surely they know that we're coming with the cattle. But where are they? Where the hell are they? I know that old sonofabitch and his bastard son! They've gotta be there somewheres.

Then he could wait no longer, and he took a pair of wire cutters from his back pocket and moved to the wooden post down from him. He carefully placed the wire cutters on the top strand and squeezed the handles. The wire parted with a loud ting! and the post vibrated and something slapped into it beside him. He stared uncomprehendingly, for a brief second, then the sound rolled to him and another bullet smacked into the wooden post. He backed away reflexively, and a third shot landed where his boots had been.

"Shit!" he yelled and dropped the wire cutters. He turned and ran for his horse. Bullets spattered the ground in front of him, and the horse reared, turning, and galloped away, the reins rising to its chest.

"Goddamn it!" he hollered. He started after the horse. A bullet ricocheted off the ground in front of him, and he froze. Sweat trickled down his shirt, soaking into the top of his blue jeans. Slowly, he turned and stared back across the fence into the Morgan pasture.

"All right! All right!" he yelled, throwing up his hands. "Don't shoot!" A bullet landed next to him. He flinched. "What the hell do you want?"

"Fix the fence!"

He turned, looking up to where a pile of rocks stood on top of the hill. The shout seemed to have come from there, but he couldn't be sure. Another bullet whined off the ground on the other side of him.

"All right, goddamnit!" he yelled. He scurried forward and grabbed the wire he had cut. A barb sliced through the palm of his hand. He swore and unwound the coil as he made his way back to the post. He bent and picked up the wire cutters. He tried to pull the wire to the post, but the tension was gone, and he came up inches short.

"I need a splice!" he yelled.

"Fix it!" the voice came.

"I can't! The wire's too short!" he yelled desperately.

"Then, hold it until you figure out a way!" the voice shouted.

"Fuck you!" he yelled, then flinched as a bullet slammed into the post around his knees. Suddenly, he had to pee. "Goddamnit!"

"I'm not joking!"

"Oh shit!" he moaned and looked over his shoulder as the first of the cattle came up over the hill. He saw Grayson pull up short, then clap his heels to his horse's sides and ride down toward Stumpy, holding tightly to the wire.

"What the hell are you doing?" he demanded. "Why haven't you cut that wire?"

"We got a problem," Stumpy said. He nodded off in the general direction of Morgan land. "Someone's shooting at me. I think it's Morgan's boy."

Grayson stood in his stirrups and looked slowly over the land. He shook his head as he sat back down in his saddle. "I don't see anything," he said.

"He's there, I tell you!" Stumpy said. He squeezed his legs together as his bladder felt like it was about to burst.

"Then what the hell are you holding onto the wire for?" Grayson asked.

" 'Cause he won't let me let go!" Stumpy flared.

"Who won't?"

"Whoever the hell is shooting at me!" Stumpy said, frustration making his voice climb. "Gimme a splice, will you?"

Grayson shook his head and swung down from his horse. He crossed to Stumpy.

"Give me the cutters and stand back," he said.

"You can have the cutters, but I ain't letting go of this wire until I know he's gone. That sumbitch's too good with that rifle," Stumpy said, letting Grayson pull the wire cutters from his belt.

"There ain't nobody there," Grayson said. "Maybe he was, maybe he wasn't. I don't know. But he ain't there now." He cut the second strand down, and the wire snapped away from him. At the same time, a bullet slammed into the earth by his boot. "JEEESUS CHRIST!" he yelled, jumping back.

"Oh, shit!" Stumpy said, and his bladder released hot urine down his leg, filling his boot.

A second bullet whined away from them and Grayson froze, shoving his hands up into the air.

"Fix the fence!" a voice came faintly.

"That you, Morgan?" Grayson yelled.

"Now, who the hell you think it is?" Stumpy said disgustedly.

"Shut up," Grayson said. He raised his voice. "All right, Morgan. Knock it off. You know you ain't gonna shoot us. There's too many witnesses with the herd." He turned to gesture, and a bullet plowed into the ground beside the toe of his boot. He jumped reflexively, then swore. "Goddamnit! Quit that!" he yelled.

"Fix the fence!" came the yell.

"I'll be damned—" The bullet came close to taking off his toe. He swore again, and turned toward his horse. A bullet drove between the horse's legs, startling it.

"Whoa! Goddamn, whoa!" Grayson shouted. The horse turned, wall-eyed, and ran away. Grayson whipped off his hat and slammed it into the dirt. A bullet drove it away from him. He drew a deep, shuddering breath, then turned back toward Stumpy who watched him, wondering.

"Just what the hell do you think you're gonna do, Morgan?" he yelled. "Shoot us? Shit! You ain't gonna do anything! You shoot us, and they'll fry your ass for murder! I ain't gonna fix your damn fence! What do you think about that?" A bullet came close to his boots, but he was expecting it this time, and although he flinched, he didn't move. "Go ahead! Shoot, you sonofabitch! Shoot! Tell you what I'm gonna do! I'm gonna cut that other strand of fence!" He stormed over to Stumpy and grabbed the second strand of wire.

"Boss," Stumpy whined. "I wouldn't—"

"Shut the fuck up!" Grayson snarled. He lowered the wire cutters and snipped the last strand of barbed wire. He looked at Stumpy. "Let go of that wire!"

"Boss," Stumpy began.

"Let—it—go!" Grayson said. Tiny white spots appeared high on his cheekbones.

Stumpy stared at him for a minute, then sighed, and let the wire go, tactfully stepping behind the lanky foreman. He held his breath, but no shots came. Behind him, he could hear the cattle begin bawling as they smelled the water. He glanced over his shoulder as they began to trot down the hill toward the opening in the fence.

"Well, I guess that's it," he said. He stepped away from Grayson and turned to trudge around the herd as it began to bunch together. The first steer crossed the break in the fence and a shot came. The steer stumbled, fell to its knees, then onto its side, blood pouring from its mouth.

"What the hell," Grayson began, then the shots came rapidly, and the cattle began to fall. A couple raced past the fallen steers, then quickly folded and fell to the ground. The cattle in front tried to turn, to stampede back, but the smell of water drove those behind eagerly forward, pushing them through the fence. The shots came faster, now, and the cattle began to pile up, and then the smell of blood halted the rush for water. The cattle began to mill. A couple ran down the length of the fence on Reynolds's side and suddenly, they turned and began to bolt away, heading back over the hill.

"Whoa!"

"Look out!"

The cowboys tried to turn the cattle, but crazed by thirst and the smell of fresh blood, they ignored the curses of the cowboys and stampeded away from the fence. Grayson watched helplessly, coughing as the dust built around him. Then the cattle were gone, and he was alone with Stumpy as the other cowboys raced after the herd, trying to turn them before they could run across the flats and through the fence on the other side of the pasture.

And then it was silent.

Slowly he turned and stared up the hill toward the pile of stones marking the old Indian camp. Morgan stood there, his rifle over his shoulder. Grayson watched as he turned and walked over the hill. Then, he appered on the roan horse and rode down to them. The horse skittered when they neared the pile of dead cattle, but Morgan eased it around the carcasses and reined in beside the fence. Grayson stared up at Morgan.

"You've gone too far, Morgan," he said quietly. He gestured at the dead animals. "Reynolds will have you in court over this."

"They call it trespassing," Morgan said quietly. "Now, catch up your horses and drag these carcasses over on your own land. If I have to do it, I'll be coming to collect charges for labor and trespassing."

"There's not a court," Grayson began, but Morgan cut him off.

"Out here, I'm the court," he said quietly. An edge came into his voice. "You beat up my father, burned down our bunkhouse, harrassed my sister-in-law and her son. I warned your boss,

Grayson. Now, I'm warning you. It's the last time. Out here, we still have laws against trespassing. And taking a man's water is theft. Remember that, Grayson."

"I'll remember," Grayson said quietly. His eyes burned out of the dust-covered mask of his face. "But you won't always be on your land, Morgan. Not always. And then—"

"Let it lie, Grayson," Morgan said. "You don't want to mess with this any further. You can't win."

He turned the roan and rode away. Grayson watched as they disappeared over the hill. Then he turned to Stumpy and sighed.

"Our horses?"

Stumpy shrugged.

"Yeah," he said. "Well, come on. It's a long walk back." He glanced down at Stumpy's wet jeans. "What the hell?"

"Fuck you," Stumpy said, and Grayson turned and walked away, pausing to collect his hat. Stumpy fell in beside him and together, they trudged up the hill, following the path of the cattle.

Dog

We were very lucky that day, although I do not think Grayson and his friend knew just how much luck they had with them. Grayson and the other caught their horses and pulled the dead cattle back onto the Rafter land and left them lying there next to the fence. At night, I watched the coyotes come to feast on the dead animals and by day, the birds were thick and heavy around the slaughtered animals. They did not mind the stink that rolled like a fog over the hills.

Reynolds sent the sheriff to the ranch to arrest Henry. Henry refused to go with him but told the sheriff to let him know when the trial came and he would go into town for that. He told the sheriff that the cattle had been on our land when he shot them and offered to take the sheriff back into the hills so he could see for himself, but the sheriff did not want to do that. Timmy and I were there with our rifles, and I think that made him nervous. The sheriff was not a brave man. I could see that in the way his eyes refused to look at another's eyes. So he went away without Henry.

When we went into town, we went two at a time after that. The Rafter cowboys saw us, but they did nothing except say words trying to get us to fight them. This we would not do, although I could tell that Timmy wanted to very badly. That was when I sent for help from the reservation, and Billy Spotted Horse and Tom Standing Bear came to help us. Billy had just been released from prison for manslaughter before the time in Gordon and everyone knew that Tom Standing Bear was crazy. Nobody likes to bother a crazy Indian. They went into town when we needed things, and people left them alone.

I knew, however, that Reynolds was not finished, yet. Many nights I would sit on the hill and look across to where I knew his house to be and imagine myself in the house, walking silently past the long, polished table where he once held dinner parties for men who came to see him from Chicago, past the well-polished black mahogany desk, down the hall lined with old photographs of cowboys and cavalry officers and one of Big Foot dead in the snow at Wounded Knee and into his bedroom. He will be sleeping alone, now, because he is too worried about his cattle to bring his secretary out from town to stay with him. I slip up to the bed and listen to his drunken snoring until he senses I am in the room and he opens his eyes and sees me standing there and when I see the puzzlement begin to disappear from his eyes I strike hard with my knife, slicing through the thick fat of his breast, turning the blade so that it will glance off a rib and cut cleanly into his heart.

For many nights I sat like this, dreaming myself into his dreams, seeing Henry ride on his death horse galloping mystically over the clouds, black clouds filled with rain, but I never saw the end of the dream and then the dream stopped altogether. The Moon of the Changing Seasons was over. The Moon of the Popping Trees began.

This is the tongue of the dead men. I heard it that night on the hard breath of wind, smelling of burnt grass, that blew across the pasture to the hill of the warrior's ring. My pony heard their voices, too, for he knickered uneasily in reply and nervously stamped his feet as if he could stamp them into the stony ground. The wind came from the Badlands so I knew that it was the voices of spirits.

It is time now, the voices said. Now, they are calling you.

I did not know what they meant by that for many voices have spoken to me over the years. Then, a man came riding on a bay horse out of the dark clouds below the Great Bear, slanting down toward me on the ground. I tried to rise, but my legs would not work and so I sat there, numbly, waiting for him to come. A strange, sickly, greenish light surrounded him and the crickets ceased singing and all was silent. I thought I heard the flapping of a bird's wings, but I could not have heard this for all was silent. And then, he was beside me, looking down upon me from his horse in the visible darkness and he said: Now you shall walk the black road and many will walk the black road with you. But do not be afraid of this black road and do not be afraid of those who walk with you as they will fear you more than you fear them.

And then he raised the reins of his horse and together they rose silently into the air and disappeared into a mist that began to gather around me. I rose in that mist and walked down from the warrior's ring to where my pony was tethered and mounted him and rode him back toward the ranch house. As I came up on the hill where the lightning-struck cottonwood stood, I looked down upon the creek that wandered through our land to Bad River. Flames rose from the waters and in the flames I saw Kate dancing a strange dance, nude and alone. The short grass was withered, but where her feet touched, a greenness appeared and I heard crickets singing and an owl crying a name I did not know.

And I heard the cattle—

Chapter Fifty-two

Reynolds came at noon in his big Cadillac, a plume of dust rising angrily behind him. He slowed when he neared the gate but still was going too fast for the turn, and the big car slid when he turned the wheel into the lane leading to the ranch house, the back bumper narrowly missing the latch post, and careened down the lane, the car lurching in and out of the ruts.

Tom Morgan heard the roar of the big motor before he saw the car and watched as Reynolds slid up to him. He turned the motor off and opened the door, levering his bulk up from behind the wheel. The engine pinged, and metal settled as he slammed the door behind him and strode up to Tom, his big belly bouncing over the huge buckle, his beefy face red with anger. He shook his finger in Tom's face.

"Goddamn you! Goddamn you!" he panted. "Your son killed eight of my steers yesterday! Eight! I'm sending you the bill, and you will goddamn pay it or I'll come collecting! I won't be coming with the law anymore! You want to do this—"

"Seven," a voice said quietly behind Tom. Reynolds looked over Tom's shoulder. Henry stood, his hands in the back pockets of his jeans.

"Huh?" Reynolds said, confused. Behind him, Grayson stepped quietly from the passenger side of the Cadillac, leaving the door open, his hands not visible. Morgan smiled thinly at him, then looked at Reynolds.

"It was seven, not eight. I killed seven Rafter steers that were on our land after your people cut our wire. Wire cutting's still pretty serious around here, Reynolds. People take a dim view of someone taking liberties with their land."

Reynolds placed his fists on his hips and leaned forward on the balls of his feet. His lips curled in a tight sneer. "You think so, Morgan? Have have you looked around this range? You ain't got a clue, off playing your games while others around here are scratching for a living. The grass is burnt. Can't even put it up for hay. Try to rake it and it crumbles into dust. Can't bale dust. Can't sweep it and lay it up and even if we could, cattle won't eat it 'cause ain't nothing in it for them. Might as well eat air.

"But you don't see that and you don't know what these people have gone through. You ain't gonna get any sympathy from these folks. You ain't gonna get any help from these folks. Fact is," he glowered. "I start pulling in mortgages and then hint around that I might give extensions if something should happen here and I just might get a lot of help against the Morgans." He spat contemptuously. "You stayed away too long, war hero. People around here don't care about your damn war and they don't give a damn about you. They got themselves to think about."

Henry turned away silently and walked down to the corral. He disappeared into the barn. Tom turned to Reynolds, the deep lines in his face taut with anger.

"I think you'd better go," he said quietly. "You have no business on Morgan land. Now, get the hell out of here and don't come back."

"What about the water?"

"My land, my water. There's nothing more to be said."

Reynolds rocked back on the heels of his boots. His eyes narrowed as he studied Tom. He sucked in his cheeks, pursing his lips. "I go now, I won't be back in a peaceable state. This is your last chance, Morgan."

"You're right about that," Tom said. He looked over at Grayson. "And you can take him with you."

Henry rode out of the barn on the roan and turned down toward the home pasture. He paused, staring for a long moment at Grayson and Reynolds, then gently pressed his heels against the roan's ribs and rode away. Reynolds watched him go and shook his head.

"That don't leave you much around here," he said smugly.

"Billy! Tom!" Tom said, raising his voice. The screen door opened behind him, and Billy Spotted Horse and Tom Standing Bear stepped out of the house. The door slammed shut hard behind them, the sound whapping the silence, startling Reynolds. Billy held a bacon sandwich in one huge hand and slowly ate it as he ambled over to Morgan. Standing Bear crossed over to the Cadillac, coming to a halt in front of Grayson. He nodded.

"You want something here, white boy?" he asked. His black eyes glittered like obsidian.

"I don't know," Grayson said, staring back. "I reckon that depends upon the boss."

"Only one boss here," Standing Bear said. His mouth drew down at the corners. "And I ain't heard him say he wanted you to stay."

"You thinking about throwing me off?" Grayson asked. His lips turned up in a slight smile, his eyes glinting dangerously.

Standing Bear shook his head. "Thinking ain't got nothing to do with it."

"You want these people gone, Mr. Morgan?" Billy said. He shoved the sandwich into his mouth. His cheek bulged like a chipmunk's. He wiped his hands across his blue workshirt and shrugged. His massive shoulders rolled and huge slabs of muscle threatened to burst through the seams.

"Yes," Tom said, and turned on his heel and left, walking toward the house. Billy started at Reynolds.

"You're trespassing, white man," he grinned.

Reynolds swore and stomped back to the Cadillac. "Get in the fucking car," he snarled at Grayson.

Grayson gave Standing Bear a tiny smile and slid down inside the Cadillac as Reynolds ground the motor and turned the huge beast in a wide circle, throwing dust high, as he roared down the lane toward the gate. It was only when he entered the Cadillac that Standing Bear noticed the pistol held low beside his leg.

"Guess they didn't want to mess with a couple of Injuns," Billy grinned.

"I think we're gonna have some serious trouble," Standing Bear said thoughtfully.

Billy frowned and stared at him. "What do you mean?"

"I think it was a setup," Standing Bear said. "Grayson had a pistol down behind. I didn't see it until he got in the car."

"Shee-it!" Billy exclaimed slowly. He whistled. "So. What should we do? Tell Henry?"

"Tell Mr. Morgan," Standing Bear said. "And Dog. Let him tell Henry." He shook his head. "Man, these fucking white men don't know when to leave well enough alone."

Dog

I found Henry sitting in the warrior's ring, staring across our land into Reynolds's land. It was not easy to find him as fog had rolled in from Bad River, wet and clammy, and I did not like the fog because it stank like the dead cattle, but only bones remained of the dead cattle now. The scavangers had seen to that.

I left my pony with the roan at the bottom of the hill and climbed to the warrior's ring. Henry did not look at me, but I knew he had seen me. He was looking far away with that look that does not have to see something to see everything. I sat beside him and waited for him to speak. But he did not speak and, I knew he was god-filled and waiting for the moment to lift the blanket of illusion and join with the Grandfathers and move with the earth's heartbeat.

At last, he sighed and turned to look at me. I told him what Billy Spotted Horse and Tom Standing Bear had told me about Grayson and the pistol and that they thought Reynolds had been trying to get Tom Morgan angry enough to attack him and then Grayson would have killed Tom Morgan with the pistol. Henry nodded and stared down at the fog moiling around at the bottom of the hill.

Chapter Fifty-three

Reynolds slammed on the brakes and the Cadillac skidded to a stop in a rush of gravel in front of his ranch house. He switched off the engine and opened the door, stepping out. He slammed the door shut and stomped up the three steps leading to the porch. A bottle of bourbon and an ice bucket and glasses stood on a small table beside a captain's chair. He dropped into it, spilled ice cubes into a glass, and filled it with bourbon.

Grayson quietly shut the Cadillac door and climbed the steps. He dropped into a chair next to Reynolds and took a glass, dropped in two ice cubes, and filled his glass half-full with bourbon. He tilted back in his chair and shoved his hat back off his forehead. He sipped, staring out over the ranch yard to where the cattle milled in the feedlot. A slight breeze brought the smell of ripening manure and seed cake and corn to him.

"You really shouldn't have gone into the feeding business," he said to Reynolds. Reynolds glared at him.

"What the fuck do you know about it?" he demanded. He slurped at his bourbon. His eyes appeared blood-red and tiny veins showed high on his cheeks and across his bulbous nose. "You don't know a goddamn thing about much."

"I don't have to take that," Grayson said, starting to rise.

"You'll take it and like it!" Reynolds said harshly. "If it wasn't for me, your sorry ass would be in the state prison! There's a lot of big Indians there who'd take a dim vision of your habit of riding down on the reservation for a little Indian poontang. The last time cost me a couple of thousand to hush up. So, don't be trying to tell me shit. And what about that fracas you got into over in Laramie? Beating the shit out of a couple of queer college boys. You're lucky you got away from that! What the hell do you know?"

"I know ranch land, and I know farm land, and I know land that can be used both ways," Grayson said quietly. He sipped. "This is ranch land."

Reynolds grunted. "There's enough corn on the bottom land along Bad River to give us feed. Or, there would have been if not for this damn drought."

"Uh-huh," Grayson said. "And so you bought all the corn before it came in and convinced Neiderssen to plant additional corn instead of oats and Stuggard and the others whose mortgages you hold. And now you are committed to crops that won't come in, and you got the farmers going under. Right now, you got Morgan as a common enemy, but if those farmers get to thinking about who talked them into planting corn in a wrong year, you might find them swinging over to Morgan's side."

"I'll foreclose on their places, then," Reynolds growled.

"And then do what?" Grayson said acidly. "What will you do with land in the middle of a drought? And what will the bank examiners think when they go through your books and discover that you hold mortgages on about everybody around with no way of collecting interest let alone principal 'cause of the drought?" He shook his head. "You're overextended, boss. Big time. You need water, and you need water now." He pointed at the cattle. "They're starting to die. You've got two choices: ship them, take what you can get from the buyers, and post your loss to bad investment, or get the Morgan water." He shrugged. "Your choice. I don't know your finances, but I'm thinking you're getting close to being strapped. You got a lot of capital going out each day and nothing being produced to earn it back even over the long run. 'Course"—he laughed and shaded his eyes as he glanced up into the bright-blue sky—"you could always pray for rain. But I don't think you and the Almighty are on good speaking terms."

"You leave that to me," Reynolds growled. He gulped his bourbon and pushed his hat back off his forehead. He pursed his lips and blew like a whale. "You take care of the Morgans, and I'll take care of the money."

"Whatever you say, boss," Grayson said. He grinned lazily and finished his drink. He set the glass on the small table and stood, pressing his hands against the small of his back and stretching. He nodded and stepped off the porch and walked with a loose hip swing to his gait to the barn and disappeared inside.

Reynolds grunted and sipped quietly at his bourbon, staring off across the burnt prairie, the sun's brightness bouncing hard against his eyes. Not a wisp of grass remained in the main feed yard. Not a single prickly pear cactus, no wallflowers, not even salsify grew and if no dogweed grew, then nothing was going to grow. Salt blocks stood starkly against the barren pasture. The cattle had eaten everything, stripped his pastures down to dust and shale, and where water once stood in a large tank, only cracked slabs of dried mud remained. A small dust devil blew across, sweeping up fine dust in a swirl, then disappearing over the fence toward Old Man Stone's place. He watched as two cowboys listlessly spread out cottonseed cakes in the feed trough, but only a few of the cattle moved toward it. The rest stood mutely, staring across the land to the west, and he knew that they could smell Morgan's water, and the thought made him angrier.

He drained his glass and refilled it with bourbon, ignoring the ice bucket. He looked down at the wisps of grass in his yard. Old grass, with a touch of green at its base, but he knew that without water, that green would climb no higher. A few listless purple asters and one or two clammyweeds still showed in the beds on either side of the steps leading to the porch, but those were hand-watered daily by Sally, his housekeeper.

He sighed and looked out again over the cattle to where his seed bull stood on the low rise leading up to the Morgan pasture. He was staring out over the hill, down to the wire separating him from the water, a magnificent hereford that Reynolds had bought in Cheyenne during the spring sales the year before. He had spent more than he should have, but when Reynolds saw that bull in the ring, a powerful feeling came over him, and he had bid recklessly, arrogantly, ignoring the shill who made him bid higher, until the crowd fell silent in awe at the money being offered for the bull. Sunlight glinted from the red of his hide. Thick muscles rolled in cables away from his shoulders down to the square block of his hips. His chest pushed forward in a massive juggernaut.

But there won't be much use for you, Reynolds thought, I can't buy the heifers I need for you. Hell, if things don't break soon, I'll have to go into the feed program along with the others the drought has busted. And how will that look to the others, their own banker forced to take a handout from the government?

And his face tightened as he knew that he could never go into the feed program and alarm the others who looked to him as the cornerstone of the county. If he went on the program, there might be a run on the bank and that would bring the auditors.

Slowly he raised his glass and deliberately drained it and reached for the bottle of bourbon. He couldn't go into the program, and he couldn't live without it. His cattle were dying, and he couldn't afford to truck in the water they would need to get through the drought.

A dull pounding began behind his eyes, and he dug his knuckles into his temples, trying to push the pain away. Those goddamn Morgans!

He heard the telephone ringing behind him in the living room and, turning, stomped into the house. He snatched the telephone from its cradle, growling, "Yeah?"

"Mr. Reynolds? This is Sheriff Wilson."

He closed his eyes against the whine of the sheriff's voice. "What is it, Wilson?"

"Well, Mr. Reynolds, I don't know how to put this—" Wilson began, but Reynolds cut him short.

"Just spit it out, Wilson! Goddamnit, I don't have time for any of your lame whinings and moanings! What is it?"

"I got a telephone call from Washington, D.C., this morning,"

Wilson said apologetically. "Someone told me that it would be in the best interests of my office to stay away from the Morgans."

"What?"

"I said—"

"I heard you, you dumb fuck! You think I'm deaf? Who the hell told you that? No, never mind! It doesn't matter! You just do what I tell you and everything will be fine!"

"I dunno, Mr. Reynolds. I think we'd better lay off them Morgans. The way I understand it, bad things could happen to us if we don't. And I got enough trouble coming up with the election next year. I don't reckon we would want to rock that boat, would we?"

Reynolds slammed the telephone down without answering and turned, staring angrily through the screen door at the sun-baked prairie. The glass broke in his hand and he stared down at the blood beginning to well out of his palm.

"Shit!" he yelled and threw the glass at the fireplace, then turned and, holding his hand up to keep the blood from dripping on the floor, made his way into the bathroom.

Chapter Fifty-four

Timmy rode slumped over in his saddle. Sweat bundled beneath his hatband then slowly trickled down his face. His shirt was nearly soaked through as was the crotch of his jeans. The material rubbed on his thighs and he knew he would have to use cornstarch after he showered.

The thought of water made him crane his head and look at the sky. The sun blazed like a blood-red ball. He shook his head. Nothing but blue sky and prairie, he thought. He glanced down at his horse's hooves as they plodded through the dried grass, powdering it, kicking up tiny dust clouds. The land is burnt. Ain't nothing up here for the cattle. We'll have to buy feed in November, December if we don't get some rain quickly.

A soft *chunk-chunk* reached him. He drew rein and sat straighter, looking in each direction for the sound. He nudged the sorrel with his heels and rode over a small rise and looked down at the bottom. Dead steers lay on the ground, bloated by the sun. Crows clustered around the carcasses. The pickup stood close to the fence, its doors open. Henry took a staple from his shirt pocket, centered it on a strand of Glidden wire, and hammered it into place.

Timmy watched for a minute, then rode down the hill to him. The stench of the rotting carcasses made him swallow heavily. He reined in beside the truck and crooked his knee around the saddle horn, letting the reins lax. The sorrel swung its head to the ground nuzzling half-heartedly at the grass, then gave up and hung its head sleepily.

"Pretty hot for that," Timmy said.

Henry squinted up at him, smiled faintly, then turned back

to his work. He took a fence stretcher, clamped it onto the second strand. Timmy could see where he had already spliced the wire. He pulled the rope, tightening the pulleys, then leaned back against the tension and hauled on the rope until the wire stretched tautly behind him. He pushed the lock with his thumb, then stood back for a moment to check the wire splice.

"Yes," he said. "It's pretty hot. But work don't wait for cool breezes. And I don't think Reynolds's men will come by to repair the wire."

"Want some help?"

Henry paused, glanced up at Timmy for a moment, then nodded. "Sure. Glad to have it." He swung the hammer in his hand toward a windmill down by the creek. "Afterwards, there's a six-pack in the tank, if you want."

"Sounds good," Timmy said. He swung his leg back over the horn and stepped down. He dropped the reins, knowing the sorrel wouldn't go far ground-tied, and went to the pickup. He pulled the seat back and took a pair of leather wire gloves out and slipped them on. He glanced at the rifle rack over the seat and paused, recognizing his grandfather's .308 Winchester. He picked up a pair of wire pliers and came to join Henry at the stretcher.

"I see Grandpa's rifle got back," he said.

"Uh-huh," Henry answered. He leaned into the stretcher again, plying more tension, holding it while Timmy centered the strand and hammered it into place with a staple.

"How'd that happen?"

Henry remained silent for a moment. "I just asked politely for its return."

"You *asked*?" Timmy said, looking up from his work.

"They were willing to listen to reason," Henry said. He unclamped the stretcher and carried it back to the third strand curled next to a post. He laid the stretcher out, carefully keeping the ropes from crossing, then began to uncurl the wire. Timmy came to help him.

"None of that Rafter bunch would ever listen to reason," he said after a moment. "You should have taken me along."

Henry smiled for a moment. He carefully attached the strand

to the stretcher and pulled it up, leaving it sagging in the middle.

"You seemed a bit restless for that," Henry said. He walked to the second strand and lay out another stretcher, clamping the wire into it. Timmy took the anchor loop and slipped it around a post. Henry pulled the wire straight.

"Maybe. But I can hold my own," Timmy said.

Henry glanced at him, then paused and took off his hat, wiping his denim sleeve across his forehead. He glanced up at the sun. "Going to get hotter," he said. He resettled his hat and looked at Timmy. "Don't take it personal," he said. "It's just that some people are good at things others aren't."

"And you're good at things like getting Grandpa's rifle back," Timmy said.

Henry paused, gazing thoughtfully at the pickup. He shook his head. "No, the rifle was just a symbol. That's all."

"I don't understand," Timmy said.

Henry sighed and leaned a forearm on top of a fence post. He looked at Timmy, "No," he said. "You wouldn't. And there's nothing wrong with that. But a person has to learn what he's good at, recognize it, and live with it. It may not be something that he wants to be good at, but he is. Maybe he's a banker and wants to be a cowboy, but he has to stay a banker. He wants to be a cowboy, but he just isn't good enough to be one. Yet, he's real good as a banker."

"And you?" Timmy said. "What are you good at?"

Henry's eyes became flat and hard and Timmy looked away reflexively, then forced himself to look back into Henry's eyes. Immediately he looked away again.

"Things I'd rather not be good at," Henry said softly.

Timmy frowned, puzzled. He kicked angrily at a clump of dried earth and watched the tiny balls of clay break apart. "I don't understand."

Henry smiled and cut a piece of wire and began to twist its strands into the cut wire's strands. "You are not meant to understand, then," he said. "Don't take it hard. Some things you can never hope to understand." He shrugged.

They worked quietly for a few minutes, then Timmy said, "Mom says I favor you more than Father."

Henry's hand slipped and the hammer struck his thumb. He pulled the glove off and stuck it into his mouth. "Damn!" he mouthed around his thumb.

"Keep your hands in your pocket, you won't hit 'em," Timmy said, grinning. Then, he sobered. "So what do you think about what Mom said?"

"Frankly, I don't see much resemblance," Henry said roughly. "Maybe it was something deeper your mother was talking about."

"All right," Timmy said. He pulled back against a rope strand, bringing the wire taut. Henry took a staple from his pocket and began hammering it in place. "I'm just a dumb cowboy. I guess you're going to have to spell it out for me."

Henry smiled and shook his head. "You'll find that out. But it is something that you have to find out for yourself, I can't tell you."

Timmy glanced back at the pickup. "It has something to do with Father and Mom and you, doesn't it?"

Henry remained silent.

"You really aren't going to tell me, are you?" Timmy said after a moment.

"No," Henry said. "It's something that you don't need to know." He looked up at Timmy and smiled. "But that sort of makes us even, doesn't it? There are things about you that I don't know, either."

"Would you like to?" Timmy asked quickly.

The smile slipped from Henry's face. A strange soft light seemed to shine from his eyes for a moment and the lines around his eyes eased. "Yes," he said quietly. "Very much. I've lost a lot that I will never get back. But I would like to know what it is that I lost."

They finished fixing the fence and Timmy mounted the sorrel and followed Henry in the pickup down to the windmill. A six-pack of Hamm's Beer rested on the moss-covered bottom of the tank. Henry rolled his sleeve back and reached down to snag the

beer. The water was cool against his arm and he splashed a handful on his face, sighing deeply. Timmy draped his hat on the
saddle horn and dunked his head, blowing bubbles. He rose
quickly, throwing his wet hair back out of his eyes with a quick
toss of his head.

"Here," Henry said roughly. He handed a can of beer to
Timmy, then opened one for himself and turned to look at the
long line of sky along the hills where the sun was turning it
orange and red. Two hawks glided low over the hillside, dipping
and swooping, then held almost steady in the air. The sky became a country of changing colors like the land: red in the west
toward Reynolds's place, a wrapping gray twilight in the east.
Somewhere, a bull bellowed, its roar falling faintly away. A few
steers moved slowly along the hillside, working their way toward
the creek and tank. Two young coyotes suddenly appeared out
of a plum thicket and the steers stopped, studying them carefully.
The coyotes trotted up the creek away from the tank. Henry
whistled. They stopped, heads up, alert, searching for the sudden
sharp sound. Then they loped up the hill, around stands of soapweed.

"You know," Timmy said, "I've never roped one of those." He
quickly drained his beer and tossed the empty can into the bed
of the pickup. He grabbed the reins and swung up in the saddle.
"Think I'll give them a try."

"Why not leave them alone?" Henry asked.

Timmy flashed him a crooked grin, and drove his heels hard
into the sorrel's ribs. The sorrel leaped forward, startled. Then he
steadied himself and broke into a dead, tearing run, stretching
out low to the ground, his red legs a blur as they gathered ground
and threw it behind them. Timmy leaned low in the saddle, his
fingers slipping the rope off the saddle, building a loop. The
sorrel streaked over the brown grass.

Henry swore, threw his can of beer into the back of the
pickup and leaped in, fingers fumbling for the keys in the ignition. He stomped on the accelerator and swung the pickup in a
tight circle, heading up the hill toward Timmy. He came up on

the hill in time to watch Timmy ride down toward the coyotes, the loop trailing behind him in his fingers as he came down the hill. The coyotes broke into a run and suddenly split, one going left, the other right. Timmy leaned automatically toward the right one, his arm going up over his head, wrist flexing as the rope began to swing, but the sorrel felt the pressure of his knee and turned sharply to his left. Too late, Timmy realized the mistake he had made and rose in his stirrups to slow the sorrel, but the horse slipped away from between Timmy's legs, the reins burning through his hands. He flew through the air, seemed to hang for a moment, then he hit the ground, rolling, tumbling across a small patch of prickly pear cactus.

He lay quietly for a moment, then started to push himself up, and quickly turned to his left and fell flat onto the ground. Henry slammed on the brakes, killing the engine and leaped from the cab.

"Lie still," he said sharply. He grabbed Timmy's shoulders, pushing him flat against the ground. "Lie still. You may have something broken."

Timmy gagged, and took great gulping gasps of air. Henry gently ran his hands down Timmy's sides, pressing softly with the pads of his fingers, checking for broken ribs, then down each leg.

"I . . . think . . . I'm okay," Timmy gasped. Then, he winced. "My butt hurts."

"Stay flat," Henry ordered. He rose and stepped to the pickup, throwing the seatback toward the steering wheel. Timmy started to sit up, then yelled and fell flat again.

"I told you to stay down," Henry said, coming back with a pair of pliers in his hand. "You got a mess of needles in your butt." He clamped on one and jerked it. Timmy twitched and yelped.

"Goddamnit!" he exclaimed. Then he yelped again as Henry yanked another free. He craned his head over his shoulder, trying to see as Henry pulled a third one free.

"I thought you broke your neck and both legs," Henry said

roughly. He clamped on another thorn and pulled it free. "I haven't seen anyone take a tumble like that."

"It wasn't as bad as it looked," Timmy whimpered. "I've hit harder in rodeos." He winced as another thorn was jerked free. "That hurts more."

"I didn't know you rodeoed," Henry said. "You like it?"

"Yeah," Timmy said. "Well, most of the time. Sometimes, though, you get to see that road coming up at you in the morning and still coming in the evening and you get to wishing you were finished and back home."

"I'll bet you meet a lot of girls." Henry said.

Timmy nodded, winced, and slapped the ground with his hand. "Oh yes. Especially when you win. But after a while"—he paused and gasped as a deep thorn was yanked free—"it gets to be old. That's when I come home. But then I get to remembering the good times and . . . well, you know."

"There," Henry said. He pulled away and stood up. "We better get you back and pour some iodine on those. Don't want to get lockjaw." He held out his hand, raising Timmy to his feet. Timmy took a couple of experimental steps, then walked toward his horse.

"I'll be all right," he said. The sorrel shied away, but he clucked soothingly as he moved slowly to gather the reins. He mounted slowly, then leaned gently back and forth in the saddle, finally sitting half-cocked. He glanced down at Henry. "You ever rodeo?"

Henry shrugged and walked back to the truck, dropping the pliers behind the seat. "Some," he said. "I think every boy's got that in him for a while. But there's only one Casey Tibbs or Jim Shoulders that comes along." He stepped into the truck and settled behind the wheel. "You be okay?" Timmy nodded. "I'll see you back at the house." He started the pickup, then leaned out the window. "You get home, you go up and sit in a bath of Epsom salts for a while. Then, have your mother dab some iodine on."

"Where you going?" Timmy said.

But Henry didn't answer as he drove away. Timmy watched

him disappear back over the crest of the hill, then turned the sorrel's head toward home. For a moment, Timmy thought of his father, then blinked and wondered why his father had slipped into his mind.

You know, you favor your uncle more than your father.

What? Why do you say that?

She shrugged and he could see that she was uneasy with what she had said. Many things, she answered evasively.

No, really. Why?

She laughed nervously and pushed a lank strand of hair back along her temples, pressing it into place with the pads of her fingers.

My, aren't you full of questions this morning?

It's only two. Why?

She sighed and looked at him sadly. She reached out and touched his cheek and he pulled back away from her. A hurt look spread over her face and he was instantly sorry for his action. He jammed his hands in the back of his trousers and looked down at the linoleum.

Why?

I don't know, she said lamely. The way you look at someone as if you could stare right through their eyes to the back of their minds and read the answers you want there. The way you walk. She shrugged, sighed, and looked out the window above the sink. The way the dimples show when you smile, she wanted to say, but bit the words back.

Dad did that, too, he said quietly. But you never say I look like him. Always Uncle Henry.

She felt the flush flow up her neck and into her cheeks and laughed. Well, he is your uncle. They both were the fruit from the same tree. Bound to be something of each of them in you.

And now he wished he had pressed her for more, but the time hadn't been right. He stood in the stirrups a moment, still staring where the pickup had disappeared over the hill, feeling a sudden closeness with his uncle that he hadn't felt before and the feeling confused him. He tried to pinpoint what was bothering him, but the sorrel moved restless beneath him, giving his head a shake as if to remind him of home waiting and the pail of oats waiting for him after Timmy rubbed him down. He blew air noisily through his nose and stamped his hoof impatiently.

"All right. You're right. Come on, boy, let's go home," Timmy said softly. He winced as the sorrel broke into a trot. He stood quickly in the stirrups. "I think I've had enough excitement for a while.

Chapter Fifty-five

Henry drove down the hill and turned back west toward the high hill and the ring of stones. He took a deep breath and lifted one hand from the wheel, noting its tremors. He shook his head and eased down in the seat, driving slowly across the prairie.

Lucky, he thought. That boy could have broken his neck on that ride. Then, you'd have another on your conscience. Why the hell did he do that?

But he knew the reason, and a lump came into his throat as he realized that Timmy was trying to win his approval. He smiled, remembering when he had tried the same thing, going into Fort Pierre in the summer for the rodeos when he was still in high school, remembering the walks along the streets beneath the tall cottonwoods down where Bad River rolled into the Missouri River, the lights flashing from the Silver Dollar Bar and the Hop Scotch Bar. The whole world had seemed rich to him, then, and he would work his way along the main street, past the Chectik Liquor Store, the town hall, the dentist's office, going into the drugstore to look over the racks of shiny-covered paperbacks. He liked the smell of the drugstore, with its clean antiseptic odor, the door left open so the faint sounds of the jukebox from the Hop Scotch across the street drifted in. Gradually, he would work his way back toward the Silver Dollar, watching the cowboys who would ride in the evening rodeo talk up the young girls, the hobos zigzaging slowly along the sidewalk, clutching bottles of wine in brown paper sacks. Then he'd walk back down and across the steel-girded bridge over Bad River and follow the street down to the arena in the fairgrounds. Usually a small four- or five-ride carnival would be down there along with a few booths.

Several cowboys and workers off the Oahe Dam would cluster around the shooting tent, betting on who could hit the most of the steel ducks painted white that lined along a steel trough in the back of the tent or the white rabbits whirling around and around on a bullet-scarred disk with one of the battered .22s chained to the counter. He would listen to the splat! of the bullets spattering against the metal. Occasionally, one would try to hit the bell through a tiny hole in a target above the ducks and rabbits. Sometimes one would and a loud piiinng! would ring out and cheers and swearing would follow. Country music poured from the beer tent where musicians in straw hats made music for everyone, singing old Hank Williams and Ernest Tubb songs while men and women sat beering and talking on folding chairs or dancing in the middle of the tent, their boots kicking up clouds of gray dust from the hard-packed ground. A few cowboys who lost their rides in the afternoon stood in small clusters at the makeshift bar of three wooden planks stretched over sawhorses, nursing their beers and talking about how they had made the one tiny mistake that had let their horse throw them.

It was an exciting time for a boy on the threshold of manhood. The shattered nights seemed exciting as laughter and curses and repeatedly rang through the night, punctuating sporadically the Williams and Tubb tunes. Across the Missouri River, the lights of Pierre blinked red and green and yellow through the dense tree line.

An illusion, he thought as he parked at the foot of the hill and got out of the pickup. He began walking up the hill toward the ring of stones. But illusions are real when you are eighteen and twenty and just as important as the reality of what you had seen when you remember it when you are forty or fifty.

A sadness fell over him as he came to the top of the hill. From here, he could see the lights of Reynolds's house flicker on and the lights of home to the east. Twilight threw long shadows between the hill and home and he sat and crossed his legs, placing his hands on his knees, staring at the house and back through time, remembering being young.

Chapter Fifty-six

Oly Anderson drove his battered pickup slowly past his fields as he made his way over to County 6 that would take him into Ithaca. Air, still morning cool, slipped past his open window, touching the side of his face. A north wind scooped up a cloud of dust and flung it through the open windows of his pickup into his face. He blinked and knuckled the grit from his eyes. He looked again at the fields and pursed his lips, studying them, trying to decide if he should plow under and sow winter wheat and hope for a spring gather. Stumpy cornstalks stood browning, leaves curling under, in the sun. A few had tasseled out, but they were the only ones that had even come close to being knee-high.

Not even enough for silage, he thought and shook his head. He could lay irrigation pipe and pump from Bad River that bordered his land on the south, but he knew that irrigation pipe was expensive and should have been laid in the spring when he had first felt the warm, dry wind from the southwest and hesitated before taking the big green John Deere tractor into the field and discing the land. But there had been enough ground moisture, then, and although vague misgivings stirred in him, he had thought there would be enough ground moisture to carry the seed through to the first rain.

But the rains never came.

He shook his head, deciding. Nope, too risky. Best to ride it out and cross this year off. He and Gretta, his wife, were comfortable enough and they had no children. They could make it another year on their savings and still have a little left to buy seed in the spring. There was bound to be snow this winter and that would give a little moisture back into the ground. Maybe not enough for corn, but enough for a quick crop of oats and maybe a little rye that would give them a cash crop. Then, if the rains did come again in the spring, there would still be time to plant the corn. It would mean working the ground twice—something he hadn't done for ten years—but he was still young enough for one season of long hours.

He sighed resolutely and gently tapped the accelerator, driving faster toward Ithaca. It would be best to act now before he second-guessed himself. A tiny smile touched his lips. Yes, he would do that. And to ease the disappointment, he would take Gretta to the Black Hills and spend a little time at Sylvan Lake, fishing during the day and lazing around at night in the lodge. It had been a long time since they had had a vacation. Maybe God was trying to tell him something.

He laughed and sat up straighter in his seat, already anticipating sitting on the terrace of the lodge, a cold glass of beer on the table beside him, enjoying the cool night in the Black Hills. Gretta would be pleased.

Chapter Fifty-seven

The morning had almost slipped away before Kate opened the door to the hen house and entered and took a basket from a hook just inside the door. She moved slowly from nest to nest, gently pushing the hens from their nests to gather their eggs. She spoke softly to them as she moved among them, and they reluctantly left their nests as she reached under them for their eggs. A couple clucked with disappointment, but she ignored them.

She stepped out of the hen house and set the basket on the ground. She opened a large wooden box next to the door and, taking a small scoop hanging from a nail beside the box, scattered seed across the ground for the hens. They moved greedily forward, heads darting swiftly to the ground, stabbing for the seed. She smiled and closed the lid on the box and hung the scoop back on its nail.

"Thank you," she said to the hens and left, heading toward the barn where one biddy had taken up refuge in the hayloft after scorning the hen house. Kate had often been tempted to leave the hen alone, but gathering the eggs had now become a game between them. The hen kept moving its nest around the loft, covering her eggs with wisps of hay in an attempt to keep Kate from finding them.

"All right, you old terror," Kate said as she pulled the barn door open and stepped inside. "Let's see what you have for me today."

She carefully placed her basket to the side of the door out of the way, then walked to the ladder leading to the loft and climbed it. She paused to catch her breath after hoisting herself up onto the floorboards, then stood and peered through the gloom.

"All right, where are you?" she asked. A low cluck answered her from the back of the loft. She smiled and moved carefully to the back. A white hen rose from behind a clump of hay and stalked toward her, beady eyes fixed on her legs.

"Now, mind your manners," Kate said. The hen clucked angrily in answer and came to a halt in front of her, its head moving jerkily from side to side. Kate waited patiently, then took a small step to her right. The bird jumped and stabbed at her foot with its beak, but Kate was familiar with the dance and easily moved out of her way, stepping around and over to the clump of hay. She found an egg and plucked it from the nest.

"Gotcha," she said in triumph. The hen cackled indignantly and stalked away. Kate sighed in disappointment, checked to see if there was another egg and, finding none, moved back to the ladder and carefully stepped down.

"Well, well," a voice said mockingly.

She gasped and stumbled off the last rung, nearly falling. She caught herself with one hand and turned toward the voice. Grayson grinned at her. A white band gleamed from his forehead where he had pushed his hat back. His eyes mocked her.

"You startled me," she said, laughing nervously.

"I did? Why's that?" he asked.

"I wasn't expecting anyone," she said. "If you're looking for Tom, he's gone with Timmy up north to check the cattle."

"Uh-huh," Grayson said. "I saw them up there when I drove past. Henry just rode out."

"Oh? Then—"

"I came to see you," he said. He took a step toward her. She stepped back involuntarily away from him. He gave her a small smile. "What are you afraid of?" She shrugged and shook her head. "You know, we never got to finish that dance."

"I think you'd better leave," she said quietly.

"Why?" he asked. He canted his head, staring at her. "Because your brother-in-law is home?" He laughed. "Why should that make a difference? Oh yes," he said, grinning at her indignant gasp. "I figured that out after your husband was killed, and you never gave any of us around here a tussle. That ain't natural, you know. You may have been married to his brother, but you had something for him, didn't you? But, now, what can be left for you with him anyway? How long was he gone? Twelve years? Fifteen? Longer? Whatever was between you two ain't there anymore. Too much time has passed. You're both different people. Has he slept with you since he's returned?"

"I don't think that's any of your business!" she said loudly. Hot tears came to her eyes. She took a step to the side and tried to walk around him, but he cut her off. He grabbed her arms, but she jerked away, stumbling toward the back of the barn. He came toward her, his face tight with anger.

"You know what you are? Stupid crazy! Any sane woman would have run away from here years ago! Or found someone else! Yet, you stay on here. Why?"

"Let me pass," she said.

"Answer me," he returned. She remained silent. He grinned. "Can't, can you? You probably don't even know yourself. All this time, hanging around, playing the martyr. Flirting—"

"I never flirted with you!" she replied hotly.

"Just being here was enough!" he snapped. "Everybody knew your husband was dead, and your brother-in-law gone for good! I've been trying—"

"I know what you've been trying to do," she said.

"Yes. And the way you looked at me told me that you didn't mind one damn bit what I was doing!" he said. "You were too long without anyone."

She tried to rush past him, but he seized her arm and pulled her close to him. She smelled the dust on his clothes, the faint hint of spice, then his lips pressed against hers, and she struggled to free herself. He lifted his head from her, and she took the moment to crush the egg in her hand in his face. He swore and released her, pawing the egg from his eye. Again, she tried to run away and nearly made it to the door before he caught her and threw her hard to the floor. She lay, stunned, while he dropped beside her, his hands ripping her shirt away. She felt his hands upon her breasts, then at her pants as he pulled them down from her hips.

"You goddamned bitch!" he snarled.

"No!" she gasped. She tried to push him away, but his weight bore her back against the floor. Whisker stubble scrapped across her face. His knee pressed against her legs, forcing them apart. She wept and cried out as she realized she was exposed to him.

"God!" she moaned.

And then she felt his weight lifting from her, heard his startled yell, then a grunt, and a meaty thunk! She sat up and stared as Grayson slowly picked himself up from the ground. Henry looked at her, his eyes flickering to her shirt. She pulled it together with shaky fingers.

"Are you all right?" he asked quietly.

She nodded. She reached for her pants. Her shirt gaped open, and she grabbed for it, then paused, frowning, trying to figure out how to do both without exposing herself.

"You—son of a bitch!" Grayson said. He lowered his head and charged. Henry stepped smoothly aside, his hands propelling Grayson past him. The foreman slammed into a post and fell to a knee, shaking his head.

Grayson stood and turned. "All right, Morgan. Let's do it," he said.

He clenched his fists and moved slowly forward, balancing himself on the balls of his feet. Henry stood, relaxed, his hands at his side, watching him, a sad smile tracing his lips.

"Don't do it, cowboy," he said softly. "You can't win."

"Yeah?"

Grayson flicked out a quick jab, then quickly brought his right hand up and over, grunting, and staggering as Henry weaved left then right, slipping the punches. His hands flicked up, catching Grayson's right wrist. He spun, slapping his hip into Grayson's stomach, then lifted and jerked down. Grayson found himself flying through the air, then landing hard on the floor.

"You can't win," Henry said again softly.

"Fuck you," Grayson said thickly. He rose again, clenching

his fist. His breath came in hard gasps, then leveled off. He pushed forward off the balls of his feet, leaping for Henry. His hands grabbed wildly but Henry had slipped to the side. Grayson stumbled, catching himself and whirled, holding his arms in front of him protectively. He heard a noise behind him and turned toward the door. Dog stared silently at him. He held a Winchester, the barrel slanted across his body, centering on Grayson. Grayson wiped his hands across the front of his shirt, and looked at Henry.

"I can't fight that. You win." He stared at Kate and winked lewdly. "Too bad. You might have enjoyed it. Maybe next time."

"All right," Henry said. Grayson swiveled his head to stare at him. "All right, cowboy. You wanted it, you've got it." He looked over Grayson's shoulder. "Dog, stay out of this." The Indian grunted and lowered the rifle.

A broad grin lifted Grayson's lips. "That was a big mistake, Morgan." He looked back at Kate. "Maybe it's not too late yet."

He took a sudden step and snapped a left at Morgan, feeling the blow connect. He grunted with excitement, then came forward, hands moving quickly. Morgan caught his arm again and again Grayson felt himself flying through the air. He rose shakily then staggered backwards, falling through the door outside the barn. Morgan's roan moved nervously, rearing, and Dog slipped around Grayson to catch its reins, soothing it.

Again Grayson rose and came forward, his fists stabbing toward Morgan, but Henry slipped through them, his palm moving upward, hand cupped. The heel of his hand caught Grayson on his chin, staggering him. Grayson threw a punch blindly, felt his wrist caught, then his arm being straightened. He braced himself, pulling back as he thought Morgan would try to throw him again, then Morgan's hand smashed into his extended arm at the elbow, dislocating it. He screamed with pain and back-pedalled hastily. He bumped into the roan, and it danced away, kicking. Dog held on grimly to its reins with one hand, the other still awkwardly holding his rifle. A foot flashed up, slamming down against Grayson's knee and pain exploded in the joint. He screamed again, and tried to lever himself up from the ground. Another foot exploded in his side, and he felt his ribs snap. He fell, moaning to the ground.

"Don't, Henry!" Kate cried as Morgan slipped gracefully to the side of the fallen man. He ignored her and grabbed Grayson by the collar, jerking him up. His fist smashed into Grayson's nose, pulping it, drew back, and flashed forward. She could hear Grayson's jaw crack like a broken stick. She rushed forward to try and stop Morgan, but the dancing roan horse crawfished, and a hoof flashed up and caught her against her head.

A blaze of light flashed across her eyes.

Pain.

And she fell to her side into darkness.

Chapter Fifty-eight

Oly frowned at the teller and shook his head. "I don't understand."

The teller pressed his lips together and said, "I'm sorry, Mr. Anderson, but you don't have that much money in your account. In fact, you only have twenty dollars and seventy-six cents showing in your savings account."

"That is impossible," Oly said. "We haven't used that account for months. There should be thirty thousand dollars in there."

The teller shook his head. "I don't know what to tell you," he said. His fingers flew across the keyboard. He stared at the computer screen. "No, sir. That is correct: twenty dollars and seventy-six cents."

"When was the last withdrawal?" Oly asked. The teller's fingers touched a few buttons.

"Over a year ago," the teller said. He frowned and tapped the keyboard again. "That's odd."

"What's that?"

"The date of the transaction doesn't match the automatic dating. Hmm."

"I think I would like to see Mr. Reynolds," Oly said quietly.

"I'm afraid that is impossible," the teller said. "Mr. Reynolds is out at his ranch."

"Call him. Now," Oly said. "Tell him to come in. I'll wait."

He turned and lumbered over to a small, red vinyl chair by the front window and lowered himself into it. He sat straight, his hands resting over his knees. The teller stared for a minute, then sighed, slid a CLOSED sign in front of his window, and stepped to a telephone behind the teller cage. He dialed and listened, then said, "Mr. Reynolds? This is Barry Stahl at the bank? Yes, sir. I'm sorry to bother you, but Oly Anderson came in to withdraw some money and well, there's a discrepancy in his account. He only has twenty dollars and seventy-six cents showing, but he claims that he should have somewhere around thirty thousand dollars. I checked the withdrawal records and"— he lowered his voice and turned his back to the room—"the withdrawal date and the date of the automatic transaction date don't match, sir. Yes, sir. I'll tell him."

He placed the telephone in the cradle and stood frowning at it for a minute, tapping his fingers on the countertop. Then he shrugged and walked around the counter out to where Oly sat. He paused.

"Mr. Anderson?"

The big farmer looked up, staring calmly at him. The teller cleared his throat.

"Mr. Reynolds apologizes and says that he can't come in right now, but he will take care of the problem personally in the morning. I'm sorry, sir, but there is nothing else that I can do."

Oly nodded, slowly. He pushed himself erect and stared levelly into the teller's eyes. The teller moved away from the hardness showing there.

"You call him back and tell him that I will be here at nine o'clock in the morning," Oly said slowly, spacing his words out as if speaking to a child. "And you tell him that I want an answer by nine o'clock, or we will call someone in Pierre to come out and have a look at his books. You understand?"

"Yes, sir," the teller began, his mouth suddenly dry, but Oly had already turned away from him and lumbered toward the door. "I'll call him back right away, sir," he called as Oly stepped through the door. He shook his head and walked back around the teller cage toward the telephone, then paused, frowning. Slowly he walked back to the computer at his station. A woman stepped out of the line and walked to his window. He looked up at her, recognizing her, then shook his head.

"I'm sorry, Mrs. Martin, but I'm closed," he said. Her eyes tightened, and she huffed and said that since only Mrs. Neumeyer was working that she thought it would be in the best interest of the bank to open another line. He shook his head. "I'm sorry, but I have to balance some accounts before I do anything else. Mr. Reynolds's orders," he added, nodding toward the telephone, knowing that she had seen him on it only moments before. She shrugged and moved back in line. Old Pete Dexter let her slip back in front of him, and she gave him a tiny smile of thanks and then turned to freeze Barry with a stare, but he ignored her.

He stared intently at the screen as he called up the accounts of the largest depositers, sorting through them. His eyes widened, and he pulled a pad of paper to him and began jotting numbers, filling the pad rapidly with three columns—names, accounts, and balances. After fifteen minutes, he took the pad of paper and let himself into Reynolds's office, closing the door behind him. He crossed quickly to the desk, seating himself behind it, and reached for the telephone.

Dog

I helped Henry move Kate into the back of the Oldsmobile and sat with her as he drove. She was in a bad way. Very bad. Her face was white and shiny with sweat, and when I pushed up her eyelids to look into her eyes, the right one did not move when the light hit it. It stared at me like a fish eye. I had seen eyes like that when my cousin Leonard Yellow Eyes had been killed after his horse stepped into a prairie dog hole and threw him. Leonard's neck was broken instantly. Dead eyes. Henry did not bother to drive to Phillip but went the other way to the hospital in Pierre. I thought he had made a bad choice, but her breathing did not change after the first thirty miles. I knew then that there was a good chance that we would make it into Pierre.

It was late afternoon when we sped down Dakota Street, crossed main street, and sped past the park along the Missouri River. A policeman chased us, but Henry did not stop and pulled up into the hospital's emergency entrance. The policeman came up to talk with him, but Henry ignored him and when the policeman tried to stop him, I stepped between them and told the policeman that I would speak with him until Henry had finished his business. I told the policeman that Grayson had tried to rape her and that Henry had fought him and that I had tied Grayson to a post in the barn with a pair of horse hobbles, but I did not think he would be going anywhere as Henry had beaten him very badly for what he had tried to do. I did not tell him that Billy Spotted Horse and Tom Standing Bear would keep him until Tom Morgan and Timmy came home.

I could see that the policeman did not believe me, but I did not care. I knew that Tom Morgan and his grandson would bring him into the hospital, and he would be my proof that I was not lying.

The policeman wrote out a speeding ticket for Henry, then another ticket when Henry said he did not have a driver's license. I told him I did not have one, either, and he could give me a ticket also if he wanted to. I think the policeman wanted to hit me, but he did not because Henry had a crazy look in his eyes, and I do not think the policeman wanted to chance making a crazy man mad.

We stayed there for a long time until the doctor came and told us that Kate had to be operated on right away. He gave Henry a bunch of papers to sign. I tried to find out what was wrong with Kate, but no one wants to talk with an Indian about a white woman. It was only later that Henry told me that something had gone wrong when the roan kicked her, and the doctors had to operate to relieve pressure on her brain. He did not say anything more about that, but I could tell that he was worried from the way his eyes stared at the tile floor.

Shortly after that, Tom and Timmy came in with Grayson, and the people in the emergency room gave Henry a strange look when Henry came down from the waiting room and told them to call the police. When a nurse tried to push Henry from the room, Henry told her to either call the police or else they would not have to fix Grayson.

She called the police and the police came and heard what Henry had to say and what I had to say, but I knew that they were listening to me only because I was telling them the same thing that Henry was telling them. If I had been alone, they would not have listened. I began to feel the spirits of the ancient ones again and knew that I could not stay in that hospital. I went out and went into the park and sat down on a bench and watched some men play horseshoes. The ancient ones moved with me, and I could feel their spirits in the willows beside the river and knew that they were waiting until we were alone so they could talk with me.

I stayed there until Henry came for me early in the morning. I did not worry; I knew he would find me. He told me that the operation was over, but that the doctor was not pleased with what he had found. He asked me if I had given her any medicine. I told him I had given her walnut water for her headaches, and he nodded and looked away from me at the river. I knew what he was thinking; the old ones had told me what would happen, and so I waited quietly for him to decide. It was something that he would have to do. Warriors know these things, and although it had been a long time since he had been a warrior, I knew the warrior's spirit was still with him and that we would soon be going back to the ranch.

At last, he stirred and said we should go. We walked back to the hospital, and Henry told his father and Timmy that they were to stay there while we went back to the ranch. Timmy started to argue, but Henry shook his head and said this was something that only he could do. He meant the two of us, but I did not bother to correct him. He would realize that while we drove back to the ranch.

He would know that when we went hunting.

Chapter Fifty-nine

Reynolds slowly placed the receiver back in the cradle and stood back from the telephone, staring at it as if it were an evil thing. He glanced down at the drink in his hand and raised it to his lips, but he did not drink and placed the glass on the small table in front of the fireplace next to the telephone. He walked aimlessly around the room for a while, idly touching things: a book, a set of leather coasters bearing the Rafter R brand, an old bullet he had found while roaming the Bad River bottoms, an old Indian arrow. He straightened a Remington print hanging over the fireplace and stood back to look at it: It was his favorite, a Pony Express rider standing beside his fallen horse, holding off Indians with a pair of pistols. He had found the print in the art museum in Chicago and bought it and had it framed in a frame covered with gold leaf. It was a good print and several visitors had thought it was real because some of the artist's brush strokes could be seen in the brown land and blue sky.

It's over, he thought.

He turned and walked out through the front door to stand on the porch. He stared over his land, ravaged and torn. The cattle lowed pitifully, and he swiveled his head to look at them. Up on the hill, the bull stood alone, staring across to Morgan's water. He slammed his fist down hard on the porch railing. The sun's heat pooled in the middle of the baked yard. A fine wind blew grit and dessicated manure across the yard in a tiny dust devil.

It's over. He would be able to switch a few funds around and cover that fat farmer's account, but he knew it was only a matter of time. The story would leak out, and the other depositers would come in to check on their accounts. He would be able to hold them off for a while by moving a block of money back and forth as he needed to, but he would not be able to do that for long. One, maybe two, certainly three large withdrawals would sink him.

He glanced up at the sky. A lone buzzard sailed on a small air current high up, circling the yards.

All he had needed was time. Just a little time. Until the rains came. And then he would have been able to fatten the cattle and get them to market and cover the accounts from the sale of the cattle. But the rains had not come, and now they would not come in time to save him. Even if they came today, they would not have come in time. He stared off toward the Morgan pasture.

And all because of a little water.

The anger washed over him like a red flood.

Morgan.

He turned and walked back into the house and went to the den. He opened his gun cabinet and selected a .270 caliber Winchester. He took a box of cartridges from the shelf above the guns. He closed and locked the cabinet and left. He crossed the yard to the bunkhouse and opened the door.

"Anybody seen Grayson?" he asked. They looked curiously at the rifle in his hand.

"Nope," Stubby Wilson said. "Leastways not since morning. He said he had a little date he had to keep." The others laughed.

"Any idea where?" Reynolds asked.

"Well," Stubby said, winking at the others, "he has been pretty sweet on that Kate Morgan. He might have gone over there. Or maybe he went over to the Bledsoe place. I understand her husband has gone for a couple of days out fishing at Belle Fourche. Hell, boss. You know Grayson."

"Yeah," Reynolds grunted. "He comes back you tell him I'm looking for him."

"You going huntin', boss?" one of the cowboys asked.

"Coyotes," Reynolds said. "Thought I might sit up on the

ridge over by the Stone place and see if I can't pop a few. This damned drought's making them nervy. A couple might come down out of the hills."

He closed the door upon a chorus of "good luck" and walked over to the Cadillac. He placed the rifle barrel down on the floorboard beneath the passenger seat and pulled himself behind the steering wheel. Within minutes, he was driving down the lane and across the cattle guard. He turned left toward the Morgan ranch.

Chapter Sixty

The big Hereford bull watched the Cadillac disappear down the road then turned back to stare across to where he smelled the water. A small wind danced across the burnt grass toward him, carrying with it a hint of dampness, the smell of bull rushes, and the heat of cows. He filled his chest and bellowed a challenge across the plains. The steers looked up from the feeding troughs below, but did not move toward him. His coat glowed blood-red in the sunlight. His huge shoulders, nearly a man's height, bunched, the muscles bulging like two-inch hawsers. He bellowed again, and angrily shook his head. He pawed the ground. He bellowed.

Dog

"You do not have to do this, Dog," Henry said. I told him that I knew that, and I knew that the police would probably come and would like nothing better than to arrest an Indian and take him in to Pierre or Rapid City and put him in jail. But the reservation was a big place, and the Badlands were just as big, and that was a lot of land for a man to disappear into if he wanted.

"All right," he smiled. He put his hand upon my shoulder. "You have your reservation; I have the monastery. I guess it doesn't make much difference, does it?"

It did make a difference, but I did not try to explain that to him. The walls of a monastery are like the walls of a prison. A man is still locked inside of them and cannot smell the wind and the rain or the grass or hear the sound the earth makes. But I knew this was not the time to explain this to him. When we had finished our hunt, then he would have enough time to discover this for himself when we went into the Badlands.

It was noon when we drove into the ranchyard. The pickup and tractor and mower were gone and I knew that Tom Standing Bear and Billy Spotted Horse had gone to the pasture along the river to cut the sweet grass there for hay. The horses heard us and whinnied from the corral. I went down to saddle the roan and my pinto while Henry went into the house to take a shower and change his clothes. He would, he said, pack supplies for us. He pulled the Oldsmobile up near the house and parked. I walked down to the corral, automatically looking at the windmill at the end of the yard. The blades stood still. I could hear a couple of cattle in the lower pasture. For some reason, the light appeared golden and I saw the machine shed and barn with a soft glow around them.

The roan waited patiently for his saddle, but my pinto was cross because he had not left the corral the day before, and he danced away from me when I tried to place the saddle on his back. I sang to him and told him how sorry I was that I had not ridden him the day before, but that I could not as there was a bad thing that happened. Eventually he quieted, and I saddled him and rode him down the hill to my cabin by the creek. I brought the roan with me and tied both behind the cabin so that they could drink all the water that they wanted while I made myself ready for the hunt.

I picked up my rifle and checked it. That was when the first shot came. The horses moved uneasily behind the cabin. I slipped up to a window and looked out quickly as I heard another shot. I could see a man up by the lightning-struck cotton-wood. He was aiming down at the house. I heard another shot and glass break.

"Come out, Morgan, goddamn you!" he yelled. I recognized Reynolds's voice and a great happiness swept over me because I knew that we would not have to hunt him. He had come to us himself.

I slipped out the door of my cabin and around to the back. Another shot sounded. I soothed the horses, and waded across the creek. I heard another shot, this one different, and I knew that Henry was shooting the old .308-caliber Winchester. I smiled as Reynolds fired again.

I slipped through the willows and made my way up the other side of the tank to where a group of old cottonwoods stood together. Reynolds was across from me and up a little. I settled down behind one and sighted carefully on a branch above his head. I squeezed the trigger. The rifle bucked against my shoulder, and I levered another cartridge into the chamber and fired again. He scurried around behind the other side of the cottonwood. I heard Henry's Winchester and saw Reynolds try to come back to my side. I fired again, then ducked behind the cottonwood as Reynolds fired twice, once at me and again at the house. I glanced out and saw Henry suddenly slip out the door and duck down behind the Oldsmobile. Reynolds fired, and I heard the bullet strike the Oldsmobile. I fired again and ducked down as he shot at me. The bullet slammed into the cottonwood, and I grinned and rolled to the other side of the cottonwood and pumped two shots into the tree above Reynolds's head. Henry's Winchester fired again, and then I saw Reynolds break from behind the tree and run down the hill away from us. I fired at him, but missed and then he was behind the hill and out of sight.

I stood and yelled at Henry and pointed. Henry waved and jumped in behind the Oldsmobile and tried to start it, but it would not start and I knew that Reynolds had killed it. I ran back to my cabin and grabbed our horses. I stepped into the pinto's saddle and galloped up the hill to Henry, leading his roan behind me. Henry mounted and together we galloped across the yard and out onto the road after Reynolds.

Chapter Sixty-two

Reynolds glanced into the rear mirror and saw Henry and Dog chasing after him on their horses.

"Dumb sons a bitches," he said. He pulled a flask from the glove box, opened it, and drank deeply of the bourbon. He floored the accelerator and felt the Cadillac leap forward. Two horses against four hundred. "Dumb sons a bitches," he said again. He took another drink as he guided the Cadillac around a curve.

He didn't see the bull until he was nearly on it.

The bull turned and lowered its head as the Cadillac raced to it.

The crash sprayed a fine mist of blood up over the hood of the Cadillac, spattering the windshield, moving the engine block back through the firewall. Reynolds flew forward, his bulk bending the steering wheel. He slipped over the wheel, his head breaking the windshield, ramming the flask back against his teeth. He went up and over the wheel before the airbag broke, flying along the crumbling hood. A scream began bubbling from his throat and then a huge horn hooked him in the chest. He gurgled, eyes bulging.

And then the Cadillac exploded in a ball of flame, spreading out and over the dirt road, setting the dry grama grass afire.

Dog

We did not tell the police what had happened at the ranch. We rode back and Henry telephoned from there and told the police what had happened. They came and took Reynolds away. Two days later, the auditors from Pierre went into the bank and then the federal auditors came from Sioux Falls.

The state sent its people to the Rocking R and began trucking in water for the cattle after the auditors seized the property. Three weeks later, black rain clouds began building on the edge of the prairie, and the next morning, the sun rose blood-red through dark clouds, its red light mushrooming along the horizon, then leaping into the sky, burning in the center like a fiery cross and the water in the tank turned dark like blood.

And then the rains came.

Two months later, big trucks came to the ranch and began to haul the cattle away. The market was not right for the cattle, but nobody asks an Indian such things.

Then the state auctioned off everything, and the federal government took the money and mixed it with the money the insurance companies were forced to turn over and started to pay off the creditors. It took a long time, and the people did not receive all the money that they had put into the bank. Someone told me later that they got only fifty cents on the dollar. I was not surprised. The Indian has been short-changed by the government all his life.

Henry told Billy Spotted Horse and Tom Standing Bear that they could stay on the ranch if they wanted. They agreed and Henry had a load of lumber brought out to the ranch and told them that they could build their own cabin wherever they wanted. They chose a place by the creek not far from my own cabin and their relatives came up to help them put up their cabin before the snows came.

In December, the first snows came, and we received a call from the hospital telling us that we had better hurry into Pierre. When Henry hung up the telephone, I could tell from his face that Kate was dying.

When we arrived in Pierre, the doctor tried to keep me out of the room, but Henry told him that we were her family, and we were going into the room. The doctor looked at me, and I could read his thoughts. I turned to leave, but Henry took my arm and told the doctor that all of us were her family. The doctor did not argue, and we went into her room.

She lay on the bed, much thinner than I had seen her last when we first brought her to the hospital. They had removed her bandages but she wore a cap over her head because they had cut off all her hair when they tried to fix what happened in her head. She was awake and tried to smile when Henry took her hand. Timmy moved to the other side and took her other hand, and Tom stood at the foot of her bed, shifting his weight from one side to the other. At last, he coughed and said he needed a drink and left the room. Tears sparkled in his eyes when he walked past, but I pretended not to notice them.

"Mom," Timmy said, but she shushed him and squeezed his hand. He bent down to kiss her, and then turned his head away.

She looked at Henry. She smiled and closed her eyes. "You have come home," she said.

"Yes," he answered.

A tiny tear trickled out from the corner of one of her eyes. "So long," she said. "So very long."

"I'm home," Henry said huskily.

"And you'll stay?" She gestured at Timmy. "He needs you. It's his place now, but there's a lot that he needs to be taught. Things I couldn't teach him." She paused, her breath coming shallower and shallower. "You . . . will tell him? . . . Someday . . . when it . . . is right? About . . . his father?"

"I'll stay," he said. "And someday I'll tell him. This is where I belong. I'm sorry that it has taken me so long to realize that. I'm sorry for—everything. Most of all, I'm sorry for what we didn't have."

She opened her eyes and smiled at him. "Welcome home."

A deep sigh came from her lips.

Her eyes closed.

And so she passed quietly from us and her spirit, her white soul, billowed up and away from her like a fine milk-white mist rising toward the sun.